Dear Reader,

A cowboy poet. A women paleontologist. And dinosaurs — the very word excites the imagination of young and old alike. I chose to bring these elements together for *Past Promises* when I read about a schoolmaster in Colorado who, in the spring of 1877, discovered the gigantic bones of ancient saurian creatures, better known to us as dinosaurs. Like the Gold Rush of 1849, the discovery led to a "Bone Rush" among men in the scientific community.

If Jessica's quest for dinosaur bones seems an unusual choice, you need to know that in the mid-nineteenth century in some places in the West, the ground was virtually littered with saurian bones. Little wonder, then, that the imagination of even the most studious scientist would be tempted by the offerings of the wide-open frontier. In this exciting time in history, the possibilities were free for discoveries of all kinds, even — as Jessica and Rory prove — a true and unexpected love!

I hope you enjoy reading *Past Promises* as much I loved researching and writing it for you!

Peace and joy,

Jill Marie Landis

Turn the page to read the critical acclaim
that has made Jill Marie Landis "ONE OF THE NEW STARS"* ...

*Romantic Times

COME SPRING

Snowbound in a mountain man's cabin, beautiful
Annika vowed to resist his wild nature, his hungry
glances . . . But as passion's fire flares, love grows
as sure as the seasons change . . .

"A BEAUTIFUL LOVE STORY."
—Julie Garwood

"WOW! . . . THIS IS A WORLD-CLASS
NOVEL . . . IT'S FABULOUS!"
—Bestselling author Linda Lael Miller

"A WINNER!"
—Dorothy Garlock

JADE

Her exotic beauty captured the heart of a rugged
rancher. But could he forget the past—and love again?

"JILL MARIE LANDIS PROMISES TO
BECOME A FAVORITE!"
—*Affaire de Coeur*

ROSE

Across the golden frontier, her
passionate heart dared to dream . . .

"A GENTLE ROMANCE THAT WILL
WARM YOUR SOUL."
—*Heartland Critiques*

Jove titles by Jill Marie Landis

COME SPRING
JADE
ROSE
SUNFLOWER
WILDFLOWER

PAST PROMISES

JILL MARIE LANDIS

JOVE BOOKS, NEW YORK

PAST PROMISES

A Jove Book / published by arrangement with
the author

PRINTING HISTORY
Jove edition / October 1993

ISBN: 0-515-11207-0

A JOVE BOOK®
Jove Books are published by The Berkley Publishing Group,
200 Madison Avenue, New York, New York 10016.
JOVE and the "J" design are trademarks belonging to
Jove Publications, Inc.

PRINTED IN THE UNITED STATES OF AMERICA

10 9 8 7 6 5 4 3 2 1

To my two Janets, Janet Carroll and Janet Melton,
with love and thanks for all you've done;

to Mary (Myra) Thoits,
a point of light within a greater light;

to Rita, Lou, Gini, Susan Leslie, and Natalie,
for friendship and laughter.

PAST
PROMISES

CHAPTER

1

Southwestern Colorado
1890

They were watching her again.

Six Ute men. Four stood, two hunkered down into a squat. All of them kept their distance; none attempted to approach her after the one in a tall black hat asked in broken English and sign language what she was doing on the reservation. Clutching a well-worn copy of Captain William Philo Clark's book on sign language, she tried to explain. After Tall Hat left, she had tried to hire some of the others to help, but they shook their heads and chose to watch in silence.

Now, miles from nowhere, Jessica Stanbridge sat on an upturned crate near a half-unloaded wagon and asked herself if making a name in the annals of paleontology was worth such dusty, sweaty, muscle-aching misery.

In frustration bordering on anger, she ignored the silent

scrutiny of the Utes, took off her spectacles, and squinted against the sunlight. Finally Jessica shifted and shaded her eyes as she stared off across the mesa. The Spanish word was an apt name for this land that was as high and flat as a tabletop. She felt vulnerable and exposed sitting atop the world, gazing out over the endless expanse of browns and tans, taupes and reds of the desolate land that shifted and came vibrantly alive whenever cloud shadows played across it.

It was an ancient land. A place that in its very silence spoke clearly of its past. The earth was parched and seemingly barren, studded by stone columns and high plateaus of sandstone and clay sculpted by water on its downward journey from high green mountains in the distance.

Pygmy forests of twisted juniper and piñon pine dotted a landscape spottily carpeted with tough grama grass and the sage that scented the breeze. The twisted, roughened plants survived not only summer sun, but winter drifts that sometimes mounted up to thirty feet. Wiping a trickle of sweat from her temple, Jessica wondered how long it would be until she, too, withered like the dry sage. The way she felt right now, she feared that might happen before she unpacked the rest of the supplies.

An eagle circled overhead then banked east. She tried to imagine what she might look like from its vantage point—a young woman seated forlornly on a crate not far from a wagonload of boxes and barrels. A lopsided tent on the verge of tumbling over was pitched a few feet away. Farther on, tied to a picket line, a horse and two mules munched on grama grass.

Jessica's long blond hair, once neatly coiled in a bun, had worked itself free of its delicate hairpins. Most of it was still trapped beneath her veiled pith helmet, but one long tendril had escaped to drape itself over her shoulder.

Halfheartedly she tried to wedge the curl beneath the

helmet, then surrendered and let the resistant skein slide back down her neck. Her once stiffly starched shirtwaist and panama skirt were crumpled and dusty, her face smeared with the grime that stuck to her sweat-soaked skin.

Without thinking, Jessica reached up and unbuttoned the high, prim collar of her blouse. A mule brayed. She glanced up at the sound and wished the Utes would leave, for she longed to slip three more buttons open and wave the neckline of her blouse to cool herself off. Instead she stood up and placed her hands against the small of her back and stretched in as unprovocative a manner as she could manage with six pairs of dark eyes moving over her.

Lord, but her back ached. Unloading some of the heavy supplies yesterday had cost her more than she had bargained for. At this rate she would be too stiff to move a muscle when the time came to begin an actual excavation—provided there would be an excavation. A discovery of any size in southwest Colorado hinged on her instincts, and so far her instincts had proved to be useless. When she and her companion, Myra Thornton, had arrived at the Ute agency in Ignatio, no one had been willing to help them. On top of that, the inadequate geological maps she was depending on had proved to be highly incorrect. And along with everything else, there was still much to unpack before she could even begin her fieldwork. And now every muscle in her body was screaming for relief.

Unwilling to add any more doubt to her worries, Jessica called out to Myra Thornton, who was seated on a boulder not far away, sketching one of the ever-curious Utes. "May I speak to you for a moment, Myra?" Attempting a smile, Jessica waited while the older woman closed her sketchbook and hurried over.

Stocky, buxom Myra was over sixty. Just how far over, Jessica had never deigned to ask, because age never hampered her companion. "Time is irrelevant," the philosophical spinster often told her. "It's merely a restriction man puts upon himself. How can it really matter what year it is in the grand scheme of the universe?''

Jessica wanted to believe time didn't matter at all, but unfortunately, for her it did. Two months ago she had vowed that before the end of summer she would make a paleontological discovery that would delight both Harvard Museum and its generous benefactor, Henry Beckworth, but it was already mid-June and time was fast becoming her nemesis.

"What is it, my dear?" Myra asked. Her bright brown eyes peered at Jessica above lopsided spectacles looped over only one ear. Although she possessed at least four pairs, Myra Thornton's spectacles were always missing a stem, yet she never seemed to notice.

"As much as I hate to admit it, I'm afraid we are going to need some help," Jess said, her words low enough not to be overheard by the Utes.

Myra peered up at Jessica, who stood a good four inches taller, and started to smile. "What kind of help?"

"Male help," Jess mumbled.

"Did you say *male*?"

"All right, I'll admit it. We do need a man around to help out."

Myra rocked back on her heels, crossed her arms under the wide, ample shelf of her bosom, and nodded sagely. "I told you so."

Jessica abruptly turned away and headed toward the wagon. "You don't have to gloat, Myra. It isn't at all becoming."

"At my age I am free of the worry about what is becoming and what is not. Sometimes one must overcome one's persuasions and let common sense prevail, Jessica. I told you as much when that pompous young assistant of yours took ill on the train and you all but forced him to go back to Cambridge. What *was* his name? I've forgotten it entirely."

"Stoutenburg. Jerome Stoutenburg. And I didn't choose him to be my assistant. The museum insisted he come along with me." Jessica thought of the overeager third-year student who had suddenly become deathly ill with influenza on the train. Blessing fate, she finally convinced Stoutenburg that she could get along without him. Although terribly disappointed in having failed on his first real assignment, he had left them in St. Louis to return to Harvard.

Once she reached the wagon, she uncovered the water barrel, lifted the long iron ladle from its nail, and dipped it in. "I insisted then—and *still* contend—that I don't need a trained assistant. What I do need is someone willing to do the heavy work, to act as a guide, to help set up and break camp. When I make a discovery, of course, I'll need professional help with the excavation." She took a long sip and offered a refilled ladle to Myra.

Water sloshed on the front of Myra's shirtwaist blouse. She seemed not to notice. "You need a man."

Jessica glowered and ignored Myra's comment. "What I need is a porter. A guide. A servant."

Myra smiled. "And just where do you propose to find one, my dear? We are, in case you haven't noticed, in the middle of nowhere, and the only available male assistance"—she nodded toward the Utes—"doesn't know the meaning of the word 'chivalry.' I have read that in the society of the red man, women are expected to do all the heavy work. Such lifting, toting, and unpacking is deemed quite unmanly." She glanced at the Utes again. They were all holding the reins of their mounts, patiently waiting for something interesting to happen. Myra finished, "I don't think you'll find any help in that quarter."

Worrying her thumbnail with her teeth, Jessica shrugged in agreement. "Agent Carmichael was no help either," she said, remembering the cold reception they received at the government agency upon entering the Ute reservation at Ignatio. The sight of her numerous official documents and permits from Washington did little to ingratiate her to the man who guarded access to the land as if the reservation and people on it were his very own. He had been barely civil.

"We'll just have to ride into Cortez and inquire at the trading post," Jessica concluded out loud.

"Not me. I'm staying here," Myra said stoically.

"Horsefeathers."

"Try to budge me."

"Myra, this is no time to be difficult."

"I'm merely stating my choice." Myra walked back to the boulder and opened her sketchpad.

Rubbing her temples, Jessica let go a heavy sigh. Myra Thornton had been an influence in her life since the very beginning. A close friend of her mother's, Myra had been there to comfort and guide her ever since Elsa Stanbridge had succumbed to rheumatic fever. Jessica had been eight at the time, but she could still remember the years before her mother's death when her father would spend his hours away from the museum teaching her paleontology while her mother and Myra sat at the dining table and debated philosophy.

One thing had become quite clear on the journey west. Myra Thornton was a woman accustomed to living alone. She did what she wanted, when she wanted. But this time Jessica was determined to have her way. She drew herself up and followed the older woman across the encampment, unwilling to raise her voice in front of their uninvited audience. She stopped directly in front of Myra, disrupting her view of the men colorfully garbed in plaid woolen shirts to which strips of fringe had been added, striped, hand-woven blankets over their shoulders, ill-fitting boots, and long braids that sported weasel tails, feathers, and beads.

"I won't leave you here alone, Myra. I absolutely refuse."

Myra sighed. "We've been here three nights. Our tent seems to be secure enough and unlikely to fall over *again* to awaken me from a sound sleep. I have an abundant supply of food and water and enough scenery to provide a lifetime of landscape subjects. I do not desire to be trundled off anywhere in the wagon as the bruises I have sustained on my backside on the way from Durango are far from faded. You forget you are a good forty years younger than I. Besides, you will make better time if you take the horse, not the wagon, and go without me."

"What if I'm not back by dark?"

"I will simply make myself a cold sandwich, light a lamp, and turn in early with Mrs. Corelli."

Marie Corelli, the author of Myra's favorite novel, *A Romance of Two Worlds,* was not with them, of course, but Myra *was* reading the book for the third time. "Mrs. Corelli's work might be entertaining, but it offers scant protection."

"Good heavens, Jessica. The last Indian uprising in Colorado was nearly ten years ago. If you mean to imply that our friends over there might cause us harm, wouldn't they have done so by now?"

Jessica shook her head. "I don't know. I guess so, but I'm out of my element here, Myra. Ask me about the Mesozoic era, ask me about leaf imprints from the Cretaceous period, ask me to describe in detail the Jurassic and Triassic periods and I can answer you without hesitation. But don't ask me if I think you'll be safe all alone in the middle of the Ute reservation."

Myra lowered her glasses and folded the one remaining stem. "Jessica, you know how completely I believe my fate is in the hands of the universe. I jumped at the chance to accompany you on this adventurous trek west, and now that the train trip and that horrible wagon ride are over, I am not about to budge, even for a few hours." Myra straightened and the buttons down the front of her blouse strained against their holes. "In making my choice, I have made a silent commitment with the universe to put myself in its care."

She pointed heavenward to make a grand pronouncement. "I am *not* afraid."

Jessica knew by Myra's set expression that it was time to admit defeat.

Myra glanced at the sun. "If you hurry, you can reach Cortez and be back before dark."

Jess pulled off her helmet, wiped her brow with the back of her arm, and slammed her headgear on again. "I should do it, Myra. I should just leave you here."

"I wish you would, dear. As Emerson so aptly put it, 'It is easy to live for others. . . . I call on you to live for yourself.' "

Jessica opened her mouth to respond and abruptly closed it. It did no good to argue once Myra's mind was set, especially when she began quoting Emerson. "If I'm going alone, I'll have to leave right now. I'll get my knapsack and set the pistol right here beside you."

"Perhaps you should take it. What if you come across something wild—a bobcat or a snake?"

"I'll be on horseback, Myra. Hopefully I can outdistance any predator."

"What if a wild animal leaps from a tree onto your horse? What if—"

Jessica crossed her arms. "What tree? There are not many trees over six feet out here. I insist that if you stay, it is with the gun or you don't stay behind at all."

"Can you really imagine me shooting anyone?" With a dismissing smile and an absentminded nod, Myra bent over her work once more. "Have a safe trip, my dear. And remember, everything will be fine."

It took another half hour for Jessica to locate the saddle amid the crates in the wagon and saddle the horse she had rented at the stable where she obtained the mules and wagon. By the time she repinned her hair, donned and buttoned up her fitted jacket, and pulled on her chamois gloves, she had used up another quarter of an hour. She glanced up at the sun, slipped the leather strap of her knapsack over her shoulder, checked the time on the watch dangling from a ribbon molded in gold, and then mounted up.

Quite an accomplished rider for a young woman born and bred in Massachusetts, Jessica adjusted her skirts until the tops of her high, laced boots were covered, and with a last wave to Myra, she headed north.

A few yards from the camp, she paused to take stock of her friend still perched on the rock. The Ute men seated themselves in the dust not far from Myra, who was still intent on her sketches. Jess looked at the lonesome tent standing all too white against the high desert color and hoped she wasn't making a very serious mistake.

> I sing in the saddle
> When days get too long.
> I sing when I'm happy
> And when things go wrong.
> The cattle don't mind it,
> It settles 'em down.
> I sing in the tub
> When there's no one around.

Rory Burnett recognized Cortez in the distance, kicked his horse into a gallop, and chuckled as he repeated the stanza again, well pleased with himself. He didn't fancy himself a true poet, not like Keats or Shelley anyway. Hell, he wasn't more than a cowhand turned rancher, but he enjoyed rolling words that rhymed around on his tongue. Every so often, when they seemed to "take," he wrote the words down.

As he watched the newly established trading post grow larger on the horizon, he hoped this unexpected trip would not keep him away from the Silver Sage Ranch for long.

With only six full-time hands he didn't have a lot of time to waste gallivanting around the countryside.

For the past week and a half he and his men had been trying to combat the blowflies that were infesting the cattle as they did every summer. It was a dirty job, but it had to be done. Branding and castration left the herd with open wounds that soon festered with the screw worms that hatched when the flies laid their eggs in the open flesh. Axle grease mixed with carbolic acid was the only way Rory knew of to kill off the worms, but the mixture had to be hand-daubed on every unwilling animal.

Before he left that morning, he set the men to the unpleasant task again, and if his errand had been anything else, he would have declined and been working alongside them. But Piah Jackson, a Ute subchief, had appealed to him for help, and in Rory's mind there was little he could do but answer the call.

Just after dawn Rory had been in the still-cool shadows that lingered in the corner of the barn holding a bridle with braided reins when Piah Jackson soundlessly entered the building.

Rory had set aside the bridle and given the Ute his full attention. The man's eyes blazed with barely concealed anger, his usual forbidding countenance darkened by irritation. His braided black hair was intricately woven with lengths of colored ribbon. A government-issue shirt was covered by a jacket that had no doubt come from a box of clothing donated by some wealthy churchgoers in the East—the coat had obviously been fashioned for a heavyset man. His leggings were of woolen flannel, close-fitted and trimmed with fringe and beads. Fastened about his waist was a hand-tooled belt and his tall black hat sported a band of silver conchos, a Navajo trade item.

"I have come to ask you to keep the promise made by the man who called you son," Piah said without salutation.

"I'll do what I can," Rory said. Miles of the Silver Sage

Ranch bordered the Ute reservation. Now that Wilner Burnett had died and passed on the ranch and his name, Rory intended to continue to help his closest neighbors, be they red or white, whenever called upon.

Piah visibly relaxed. "Strangers have come to the reservation. They have many papers that give them the right to search our land, to dig for bones and disturb the ancient ones buried on Ute soil."

Rory took a moment to sort out what the man was trying to tell him. "Have you asked Carmichael for help?"

"We have asked. But they have papers. The agent says there is nothing he can do."

Perplexed, Rory crossed his arms over his chest and leaned against the scarred wooden rail of the nearest stall. Domino, his big Appaloosa, nuzzled his shoulder. He reached back to scratch the animal's nose. "If they have government permits," he said slowly, "I don't see how I can help. What else do you know?"

"She said they are looking for bones. She wanted to give us money to help her dig them up."

She? "A woman?"

Piah held up two fingers. "Two women. One old, one not so old. No man."

Shoving away from the stall, Rory ran a hand over his eyes and said half to himself, "Two women are on the reservation to dig up bones." It didn't surprise him. Since two ranchers had stumbled on the cliff dwellings at Mesa Verde two years before, the area had been crawling with treasure hunters, archaeologists, and curiosity seekers. His own opinion was that the discovery had turned the place into a circus. To Piah he said, "Did you tell these women that grave sites are sacred to your people?"

With a shrug, Piah turned and squinted out into the sunlight before he looked back at Rory. "They have papers. They didn't understand the signs I made."

"Then why didn't you speak English?"

Piah smiled. "I spoke a little, but sometimes it is better not to let a stranger know all that one knows. They are camped on the high mesa close to your land." Piah paused a moment before he added, "Near the cave."

Rory suddenly knew all too well why Piah was so disturbed. The strangers were camped atop an extensive cavern in the sandstone wall of one of the many canyons carved into the mesa.

Situated on land that technically straddled the boundary between the Silver Sage and the reservation, the huge cave was a sacred site to the Indians and had been for centuries. Years back, when Wilner Burnett was out rounding up stray cattle and had innocently stumbled across the place, he immediately approached the Ute elders, told them what he had found, and swore to keep the location a secret. No one, he promised, as long as he and his descendants owned the land, would ever disturb it. Because of his open sincerity and willingness to help, the Utes had believed him. To Wilner, a man's word was sacred. He had always kept his word.

Now Wilner was gone and not only had Rory inherited the Silver Sage, but the promise to the Utes.

"Maybe Carmichael will listen to you and make the women go," Piah suggested.

"Not after the run-in I had with him this past April," Rory admitted as he tapped a hand against his thigh. "Our *discussion* over that rotten beef he tried to hand out to your people exploded into a shouting match."

"You gave us cattle of your own so we would not go hungry. I ask for your help again."

Rory knew Piah wouldn't budge until he agreed to at least try to help. Giving away a few head of cattle had been easy. Interfering in government-sanctioned work was more than he had bargained for; still, if he could find the women and explain to them just what their intrusion mean to the Utes, he thought it was worth a try. "What exactly do you want me to do?"

"Make them go."

Reduced to three words, the task sounded simple. Rory shoved back his hat and shook his head. "Not very easy if they have government permission."

"If they stay, if they disturb the bones of our ancestors, they will raise evil spirits. It is not right to disturb the dead. We hide the graves of our people because the spirits that survive them must stay buried. Nothing good will come of these women digging on our land. Only disaster."

Now, as Rory unwillingly approached the outskirts of Cortez, he frowned against the noonday sun. He hadn't promised Piah he would succeed, only that he would try to talk to the women and explain the sacredness of the Ute grave sites to them; he had to be careful how he went about it. If he told them about the cave outright, it might just send them running in that direction. More than anything, he wanted to reach the interlopers before they stumbled upon it themselves. If any "disaster" befell them, the Utes would take the blame and the surrounding countryside would be up in arms.

He wondered what in the hell possessed two idiot women to venture onto the reservation alone. True, there had been no major problems with the Utes since the uprising at White River back in '79. Agent Nathan Meeker had been murdered along with eight of his men, and his wife and daughter taken captive. Still, no one in Colorado had forgotten about the incident. In order to prevent trouble, the very least he could do was ask around, see if he could find the two women, and then try to set them straight. He hoped it wouldn't take more than a day or two.

As he reined in before the general store and trading post and dismounted, Rory wondered if it was too much to hope that everything would be settled by nightfall.

The rowels of his spurs delivered a metallic whisper as he

crossed the lopsided pine sidewalk that bordered the front of the store. He ducked through the low door frame, took off his hat out of habit, and spun it around on his finger as he walked toward the counter. The entrance area of the elongated room was well lit by the front windows, but near the back, only hanging oil lamps dispelled the shadows.

Rows of canned and dry goods lined the shelves behind the counter. Barrels of flour, sugar, salt, and cornmeal with scoops and sacks beside them stood like infantrymen along one wall. Grain, seed, and feed were stored in the back corner, while household goods, ribbon, and fabric, along with pots and pans were up front where they would catch a housewife's hungry eye.

As Rory approached the counter Willie Henson, the proprietor, straightened his apron strings and stepped forward expectantly. "What can I do for you, Rory? Come in to collect your mail?"

Rory leaned one elbow on the cash register and continued to twirl his dusty black Stetson. "Well, that, and I'm hopin' you can answer a question, Willie. You had any women through here, travelin' alone, maybe buyin' supplies?"

Henson shook his head as he reached for the box of mail he kept under the counter. "Nope. An' I'da remembered any unattached females, that's for certain." He began to sort through the envelopes.

"Thought maybe you would," Rory said.

Willie lay two letters on the countertop. "What's up?"

"Oh, just curious. Heard there's a couple of them up the reservation digging around."

"You in the market for a wife?" Henson asked.

The Stetson stopped twirling. Rory straightened. "Nope. The Silver Sage is about all I can handle right now."

"How you been doin' since ol' Wilner died?"

"Not bad." If you consider working from sunup to sundown and always coming up short of money good, he thought. "But I miss the old coot more'n I like to let on."

Willie smiled. "Nobody could ride down a steer like Wilner Burnett. Leastwise that's what they say."

"What they say's the truth." Rory shoved the letters in his back pocket. Since Willie had not seen the women, he was at a dead end. There'd be nothing to do now but ride all the way down to the mesa that bordered the reservation on the south end of his land and search for them.

"With Wilner not long dead you still plannin' on holdin' the barbecue on the Fourth?" Willie wanted to know.

"Sure am," Rory assured him. Wilner had been dead six months, but the annual Fourth of July barbecue and rodeo for all the ranchers and neighbors was a tradition Rory intended to keep. "You be sure to come on out and bring your ma."

"I'll sure do 'er."

Before he left, Rory remembered to ask, "You get that new feed mix in?"

"It's in the back corner. Open up a sack if you want to see it," Willie offered.

Rory heard the sound of hooves out front as he sauntered over to the darkened back corner of the store. Just as he bent over a burlap sack of grain, he heard the distinct sound of a woman's heels tapping across the floorboards followed by Willie clearing his throat. Curious, Rory paused to peer around the end of a row of shelves and there she was, a woman the likes of which he'd never seen. He knew immediately she was one of the two he was looking for.

Willie glanced his way. Rory quickly shook his head and held a finger to his lips, aiming to study the woman before he approached her. The clerk turned his attention back to the woman at the counter. She was of medium height, slender, but not bony. From what Rory could see, she neatly filled out her fitted brown jacket. The trouble was, she had the damn thing buttoned nearly to her eyebrows. That was an exaggeration, he knew, but despite the warm June weather, the woman had the jacket closed all the way to her chin. A hint of cream-colored lace edged all that was visible of the collar. It brushed against the underside of her jaw.

He couldn't see her hair because she had it shoved up under a stiff-looking hat, but he guessed it was probably brown, or a watered-down derivative of it, just like everything else she wore. The hat itself reminded him of a picture he'd once seen, a seed-calendar painting of a hunter on African safari. She had on chamois gloves and sturdy, lace-up boots—again of brown. On the bridge of her perfectly tapered and slightly tilted nose rode a pair of thick, wire-frame spectacles.

The woman silently studied Willie Henson, who was smoothing down his parted, well-oiled hair with both hands as he stared back wide-eyed at his surprise customer.

Finally she spoke. "I'm Jessica Stanbridge and I'm here in Colorado to conduct a scientific search, Mister . . . ?"

Willie looked startled as she paused, then quickly supplied his last name. "Henson. Willie Henson, ma'am."

"Yes, well, Mr. Henson, I'm here on behalf of the Harvard Museum. You've heard of it, haven't you?"

"No, ma'am. I'm sorry I ain't. I mean, haven't never."

"I see. Well, at any rate, I'm a staff assistant paleontologist, and I've come to comb the area for signs of huge reptiles that inhabited the earth millions of years ago."

"They move back to Colorado?" Sudden concern marred Willie's usually bland expression.

Rory swallowed a laugh and noticed the woman missed the levity of the moment. She merely looked perturbed.

Miss Stanbridge shook her head. "On the contrary, Mr. Henson. I'm searching for the fossilized remains of saurians that have been dead for centuries."

"I see," said Willie, who obviously didn't see at all.

"I wonder if you can be so kind as to suggest someone hereabout that I might hire as a guide?"

She asked so softly that Rory could barely hear her. He leaned closer.

Willie swallowed and acted as if he'd never heard the English language spoken before. "Guide?"

She nodded. "Yes. Guide. Scout. Whatever you like to call it. I need a male. Preferably strong. Someone who knows the area well, especially the mesas on the Ute reservation."

Behind a full shelf of tins of cookies and soda crackers, Rory shifted. The woman fanned herself with her hand, blew at a stray wisp of hair that was hanging over her glasses, and then went on to explain, "I've tried to get some of the men at the reservation to help, but they seem unwilling to do so, even for pay."

"They tend to be a stubborn bunch," Willie editorialized.

"So it seems. I came to see if you have any suggestions. Perhaps someone who lives nearby. By the way, I saw your sign out front and will have my mail forwarded to your store. I would appreciate it if you could hold any letters that might arrive in the next few weeks, as I don't know how often I'll get into Cortez."

"Be happy to take care of your mail, ma'am, but as to gettin' somebody to guide you, I just don't—"

Rory suddenly saw his chance yawning as wide as the very mouth of the cave he hoped to steer Miss Jessica Stanbridge clear of. Signing on as her guide would give him a perfect opportunity to lead her away from the cave and off the Ute reservation. Once he had her on his land, he could keep her busy searching the high plateau for bones while he checked in at the ranch house. By getting to know her better, he could gauge whether or not she might be sympathetic to the Ute concerns.

He quickly stepped around the end of the shelves and over to the counter. When she swung her gaze toward him, he saw that she was startled to discover someone else was in the store. He was almost as startled as she, for he hadn't expected her eyes to be so blue, so wide, or so beguiling. Nor had he expected the mysterious bone hunter to be so

very beautiful. In spite of the dirt that streaked her face and
the owlish look the round spectacles gave her, her loveliness
was still apparent. For a fleeting moment he couldn't for the
life of him remember what he was going to say.

Then it hit him. "You say you're looking for a guide,
ma'am?"

"I am."

"Then I'm your man."

CHAPTER

2

Jessica tried to ignore the tall, dark-eyed stranger's intense stare. Instead she focused on the row of buttons down the front of his red plaid shirt and followed them down to his shining belt buckle. For a split second she wondered why a gun and holster rode his hip. It was hard not to notice the weapon—not when the handle was inlaid with turquoise and silver. Her gaze flicked lower. She immediately felt her color rise and looked up again. The entire perusal had taken no more than a second, but from the smug look on his face she knew it had taken too long.

"Who *are* you?" She put it bluntly, but he didn't seem in the least offended.

"Rory Burnett. I own the Silver Sage Ranch just south of here. It borders the Ute reservation."

"I see."

"And you?"

"Jessica Stanbridge, but since you seem to have been lurking somewhere nearby, I must assume you overheard my entire conversation. What I'd like to know is why would a rancher want to hire on as a guide?'' She reached up to straighten her hat.

''Why not?''

''Surely you must have enough work of your own. I was thinking of someone more in need of a job—''

''Miss Stanbridge, in case you haven't noticed, aside from this trading post and the livery, there's no one else around. Just how long are you willing to wait for someone to wander in here?''

Her last sight of Myra seated on the boulder surrounded by Utes forced her to answer, ''I can't wait at all. Do you have any references?''

''None. Aside from Willie here.''

''Oh, he's Rory Burnett all right,'' Willie volunteered as he felt along the part that split his hair down the middle.

''And I'm definitely strong,'' Rory added.

Jessica ignored Rory and turned back to the storekeep. ''Can he be trusted?''

''He sure can,'' Willie assured her.

''I'd appreciate it if you didn't talk about me like I wasn't even here.'' Burnett moved closer.

Jess took a step back and looked from one to the other. Perhaps the casually dressed, albeit dusty rancher was down on his luck. Besides, judging by appearances, she didn't look much better. What choice did she have? Two hours ago she had been willing to hire the Utes. At least this man could understand her when she gave him instructions, even if he didn't seem the type to take direction well.

Half hoping he would decline, she told him, ''Mr. Burnett, if you're willing to start right now, I'll agree to hire you on. I can pay you half a dollar a day, plus meals.''

''Why such high stakes?''

''Because the museum's benefactor wants results. Do you have access to any more help, should I need it?'' She felt oddly disappointed when he leaned against the counter, dropped his dark gaze, and began the irritating habit of spinning his hat on his finger.

"That depends on what kind of help you're talking about," he said quietly.

When he looked her directly in the eyes again, she realized he had a very disturbing way of seeing right past her spectacles as if he knew they were unnecessary. Indeed, they were no more than thick, clear glass. It was hard enough being a woman in a field of men without having been born with uncommon good looks. As the rancher continued to stare Jess reached up to make certain her jacket was still closed at the throat. It was, but somehow Rory Burnett made her feel as if all the buttons had just melted off.

"If . . . *when* I make the discovery I expect to make, we'll need men to help unearth the fossilized skeleton of the largest Jurassic saurian uncovered to date."

"Giant reptile bones, right?"

Surprised he knew that much, she nodded. "Exactly."

"And that's all you're looking for?"

"That's what our benefactor is funding this expedition for. Why do you ask?"

His stance was nonchalant, his expression carefully blank, but she couldn't help but feel he knew more than he was letting on. She watched him straighten to his full height and calculated that he was well over six feet tall.

The hat continued to spin, but slower now. "If all you want is bones, then you wouldn't be interested in seeing some tracks, would you?"

"*Tracks?*" Her cool, authoritative demeanor fled. Jessica clasped her hands in order to keep from grabbing him by the shirt front and shaking information out him. "Fossilized saurian tracks? More than one? What type of stone are they preserved in?" Her glasses slipped down her nose. She pushed them back up and waited impatiently for him to respond.

"About half a dozen. In sandstone."

Excitement bubbled inside her, so much so that she wanted to bolt from the store dragging Rory Burnett behind her. She was headed for the door before she realized he was not following her. Jessica paused in a patch of sunlight that spilled in through the opening and glanced over her shoulder.

"Well, Mr. Burnett? Shall we go?"

Rory watched the haughty twitch of Miss Jessica Stanbridge's beige-skirted backside as she hurried through the doorway. Once outside, he shoved on his hat to shade his eyes from the intensity of the noonday sun. So far, so good, he thought as he tried to remember exactly where it was he had seen the huge, birdlike tracks. As he recalled, they were in the sandstone floor of a wash that ran across the southwest corner of the Silver Sage.

He found her waiting for him beside her horse with a knapsack slung over her shoulder. Her helmet shaded her eyes as well as the spattering of freckles across the bridge of her upturned nose. He tried to guess her age and wondered how far past twenty she might be.

"Exactly where are these tracks, Mr. Burnett, and how long will it take us to get there?"

"You can call me Rory, Miss Stanbridge. They're about a two-hour ride from here. Did you say you're camped on Ute land?"

She paused, the reins of her chestnut gelding looped about one hand. "I didn't say, but we are. Is that anywhere near the tracks?"

"That depends on where you're camped."

She put her hands on her hips and sighed. "I've set up a field camp on the mesa near McElmo Canyon." When her mount tossed its head, she calmed it expertly.

"You'll have to move," he informed her bluntly.

"Why?" she demanded, focusing on him again.

He shook his head. "Too far away. If you're going to do more than look at the tracks, you'll need to move to the area." Before he was through, he saw her stiffen stubbornly and added, "But maybe a quick look-see is all you want."

She started scraping her thumbnail with her teeth, caught him watching, and stopped. "I'll need more than a 'quick look-see,' as you so colorfully put it. I'll need to make plaster impressions, measure them, and make note of the exact location and land formations. Then, of course, I'll study the surrounding area for fossilized skeletons."

"Then we'd best get going and collect your things."

Refusing a hand up, she used the wooden porch in front of the store as a mounting block. Once he was certain she was at home in the saddle, Rory rode slightly ahead and mentally reviewed his plan in detail. He'd see that the women were moved off Ute land as quickly as possible, get them settled on the plateau, and then have his men occasionally keep an eye on them while he got back to running things at the ranch. If Miss Stanbridge needed more help, he could spare Whitey, the young wrangler, but none of the more seasoned hands.

Until he had time to sit Miss Jessica Stanbridge down and explain the ramifications of prowling around Ute land and sticking her nose under every rock for bones that might unfortunately prove to be human, he was bound and determined to keep her and her friend busy. And until he knew for certain that his warning might not send her after the very thing he didn't want her to find, he intended to keep quiet.

"Excuse me, Mr. Burnett?"

"Miss Stanbridge, I'd appreciate it if you called me Rory."

He waited while she hesitated, obviously mulling over her response.

"I would prefer you call me Miss Stanbridge and I will

continue to address you as Mr. Burnett. I feel it's important to keep this an employer-employee relationship.''

He slowed up until their horses were side by side. ''No sense in being so formal out here.'' Rory couldn't help but notice her immediate discomfort. It had been a long time since he'd been with a woman. He couldn't help dropping his eyes to her lips, her breasts, the hem of a petticoat that was no more than a froth of lace against the top of her dusty boots.

He knew instantly that she hated his perusal. Fear flashed behind her eyes when he looked in the blue depths. He watched her glance around the open countryside as if realizing for the first time she had put herself into a vulnerable position with a complete stranger. When she put her hand to her throat to feel her top button, he could feel her fright, and it galled him that she thought he was the kind of man who'd be capable of hurting a woman.

''You've read one too many dime novels, Miss Stanbridge, if you think I aim to carry you off and outrage your person,'' he assured her coldly.

Her cheeks flamed. Her hands clenched the reins. ''What gives you any reason to think that I think any such thing, Mister—''

''It's Rory,'' he corrected again. ''And I could tell by the look on your face.''

When she picked up her reins as if to ride off and leave him, Rory reached out and put his hand over both of hers. ''Hold up, little lady. I couldn't help but notice the high-handed way you dealt with Willie back there, but don't ever try it on me.''

''Please, sir, I demand you let go immediately.''

''Do you ever let down your guard, Miss Stanbridge?''

''What do you mean by that?''

''Is this just some act to impress a no-account rancher with your stuffed-up, pompous ways, or are you really the tight-assed priss you pretend to be?''

Her lips pruned. She blinked twice. "You're fired."

"Fire me and you'll never see those tracks you were so hell-bent on seeing."

"Why should I even believe there are any tracks after this display of uncalled-for vulgarity, *Mister* Burnett?"

"Since when is being honest vulgar?"

"If I were a man, would you speak to me like this?"

"Hell yes. I like to think I deal the same hand to everyone."

"How's that? With insults?"

"No. With honesty."

Rory kicked his big Appaloosa into a canter, hoping he hadn't ruined everything with his big mouth. He hadn't meant to get her so riled up that she'd fire him—at least not until he had convinced her to move off the reservation. Up ahead, he saw the flash of the whitish tail patch of a rock wren and heard the songster trill. Not until he finally heard Jessica's mount pounding to catch up did he relax and start another poem.

As she blinked back tears Jess tried to tell herself Burnett's crude accusation didn't matter. Why should she care what some ill-mannered rancher thought if he had nothing better to do than torment her? More than his taunt, she hated the tears that escaped from that fragile part of herself she tried to hide from the world. There was no room in her life for vulnerability, or softness, or tears.

Damn Rory Burnett. Damn him for making me feel this way. Jessica turned her head and brushed her cheek against her shoulder before a telltale tear made its way any closer to her jawline.

A year ago when her father died, she hadn't even cried. But since then she had struggled through each and every day. Very often she still had to remind herself that he would not be waiting when she ran up the stairs to the two-bedroom flat they had shared in Cambridge.

Crying, he believed, was a waste of energy, so she drowned her sorrow in other pursuits like rearranging the furniture so that his overstuffed chair was no longer the focal point of the parlor. It helped ease the pain not to see the ruby-red chair standing in the bay window facing the boulevard and the park beyond. Cataloguing Uriah Stanbridge's books and charts, organizing his notes, and reading through his journals had kept her occupied during long, cold winter evenings. Had he lived, they would still be spending quiet hours in front of the fire discussing the latest finds in the field. Despite all the work she had surrounded herself with, her time alone in the all-too-silent apartment had been filled with aching loneliness.

Uriah Stanbridge had been her father, her mentor, her friend. And now he was gone.

Instead of giving in to the yawning void in her life, she often reminded herself that her father's knowledge lived on through her. That knowledge was his legacy, the talisman she carried as she continued his work at the museum. No other woman could claim such an opportunity; his name alone had opened doors to her that would otherwise remain closed.

But her entrance into the scientific field had claimed its own price; in a field of men, she was always afraid to let her feminine, emotional side show. Nor did she want anyone to take her less seriously because—to be perfectly honest with herself—she possessed more than passing fair looks. She considered it a disadvantage she would have gladly traded away, but since that was impossible, Jessica worked hard to camouflage her appearance. But now this man, this Rory Burnett, seemed able to strip away her disguise with a mere glance.

Once she was certain that she was not about to cry again and humiliate herself, she rode on, but held her horse back so that she wouldn't be forced to ride beside Rory Burnett. From this vantage point she could study him without having to suffer his perusal of her. He was a tall, muscular man whose black, high-crowned hat gave the appearance of even greater height. She couldn't help but notice his wide shoulders, narrow hips, and straight spine. She noted the way he confidently held the reins of his mount, the way his knees worked the beautiful black-and-white-spotted horse.

Although his features were sharply chiseled, his skin tanned and weathered, he was still handsome. His eyes were black. Piercingly black. As deep and fathomless as a moonless night sky. There was no denying it; confidence and competence radiated from Rory Burnett.

Jessica knew exactly what Myra would say when she saw him, for her companion's aim in life—aside from trying to see the world and learn as much as she possibly could before she "made her transition to the other side"—was to see that Jessica made a romantic attachment. And if there was one subject over which she and Myra continually clashed, it was the fact that the farthest thing from Jessica's mind was forming any sort of romantic entanglement. Ever. Her own path in life was clearly laid out for her; her one goal to establish a name for herself in the scientific community. It was hard enough being a woman in a man's field without the additional stigma of being a wife and mother.

To her chagrin, Jessica looked down and found Rory Burnett's knee very near her own. Somehow they had drifted into riding side by side again. She looked up and met his gaze and was startled when his hand grazed her arm. He pointed to a spot somewhere in the distance.

"What?" she said, squinting through her dusty glasses. She wished she could take the damned things off.

"Tortoise. Over there by that sage."

There was sagebrush nearly everywhere she looked. "I don't see anything."

He pointed again. "There. Beneath the big clump on the right. In the shade."

They drew nearer until he indicated to her that she should stop. Rory dismounted, walked over, and picked up a tortoise the size of a dinner plate and handed it up to Jessica. She took it in her gloved hands, held it at arm's length, looked the aged creature in the eye, and smiled. "Hello, old thing."

"Since you're in the reptile business, would you like to have it?"

Striving to keep their relationship cool, she made no comment.

"You want to keep him or not?"

Jessica thought he might be making a peace offering, and in the interest of peace she accepted with a nod. "How shall I carry it?"

Rory reached up and took the tortoise and walked with it under his arm to his own horse. He pulled a folded burlap sack out of his saddlebag, gently slipped the tortoise inside, and then held it on his lap in front of him once he remounted.

When he spurred his horse on again without another word, Jessica decided she should make some effort to try to smooth the ruffled waters between them. Trying to avoid another argument over the use of his given name, she asked, "Have you lived here long?"

"All my life."

"And your parents?"

"I was orphaned when I was less than a year old. The Burnetts adopted me. They're both dead now." He didn't offer any more information.

Two questions into it and she'd reached a barrier. Jessica tried another tack. "I suppose ranching can be a very demanding business."

"It can."

"What do you raise?"

"Cattle."

"Ah."

"Yep. That about sums it up."

She guided her horse across a gully, leaned forward as the gelding cantered up the other side. The challenge was great, but she'd met stiffer. After all, she had convinced the museum board that she was capable of bringing back a find. Jessica forged on with her line of questioning. "Do you have any hobbies?"

He was silent for so long that she wondered if he refused to answer or if silence simply was the answer. Finally she watched his shoulders shift beneath the plaid shirt and then heard him say, "Poetry."

She was as shocked as if he'd just said knitting. *"Poetry?"*

"You've heard of it, haven't you? Words that rhyme?"

"I'm sorry if I sounded somewhat taken aback, Mr. Burnett, but you don't seem at all the type to be interested in poetry."

"Why not?"

Why not? "Well . . . I don't know, I just never thought of anyone so . . . so . . . ."

"Uncivilized?"

"I didn't say that."

"Backward?"

"I wasn't thinking that either!"

"So *what*, then?"

She didn't dare say what she thought. She glanced at the turquoise on his gun butt, his spurs, his worn hat. "So colorful, I suppose."

He smirked. "You'll have to do better than that, Miss Stanbridge."

"All right. So *rough*, then."

"Rough?"

Finally her temper snapped. "I just never thought of anyone who wears a gun belt and farms cattle as being interested in poetry, that's all. I'm entitled to an opinion."

He reined up again. Her mare stopped immediately. With

a look that would have withered anyone the least bit faint of heart he said, "You have a lot to learn then, *Miss Stanbridge*. And you ought to know I don't *farm* cattle, I *raise* cattle."

With that he rode down another shallow wash and up the other side. Jessica stared off into the distance, watched the reddened sandstone mesa where she had left Myra grow larger on the horizon, and hoped, not only for the sake of Henry Beckworth, the museum's impatient benefactor, but for herself, that her time with Rory Burnett would be short.

> Some women give comfort
> Some just give pain.
> Some are stubborn enough,
> To stand out in the rain.
> But when I find a woman,
> A gal I can love,
> We'll both fit together
> Like a hand in a glove.

Not bad, he thought. Rory turned the phrases over and over in his mind. Not bad at all. He always found that the right words came to him fastest when he was pissed off, and if the last two hours alone with Jessica Stanbridge were any indication, he was probably going to do one hell of a lot of composing over the next few days.

He watched as Jessica's female companion put down a book and hurried across the campsite to greet them. She was shorter, a sight wider, and far friendlier than Jessica, if her welcoming smile and enthusiastic shout of hello was any indication. Sporting a getup much the same as Jessica's, the elder woman waited while Rory dismounted. The woman beside him was out of the saddle before he could offer to help her, which was just as well as far as he was concerned.

Rattlers came in pretty packages, too, but a man didn't rush to touch them.

With the burlap sack in his hand, Rory stared around the pitiful excuse for a campsite and listened while the two women exchanged greetings.

"How did everything go, Myra?" Jessica asked.

Rory felt the older woman's eyes on him even though she spoke to her friend. "Lovely. Our Ute friends left shortly after you did. I gave away the sketch of the youngest and they seemed well pleased. Aren't you going to introduce me?"

When she moved up beside him, Rory gave Myra his full attention. Jessica offered brief introductions and then Myra bluntly asked, "Are you married, Mr. Burnett?"

Jessica Stanbridge turned scarlet and whispered, "Good heavens, Myra."

Rory was hard pressed to hide a smile as Myra turned back to her companion. "I'm only asking because I'm sure you didn't think to."

"No, I didn't. Besides, what difference does it make?"

Myra turned to Rory and offered an apology. "I'm sorry, Mr. Burnett, it's just that I'm curious about everything. Jessica always forgets the details where mundane things are concerned. But just ask her anything about paleontology and she's got the answer on the tip of her tongue." She gazed at him over a pair of lopsided spectacles. "So, you're to be our guide?"

"Yes, ma'am." He shot a cool glance at Jessica. "If you want, you can call me Rory. And you'll want to start packing. I'd like to have you two moved by sundown."

"Wonderful!" Myra started to hurry off in the direction of the lopsided tent then stopped and looked over her shoulder. "By the way, where are we going?"

"I promised to take Miss Stanbridge to see some saurian tracks on my land, but I'm afraid it will entail moving your camp."

Myra glanced at Jessica and back to Rory. Then she

smiled. "Saurian tracks? What luck! Marvelous! I knew everything would work out. I'll be ready in no time."

Jessica trailed after Myra. He heard her say, "How come you are so willing to pack up and leave? You wouldn't budge this morning when I asked you to go into town."

Myra looked back at Rory, then at Jessica, and shrugged. "I suppose being rested makes all the difference. Besides, things may prove to be far more interesting from now on."

The sun slipped over the edge of the land before the relocated travelers had time to cook their dinner. Myra made a rock pen for the tortoise she named Methuselah while Rory stoked the fire, opened two cans of beans, dumped them in a pot, and got the coffee going. When Myra joined him at the fire, he handed the bacon duty over to her.

Across the fire Jessica pulled four crates together into a makeshift table, hefted two caneback chairs out of the wagon, and carried them over. The smell of the frying bacon made her stomach grumble, and until it had, she thought she was too tired to eat.

Even though Burnett had pushed them all afternoon, by the time they had set up the new camp, she still had not had a chance to see the promised saurian footprints. They had barely had enough light left to choose a clearing.

Jess felt the strain in every muscle as she set the two chairs in place and then reached for the chisel in her pocket. She had done as much lifting as Burnett, only relinquishing the heaviest crates and barrels when she could not budge them. Now she pried open a low crate that stood with a pile of others near the tent. Inside lay her china and cutlery, carefully packed between wads of burlap she would later use to make plaster casts for fossils. She took out a stark linen tablecloth, shook out the wrinkled folds, and let it settle over the table. Piece by piece she unwrapped three plates, cups, and saucers, then lined the monogrammed silverware up alongside it.

She snuck a glance at Rory Burnett and found him hunkered down by the fire, watching expectantly as Myra fried the bacon. The two of them were talking softly. Jessica envied them their growing camaraderie. Despite the trying move, Myra was still full of spark. She had complained a few times when the wagon had jolted sharply over the rocky ground, but had done her share to help them get moved.

In the dim light cast by the fire, Jess turned back to her task and, once satisfied, went into the tent to freshen up. The oil lamp on a box between two cots was already burning. Tossing her helmet on the bed, she turned up the wick and then poured water from the pitcher on the makeshift stand into a wide, porcelain bowl. Having finally discarded her jacket during the unpacking, she reached up and unbuttoned the collar and top buttons of her blouse. The pins that held the tight knot atop her head fell to the cot one by one as she pulled them out and then shook her hair until it swung free to her hips. She set her spectacles beside the basin. As she began to splash the refreshing, tepid water over her face and neck, Jess sighed with relief.

It was definitely foolish, she decided as she massaged her throbbing temples, to let Burnett get to her. He was only hired help. A necessity. A means to an end. When her work was complete, she would happily see the last of him. There was no need for her to worry about what he thought of her or to let him shake her carefully controlled composure.

No need at all.

"Supper's on."

She nearly jumped out of her skin at the sound of his voice and whirled around to the open tent flap. He was head and shoulders inside, unabashedly staring at the open throat of her blouse and the water stains spattered over the bodice. Her hands flew to the buttons. She fumbled one closed and then caught herself overreacting to his open appraisal. Straightening as far as she could in the low tent, she drew a deep breath, shot him an indignant glare, and said, "If you'll excuse me, Mr. Burnett, I'll be right there."

He smiled. A slow, wide, knowing smile. Without a word he withdrew.

Jessica thrust the remaining buttons through the button-holes, quickly wound her hair into another tight bun, and then picked up her pith helmet and jammed it on her head.

She found them waiting at the table, the plates already filled with beans and bacon. Coffee steamed in the china cups. A tin of crackers completed the meal. She noted Burnett's portion was double that of hers and Myra's.

Myra asked no one in particular, "Smells wonderful, doesn't it?"

Conscious of the fact that Burnett was waiting for her to take the first bite, Jess lifted a forkful of beans to her lips and stared down at her plate as she chewed. "I'm so tired it doesn't matter what I'm eating," she mumbled.

"You shouldn't have done so much heavy lifting, my dear," Myra admonished.

Jessica made no comment, but just as she expected, Burnett did.

"Never saw so much stuff for a short stay in my life." He shoved a cracker into his mouth and bent over his plate.

Jessica stared at his big hand wrapped around her delicately patterned silverware. "You think I'm foolish for carrying the comforts of civilization with us?"

Rory glanced at her for a second and then shrugged.

"Perhaps I did bring one too many books," Myra admitted.

"*One* too many?" Still feeling quite testy, Jessica turned to her friend. "I didn't know you left any at home."

Undaunted, Myra smiled. "Reading is my life," she told Rory. "I can't imagine going anywhere without my favorite books. Just now I'm rereading a wonderful tale of reincarnated lovers who—"

"I'm sure Mr. Burnett isn't interested—"

"Sure I am. Go ahead, Myra."

Jess was seething. The two of them were on a first-name basis, discussing reincarnated lovers. Staring down at her beans, she shoveled up a forkful as she fought to maintain her dignity and silently cursed Burnett for getting under her skin so easily.

Finally, as if they sensed her unease, the conversation dwindled into silence. Rory Burnett picked up his empty teacup, turned it over, read the bottom, and then carefully put it back on the saucer.

"You do think I'm crazy for carrying all of this with me, don't you?" Jessica challenged.

Myra tried to stem the argument with a low warning, "Jessica, dear . . ."

"I didn't say that," Rory said.

"You didn't have to," Jess snapped irritably.

He sat up and shoved his hat back on his head, ready for a fight. "Look, lady, I didn't say anything about anything."

The firelight flickered over his features. The tension around the table increased as the silence lengthened. Jessica was determined to get hold of herself. Rory Burnett merely stared back.

"Where did you go to school, Rory?" Myra asked, trying to change the subject.

To Jessica's relief he finally looked away. "There wasn't any school around here when I was small. My mother taught me to read and I've done some learning on my own."

As if there was nothing wrong between her two dinner companions, Myra chatted on. "I imagine you're a busy man, being a ranch owner and all. What do you do in your spare time?"

"I like poetry."

"Really? Who do you admire most? I must admit that Whitman is a favorite of mine. So is Ralph Waldo Emerson."

"I don't read much poetry, ma'am. I write it."

Jessica **dropped her** fork. It clattered loudly against the china plate. Her **cheeks** burned with raw embarrassment.

When she **looked** up again, Myra was displaying a satisfied smile **and** Rory Burnett was concentrating on ignoring her.

"Please, give us a sample. I'd love to hear some of it," Myra coaxed.

When Burnett became visibly more uncomfortable, Jess couldn't help but feel satisfied. It served him right. "Yes, please do recite something, Mr. Burnett."

"I don't think so." He glared back at her.

Myra polished off the last of her bacon, wiped her lips with a linen napkin, and leaned forward. "Are you sure? I think it's very encouraging that there are so many young people about with such talent these days."

Rory didn't take his eyes off of Jess. "I'm sure you'd find my poems . . . *rough,* to say the least." Deftly he switched the subject. "I'd like to show you the tracks first thing tomorrow, Miss Stanbridge, so that I can get back to the ranch house."

For the third time in an hour he caught her off guard. "What do you mean, get back to the ranch house?"

"You didn't think I'd be staying here full-time, did you?"

She stared at him, blinked twice, and adjusted her glasses. "But I hired you as a guide."

"And I guided you. When you're ready to move camp again, I'll be back."

"As far as I know, you merely led me *away* from an area I intended to explore fully. This is no haphazard jaunt I'm on, Mr. Burnett, this is a field expedition for the Harvard Museum. I have been given the responsibility to report back with what I hope will be the major find of the century and I do *not* intend to go traipsing around at your whim. You brought me here to see saurian tracks that you *claim* are 'over yonder.'" She pointed to the northern edge of the campground. "I trusted you to be ready to help us pick up and move whenever I see fit. *Is that clear?*"

She watched him sit back and fold his arms across his chest.

His voice was low, his tone held no menace—but it was obvious he meant to put her in her place. "Let's get one thing straight, Miss Stanbridge. You obviously don't like me and I don't like you. I don't intend to drag this out any longer than I have to. I have a ranch to run, you needed someone to point you in the right direction and see you get there. You dig around here for a couple of days, I'll send my men out to check on you, and then—*when* and *if* you're ready to leave—I'll see that you get moved. Is *that* clear?"

"Exceedingly." She nearly choked on the word.

"Good. I'm going for a walk. When I get back, I'll bed down in the empty wagon. I'll see you at dawn." He stood up and turned to Myra, who had become ominously quiet as she began stacking the plates. "Good night, Myra." He nodded curtly at Jessica. "Miss Stanbridge."

As she watched him disappear beyond the glow of the firelight, Jessica leaned her elbows on the table and cooled her burning cheeks against her palms.

Tomorrow morning she intended to fire Rory Burnett again.

This time for good.

CHAPTER

3

The tent was dark. Jessica heard Myra breathing softly and knew that her friend wasn't asleep yet, but she didn't feel like engaging in conversation. As quietly as she could, she washed her face and hands, then sat down carefully on her cot and bent down to unlace her boots. She heard a sound outside near the edge of the camp and stiffened. A quick glance told her that the tent flap was still securely closed.

Firelight flickered on the tent's canvas walls, playing over the fabric. The smell of burning piñon mingled with the pungent, ever-present sage.

The sound of footsteps warned her Rory Burnett had finally returned from his walk. Perfectly still, she held her breath, listening to the creak of the wagon bed as he climbed inside and imagining the tall man stretching out with only a bedroll on the hard plank flooring.

Thankful that he had stayed away while she helped Myra wash and stack the tableware, Jess relaxed and dropped one boot to the ground. When the other was finally unlaced and carelessly tossed aside, she wriggled her stockinged toes and sighed, then she flopped back onto the cot.

Myra's voice floated to her from the darkness. "Aren't you going to change clothes?"

"I'm too tired."

At first there was no response, and then came a hushed, "I'm worried about you, my dear."

Jess draped her arm over her eyes. "Please, don't be. I'm just exhausted."

Myra continued to whisper. "I can't help but think you weren't ready for this journey, Jessica."

The quiet statement jolted her so that all the cobwebs of fatigue momentarily dissolved. Jessica turned her head toward Myra's silhouette outlined against the tent wall. "How can you say that when I've been training for just such an expedition for half my life?"

"Don't be offended, dear. I meant no slight to your professional ability. Heavens, no. What I'm worried about is your frame of mind. You're driving yourself. Perhaps it's too soon after your father's death for you to be under so much of a strain."

Rolling to her side, Jessica drew herself up on an elbow and propped her head in her hand. "What makes you think I'm under any strain? A time limitation, yes, but really, Myra—"

"Let's just say you're not yourself. Why, your behavior tonight toward Mr. Burnett bordered on rude. I've never seen you act that way before."

Trying to find a comfortable position, Jess wriggled her bottom and then punched her pillow. "You've never seen me at work. Besides, Mr. Burnett just seems to bring out the worst in me." Wishing it was his smug face, she gave the downy pillow another good whack.

"Why?"

Why? "He just does. He's . . . he's arrogant. He's . . . crude."

"Are we talking about the same man?" To Jessica's irritation, Myra sounded astounded.

"He said some terrible things to me on the ride from Cortez, Myra." Jessica heard a swift intake of breath.

Then, ever curious, Myra whispered, "Can you repeat them?"

Jess thought it was high time Myra lost some of her growing admiration for the man. Her face burned even in the darkness when she admitted, "He called me *stuffed up*."

"Oh, my!"

"And"—she paused for emphasis and lowered her whisper until it was barely discernible—"*tight-assed*."

"Oh!"

"Exactly."

"Why didn't you fire him?"

"I did. But he didn't take me seriously. And I didn't press the issue. I need him until he shows me those saurian tracks and he knows it."

The frame of Myra's cot creaked as she shifted. "I have to admit, you did act a bit pompous tonight at supper, dear."

"Well, now you know why."

"Since we need Mr. Burnett, don't you think it would be a good idea to put aside your offended pride and—"

"—ignore his hostility? I don't think so."

"He's not so bad. Maybe you offended him in some other way."

Jess thought of how she must have appeared on the ride back from Cortez when she let him know she felt frightened of him. And after all, he really hadn't done anything to lead her to think he might do her bodily harm—if one called staring her up and down nothing. Perhaps she had offended his male sense of honor with her unspoken accusation, but then again he didn't look the sensitive type.

Tomorrow she'd examine the tracks, if there were any, and Rory Burnett would go back to his ranch house, if his word was good. Then, if the man he sent out wouldn't help her when it was time to break camp, she'd simply return to Cortez and hire another guide. In fact, she thought as she relaxed onto her back again, this time she would be willing to ride all the way to Durango to find someone more suited to the task.

"Jessica?" This time hesitant, Myra's voice summoned her back from the edge of sleep.

"Yes?"

"I hope you aren't upset with me. I know how much your privacy means to you. I didn't mean to pry. I have nothing but admiration for what you've set out to do. It's a monumental task."

"It's an opportunity for me to finally prove myself, Myra. But not monumental. All I have to do is locate as complete a skeleton as possible before the museum loses confidence in me and sends someone else to fulfill Beckworth's wishes."

"But you're the most qualified."

"I'm a woman." Jess said the word as if it were a curse.

"You're Uriah Stanbridge's daughter. He was renowned in the field."

"That didn't seem to matter to museum director Ramsey. It took every argument and far more research than anyone else would have had to come up with just to convince him I could do the job. I had to show him extensive notes, report on nearly nonexistent geological surveys of the area, give a detailed plan of study, and if Wilson and Hedges hadn't already been busy in the field in Montana, he would still have sent them instead of me."

"It makes no sense."

"It makes perfect sense. Why would a millionaire like Henry Beckworth want to grant money to a museum with a director foolish enough to send a woman out to locate what he wants?"

"Because you're the best."

"That may be, but I haven't been able to prove it yet. As

far as Ramsey is concerned, all I've done is spend three years working in the museum basement gluing together thousands of fragments of fossilized bone, some no bigger than a thumbnail. If it hadn't been for Father, I'd never even have been accepted on staff.''

"But now is your chance to shine, my dear. Everything is going to work out, I can feel it. Fate has sent you Mr. Burnett and his saurian tracks. Success is in the air!''

She knew that if she didn't douse Myra's spirits quickly, her friend would be up marching around the tent. Jessica yawned out loud, pulled the blanket over her to guard against the night's chill, and murmured, "I hope so.''

As he lay on the rough wagon bed partially covered by a blanket that was far too small for his frame, Rory heard the hushed sounds of the women's voices but couldn't make out their words. The hard wood didn't give under the weight of his shoulder, so he shifted to his other side and tried to find a more comfortable position. Lord, but he felt ancient.

Only thirty and already he felt like an old man. Life had flown by on swift wings of late, an endless round of work on the good-sized spread. Ever since Wilner Burnett had died and left him the Silver Sage, he had been trying to live up to his adoptive father's name. It was a big pair of boots to fill. Wilner had made running the Silver Sage seem easy; he was always on top of the men, the accounts, the cattle, and the hundred other jobs that had to be done. Rory credited himself with keeping up with it all, but the task had left him no time for anything else.

It had been months since he had any time to himself and now he was wasting precious hours hauling the little bone hunter and her ridiculous wagonload of rubbish about, listening to her high-handed talk and putting up with her contempt.

Rolling onto his back, he folded his arms across his chest and crossed his ankles. Tomorrow, first thing, he'd show her the cursed tracks and head back to the ranch house, then he'd send Whitey to watch over the women until they were ready to pull up stakes again. As low man at the ranch, the wrangler usually preferred any job to his own. Sixteen-year-old Whitey might like nothing more than having the responsibility that Rory couldn't wait to shed.

Welcome to it, Rory thought. With any luck at all, his own experiences with Miss Jessica Stanbridge would be few and far between.

Jessica Stanbridge.

Damned if he could figure her out. What was she hiding behind her tightly controlled emotions and thick glasses? What was it he'd seen lurking behind her confident facade? Fear? If so, of what?

Surely she still wasn't afraid of him?

He went back over the day's events. Sure, he'd given her a good once-over, no more than any other red-blooded man would have done, and she'd reacted as if he intended to throw her down and toss her skirts up over her head. Which, if she knew him well, would prove to be a ridiculous notion. Sometimes it took him half an hour to work up the courage to ask a woman to dance.

She was a damn pretty woman. A beauty really. He reckoned she would have to be a fool to be unaware of her good looks. Maybe she didn't want to draw attention to it, but why try to hide it all together?

Even with her modest, drab outfit and those ridiculous glasses, Jessica Stanbridge was still an eyeful—slim-waisted, rounded hips with a hypnotic sway that she would have surely corrected if she knew it existed, straight shoulders, and a proud carriage. Beneath the jacket were breasts that were just the right size for her frame, not too big, not too small. Probably a very good handful.

Staring up at the star-spattered sky, Rory felt a swift tightening in his crotch and knew he had better change the direction of his thoughts. He forced himself to think of the job facing him tomorrow, but somehow it didn't hold a candle to the memory of a day spent with his new employer.

He closed his eyes, only to see her as she had appeared at the table highlighted against the golden firelight. Seated on a cane chair in the dirt, using sterling silver to fork beans into her mouth off of a china plate, she had made eating in the open a sophisticated ritual. He remembered the smallest details of the way she'd appeared in the tent when he had caught her unaware—her face glistening with water droplets, her sky-blue eyes wide with shock—his own surprise when he discovered that instead of the mud-brown hair he expected, she had thick, golden blond hair that hung all the way to her hips.

She hadn't been buttoned up to the hilt then. She had been natural, spontaneous, and all too inviting.

Rory stifled a groan and rolled onto his other shoulder.

Hopefully, dawn would come early.

Jessica awoke when daylight crept in with the early-morning chill and Myra was still snoring. She sat up slowly and pushed her hair out of her eyes. It was a hopeless tangle. She found pins scattered across her pillow and on the floor beside the cot. Her ecru blouse was wrinkled beyond hope, her skirt twisted up around her thighs. Now that the light of day was upon her, she wished she had taken the time to change into her nightgown.

As she rose stiffly from the narrow cot, moving silently so as not to awaken Myra, she heard the soft sound of a melodious whistle. Carefully opening the tent flap a mere fraction of an inch, she peered out and spied Rory Burnett hunkered down over a low fire. He whistled a cheerful tune as he concentrated on his task. Not more than four yards away, he was dressed in the same outfit he had worn yesterday, faded denims and a plaid shirt. He, too, must have slept in his clothes, but instead of looking like the bottom of a laundry basket like she did, he didn't appear any worse for wear. His inky hair was carefully combed, still damp from a morning wash and as shiny blue-black as a crow's wing.

She watched a moment longer while he deftly moved a Dutch oven closer to the fire and then flipped open the lid of the enamel coffeepot to look inside. He was definitely at home around a campfire.

At the sound of a magpie, he looked up and whistled an echo to its call. When she saw his dark eyes flash toward her, Jess snapped the tent flap shut before he saw her and stood perfectly still. With her hands still clutching the edges of the opening, she closed her eyes and took a deep breath. *Today,* she promised herself, *I will not let Rory Burnett upset me. I will remain calm and in control. I will not lose my temper. I will try to be civil—no, friendly—toward him.*

Jess stopped in the middle of making vows to herself and opened the flap just the tiniest bit. Maybe friendly was taking it a bit too far. She would start with civil, and see how the day progressed.

In no time at all she had changed into clean clothes, identical to the ones she had on yesterday. Fresh cotton stockings and a change of petticoat and chemise were wonderfully refreshing after removing the bedraggled, limp underclothing she had worn for three days.

As she pinned on her brooch Jessica noted that it was just a little past six. Certain it was still early enough to take a few extra minutes, she brushed out her hair until it crackled and shone and then plaited it into a long braid that she left hanging free. As thick as a man's fist, it almost reached her hips.

Her stomach rumbled and her mouth watered when the smell of fresh-brewed coffee wafted into the tent. She quickly put on her helmet, then took it off again and set it on the bed while she hunted for her knapsack, hidden beneath the pile of rumpled clothing. From a small trunk at the end of her cot she took a notebook, pen and ink, a neatly rolled measuring tape in a brass case, pencils, and her maps. She packed them into her boxy leather knapsack that already contained the tools and binoculars she had inherited from her father, and buckled it closed.

Shrugging the strap of her knapsack over her shoulder, Jess put on her helmet and took one last look in the oval standing mirror on her makeshift washstand and considered herself ready to greet the day—and Mr. Rory Burnett, rancher turned guide.

> You can ask anybody,
> What time they love best,
> And they'll all answer different,
> North, south, east, or west.
> But the time of the day,   ·
> That I love best of all,
> Is mornin'—be it summer, winter, or fall.

Or spring. How am I gonna work in spring?

"Good morning, Mr. Burnett."

Rory nearly spilled coffee all over his thigh at the sound of her voice. He glanced up from the crate of books he'd pressed into service as a seat and found Jessica Stanbridge standing over him. How or when she had crept up on him he didn't know, but he did wonder why in the hell his heart bolted at the sound of her voice. He was starting to act as jumpy as she was and he wasn't the sort to get riled over nothing.

With his legs spread wide, he let the coffee slosh over the edge of his cup and drip onto the ground between his boots. He looked at her from beneath the brim of his black Stetson.

"How are you this morning?"

He didn't know what to make of her chipper greeting, so he answered slowly, suspiciously, "I'm doing just fine, Miss Stanbridge, how about you?"

"Much better, thank you. In fact"—she took a deep

breath and looked up at the brilliant cerulean sky and then off toward the high mesa, the sight of her previous camp— "I feel quite rested."

"That's good, ma'am." He waited to see if her good humor would dissipate. She stood waiting expectantly, looking down at his tin coffee cup.

He stared up at her, his steaming coffee forgotten, wondering how anyone had the right to such clear, glowing skin or such vibrant blue eyes, eyes that mirrored the expansive sky above them. More freckles than he had noticed yesterday peppered the bridge of her nose. Her lips formed a dainty pout. Her lashes were thick and dark, a sharp contrast to her light eyes. Deeply appreciative of the sight, he watched as she worried her bottom lip with her teeth and stared back at him.

Rory shook himself into action. "Would you like some coffee?"

"Thank you, yes. May I ask where you got that tin cup?" She was digging through the dishes they had carefully stacked inside a barrel, trying to locate a cup and saucer. When she returned to the fire, he lifted the pot and poured while she held her fragile, flowered cup beneath the spout.

"I carry it tied in my bedroll."

"What a good idea. It's probably very useful."

He lifted the lid of the Dutch oven and grabbed a warm biscuit. Tossing it back and forth in his hands, he blew on it and then set it on his knee. "Want a hot rock?"

"A hot rock?"

"A biscuit."

When she actually smiled, the first smile he'd ever seen on her lips, he forgot what he'd even asked her.

"I would love one. I see you found the cooking supplies."

"That I did. Scratchy'd be proud of me."

"Scratchy?"

"He's the biscuit shooter at the Silver Sage. Been there longer than anyone can remember."

"Biscuit shooter?"

"The cook. Orneriest old cuss you ever saw." He lifted his coffee cup up off the ground and took a long swig. "He doesn't make the greatest housekeeper, if you're at all particular about dirt, but we have to eat and there's nobody else around to do it."

"You seem quite at home around a campfire."

"Spent a lot of time on the range. I'm afraid you've sampled everything on my menu—thunderberries, bacon, and biscuits."

"Thunderberries?"

He cleared his throat, embarrassed about having to explain. "Beans."

"Oh." She looked around for one of the bentwood chairs and dragged it over before he could get it for her.

Wonderful, Burnett. She's making an attempt to be friendly and you can't get up off your ass in time to get her a chair.

If she was put out, Jessica didn't let on. He watched her seat herself, arrange the hem of her skirt until it covered her ankles, and then pick up the dainty cup and saucer. She took a sip and looked over the gold-edged rim of the cup and acted as if his poor show of manners didn't matter to her in the least.

Rory wiped his hands on his pant legs, took another biscuit out of the cast-iron pot, tossed it back and forth, and then passed it over to Jessica, who dropped it onto her lap to let it cool.

They sipped and ate without talking while the magpie scolded them from a twisted juniper nearby. Rory found himself at a loss with this new Jessica Stanbridge. Somehow it had been much easier to deal with the quick-tempered woman she'd been yesterday. He had known just how to act and what to say.

Today she seemed softer, more vulnerable—maybe, he reckoned, it was the fact that she'd braided her hair instead of shoving it all up out of sight beneath her silly veiled helmet. Or it could just as easily be because she was no longer acting so waspish. Maybe it was the open way she met his gaze and looked at him instead of through him with her big blue—

"You're not wearing your spectacles!" The realization burst from him without warning.

She stood up so fast that the second biscuit he'd handed her catapulted off her lap and arced into the air before it landed with a soft thud in the sandy soil. The teacup rattled in the saucer as she banged it down on the seat of the chair and hurried off toward the tent with what sounded like a mumbled, "Excuse me."

He watched her feet fly across the ground, whipping her skirt and petticoats around her ankles. Rory hid a smile behind his tin cup and chuckled to himself, fairly certain his guess had been right; if she had forgotten to don the spectacles, perhaps she didn't need them at all.

When she returned, he couldn't help but notice the way her cheeks were two bright red spots against a field of white. Jessica cleared her throat, looked around for the biscuit he'd already tossed away, and picked up her cup again.

Aware of her discomfort, Rory made no more mention of the spectacles. Instead he nodded at her knapsack hanging over the back of the chair and said, "I see you're ready to go look at the tracks."

"I am, if indeed they exist."

"They're about five hundred yards away. We can walk, or ride if you prefer."

"I think walking would be best. That way I can study the outcroppings along the way and make notations. I must tell you I'm quite surprised that there is anything down here at all. Given the geological makeup of the land on the high mesa behind us, I'm fairly certain that is where I'll make a major find. But it will be interesting to see what you call saurian footprints."

He glanced over his shoulder at the mesa before he offered her more coffee and another biscuit. Red and pink in the early-morning light, the mesa rose like an impregnable castle wall in the distance. Rory frowned down into his empty cup and stared at the loose coffee grounds stuck to the bottom. From the little she had already told him, he knew that finding a set of saurian bones was of utmost importance. His problem, he decided, was not only the fact that he was wasting valuable time away from the ranch, but that he was also leading her away from the very thing she needed to find—and because of Wilner Burnett's promise, there was nothing else he could do. He was bound to his promise to keep the cave secret.

Rory stood up and tried to flick the moist coffee grounds out of his cup. He walked to the water barrel strapped to the side of the wagon and poured half a dipper into his cup, swirled it around, and chucked the water out onto the thirsty soil.

He watched Jessica walk toward him. With the knapsack slung over one shoulder and her gloves on, she was ready to go. "I'll just tell Myra we're leaving," she said as she walked past him toward the tent.

The fresh, powdery scent of her soap flavored the air around her and he breathed it in as she passed. It was a welcome experience; it had been a long time since he'd had the pleasure of a woman's company.

By the time he had tied his cup back in his bedroll and was leaning against the wagon wheel, Jessica walked out of the tent and crossed the open ground toward him. She was holding a folded page in her hand.

"Myra is awake, but she's reading. She said she'll go with me later to see the tracks." Jessica reached down and began to unfold the page. "Before we start out, I'd like you to point to our exact location on this map."

"We're here," he said, bending near to savor her floral scent. "Southwest of Cortez, just off the Ute reservation." He held on to a corner of the map while she studied it. "Where did you get this?"

"Why?"

"It's not complete."

"I realize that, Mr. Burnett. This isn't a well-documented area. That's precisely why I hired a guide."

He smiled. "Well then, I'd best start guiding." Without another word, Rory started off toward the northeast. The sun was higher in the sky, its warmth quickly heating the crisp dry air. Here below the mesa on the arid floor of the high plateau, the land was carpeted with silver sage and mesquite. Yucca, with its deep green, sword-shaped leaves, was scattered amid the rocks and low-growing dwarf piñon. As he walked along, careful to shorten his stride so that the woman beside him could keep up, Rory wondered what she thought of this land that he loved so much.

To the untrained eye it was barren and lifeless, but in reality the high desert teemed with life. Mourning doves nested in the low trees or on the ground and filled the air with their mournful *coo-ah, coo, coo, coo*. A spiny swift lizard, as rough in appearance as the rock-littered ground, scurried across their path.

Rory glanced over at Jessica. If she noticed the lizard, she didn't comment. Instead she kept her gaze on the ground. He could tell she was thinking, making note of the path they traveled, often glancing back at the camp. He wondered if she was still afraid of being alone with him. If so, she was doing her damnedest to hide it.

"We're almost there," he said, hoping to reassure her.

"That flat sandstone slab in the distance?"

He nodded. "Right. The prints are on top of it."

The stiff material of her skirt brushed the ankles of her boots as she picked up her pace. She was concentrating on the mass of stone that they were fast approaching. He could hear her breathing rapidly now as she trotted along. With one hand she kept her hat on while the other clutched the shoulder strap of her knapsack.

He was forced to lengthen his stride just to keep up with her. "Don't turn a heel," he warned. "That rock isn't going anyplace."

She looked back at him, her cheeks deep pink from exposure to the sun. Excitement shone in the blue eyes trapped behind the thick, clear glasses. Half of the veil wound around her hatband was sagging over the brim and one eye. Excitement radiated from her until it charged the very air around her.

Rory found himself actually looking forward to her reaction to the tracks imprinted in the rock. He tried to convince himself that showing them to her would make up for leading her away from the cave on the mesa.

She ran the last few yards. He ran beside her, his heavy boots pounding the dusty soil.

When they finally reached the slab that lay nearly four feet thick and thirty feet long, she slowed down and approached it as reverently as an acolyte approached an altar.

"I can't remember how many there are, but they run from west to east across the top," he said.

She shushed him.

In silence, Jessica stepped forward. One, two, three steps. Then she halted. He heard her sigh. Slowly she reached up and removed her spectacles, carefully folded the stems, opened her knapsack, and dropped them in. Slipping the strap off her shoulder, she handed the heavy bag to him without a word. He took it without comment and watched her step up to the waist-high stone platform.

Worshipfully she reached out. He could see her fingers trembling as she traced the outline of one of the closest, birdlike marks in the sandstone. Then she laid her open palm in the hollowed-out print on the warm rock. Standing perfectly still, Jessica closed her eyes and sighed.

A second later she turned to him. With a look that bespoke the depth of her sincerity she said, ''Thank you, Mr. Burnett. This is the most wonderful thing anyone has ever given me.''

CHAPTER

4

"I guess they'll do, then?" He couldn't help but feel smug after proving to her that he hadn't been lying.

"Do? They're perfect. And so many! I want to take a few measurements before we go back to camp." She was looking at the tracks now, not at him.

He leaned back on his elbows and tipped his hat further down to shield his eyes from the rising sun. "Whatever makes you happy, Miss Stanbridge."

"Might I trouble you to give me a boost?"

Rory nodded, and before she was quite expecting it, he grabbed her around the waist and lifted her up onto the sandstone rock. He set her knapsack down beside her and then pulled himself up as well. She was busy searching in the dark bag for her measuring tape; when she finally found it, she produced it with a flourish and a "Voilà!" Next she pulled out a bound notebook, a pencil, and a thick sable brush.

Rory stretched out on the rock's warm surface and

watched her from beneath his hat brim. Her once haughty demeanor was gone as Jessica Stanbridge lost herself in her work. He could only assume it was sheer excitement that caused her to chat on as she made notations.

She lifted her skirt, careful not to expose her legs to him, but he did catch a glimpse of black cotton stockings beneath her white petticoats. Scrambling forward over the rock, she paused on all fours beside the first print and lifted the brassbound case that contained her measuring tape. She held the end of the tape with one hand, measured from the tip of the middle toe to the heel of the print, and then from one side to the next.

Rory was hard pressed to hide a smile as he watched her and wondered what the ever-so-solemn Miss Stanbridge would say if she could see herself from behind with her pert, round derriere pointing skyward. He decided to remain silent and simply enjoy the view.

Jessica opened the crank handle and rewound the oiled-cotton tape, then reached for her notebook. She made a notation, then set book and pencil down and picked up the brush. As she briskly swept the loose sand and dirt out of the footprint, she glanced over at him.

"I really didn't expect to find anything at this altitude. I had singled out the grand mesa because the red sandstone bluff is striated with the white sandstone and hard clay deposits." She threw a fleeting smile his way and shook her head. "That's a sure sign of Jurassic formations. If any remains of extinct giant reptiles are to be found, that"—she nodded toward the mesa—"would be the most likely place."

"Why?" He watched as she picked up the tape again, remeasured the print, and then scooted everything over to the next one. On all fours, she bent over the next print and he smiled to himself again.

"It's very hard to explain in a few words," she began, "but the land is layered according to the body of water that once covered it. The lower marine strata contain the remains of such creatures as the ichthyosaur, which is sort of a fish lizard.'' Quickly noting the print's length in her little book, Jessica then brushed out the second one before she measured the distance between the two depressions.

He had but a vague notion of what she was talking about. ''You sound like a professor.''

She looked amazed. ''Is that a compliment or an insult?''

Rory sat up, crossed his legs, and pulled one foot close beneath him. He ran his finger over the tooled leather design on his boot. ''What got you started?''

''Probably the same way you became a rancher—it was my father's profession. Some say he was the best paleontologist that ever lived—but he was an unsung hero. Most of his work was done in the laboratory, but he did go to Egypt once. After I was born, he never traveled far to do excavations. My mother died when I was very, very young and my father stayed close to home to be with me. He included me in everything.''

He tried to imagine her as a little girl with sunshine hair and blue eyes, trying to learn the difference between rock formations and bits of bone, and found himself hard pressed. Jessica Stanbridge was so naturally feminine— despite her efforts to hide it—that she made him think of dolls and tea parties, not rock sorting and bone hunting.

''Do you know anything at all about the early saurian finds, Mr. Burnett?''

''I don't even know anything about the late saurian finds, ma'am.''

She bristled. ''Am I boring you?''

''Not a bit.'' He smiled into her eyes.

She colored and quickly turned away, but kept talking. ''A rancher like yourself picked up the first giant saurian bones ever found in the West, right here in Colorado, near Canyon City.''

''No kidding?''

"How old are you, sir?"

"Thirty."

"It was in the seventies. You might have been too young to remember, even if you had heard about it."

"What about you?" He thought it a very sly way to ask her age.

"I can still remember Father's closely following the reports. Everyone was talking about it at the time."

He was surprised at her wistful tone when she mentioned her father, and could tell immediately that she missed him deeply. She had kept it well hidden until now. She reached the end of the prints and stood up. Brushing off her skirt, Jessica put her hands on her hips and surveyed the discovery. "Five good prints, three feet apart. Much more than I expected."

"You thought I was lying."

She frowned. When she caught him studying her so intently, Jessica dug through her knapsack, located her glasses, and shoved them on again. "I did. And I apologize."

"Accepted." Rory jumped down off the rock and wondered how he was going to keep her from insisting on a trip back to the mesa now that she'd seen and measured the tracks. "Now what?"

"Don't worry, Mr. Burnett. I know how anxious you are to return to your ranch. There's plenty to keep me here for a while. I plan to make a plaster impression of the prints so that I can ship them back to Harvard, and then I'll explore the area in all directions. I may come up with a fossilized bone fragment or two, hopefully more." When she gained the edge of the rock, she started to crouch down to jump off, but Rory reached up and grabbed her, then lowered her to the ground.

She was so close he could feel her warm breath near the open collar of his shirt. Trapped between him and the rock, she had nowhere to go. He could smell her lavender scent again and for a moment he didn't budge. Then Rory took a step back and said, "I'll be sending one of the hands out to watch over your camp so that if you need anything, you can send him to get me."

"I can't pay two men," she said softly.

"I won't be working for you if I'm not here. And you don't need to pay Whitey at all. He works for me. Besides, I don't know how much help he's likely to be."

"Is he old?"

"Just the opposite. He's barely out of short pants."

"Then I insist on paying him," she said, somehow maneuvering to step around him and start on the trek back to the campsite.

"And I insist you don't."

Adjusting the slipping knapsack strap, she pulled up short and stopped. "Are we going to be at loggerheads again, Mr. Burnett?"

He couldn't help but laugh. "We are if you keep arguing. You know, Miss Stanbridge, I'm usually an easygoing sort. Ask anyone who knows me."

Jessica shrugged. "I'm used to arguing with men."

He started walking again and noticed there was something oddly enjoyable about having her beside him. "Life's a lot more pleasant when it isn't a contest of wills. I'll stick to ranching and you can stick to bones so we don't have to tread on hen fruit around each other."

"Hen fruit?"

"Eggs."

"You have a peculiar vocabulary, Mr. Burnett. I should begin a glossary."

He kicked a small rock out of the way and watched it bounce across the ground. "That's funny, everyone I know talks like me. But I guess if your bone hunting doesn't pan out, you can always write a dictionary on southwestern lingo."

The look she gave him vehemently denied the suggestion.

As they approached the campsite Rory acknowledged it was a far different time that they had shared today. There was a likable side to Jessica Stanbridge after all, one that matched her beauty and her brains. It had been just as easy to converse with her as it had been to argue, so much so that a mounting sense of guilt nagged him when he thought of how easily he had led her away from the mesa.

He'd only been in the burial cave once in his life. His father had taken him up to red mesa to hunt down stray cattle. They found a lost calf bawling nearby and Wilner had showed him the outside of the cave. He was warned never to go inside. The place was a grave site filled with ghosts, Wilner said, Indian ghosts, and there was no telling what might happen if anyone made them mad.

To a boy of eleven, the cave had yawned wide and foreboding. Just beyond the entry he could see the smoke-stained ceiling and strange rock paintings that bordered on the edge of darkness. Then Wilner led him to the left side of the entrance and made him look hard at the mesa wall.

"What do you see?" Wilner had asked.

"Rocks, I guess."

"Look harder."

Rory had shrugged. "I don't know, Pa."

Ever patient, Wilner had stepped closer to the wall of sandstone and pointed. "Look here, and here. Follow this row of dark stones back to here."

His father had pointed without touching and Rory watched in awe as the imprint of a curious creature became visible. In his young life he'd seen enough skeletons of dead cattle to recognize bone structure when he saw it. A skull bone, neck vertebrae, rib bones, pubis, femur, feet, and even toes. The outline of a gigantic beast the likes of which he'd never seen was suddenly all too clear.

"What is it, Pa?" he had whispered as he stared in awe.

"All that's left of a giant lizard. The Utes claimed these were huge serpents that crawled into the earth to hide from the Great Spirit. But he found them all and killed them with bolts of lightning that fried 'em but left their bones in the ground.''

Rory remembered falling back a few more steps so that he didn't have to stand too close to the remains of a terrible lizard who had crawled into the earth to escape the Indian god.

''I don't ever want you coming up here alone, son.''

Rory shook his head. ''No, sir. I wouldn't even want to.''

''Never forget this place belongs to the Utes. It ain't ours even though part of it runs over onto our land. This is spirit stuff, boy. Ghostly things that I promised the Utes we'd stay clear of. You'll mind me now, hear?''

''I hear ya, Pa.'' Rory could still hear his own promise ringing in his ears.

Even now, years later, he still hadn't returned to the cave on the far mesa. Not because he believed in the evil spirits or ghosts, but because he knew enough about the Utes to know their grave sites were sacred to them. Respecting their beliefs, he just never went back.

But now the woman walking beside him was searching for the very thing he had helped to keep secret from other white men all his life. What would she think if she saw the reptile skeleton, which probably was quite massive, if memory served him? The unadulterated joy that lit her face at the sight of the footprints would be nothing compared with what she would experience if he led her to the cave. She could claim the find for her museum and make a name for herself back east.

There was far more to steer clear of on the mesa than the saurian skeleton. Far more. If he led her to the cave, he would not only jeopardize the trust the Utes had in the Burnetts, but he might even be putting Jessica Stanbridge at peril. Piah's warning had made it all too clear that no good would come to an outsider who discovered the cave. He couldn't believe the man would actually harm anyone who trespassed, but he didn't want to test Piah at all.

His thoughts led him to ask, "What will you do if you find what you're looking for?"

"There's no doubt about it. *When* I find what I'm looking for, I'll telegram the museum. They'll send out a team to excavate, which could take weeks, months, or even years."

Which is exactly why I can't let you find the cave.

The whiteness of the tent in the center of the campground stood out like a beacon against the colorful land and the clear sky. They could see Myra, dressed in her customary brown skirt, high-collared shirtwaist, and sturdy, lace-up boots, coming toward them carrying an umbrella for shade. Every few feet she would stop and bend down, peer at the ground, and then continue on. Finally she was within shouting distance.

"Hello!" Myra called out gaily. "Did you find them?"

"We did," Jessica shouted.

Rory looked down and found her smiling up at him. He shoved his hands in his pockets, feeling much like a boy who had just given his first girl a bouquet of wild zinnias. He glanced away and cleared his throat.

As Myra drew near she handed Jessica what appeared to be a stone. "I knew this was a wonderful place. I feel you are on the verge of a great discovery, Jessica. Just look at that."

Jessica rolled the piece over in her hands, slid her glasses down her nose, and peered over them at the rock. To Rory it looked like sandstone with tiny fluted shapes carved into it. He'd seen many of them before.

"Lithostrotion." Jessica said matter-of-factly.

"Can I have a look?" Rory held out his hand.

She dropped the piece into his palm.

"There's bushels of this around." He rolled the rock over and over.

"I'm sure of it," Jessica said.

"It's fantastic," Myra added.

"What exactly is it? I always thought it was just rock." Rory handed it back to her.

"Now it's rock. It's fossilized coral, those little ridged cones are coralites. It lived during the Paleozoic era when red sands and mud built up on the bottom of the sea and trapped it under the layers."

He frowned. "Is that how the prints were formed?"

"Exactly, but about thirty million years after the coral was gone."

Myra spun around, nearly poking Rory in the neck with her umbrella as she threw out one arm and surveyed the landscape. "Can you imagine all this under the sea?"

"Not once but four times," Jessica clarified.

He looked around the pink-hued landscape covered with short stubborn clumps of grass, sage, and rock outcroppings. Beyond were mesas dotted with piñon and juniper. He tried to imagine this land covered with miles of water.

"I can," Myra said enthusiastically. "I can indeed imagine."

All Rory could see was a vast stretch of empty ranch land, some fences that needed tending, and endless hours of work that needed to be done. The thought spurred him to take his leave.

"If you ladies will excuse me, I'll be getting back to the house. I'll send Whitey right out; he should be here in an hour or two, if I can find him when I get back."

Remembering to weave out of the way, he shifted his weight and missed being skewered by the umbrella again as Myra swung around to face him. She sounded disappointed. "You're leaving?"

"I have a ranch to run, ma'am, but I can get here in no time if you really need me. Just send Whitey."

Jessica showed no such disappointment. "Thank you, Mr. Burnett. I am thrilled with the saurian tracks, and as I said, they will keep me busy for another day or two. When

I've finished searching the area, I'll send for you and you can help us move back toward the high mesa.''

Not if I can help it. "Right. Let me know, ma'am." He tipped his hat to both of them and, with nothing left to say, walked toward the picket line where the animals grazed.

"So?" said Myra.

Jessica knew what was coming; still, she sidestepped. "So, what?"

"Tell me all about it. How was your sojourn in the desert with Mr. Burnett?"

Kneeling in the dust, Jessica paused with one hand on the crate that contained her excavation tools. She opened the lid and carefully removed a short-handled pick and laid it on the ground beside her. "Myra, please. Our 'sojourn in the desert'—aside from the fact that the saurian prints are more than I hoped for—was highly uneventful." From beneath the brim of her beige helmet, she shot Myra an accusatory glance. "Why should it have been anything else?"

"I think Mr. Burnett is an outstanding man. I thought perhaps . . ."

Jess rocked back on her heels, took off her glasses, and shoved them into her skirt pocket. "What exactly do you find outstanding about him? You hardly know him. *I* hardly know him, and I've already spent more time with him than you have."

"He's a fine-looking fellow. Handsome, strong of limb, straight eyes and teeth.''

"You could be describing a healthy horse, Myra."

Obviously irritated, Myra snapped her mouth and then her umbrella closed and leaned the latter against the table formed of crates. "I've made some tea." She set out two cups while Jessica pulled out more of the items she would need that afternoon—a sack of plaster of paris, a roll of burlap, extra tissue paper.

"I think," Myra said carefully, as if she knew the subject

would send Jessica's temper flaring, "that you and Rory Burnett might well be suited to each other."

Jess stood up and brushed the dust and bits of weed from her skirt. "Impossible. There is not a thing that man and I have in common, Myra, and you know it. He sets my teeth grinding."

"Exactly. He elicits a response from you even when a response is unwarranted." Carried away, Myra spread her arms like a symphony conductor. "Sparks fly. Electricity fairly crackles. Explosions rock the very air between you—"

"Sounds like you're describing a war, not a romance," Jessica mumbled, deciding to locate the rest of her supplies after tea.

Her enthusiasm stemmed but not extinguished, Myra set out a sugar bowl that matched the cup and saucers, and a square, etched-glass spoon holder filled with spoons, then opened a tin of canned milk. "I would just like to see you become interested in a man before it's altogether too late for you, dear."

"Sage advice coming from someone who's never married."

"Ah, but by choice."

Jessica removed her hat and set it on the corner of the table. "Then you should have no objection if I make the same decision."

Myra grew serious, the lines about her usually smiling mouth deepened as she frowned. "My status is the result of a decision too hastily made, not from lack of choice."

"I'll fill your cup and you sit down and tell me all about it." Jessica sat down on the bentwood chair, reached for Myra's cup and saucer, then carefully poured in the steaming dark brew.

Sitting down slowly to allow the legs of the chair to adjust to the loose soil, Myra ignored the tea. She put her elbows on the table and leaned toward Jessica, speaking in a voice so low that Jess strained to hear.

"Myra, there's no one around for miles. I do think you can speak up."

After a cursory glance to be certain, Myra began again. "When I was in my late twenties, I met a man I would not normally have even been attracted to. He was attending a literary soirée at a friend's home, and seemed highly uncomfortable, as if the very walls were confining. He did not add to or pay close attention to the discussion that day—I believe the topic was Plato. At any rate, after exchanging intense stares with him all afternoon, I was not surprised when he finally took me aside and asked in a wonderfully thick Irish brogue why I was content to sit and discuss a long-dead philosopher when I could be out in the sunshine enjoying a glorious day.

"We went for a buggy ride through the commons. What he didn't know about literature or philosophy, he made up for in knowledge of the real world: plants, flowers, animals, human nature. I have never felt so instantly at ease. It was as if we had indeed met in another place and time and had just rediscovered each other. At no time had I ever been away from a book for so many hours. It was all so very wonderful."

Jessica watched the wistful enthusiasm that moved across Myra's face as she described the encounter. Racing ahead, Jessica's mind conjured up the end of the tale; perhaps the man had been toying with Myra, for she had inherited quite a comfortable fortune from a maiden aunt. As Myra's dark eyes snapped with excitement she continued.

"He came to call three days in a row. And on the fourth, he told me he had to return to Ireland at the end of the month. I was heartbroken. He wanted me to go with him, asked me to marry him—and I can say truthfully that I was tempted. But Jessica, although I often think now that I made a tragic mistake, back then I decided that although our souls were quite suited for each other, our present worlds were far too different to ever become aligned.''

Jessica took a sip of tea and then said, ''You've read Corelli one too many times.''

''No, it's true. Back then I thought our differences insurmountable; I read voraciously, he never even read the newspaper; I am hopelessly messy, he was compulsively neat; I function on a mental level, his world was physical. He was Irish and Catholic and I am American and of a very open attitude where religion is involved, as you well know.''

''It sounds to me as if you made the right decision,'' Jess concluded.

''I let him go back to Ireland, but I never met another man that moved me so again. In here''—Myra pointed to her head—''I had made the right decision. But here''—she pointed to her heart—''here is where I have had to live with it ever since.''

''Why didn't you follow him?''

Myra shrugged. ''I told him not even to write me, because my decision was final. I was very adamant about it. To have prolonged the pain would have been too terrible. He didn't write. I wouldn't let myself.''

''And so you never saw him again.''

''No.''

''If you had it to do over?''

''I would cast logic to the wind and follow my heart. I don't regret the life I've lived, Jessica. And I know that my choice was made of my own free will, but oftentimes I can't help but wonder. . . .'' Myra gazed off toward the mesa. ''You're so young, so vibrant. The world has so much to offer you. I just don't want to see you locked away in the basement of that museum until you wither up and die.''

''Like my father.''

''I didn't mean—''

''I know you didn't, but please, don't try to see a romance

where there is none. Aside from having nothing in common, Mr. Burnett and I don't even particularly like one another. Wouldn't I know if he was some sort of soul mate?"

"Perhaps not. Perhaps too many aeons have passed since you were together."

Centering her cup on the saucer, Jess stood up. "I don't think so, Myra. But for now I must get busy before too many aeons go by again. When Mr. Burnett's hired man gets here, send him out to the prints. He can help me load the casts onto the wagon."

She pulled on her gloves and put on her hat. Then she put a crate on the end of the wagon with the plaster, tissue, and two large bottles of water she wrapped in burlap to keep them from clanging together. The knapsack went in last. It took her longer than she had counted on to hitch up the mules, and by the time she was ready, she was perspiring. She wiped her dusty brow with the back of her sleeve.

Still seated at the table, Myra looked up from beneath the umbrella she had reopened. She held a book on camping open on her lap. Jess looked down at the illustrations and noted the diagrams of awnings and sun shields. "Starting a project?"

"I thought perhaps Mr. Burnett's man could rig something up. Otherwise we'll be forced to either sit in the sun all day or stay inside the tent, and I find this air so very invigorating that I hate to miss a moment of it."

"If you're so very invigorated, I should have let you hitch up the mules."

"I would have, but I don't deal well with mules." Myra sounded disappointed in herself.

"I would consider that an asset. Anyway, help is on the way, isn't it?" Jess walked past the barricade of rocks piled in a circle much like the ring that rimmed the campfire. She stared down at Methuselah, who had burrowed into a hole. "Now, take care of our friend here and I'll see you again late this afternoon."

As she clucked to the mules, snapped the lines, and got the animals moving, Jess thought about all Myra had revealed about her past and how she had intimated that there could be romantic sparks flying between herself and Burnett.

Ridiculous. How anyone could think that Rory Burnett might prove to be her love of a lifetime was beyond contemplation. Why, even Gerald Ramsey, the director of the museum, never provoked her as quickly as Burnett.

"Ha!" She let go and laughed aloud, grateful for the peaceful solitude of the open range. "Imagine Mr. Rory Burnett and me forming a romantic alliance. I'd rather be fossilized first."

CHAPTER

5

Long and low, the wood-and-adobe ranch house blended with the landscape and beckoned Rory the way an oasis attracts a thirsty man. The place appeared deserted, but he knew good and well that Scratchy was most likely sitting in some shady corner of the back porch snoozing.

Rory skirted the house proper and rode past his mother's former vegetable garden. Without care, the plot had withered and died almost as quickly as Martha Burnett had succumbed to what the doctor had simply described as "a woman's ailment." Toward the end Rory found himself praying that death would release her from her pain. Wilner had been far luckier. He had dropped dead of a heart attack. The Burnetts, always committed to one another, had passed on within six months of each other.

Rory missed them both sorely, but didn't begrudge their going together. Wilner and Martha Burnett had been as well matched as a set of bookends, and like bookends, they always held the volumes of the ranch history and business together.

Wilner taught Rory his simple philosophy of life: "Be fair, boy, and do a hard day's work. Keep your word. Love the land and everything will come out right." The old man hadn't been gone two weeks before Rory began to feel the burden of keeping the place together.

He drew his horse up in front of the corral, easily swung his leg over the saddle, and dismounted. The heavy gate opened with a creak and a groan before he led Domino in, unsaddled him, slipped off the bridle, and gave the horse a swat on the flank. As the big animal snorted and ambled toward the water trough, Rory slung his saddle over the top rail of the fence, exited the corral, and headed for the house.

Using his hat, he beat the trail dust off his pants. His spurs sang in unison as he crossed the yard and mounted the back step. The shade of the wide veranda swallowed him with its cool relief. As he suspected, Scratchy Livermore, cook and unenthusiastic housekeeper, was slouched down in an old rocker on the corner of the porch, boots on the rail, arms crossed over his chest, mouth slack. He drooled on his shirtfront.

Barely breaking his stride, Rory kicked Scratchy's feet off the rail and startled the old reprobate awake. "I'm home. Anything to eat around here?" Tossing the words over his shoulder, he hung his hat on a wall rack outside the backdoor and bent over the dry sink on the porch. He poured water out of the bucket on the drainboard and began to wash his hands.

Dressed in what remained of faded, seat-worn woolen trousers and a collarless yellowed shirt, Scratchy unfolded his lanky frame and scratched his gray bearded chin. "Yup. 'Spects I can rustle somp'in up." He shuffled past Rory and let the screen door bang shut behind him.

Rory knew better than to ask what that something might be. Since Martha died, he and the hands had taken potluck, which usually consisted of overdone beef, dumplings the consistency of paste, oversalted, canned vegetables, and lots of boiled cabbage. Hiring a real cook would mean sending all the way to Durango. That, coupled with the fact that a new cook would put the old man out of work, kept Rory from seeking someone out. He splashed water over his face and neck, reached out for the wrinkled towel that hung on a hook beneath the sink, and vigorously rubbed his face dry.

"Want coffee, too?" Scratchy yelled from the kitchen.

"Sure." Rory walked into the house and paused for a moment just inside the kitchen door. "You can bring it into the office with the food. Anything happen this morning that I need to know about?"

The cook paused, scratched the yellow shirt stretched across his belly, and frowned. "Seems like there was somp'in I was 'sposed to remember. . . ." His voice trailed away. "Must not have been too important."

"I hope not," Rory mumbled under his breath as he turned away and headed toward the office. He passed through the sitting room that took up the entire width of the front of the house. It was dark and cool inside. The thick adobe walls held the evening's chill even in the middle of the day. Woven blankets hung over every long, narrow window. The colorful Indian patterns were highlighted by the sunlight outside.

After Martha died, he and his father avoided the room by unspoken agreement. It was too painful to enter its confines and not see her knitting in the low rocker or fussily arranging her collection of curios and bric-a-brac scattered around the room. In the dim light, the dust that usually covered the once highly polished surface of the furnishings was barely visible. Rory paused in the doorway and squinted, unable to believe his eyes. Not only was the dust barely visible today, in some places it was gone entirely.

He stepped back into the room, bent over the library table, and swiped two fingers across it. A few traces of gritty dust clung to his fingertips, but they were nothing compared with the state the room had been in for weeks. Glancing around, he noticed that here and there was more evidence of a haphazard attempt at dusting. When his gaze fell on the heavy cottonwood beam that served as a mantel on the stone fireplace, he shook his head.

Scratchy had obviously waved a dust rag around, for in evidence was a photograph taken of Wilner and Martha Burnett on their twentieth anniversary. It stood upside down on the mantel beside an empty vase and a clock that hadn't been wound for months. Rory laughed at the sight of his parents standing on their heads and reached out, righted the picture, and leaned it against the fireplace again. He smiled wistfully at the happy couple. "I'm trying, Pa," he whispered before he took another look around the room. "Looks like we all are."

The office, originally intended as a nursery, was smaller than the three other bedrooms in the house. Once Rory outgrew it and Martha had failed to conceive any children, Wilner had moved his desk and ranch business into the little room. Now, whenever he was working alone in the tidy retreat, Rory often felt his father's presence.

Before he sat down on the worn leather chair, he pulled the mail out of his back pocket and smoothed the two crumpled envelopes. Leaning forward with both elbows on the table, Rory put aside the one marked "Sears, Roebuck and Company." He still had three payments to go on a set of cookware his father bought to outfit the chuck wagon.

He ripped open the second envelope and quickly scanned the page. It was an announcement of a cattle auction in two weeks at the stockyard adjacent to the Denver and Rio Grande Western Railroad Station in Durango. Rory smoothed the creased sheet until it was flat and set it on the desk. There was plenty of time to round up a good-sized herd of cattle and drive them to Durango, but it would mean long hours for everyone unless he could lay on some extra hands.

A rectangular, canvas-bound ledger rested in the center of the desk. He pulled it toward him and flipped past the meticulous entries Wilner had made until he came to his own bigger, bolder writing. His father often said that a man didn't ranch for profit, not when he had no control over cattle disease, weather, and stock prices. A man didn't become a rancher because he wanted to get rich, but because he loved the work and the land and wanted to hold on to a scrap of it for his family's future.

Rory stared at the column of numbers and decided that with some budgeting here and there, he could pay one, maybe two more men, and if he was lucky, the help he needed just might arrive in the form of a drifter riding the grub line.

As he closed the book he suddenly remembered Miss Jessica Stanbridge. He wondered if she was still crawling around on the slab of rock measuring the fossil tracks, and smiled. He couldn't recall anyone ever looking at him the way she had when they finally reached that rock. What would it be like to have a woman look up at him like that every time she saw him? What would it be like to have Miss Jessica Stanbridge look at him that way again?

Regrettably he didn't have time to find out. Since he didn't dare leave her alone for long, she would cost him valuable help if he couldn't talk her into leaving the area in the next few days. He leaned back and shouted, "Scratchy!" through the open doorway. Right now, as much as he didn't want to spare a man, he had to send someone out to watch over her.

Immediately on the heels of Rory's outburst, the old man ambled through the door with a tray in his hands and said, "Don't have to yell out my eardrums." He set down the painted tin tray that contained a slab of beef on two thick slices of bread, a cup of coffee, and a pickle.

Rory picked up the sandwich, gingerly peeked between the layers of stale bread, and then took a bite. He washed down the dry mouthful with coffee before he said, "Thanks. You seen Whitey?"

"Not since breakfast, but he ought to be in soon. I sent him out to repair that fence you wanted mended down by the far pasture."

"Send him in as soon as he gets back." Rory took another bite and stared at Scratchy, who was content to stand and watch him chew.

"I'll send him right along," Scratchy promised.

Rory glanced up from lowered brows. "You dust the sitting room?"

The cook scratched his head of short, sparse hair and shrugged. "Don't know what come over me."

"Yeah, me either. Any more surprises up your sleeve?"

"Nope. Guess that's about it." Scratchy rocked forward on his toes and then back again.

"Any drifters come along looking for work, have them wait around until I can talk to them. We'll be running fifty head up to Durango and I'll need all the help I can get."

"Will do. Anythin' else?"

Rory shook his head. "No. That's about it. Just don't forget I need to see Whitey, pronto."

"Right." Hefting his beltless trousers around the middle, Scratchy left the room.

As he ate the last bite of his sandwich, Rory couldn't help but notice that Scratchy, like the rest of the men, never called him boss, the way they had Wilner. It wasn't surprising, considering he didn't feel any different than he had when he rode the range and followed his father's orders right along with them. He wondered how long it would be before he would earn the respect and trust they had always given Wilner Burnett.

As he swirled the lukewarm coffee in the mug and then swallowed it down, he closed the ledger, set it aside, and pulled his composition book out of his top desk drawer. Setting the mug aside, he found the first blank page in the composition book and smoothed it open. The inkwell stood ready. He shook it, pulled the cork, and then took up his pen. Dipping it, once, twice, and then carefully wiping off the excess droplets of black ink, he wrote:

> Some women give comfort,
> Some just give pain,
> Some are—

Overwhelmed by the image of Jessica Stanbridge racing toward the slab of sandstone to see the ancient tracks, Rory paused and smiled. All things aside, she was some kind of woman. Exactly what kind, he wasn't quite sure. Intelligent? Highly. Lovely? To be sure. Prickly as a cactus? No doubt about it. But there was something hidden beneath her standoffishness, something that he suspected was both vulnerable and exciting. He'd seen a glimpse of it when she saw the saurian tracks. That glimpse was enough to make him curious enough to find out all there was to know about her.

If he could only find the time.

"You want me, Mr. Burnett?"

Whitey Higgins stood in the doorway, hat in hand, shifting from foot to foot, ill at ease in a body that was still growing faster than he could handle. Whitey reminded Rory of himself at sixteen, with his black hair, eyes, and olive skin tanned to a deep copper. His nickname was the exact opposite of his looks and had been given him by the other men when he first signed on. Much to the boy's delight, his given name of Buford was soon forgotten.

"Sit down, Whitey." Rory nodded toward a deep, overstuffed chair covered in rawhide in the corner.

Dressed in a faded denim shirt, Levi's, and chaps, Whitey glanced at the chair and nervously declined. He straightened the knot in the red bandanna looped around his throat. "Am I in trouble?"

Rory frowned. "Should you be?"

With an emphatic shake of his head, Whitey said, "Nope." His brow knit. "Leastwise I don't think so."

Rory smiled to put him at ease. "You're not in trouble. In fact, I've got a job for you. Something special I think you can handle better than any of the rest."

The worried look on the youth's face relaxed. He drew himself up straighter. "Yeah?" As a wrangler, he was low man around the place. Any job would be better.

Rory nodded. "There's a couple of women camped out near Dry Creek."

Whitey swallowed visibly. "Women?"

"Women. They're out there searching for old bones for a museum back east. What I want you to do is get your camp rig and ride out there, keep an eye on them until I can see my way clear to get back out and convince them to move on. It shouldn't be more than a day or so, just until I get the men busy rounding up enough head for a drive into Durango."

At the news of the drive Whitey snapped to attention. His dark eyes were both hungry and hopeful. "A drive to Durango? Will I be goin' with y'all?"

"I'm afraid that right now I need someone to keep an eye on these women."

Whitey looked disappointed. "All I'm 'sposed to do is watch them?"

Rory thought of all the crates and boxes of paraphernalia the women had brought along and the exhaustion mirrored on Jessica's face yesterday. "Do any heavy work that needs done." He glanced out the window and stared across the flatland toward the mesa in the distance. "Keep them at that site until I get there, and above all don't let Miss Stanbridge talk you into moving them back up on the mesa. Don't tell her I want her away from it, either."

"Why *don't* you want her up there?"

"Because one of the Utes asked me not to let her go snooping around on Indian land for bones that belong to their grave sites. You ought to leave as soon as you can, because I told them you'd be there before nightfall."

"Then I'd best be on my way." Whitey tapped his sweat-stained hat against his leather chaps and smiled, his teeth flashing white against his dark complexion. He hovered in the doorway as if working up the courage, then finally said, "Thanks, Mr. Burnett."

"Don't thank me yet, boy. You haven't met 'em."

The plaster casts were ready to be moved, but Jessica was in no mood to try to lift them just yet. She lay flat on her back, comfortably stretched out across the warm surface of the sandstone rock watching towers of white clouds drift across the indelible blue sky. Her stomach growled in protest of its emptiness, but she paid it no mind. Instead Jessica closed her eyes and let the sun caress her face as its warmth seeped into her bones.

While she spent the morning working alone against the empty landscape, she had become increasingly aware of the land and sky, even of the very air around her. Unlike Boston, alive with the constant clatter of carriages and the incessant hum of humanity, this raw, open land surprised her with a pulsing life of its own. As she lay in silent repose Jessica was content to listen to the electric buzz of insects in the sage, a constant thrum that kept time to her heartbeat. Feeling free as a pagan, she spread her arms wide, pressed her open palms against the ancient rock, and let the warmth of its rough, heated surface seep into her skin.

Above the insects' song she detected a second steady, rhythmic beat. This one was not of her heart. Startled, she sat up and blinked against the glare of the sun then shaded her eyes with her hand. A man on horseback rode toward her, silhouetted against the azure sky.

It irritated her to realize how her heartbeat had accelerated involuntarily when she wondered if the approaching rider might be Rory Burnett. Scrambling to gather her things, she found her glasses and carefully fit the curved stems over her ears. Quickly Jessica tried to slip the wayward strands of hair back into the tight knot at the nape of her neck and then smoothed the front of her blouse. Tugging on the hem of her fitted jacket, she looked up again to mark the man's progress and drew a sharp breath of alarm.

The rider was definitely not Rory Burnett.

As the distance closed between them she could see that this man, although dark, was not as broad-shouldered or as tall in the saddle. Nor was he riding the distinctive black-and-white horse Burnett had ridden earlier.

Jessica jumped off the rock and hurried over to the wagon where she'd left the gun tucked in her knapsack. Unwilling to be caught unaware, she slipped the gun from the bag, dropped her arm to her side, and hid the weapon behind the folds of her skirt.

The man was almost upon her.

She remained silent and watchful as he reined in his horse and then rested a forearm on his pommel. Dressed like a cowhand, he was young and lean, all arms and legs and openly curious black eyes. Tugging the brim of his hat, he said, "Howdy, ma'am. You Miss Stanbridge?"

Jessica relaxed somewhat at these words, but she didn't loosen her grip on the pistol. She nodded. "And you are . . . ?"

"Whitey Higgins. Mr. Burnett sent me to help you. Said he'll be back tomorrow, or if not, by the day after."

He was far younger than she had first realized and he was staring at her with unabashed admiration. She colored at his obvious smile, which, she noted, was a far cry from Rory Burnett's cool, unreadable assessment.

"I hope you'll pardon me, Mr. Higgins"—she withdrew

the hand that held the gun and turned to slip it back into the knapsack—"but I wasn't sure if you were friend or foe."

He dismounted with a laugh. "I'm definitely friendly, ma'am, especially to a pretty woman like yourself." When she colored, he pretended not to notice and glanced over at the slab of sandstone where she had spread out her notebook and other items. "What can I do to help?"

Jessica forgave his flirting because he was so young. "I was just getting ready to head back to camp," she said, stretching the truth some, "so I suppose we should begin by loading those plaster casts I've made of the tracks embedded in the rock."

Whitey tied his horse to the back of the buckboard wagon. She led him to the rock and gently tapped along the edge of the imprint with a curved-headed hammer until she had loosened the plaster. Then she and Whitey lifted the burlap edge that overlapped the depression. The first of the prints came away from its rocky bed. They cradled the cumbersome, yard-long object between them and carried it to the wagon bed, where Jessica wrapped it in more burlap to protect it as they traveled back to camp. With his help, the five huge prints were soon loaded, and in no time at all they were both back at the camp, where Myra wasted no time introducing herself to Whitey Higgins and getting him to erect a canvas tarp for a sun shield. Carried away with high spirits, Myra stood on a chair and tied a paisley scarf to the top of one of the support poles.

"What do you think of Zanzibar, Jessica?"

Seated at the table beneath the new shade, Jessica set out pen and ink and said offhandedly, "I've never been there, Myra. You know that."

Myra shook her head and let Whitey help her down. Puffing from the exertion, she plopped down and clarified, "I mean, how would you like Zanzibar as a name for the camp?"

Jessica glanced up. "You're naming the camp?"

"Why not?"

"Why not, indeed. Zanzibar sounds fine."

Whitey listened to the exchange in silence.

Gaining a second wind, Myra shot to her feet. "Then Zanzibar it is! Let's celebrate with tea. Will you have some, Mister Higgins?"

He lowered himself into a chair and rested his brown hat on his knee. "I'll try one, ma'am, if it please you."

"An afternoon shouldn't pass without a cup of tea," Myra told him. "That and a good book."

Jessica laid her pen aside and studied Whitey. "How did you come by your nickname, Mr. Higgins?"

He adjusted the bandanna around his neck and swallowed. "Ma'am, I wish you'd both call me Whitey. I don't much take to Mr. Higgins."

Hiding her smile, Jessica nodded. After all, this wasn't Rory Burnett. "About the nickname?"

"The boys gave it to me, on account of my hair's so dark and all."

Myra set out the cups and saucers and then carried over a pot of steeping tea and a book. She put the pot in the center of the table and drew up her own chair, shifted until it was comfortable, and then settled back. Jessica was bent over her notebook again, busily trying to describe the land and the rock formation where the tracks were located. She heard Myra say, "Tell us about Mr. Burnett, Whitey. Are you related? How long have you worked for him?"

Jessica shot her a furious glance over the rim of her glasses.

Myra ignored her. Whitey's chest visibly expanded with his newfound importance.

"Naw, I'm not blood kin to Burnett, not that I know of, leastwise. I been here nigh onto nine months. His pa, Wilner Burnett, hired me on, but he up and died about five months back. Ever since then Rory's been in charge." He leaned back and rested his foot on his knee. "He's never said so, o'course, but sometimes I get the feelin' runnin' the Silver Sage is a lot tougher than he ever knew.''

Jessica's pen stopped scratching. Head down, she hesitated to let Myra see her interest, but she found herself listening intently to Whitey as he talked about Rory Burnett.

''Is the ranch a large one, then?'' Myra inquired.

Whitey nodded. ''So to speak. Plenty of places to run the herd. Trouble is, the danged—pardon me, ladies—the cattle ain't too choosy about where they wander off to. We have to round 'em up outta some of the most unlikely places. There was the time—''

''I suppose Mr. Burnett doesn't have much time to socialize?'' Myra interrupted as she poured herself another cup of tea and motioned to Whitey for him to taste his. ''Sugar, Whitey?'' she asked.

He reached for the sugar bowl and spooned in three heaping spoonfuls. ''Nope. Rory Burnett's all business anymore. Back 'fore his pa died, he used to ride with us, worked shoulder to shoulder like he was one of us, always willin' to do a hard day's work and still play cards and jaw in the bunkhouse at night. Every once in a while he'd even have time to ride into Durango to the wh— to take in the nightlife. But now, seems like he has to put in the same long hours on the range and then burn the midnight oil in his office after supper. Kinda makes a man glad he ain't got the responsibility of a spread of his own.'' He finished the tea with a smack of his lips and nestled the cup back onto the saucer.

Jessica looked up to find him staring at her appraisingly.

''Does Mr. Burnett have a fiancée, or anyone he's partial to?'' Myra pried.

Jessica slammed her notebook shut. ''Myra, really,'' she said through clenched teeth.

''Just curious, dear.'' Her face wreathed in an innocent smile, Myra turned expectantly to Whitey.

''So far he ain't had time for a fie-on-say,'' Whitey

informed her. "No other kin, neither. He was adopted by the Burnetts when he was a boy. They never had any children of their own." He jiggled the booted foot that rested on his knee and spun the rowel of his spur. "Some of the men speculate on whether or not he's got some Indian blood, but hell—oops, pardon me again, ladies—I'm as dark as he is an' I'm pure Texican through and through."

Myra laughed.

Jessica shook her head. "You're quite a font of information, Whitey."

"I don't know about that, ma'am. But I do like to talk."

"A most rewarding attribute, especially in a man," Myra said as she gave him a pat on the sleeve. From the look of pride on the young man's face as he accepted the compliment, Jessica knew she would be sitting through many more hours of Myra's intense investigation into Rory Burnett's background. But in an odd way she found herself looking forward to it.

Whitey suddenly slapped his forehead and uncrossed his legs. "Mr. Burnett told me you were out here lookin' for old bones, so I brought you one. Forgot all about it till now." He stood up and hurried over to his horse, where he untied his bedroll and rummaged through his blanket until he pulled out the bleached white, lower jawbone of a cow, complete with three teeth still anchored in it.

He carried it back to Jessica and handed it to her. "Is that old enough?"

Myra took one look at the cow jaw and opened her novel.

Jessica turned the bone over and over, then carefully set it aside. "It's very old indeed, Whitey, for a cow. But I'm seeking something even older." She opened her notebook again and paged through it until she found a sketch she had made of the skeleton of a stegosaurus, a Jurassic-plated saurian discovered ten years earlier at Como Bluff in southern Wyoming. Handing the book to Whitey, she watched while he frowned over the drawing.

"This 'bout the size of a lizard?"

Smugly Jess shook her head. "No. It's about the height of a very tall man."

Whitey laid the book on the table and leaned over it with a whistle. "Ain't never seen one around here. Hope I don't."

"You don't have to worry, they're all dead. Have been for millions of years. That's why I have to content myself with bones."

He eyed her skeptically. "You ever seen any bones from one of these things?"

She nodded. "Not any I found personally, but I do have one I can show you." Jessica rose and went over to the many boxes and barrels stacked near the tent. She opened the lid of a low box filled with smaller cartons and soon approached him with what appeared to be an elongated piece of stone. "This is a fossilized saurian bone, from one much smaller than the stegosaurus. Fossilized means it has turned to stone."

Whitey reached for it, handled it gently, looked down the length of it, and then announced, "I seen somethin' like this before."

Myra set her book down and leaned forward expectantly.

Jessica folded her hands in her lap and tried to remain calm. "Where? On the mesa?"

Whitey looked over toward the mesa. The late-afternoon sun set it afire with a red glow. Emphatically he shook his head. "Nope. Not up there."

Jess waited for him to go on. When nothing was forthcoming, she prodded, "Then where?"

"I can't rightly remember, but I'll dwell on it tonight and it'll come to me," he said.

Reaching out to take the fossilized bone from him, Jessica sighed, doubtful that he'd ever really seen one at all. She had the distinct impression that Whitey Higgins would say anything to impress her.

CHAPTER

6

"I guess you could liken this to a logjam." Jessica straightened and looked at Whitey from beneath the brim of her helmet as she blew at a strand of hair dangling in front of her eyes. Glancing down at a chunk of fossilized vertebrae barely exposed in the dry earth at her feet, she decided she must be living under a lucky star. First the tracks and now this young cowboy had led her straight to a multiple find in a dry gully not a two-mile ride from Camp Zanzibar.

Whitey put his hands in his back pockets and puffed his chest with pride. "Just what you're lookin' for, I take it."

Dropping to her knees again, ignoring the soft soil that dusted her skirt, Jessica dug in her knapsack until she found a sable brush. Quickly dusting away loose pieces of soil and finely ground pebbles, she uncovered more of the exposed bone. "There may be something of significance here"— leaning forward she poked at the sandy soil with the end of the brush—"but it may take months if not years to uncover every fragment. From what we've learned of this sort of find, this is most likely a spot where the remains of all manner of dead creatures washed downstream, then piled up because of a sandbar or other obstacle and decayed. More bones are probably embedded in sediment far below the ground.''

''So it ain't that great a thing then?''

Unwilling to diminish the importance of his find, Jessica reassured him with a shake of her head. ''It's a wonderful discovery and one definitely worthy of further examination.'' She leaned back, pushed back her helmet, wiped her brow with her sleeve, and then sighed. ''I was hoping for a miraculous find, an entire skeleton that would be close enough to the surface for me to guarantee to Beckworth that it was just what he wanted. Such discoveries are rare, but not unheard of.''

''Shoot,'' he said, hunkering down across from her, his dark eyes serious beneath the shadow of his hat brim, ''there's plenty of these dry washes hereabouts. I wouldn't mind ridin' out from camp in all directions to see if I can come up with somethin' else. Now that I know what to look for.'' He smiled again. His long arms dangled over his knees, his wrists exposed by the too-short sleeves of his shirt.

Wishing she could be as certain of success, Jessica laid the brush down and pulled a pick the size of a small hammer from her knapsack. Leaning over the fossils and bracing herself with one hand in the dirt, she carefully loosened the soil around the time-blackened bones. ''The trouble with these ancient riverbeds is that many of the bones may have been washed away by erosion. That's how these pieces became exposed over time. A skeleton on higher ground stands a chance of being complete. ''That,'' she mumbled, ''is why I want to explore the mesa.''

Whitey watched her work in silence then volunteered, ''I can help if you show me what to do.''

Jessica looked toward Zanzibar. Myra would be content to explore the perimeters of the camp and read beneath the awning until late afternoon, so there was really nothing for Whitey to do there. From this point on, her work would be long, tedious, and lonely. "Why not?" she decided. "I'll put you to work while I make notations and map out the area." She handed him her brush. "To begin with you can sweep away all the loose soil along this ridge of bone back to where it disappears below the soil. When you get that finished, I'll show you how to dig a channel around the bone."

Eager to please, he sat down cross-legged, his back to the sun, and began to work slowly and carefully.

Jessica paused for a moment and watched him, then asked, "Will he mind you working at this, do you think?"

Whitey looked up. "Who?"

"Mr. Burnett?"

"Hell . . . pardon me, ma'am, heck no. He told me to help you out. That's what I'm here for."

Once more she dipped into her huge leather bag and withdrew her notebook, pen, and ink. Frowning, Jessica picked up a rock, examined it quickly, and tossed it aside before she sat down and stretched her legs and propped her book on her thighs. Squinting against the sun, she began to make notations.

Rory's Appaloosa splashed through a slowly meandering stream as he rode in the shadow of a high butte, pushing the remnants of a small herd of cattle. A gray-brown rock wren sang out before he startled it into flight from its perch on a wind-twisted piñon pine. He called out to the cattle, whistled sharply, and waved his hat to keep them moving into the nearby box canyon where they could graze until morning. There was enough feed and water in the canyon to keep them happy, and at first light he would return with two men to move them back to the ranch proper, where he had begun to collect the herd he intended to sell off.

Tamping down his irritation, he wondered why he hadn't seen any of his crew all afternoon. He'd told them to scatter and round up as many strays as they could, but it was odd he hadn't come across any of them yet. With Whitey over at the women's camp, he was short a good hand.

Rory wondered how the boy was faring with both women on his hands. It had been two days since he'd left them and he intended to see for himself before another day passed. He hollered again, waved his hat over his head, and shooed the last of the cattle into the canyon, then began pushing them along the creek so that they would head upstream toward the steep sandstone walls.

Within an hour he had the simpleminded creatures boxed into a canyon filled with enough sage and sparse grass to keep them happy until morning. Turning Domino about, he then spurred the big horse toward Jessica's camp. Before he'd gone more than a few yards, he drew up short at the sight of two Ute riders making their way down the steep hillside. Rory recognized Piah's tall black hat and the band of conchos, silver medallions that flashed in the sunlight. The other was far smaller, a youth Rory recognized as Piah's nephew, Chako. Unexpected irritation pricked him. His visit to Jessica's camp would have to be postponed awhile longer.

They met on a rise at the mouth of the canyon. The stream behind them chanted as it bubbled over the rocky bed. Rory dismounted and let Domino wander over to the stream, where the big horse drank heartily and then contented itself with a mouthful of thick grass growing at the water's edge. Piah dismounted and led his horse by a rough hemp halter until the two men stood within arm's length of each other. The youth remained astride a big bay and waited beside the stream, watching the cattle lazily amble along the canyon floor.

Rory stared at Piah and waited for him to speak. The man's overlarge hat shaded the upper half of his face and kept Rory from reading the emotion in his haunting dark eyes.

Piah finally spoke first. "I have come to thank you for taking the women off the mesa."

Rory thought it was far more likely that Piah and his nephew had come to rustle a wandering steer, but he knew the Utes needed the meat as much as he could afford to spare it. Toeing a curled lizard skin lying in the dust, Rory shrugged. "Don't thank me yet. They're still on my land, still searching for bones of the giant thunder lizards. I can't guarantee they won't want to go back up the mesa." He watched the other man's lips compress into a taut line.

"The spirits cannot be stopped if they do."

Rory's own expression darkened as he pinned Piah with a determined stare. "They *will* be stopped if you are wise."

"Your father was a friend of the People," Piah began. When Rory tried to interrupt, the Ute silenced him by waving his hand downward. "Because of this I will tell you what I have learned from a cousin just returned from the land of the Paiutes. A great prophet, Wovoka, has foretold of a time that will come soon—a time of miracles when the whites will die and the dead spirits of our ancestors and those of the great buffalo will rise up and take over the earth again. If these women are wise"—he nodded at Rory—"if you are wise, you will leave this land and go east, where you can stand and fight with your own kind."

"Thanks for the advice," Rory said softly, "I've read of this new religion and the Ghost Dance." Indeed, the papers were full of news of the new Indian messiah whose teachings were rapidly spreading through the reservations. Rory didn't expect that the native people would dismiss this new religion lightly—not when their old ways had rapidly deteriorated as the reservations closed in ever tighter.

"I'm afraid it's going to take more than a dance to bring

your people back—not to mention the buffalo." A niggling warning prickled the hair on the back of Rory's neck. He recognized the intense look of a zealot in Piah's ebony eyes.

In answer to Rory's casual dismissal of his warning, Piah turned away. The steady breeze that blew through the canyon lifted the man's long hair and sent his words drifting back to Rory. "You may not believe, Burnett, but things will change, and far sooner than you think. A new way is coming as surely as the coyote howls at the moon."

"I won't hold my breath," Rory told him.

Piah's warning reminded Rory of Jessica. He glanced toward the afternoon sky. It was getting late. If he was going to pass by her camp before dark, he'd best be on his way.

Piah spoke again. "If the woman finds the cave—"

"She won't find the cave." Rory looked over at the slim, long-haired youth astride the huge bay horse and wondered how many others on the reservation shared Piah's views. As he thought of many of his Ute friends, he remembered the annual Fourth of July celebration at the Silver Sage. The Burnetts had always invited all the neighboring ranchers, their hands, and any Utes who cared to join in. "Ghosts or no ghosts, I'm planning on holding the barbecue and rodeo at the ranch as usual this year. Tell your people they are invited."

Piah frowned. "Some will come."

Rory turned away and grabbed Domino's reins from where they trailed to the ground. He swung easily up into the saddle and left Piah standing in the dust. "Good. They'll be welcome. Bring the ghosts if they're back in town by then."

Jessica was certain she'd never be clean again. Sandy grit had seeped through her clothes and into her very pores. The air inside the tent was close and warm, Myra's cot and the floor around it a study in upheaval. Books lay open on the makeshift bedside table, clothing was draped over the woman's cot, her trunk stood open at the end of the bed. Jessica didn't know how Myra could function comfortably in such a mess—the woman brushed aside the pile of clothes and climbed under it to sleep—but the lack of order never bothered Myra.

In exact opposition, every item of clothing on Jessica's own side of the wide tent was either carefully folded away in her trunk or hanging from the support pole. Her toilet articles were lined up alongside the china washbowl she now filled with tepid water from the bucket they refilled from water barrels strapped to the wagon. She supposed it was her early training in paleontology that made her so organized. There was no room for disorganization in a museum laboratory.

She dipped her washcloth into the tepid water and squeezed it dry, then swabbed it across her face and neck with a sigh of relief. Leaning over the washbowl, she stared at her reflection in the small oval mirror nailed to a support pole and looked at the freckles dusting the bridge of her nose with chagrin. Try as she might, it was impossible to suffer wearing her helmet all day. More and more she had come to relish the feel of the warm, dry wind in her hair and the sun on her face. She was paying for such frivolity with the spattering of freckles and sunburn.

"Teatime, Jessica!"

Myra's voice penetrated the privacy afforded by the canvas wall of the tent.

Jessica swabbed her face again and called out, "I'll be right there."

With the day's work behind her, she started to change into a clean shirtwaist then thought better of the idea. In minutes it would be as wrinkled and dirty as the rest of her things. Instead she rebuttoned her blouse and straightened it as best she could, pulled back her hair and wound it into a tight knot, and then rammed a decorative tortoiseshell fork into it to hold it in place. The tortoiseshell reminded her that

Methuselah, still roaming his makeshift pen, needed to be fed. Hooking the wire stems of her glasses over her ears, she was ready to join the others.

Jessica bit back a smile as she ducked beneath the tent flap and saw Whitey seated on the edge of a chair with one of her fragile teacups and saucers balanced awkwardly on his knees. The dark-haired youth was always trying his best to please.

"Can I help with anything, Myra?" she asked.

"Not at all, dear. Please just sit down. You two have been in the hot sun all afternoon. I'm sure it's been draining. Me, I can't stand the hot sun." She had been reminding them of that fact for two days now. "This awning that Whitey so kindly erected for us is wonderful. Why, now I can enjoy the great outdoors all day and still be protected from the burning rays of the—"

"Myra?" Jessica interrupted gently.

"Oh, yes. Where was I?" She hustled over to the cook bench, a long board stretched out over two barrels and covered with their kitchen utensils and supplies. "I've put together a light snack of Dutch-oven-baked biscuits and tea. Actually I experimented by adding a little extra sugar and some currants and have come up with a tea scone I think you'll enjoy." She bent over and filled their plates with the biscuits and added a dollop of raspberry preserves to each.

"They look delicious." Jessica was grateful for her companion's willingness to take over the cooking, and she meant her compliment as Myra set the plate before her.

Whitey took a sip of tea and leaned back, stretching his long legs under the table. "That jam sure looks good enough to eat." He smiled and Myra beamed.

"Why, thank you, Whitey. I made it myself back in Boston."

"Sure wish we had a decent cook back at the ranch. I'm gonna miss the fine meals you put together."

Myra paused in the middle of peering down into the teapot and looked up at him. "You have no cook?"

"Oh, we got one all right, but what Scratchy sets out can't be likened to food."

Frowning with concentration as she set down the pot and then passed the sugar bowl, Myra said, "I can't believe a ranch with strong, hungry cowhands like yourself doesn't have a decent cook. Jessica is a wonderful cook—"

Jessica's voice held a warning. "Myra—"

"—she'd be an asset to any man's home, or ranch for that matter."

Whitey turned adoring calf eyes on Jessica. "I know that, ma'am."

Blushing under such intensely open admiration, Jessica fiddled with the button at her throat. "Actually, I hate housekeeping. I find it boring." She glanced up and found them both staring at her. Myra was smiling, Whitey moon-eyed. "You are both embarrassing me. I think it's time—"

She was interrupted when Whitey abruptly stood and stared in the direction of two riders silhouetted against the sun. They were approaching fast.

"Oh, my," Myra said, looking worried. "I'm not sure if I have enough scones for two more."

"That is the least of our worries," Jessica told her before she walked over to Whitey, who watched with one hand shading his eyes. She asked, "Is it trouble, do you think?"

He waited a moment longer as the two figures grew closer and took on recognizable characteristics, then he shook his head. "No. Not trouble, just a nuisance."

Jessica couldn't help but hear his disgruntled tone. "You know them?"

"Yeah. That tall one that looks like a beanpole on a horse is Fred Hench. He's like to talk your leg off. The other one, the one that looks wide as his mount, that's Woody Barrows. We call him Wheelbarrow. They ride for Burnett."

"Do you think they're bringing news?"

"Naw." He shook his head again and stomped back to his chair. He sat down hard and picked up his cup and saucer. "They're supposed to be out roundin' up cattle for the drive. My guess is they come for a look-see."

Jessica sighed, uneasy knowing she would be under scrutiny again. She tried to assume the cool demeanor that was meant to keep men at bay. The riders' mounts thundered up to within a few feet of the camp and both men swung down easily, ground-hitched their horses, and ambled up to the awning.

They tipped their hats, first to Myra and then Jessica, obviously awkward in the presence of ladies. The tall one, Fred, whose hat had served to cover a high, bald pate, turned to Whitey. "We were in the neighborhood, so we thought we'd ride by and see if there was anything you needed."

Woody, better known as Wheelbarrow, merely stared dumbstruck from one woman to the other and smiled. He sported a thick gray mustache that covered his upper lip.

Whitey's deep complexion darkened further as, forced into a show of manners, he said, "We're fine. And since you're here, this"—he indicated Jessica with a wave of his hand—"is Miss Stanbridge, and this"—he nodded to Myra—"is Miss Thornton." He sat down again and picked up his teacup with a challenge in his eyes, daring them to say anything about the delicate piece of china he lifted to his lips.

Myra broke the tense silence. "Gentlemen, we were about to have tea and scones. If you'll pull up a barrel, I'd be happy to fix you some."

Wheelbarrow's mustache twitched and his face was wreathed with smiles. "Don't believe I've ever had either one, but there's a first time to everything." He moved off to collect his seat. Fred thanked her for the invitation and did the same. Whitey rolled his eyes.

Jessica resumed her chair and vowed to get through the

ordeal. When she left Boston, she had no notion that she would ever be sitting at a table in the middle of the high plateau sipping tea with three cowmen wearing guns strapped to their thighs. She wondered if a journal article could possibly come out of the experience.

In no time at all, Myra had served their two new guests. The men, cowed by the formality of the little ceremony, ate and drank in virtual silence. By the second cup of tea, though, they were regaling Myra with their feats of daring on the open range. Finally, out of breath but not stories, Woody Barrows noted the book lying beside Myra's cup and asked, "What are you reading, ma'am?"

Jessica and Whitey exchanged a smile. Myra's favorite topic of late was the Corelli book. They sat in companionable silence and let her go on about the novel until Fred interrupted. "It's been a long time since I heard a good tale, Miss Thornton. I don't suppose you'd like to read to all of us a bit, would you?"

Myra puffed up like an orator asked to speak on his favorite subject, smoothed a hand over the straining bodice of her blouse, and took up her book. "It's a long story, far longer than we could read in many days, but perhaps, since I've filled you in on so much, I should just pick up where I left off?"

The men nodded. Woody, who was nearly as well rounded as Myra, set his cup down. Balancing his hat on his knee, he leaned forward with an elbow on the table. Fred straightened and crossed his legs while Whitey sat with his arms folded across his chest.

Jessica silently began planning a letter to the museum director.

Myra read on and on, the sound of her voice soothing and pleasant until she started to cough and took a sip of tea. If the three men were bored, it was not evident in their expressions. In fact, Jessica thought they looked very disappointed when Myra stopped.

"Would you mind?" Myra asked her.

Glancing at the encouraging faces around the table, Jessica would have been hard pressed to say no. She nodded in agreement and Myra passed the book to Fred, who handed it reverently to Jessica.

> Lonely's a word I don't often use,
> 'Cause I know I'm livin' the life that I choose.
> But more often than not, at the end of the ride
> I find myself wonderin'—if I took a bride—
> Would cold nights seem shorter?
> Would days fill with song?
> Would she keep to herself or come ride along?
> Would I ever get weary of husbandly dues?
> Or is this lonely feeling all that I'd lose?

Rory hummed to himself as he tried to rearrange line and meter to match the motion of his horse's gait. The sun was lower in the afternoon sky—it would be sunset in two hours—but he was determined to see Jessica Stanbridge again before the day was through. He couldn't account for his need, no more than any man can account for wanting to be in the presence of a beautiful woman, but the fact that his thoughts had strayed to the subject of loneliness was enough to make him wary.

As he galloped over a low rise he saw the camp outlined in the distance. The tent was still standing, but now a second, open-sided structure stood not far away. A colorful piece of scarf fluttered in the wind, a whimsical, feminine touch that instantly brought a smile to his lips. It didn't seem like something Jessica would do, so he guessed Myra must have added the festive touch. When he looked closer, he noticed quite a few people huddled around a table beneath the awning.

Rory frowned. *Who in the hell . . . ?* As he drew closer he recognized two of the horses on the near side of the camp as Barrows's and Hench's. No wonder he hadn't come across his men all afternoon. He quickly headed Domino toward the far tent and slowed to a walk so that the group seated around the table couldn't see him directly. When he was in shouting distance, he dismounted and led the big Appaloosa as close as he dared before he ground-hitched the horse and silently slipped up on the others.

Whitey and Myra were seated with their backs to him. Barrows and Hench stared in rapt attention at Jessica as she read from a book lying open on the tabletop. From where he stood, Rory had a clear view of her. With forearms resting on the table, she bowed her head and concentrated on the words. She read in a clear, melodious voice filled with emotion. Cautiously he stayed beside the tent but moved closer until he could hear her clearly.

> *"Her beautiful face, turned upwards to the angry sky, was half in light and half in shade; a smile parted her lips, and her eyes were bright with a look of interest and expectancy. Another sudden glare, and the clouds were again broken asunder; but this time in a jagged and hasty manner, as though a naked sword had been thrust through them and immediately withdrawn.*
>
> *"'That was a nasty flash,' said Colonel Everard, with an observant glance at the lovely Juliet-like figure on the balcony. 'Mademoiselle, had you not better come in?'"*

One of the oldest cowhands, Wheelbarrow, held a floral teacup loosely between thumb and forefinger; his eyes never left Jessica's face. His foreman, Fred Hench, rested his elbows on the table and his head between his hands as he listened without moving. Rory was certain that if he could see Whitey Higgins's face, it would reflect the same dazed expression, and he knew immediately that Jessica had lost herself in the reading, for she would never sit still and intentionally weave such a spell around his men. No, he thought, if she knew how she affected them, she would slam the book shut and dismiss them all.

He turned his attention back to the words.

> " 'Besides, I love the storm.' *A tumultuous crash of thunder, tremendous for its uproar and the length of time it was prolonged, made us look at each other again with anxious faces.*
> " *'What are we waiting for? Oh my heart!'* "

He saw her face slowly pinken as she began to read the tender words of a love poem.

> *"Kiss me straight on the brows and part!*
> *Again! again, my heart, my heart!"*

He watched Jessica glance quickly at Myra as if to say, "How could you do this to me?" Then he heard Myra's encouragement. "Go on. At least read to the end of the poem." This time he listened intently to the words and felt an overwhelming longing to touch her.

> *"What are we waiting for, you and I?*
> *A pleading look—a stifled cry!"*

At that Jessica slammed the book shut and set it down. The red glow of the western sky could not account for the color that suffused her face and neck.

"I'm afraid that's all for today, gentlemen," she said as she abruptly stood up, just as he knew she would, to dismiss the men.

It was impossible to forget the words she had just read as he stepped away from the tent.

"That *is* all for today, *gentlemen*," he said.

Five pairs of eyes turned swiftly in his direction. Whitey, Hench, and Barrows jumped to their feet. Barrows's hat flopped to the ground. Jessica's mouth opened and then quickly snapped shut. Myra was the only one who looked genuinely happy to see him.

Rory crossed the short distance to the table and stood beside Myra. He didn't take his eyes off of Jessica. He knew she hated his stare, but he couldn't look away. She was more beautiful than he remembered; her face was alive with color from exposure to the sun and embarrassment. She fairly glowed. It didn't matter that her full lips were pursed into a narrow line or that her huge owl eyes stared unblinkingly from behind her round glasses. It didn't matter that her clothing was dirty and rumpled. What did matter was that for the first time he was fully aware of what being near her did to him. Stunned by the overwhelming reaction, he wondered what to do next.

What did a man do when he was on fire?

CHAPTER

7

"Have a cup of tea, Mr. Burnett," Myra urged.

He nodded. It might be as good a cure as any. Afraid to let Jessica see the heat in his gaze, he kept his eyes on the men. Mistaking his intense look for anger, they shifted, as nervous as ants on a crowded boardwalk. "A little far of field, aren't you, boys?" he asked.

Barrows and Hench glanced at each other. Barrows shrugged. Hench cleared his throat and said, "We thought we'd check out this end of the range before we headed back."

When Rory didn't say anything in response, Barrows shifted. "We did round up about fifteen head and ran them back to the ranch before we rode out again."

"What about Gathers and Tinsley?" Rory asked, referring to his other two cowhands.

Fred Hench looked to Wheelbarrow to speak. "They got in an argument over an *orejana* Gathers found up the draw."

None too pleased at the news, Rory drew off his hat, wiped his forehead, and jammed the hat on again. All he needed now was to have one or the other of his best hands up and quit because of a fight over an unmarked bull. Tradition on the range was that any cowhand who was first to rope an unbranded bull could claim ownership and all monies the animal brought at market. "They settle it?"

"Tinsley ain't happy, but Gathers was there first, fair and square."

Fully aware that Jessica, Myra, and Whitey were listening patiently to the exchange, Rory excused the men. "You two head on back and I'll talk to both of them when I get in."

Myra left the table and quickly came back with a clean cup. "Here's your tea, Mr. Burnett."

As his men bid the ladies a hasty good-bye and Whitey hurried off to water the mules and horses, Rory reached down, picked up the lukewarm tea, and unceremoniously tossed it back in one gulp. The liquid did little to douse the heat in his veins. He purposely kept from looking at Jessica until he had gathered his wits about him. When he did, he found her studying him closely.

"Won't you at least sit down?" she offered.

"I have to talk to you alone. Now."

She looked startled by his curt demand but quickly regained her composure. "Fine." She led him a short distance away to a spot where they were out of sight of the others. He could smell the light, clean fragrance of scented soap about her and suddenly realized he wanted to reach out and brush aside the stray lock of hair that played across her forehead.

Instead he kept his hands jammed in his pockets. "I'll be leaving day after tomorrow on a cattle drive to Durango. Until then I expect you to stay put."

She stiffened immediately. Her intense blue eyes snapped as she stared up at him from behind the lenses. "Have you forgotten, Mr. Burnett, that it was I who hired you? You have no right to tell me when to stay or where to go."

He shook his head. "No, I haven't forgotten, but for your own good, I'd like you to stay here and forget about the mesa."

She studied him closely. "Exactly what is it you're hiding up there?"

Much too quickly he responded. "Nothing."

"Why is it I don't believe you?"

Rory realized uncomfortably that they were close enough to embrace, so close in fact that he could see the light sheen of perspiration glowing across the bridge of her nose.

He tried to change the subject. "Are you finished with the tracks already?"

She nodded. "Whitey has led me to an exposed section of petrified bone in a dry creek bed not far from here. They're all fragments, but there may be something deeper—"

"That ought to keep you busy."

Jessica shook her head. "Although I sense you'd like nothing better than to keep me well occupied, I still intend to look around before I choose a definite excavation site. Luck has been with me so far."

"If you go up on the mesa before I get back, your luck just might run out," he warned.

"Are you threatening me, Mr. Burnett, because if you are . . ."

He took off his hat again and this time made a study of the brim. With a glance back at the camp, he sighed. "I've been warned to keep you off the mesa by Piah Jackson, one of the Ute leaders."

She wrinkled her nose and he watched her freckles hide beneath the creases. "When did he tell you this?"

"Before I met you."

"Then you schemed to bring me here all along?"

He could see she was beginning to get all steamed up. If he didn't act fast, Miss Jessica Stanbridge would likely bolt and head right back to the mesa. Rory slammed his hat back on and reached out for her. Shocked, she looked down at his fingers as they squeezed her upper arms.

Her frigid stare forced him to let go. "Yes, I did. But it was for your own good," he admitted grudgingly.

"Mr. Burnett, for a long time now I've been the one to decide what was good for me. When were you going to tell me the truth? Or were you?"

"That's why I rode out here today."

"You had ample opportunity to tell me before now. Why should I believe you?"

"I didn't know if you had sense enough to listen to reason."

"And now?" She planted her hands on her hips and glared at him.

"Now that I do know you, I think you might just be pigheaded enough to go back up there just because I'm asking you not to." He shifted his weight and shoved his hat farther back on his head. "I don't have time to give you a history lesson, Miss Stanbridge, but not too long ago an ancient village site was found not far from here in the cliff at Mesa Verde. Since then there have been all sorts of people digging through the ruins. The scoundrels have no regard for Indian ways or for the fact that a burial site, no matter how old, is as sacred to Indian people as a graveyard is to us."

She cut him off. "I don't intend—"

"I don't intend to let you, either," he said. "There are graves hidden all over this area. The Utes don't want to see them desecrated."

"Nor do I. You know I'm only after saurian bones."

"And what if you find a grave site instead? What would you do if you discovered a place filled with ancient relics and primitive remains? You're telling me that as a scientist you could just turn your back on it all?"

"I'm telling you that right now such finds are not my

objective, but if I do come across any such thing, I'll notify the proper authorities. Besides, what you don't realize is that my father was one of the foremost scholars on antiquities as well as paleontology. He was very well known for his care and consideration of human remains.''

"What you're saying is that he was careful when he packed them up for the museum. If you found anything new, word would get out one way or another, and I'm not dealing with your father now, Miss Stanbridge, I'm dealing with you—''

"Just as I, unfortunately, am dealing with *you*," she told him bluntly. "I assure you, I don't intend to ravage any grave sites.''

"I have no idea if you'll keep your word.''

"Because I'm a woman?''

"No." He lowered his voice when he realized he was shouting. "Because you're so hell-bent on success. I think you'd be willing to do whatever it takes to make a name for yourself. If that means you have to destroy sacred ground or disturb a few Indian graves in the bargain, so be it.''

"What gives you the right to play self-appointed guardian of those people's bones?''

He squinted off at sun that now lazed just above the horizon. "Because my father taught me to stand up for those who can't stand up for themselves.''

The canvas tent flap rustled with the force of the same breeze that pressed her skirt against her legs. He could see by the cocky tilt of her chin and the fierce determination shining in her eyes that no matter what he said, no matter what case he pleaded, she was still set on exploring the mesa.

Sensing defeat, he tried one last tack. "Have you ever heard of the Ghost Dance, Miss Stanbridge?''

She nervously smoothed her skirt over her slim waist and shook her head. "No.''

"It's a religious movement that's sweeping through the

Indian reservations. A wrong move could stir the Utes to rebellion.''

Certain he was only trying to frighten her, she folded her arms beneath her breasts and said, ''Oh, please! This is 1890.''

''That's right. But don't forget you're in Colorado, not Boston.''

''Exactly what is it you want from me, Mr. Burnett?''

He stared down at her, still moved by the haunting words of love she had read aloud. *Kiss me straight on the brows and part! Again! again, my heart, my heart!*

''I was real sure about what I wanted to tell you when I got here, but for the last few minutes I've been thinking about something else entirely.'' Casually, his voice low so that it would not carry on the breeze, he asked, ''Have you ever been kissed, Miss Stanbridge?''

The abrupt change of subject took her aback. Had she heard wrong? ''*What?* Why, I never—''

Rory smiled. ''That's just what I thought.''

She stepped away.

He reached out for her before she escaped.

''Get ready, because it's about to happen.''

Jessica knew what was coming but was powerless to stop it. Shock mingled with an odd curiosity kept her from struggling. When his hands closed over her upper arms and he pulled her roughly against him, all she could think of was the warmth that emanated from him and the surprising fact that up close, his eyes were unbroken by any flecks of color, just as dark and fathomless as they appeared from far away. As he lowered his lips to hers, she was mesmerized by her own reflection in his eyes. Almost immediately she was caught up in the sudden realization that his lashes were so thick it was a pity they had been wasted on a man.

Their lips had barely touched when Rory pulled back and secured his hold with an arm across her shoulders. He

slipped off her spectacles with his free hand and set out to
kiss her again.

It was like nothing she'd ever imagined.

It was more than he'd ever dreamed.

Her lips were soft and pliant, so very willing beneath his
own that Rory wondered if he might be imagining the whole
exchange. The stalwart, no-nonsense Miss Jessica Stanbridge was suddenly clinging to him. Her fingers were
clutching the soft flannel of his shirt so tightly that he felt
the center button strain from the force of her hold. Obviously innocent of a man's kiss, she kept her eyes open and
her lips closed tight. Unwilling to frighten her, unable to
hold back, Rory strengthened his hold and pressed for more.
He traced her lips with the tip of his tongue. When she
opened her lips to protest, he slipped his tongue between
them and deepened the kiss.

Somewhere in the back of her mind Jessica was still able
to think rationally, even though her senses were on the verge
of riot. Her heart pounded. Her knees went weak. A deep
ache that had begun low in her middle, in a very unthinkable
place, was now radiating out and upward so quickly that she
was afraid she would become engulfed.

There was no way she could let go of his shirt.

She was inexorably drawn to this man and the sensations
his kiss evoked, so much so that she likened it to the
moment she lay on the sandstone rock and felt the pulse beat
of the desert around her. The scientist in her clinically
recorded his every move and noted every disturbing response as his lips and tongue teased hers and his arms
tightened and drew her closer against the hard lines and
angles of his body. In an instantaneous flash of awareness
she knew that no man she had ever encountered could have
produced such a blatantly sensual response in her. A
hundred questions assailed her. Why now? Why here? Why
with a man as different in temperament and situation as
Rory Burnett? What *was* he doing with his tongue?

Rory had not expected to kiss Jessica Stanbridge until the very moment he took her in his arms, and although he was just as surprised by his overwhelming reaction to her, he was that shocked at her response. And he was still fully aware of the consequences—the worst being she'd pack up and leave the minute he released her. As he lengthened the sweetest, hottest, most nerve-shattering kiss he had ever had, he became determined not to let her go.

With that end in mind, he regretfully let reason take over. Slowly he ended the kiss and raised his head, determined to salvage the situation. Jessica stumbled back two steps and he immediately reached out to help her regain her balance. She grabbed his hand and held on until she was standing on even ground. Then she instantly let go, as if touching him disgusted her.

With a hand to her breast she gasped, "What did you do that for?" Her blue eyes were wide with shock, her cheeks aglow, her lips reddened from his assault.

He pulled the brim of his hat down and feigned a coolness he didn't feel. "Beats me. Maybe I was just trying to shut you up. It wasn't so bad, though, was it?"

Unwilling to let him know exactly how much his kiss had moved her, Jessica looked down and straightened her blouse where it had come partially untucked from the waistband of her skirt.

"That was a supreme waste of time given the fact that this relationship is going nowhere." Shaking, she reached out for her spectacles and he relinquished them.

He studied her carefully. "I say you never know, Jess. You never know."

When he turned away and headed back toward the center of camp, she was forced to run after him. Jessica grabbed him above the elbow. He bestowed a smug smile at her touch and she quickly let go. "If you think that kiss has rattled me so badly that I'll forget all about exploring the mesa, think again," she warned.

He smiled. "Then you admit it *did* rattle you?"

She shook her head. "Not one whit."

Rory laughed aloud.

Jessica fumed. Glancing around the corner of the tent in the direction of the awning, she saw that Myra was setting out the dishes for the evening meal as Whitey stoked the fire under a spitted rabbit. The smell of roasting meat was beginning to flavor the air.

"Apologize immediately," she said through clenched teeth.

"No way I'll apologize for something that was obviously so enjoyable for both of us."

"Then get out of my camp."

"You're on my land."

"A situation easily remedied at daybreak," she threatened.

He sobered immediately. "Jess, I have to have your promise you won't leave until I get back."

She ignored the way the shortened version of her given name sounded like a caress when he said it. "Why should I promise you anything after the way you've just humiliated me?" She clenched her fingers together at her waist and stared at the ground.

The sight of her bowed head bothered him more than he liked to admit. "No one saw us. Besides, what's so humiliating about a kiss? Look, if you stay put until I get back, I promise to take you up to the mesa myself."

Jessica slowly raised her head and pinned him with what she hoped was her most quelling gaze. The sight of his dark-eyed perusal moved her more than she would ever let herself admit. "Why should I wait?"

"Because it's not safe for you to go up there alone, not after what Piah told me today," he said honestly.

She fiddled with her blouse again, smoothing it against the waistband of her skirt. Before she answered, she tucked a stray lock of hair behind her ear. Putting aside her pride, she told him honestly, "I'm not a stupid woman, Mr. Burnett. You've certainly given me no reason to believe you, especially after your lascivious conduct just now, but given the distinct possibility that your warning might contain the slightest hint of truth, then I promise. I won't explore the mesa until you return, but only if you swear you'll take me there yourself. After that, you're fired."

Relieved to know she would still be here when he returned, Rory smiled and held out his hand. "It's a deal."

She looked down at his hand as if it were a rattler. "On second thought, why can't Whitey take me?"

When apprehension coupled with swift anger shot through him, Rory knew he had been bitten far worse than he thought. "That kid has a hard enough time watching out for himself, let alone you. I'll leave him here to guard the camp, but don't try to charm him into any trips up to the mesa. You could both wind up dead."

As much as she would like to admit she didn't need him, Jessica knew she would feel far safer with Burnett as her guide, as long as he kept his hands, and his lips, to himself. "I won't," she assured him.

The smell of roasted rabbit made his stomach rumble. "I'd best be getting back to the ranch."

"Will you stay for dinner?" The words came out without warning. She wanted to kick herself. She needed time to be alone with her thoughts, to analyze the most disturbing exchange.

Rory bit back a triumphant smile. "Sure. On one condition."

"Is there always a condition with you?" She crossed her arms and waited.

"Stop hiding behind those silly glasses. You don't need them."

Completely disarmed, she gracefully sidestepped him and headed toward the awning with its fluttering paisley scarf.

• • •

With Whitey's help, Jessica had unearthed far more fossils in a week's time than she previously thought possible. As she stood beneath a robin's-egg-blue sky and squinted against the intense sunlight, surveying the dig, she couldn't help but take pride in her accomplishment. Carefully excavated bits and pieces of bone, all numbered and tagged, lay off to the side. The larger segments were sealed in plaster to prevent breakage, and lay like pieces of an age-old puzzle, waiting to be reassembled.

Every precaution had been taken while digging, lifting, sifting, and sorting the fossilized bones. Whitey quickly learned the importance of working slowly with the fragile pieces. They worked elbow to elbow all week long, and more often than not Jessica grudgingly admitted to herself that she was thankful to have him there for both company and assistance. Even Myra, caught up in their enthusiasm, had accompanied them to the site twice to help out.

Jessica looked down at her hands. They were a mess, she decided as she pulled off her gloves to inspect the damage. Sand and grit had sifted through tiny rips and tears in her chamois gloves, cutting her fingertips and nails. Her palms were blistered and callused. Tossing her gloves in the wagon bed, she began to unwrap the sandwiches Myra had sent along with them. At the sight of slices of bread liberally spread with thick blackberry preserves, Jessica's mouth began to water. She found the water bottle, uncorked it, took a long pull, and let the water cool her parched throat. Then she called out to Whitey.

"Time to eat! If you don't hurry I might eat it all."

He looked up from where he was digging a trench around a half-exposed section of bone and waved.

Jessica tipped her helmet back, took a bite out of her sandwich, and leaned back on her elbows against the wagon bed. The jaunty veil on her pith helmet had shredded days ago after her hat fell into the excavation pit and caught on the head of a pick. She ripped off as much as she could, wound it around the crown of the helmet, and then tied it off. The ragged hatband was just another trophy accumulated through hard work. She'd given up wearing her all-but-useless spectacles as soon as she tired of wiping dust off them every few moments.

As she took another bite and washed it down with water, Jessica hoped that wherever her father's spirit had gone to dwell, he could see her now. Not too many months ago they had pored over the notes of famed paleontologist O. C. Marsh, one of the first to have ventured west in search of saurian fossils.

She couldn't help but liken her own adventure to those of Henry Osborn and William Scott, also inspired by Marsh's writings, men who went west by rail and wagon to a land barely tamed and settled in the summer of '77. Back in her quiet flat she and Uriah Stanbridge had thrilled to the accounts of the numerous notable discoveries they made at Bridger Basin, Wyoming. Now she was in the field, dirty, gritty, immersed in the past and loving every moment. In all her life she had never been as happy or as fulfilled. As she listened to the hum of insects and watched a jay take wing, she wondered how anyone could bear to work at a task they didn't enjoy.

Yes, she thought with pride as she glanced at the neat rows of plaster-encased bone with the manila tags fluttering in the breeze, she could hold her head up among the best of them. Still, she couldn't help but wonder what Rory Burnett would think when he returned and saw the excavation pit. She couldn't wait to show it to him and tell him about the pieces they had uncovered. As much as she hated to admit it, she had missed sparring with him. And as much as she tried to deny it to herself, she had spent the better part of the week analyzing the way his kiss had made her feel.

After one last bite of sandwich, Jessica hailed Whitey again. "You must be starving!" She couldn't believe how much her own appetite was stimulated by activity, the clear air, and sunshine.

Resting against the open end of the wagon bed, she watched Whitey straighten and stretch, then brush the red dirt off his pants. As he sauntered toward her, wiping his grime-streaked face with a red bandanna, she couldn't help but admit that he was a strikingly handsome young man. Over the past week he had been attempting to grow a mustache, but all he had to show for his trouble was some sparse, dark fuzz across his upper lip.

He smiled when he reached the wagon and picked up a sandwich. With the bread halfway to his lips he paused and said softly, "We've got company."

Jessica looked over her shoulder and then turned to stare. Sure enough, six riders were approaching. She shielded her eyes and tried to keep the excitement out of her voice. Rory Burnett had been gone a week, and as loath as she was to admit it, she was actually anticipating his return. "Is it Burnett? Are they back already?"

"No." Whitey pulled his gun out of his holster and checked the chambers, then snapped it back in place. "They're Utes."

She stared down at the gun in his hand, then into his eyes. "But surely they're friendly."

"They're off the reservation. It doesn't hurt to be ready."

Jessica watched the slowly approaching riders and soon recognized the tall hat of the man who had watched her so intently when she and Myra first arrived at the reservation. Rory's warning came back to her; still, she wanted no trouble with these men.

"Put that gun away, Whitey. Until we know otherwise we'll assume they're just paying us a friendly visit."

The riders drew nearer. She recognized the one she called Tall Hat, four men, and a youth. Their ponies, with their rope halters and woven saddle blankets, were as shaggy and wild looking as the men in their colorful mixture of traditional and modern clothing.

"Do you have your gun?" Whitey whispered.

Jessica shook her head. "No. I left it behind." The past uneventful days had led to complacency.

He reached out and squeezed her hand. "Don't worry, Miss Jessica. I'll protect you with my life if I have to."

The loving gesture coupled with the sincerity of his pledge startled her. Somehow, sometime during their week together, Whitey Higgins had fallen in love. She frowned and wondered what, if anything, she had mistakenly done to encourage him. She promised herself that as soon as their current problem was resolved, she would let him know his feelings were not returned.

"Don't look scared," he advised, drawing her out of her thoughts. His voice cracked on the words.

"I'm not," she told him truthfully. Given his sudden loss of color and the way his Adam's apple bobbed up and down, she was certain that should they be in any real danger, she would most likely have to rely upon herself.

Seconds passed before the Ute riders stopped beside the wagon.

Tall Hat, with a stern, foreboding expression, dismounted before the rest followed suit.

Whitey nodded. "Piah."

Jessica recognized the name and held her breath. This was the man Burnett had mentioned. Piah was staring directly at her. She felt Whitey move up to her side.

"You are the woman who searches for the bones?" Piah asked.

She shook her head. "Not human bones. Not the bones of your people."

He pointed at the unearthed pieces behind her. "What are those?"

"Come. I'd be happy to show you," she volunteered. Whitey grabbed her elbow but she shook him off, ignoring the warning glance he threw her. "They're bones of saurians. . . ." She fought for a clearer explanation. "Lizards. Giant lizards that once—"

He nodded. "Thunder lizards. They are best left to sleep in the earth."

"They have no power. They have been dead for centuries. Millions and millions of years." Did Indians compute in millions? Jessica struggled for a way to make him understand.

Piah's gaze never wavered. Black eyes that hid ancient secrets bored into hers. She tried to remember something about primitive cultures. Perhaps he was a shaman, a magician. She wished they could communicate better, for she suspected he was a man with much to teach, but his hostility toward her work was all too apparent.

"A spirit never dies," he warned.

"Please." She beckoned him as she walked toward the carefully prepared bones. "Come and see. There are no human remains here. No Indian bones."

He followed. The others remained near the wagon. Whitey stood uncomfortably between the men and Jessica. She knelt to show Piah the bones and lifted what was obviously the pelvic bone of a creature far larger than a man.

"You see?"

Piah stared, but did not reach out to touch the fossil. Then he knelt beside her and stared at the smaller fragments, never touching, only carefully sizing them up with his eyes. "How can you be sure that some of these were not once bones of the People?"

When she had seen him on the reservation, the man had led her to believe he couldn't speak English. Now it appeared he was quite fluent. This is not, she told herself as certainty swept over her, a man who can be trusted.

"I've studied many years. It is my job to know where they came from."

"What will you do with them?"

It was a fair question. She answered truthfully, "I am taking them to the East, to a place where wise men study them to learn about the past."

"The past is better left buried. To unearth the past is to end the future."

She felt her palms grow damp. What did he mean, end the future?

"I told Burnett to keep you away from the mesa," he said.

The sensation of fear made her angry. "I know. He told me. But I don't have to listen to Burnett."

"Then you are even more stupid than I thought."

Jessica was on her feet in an instant. "Now, you listen here—"

Whitey was suddenly beside her again. "She's not going up to the mesa, are you, Miss Jessica?"

For once she let common sense override her temper. She cleared her throat, looked down at the scuffed toes of her boots, then off toward the horizon as if she had all the time in the world. "No. No, I'm not."

Piah made no comment, but his silence convinced her that he didn't believe a word. When she finally met his intense stare, he said softly, "You have been warned, woman."

Then, without another word, he turned and walked back to the others. Almost as one, they mounted up and thundered away. As the dust rode the breeze behind them Whitey threw his hat on the ground and ranted, "Damn it, Miss Jess, here I was hopin' to keep things from gettin' bad and you go and square off with one of the head honchos of the reservation!"

"Well, I'm sorry, but as I told your boss, I'm quite able to take care of myself."

"Maybe that's true back where you come from, but this is Colorado, ma'am, and well . . . if anything happened to you, why I'd . . ."

She watched him shift uncomfortably as he searched for words, then much to her chagrin, Whitey Higgins reached out and grabbed her. Her helmet tumbled into the dirt just before he smashed his lips against hers.

The entire bumbling incident took less than two seconds, but it was enough to cause her frayed temper to snap. She shoved him away with all her might and glared. "What *is* it with you men out here?"

He was beet red from collar to hairline. Once more his voice cracked. "Oh, Lordy, I'm so sorry Miss Jessica. I don't know what came over me."

She drew herself up to her full height. The sun in her eyes forced her to stoop down and pick up her helmet. She slammed it on her head so hard she winced. Reminding herself she was older, wiser, and therefore should be more in control of her emotions, she said as calmly as possible, "I'm certain it was merely the heat and the tenseness of the situation, Whitey. I think it's best if we both put this entire incident out of our minds."

"Yes, ma'am."

"I do not intend to let anything sway me from my appointed task." *I just wish I could dismiss Rory Burnett's kiss as easily.*

"No, ma'am."

"I have no room in my life for romantic entanglements." *Not with you or Mr. Rory Burnett.*

"No, ma'am."

"Definitely not. None whatsoever."

"No, ma'am." Whitey picked up his hat, dusted it off, and then brushed off the brim to avoid looking at her.

"I do not welcome any romantic advances." *Since Burnett's kiss was definitely executed with more finesse, does that mean he goes around kissing women all the time? How also does one hone such skills?*

"No, ma'am. I'm truly sorry, Miss Jessica."

"Then I take it we understand each other?" *Rory Burnett*

*did not smash my teeth. He slipped his tongue into my mouth
with ease, so much so that I nearly melted in his arms.*

"Yes, ma'am."

"Fine, then let's get back to work."

Her hands were still shaking when she wiped them on her
skirt and pushed her hair back off her face. In just over a
week she'd been kissed by not one but two men. Stalking
over to the wagon bed to retrieve her gloves, she shook her
head in disbelief. She had a lot to learn about Western men.
Even the young ones were certainly not hesitant about
taking whatever they wanted.

That's what comes of letting down my guard, she
thought. Next time, she vowed as she pulled her spectacles
out of her skirt pocket and slipped them on, she'd be ready.

CHAPTER

8

Spending Saturday in Durango was always worth the sweat, dust, and rigors of a cattle drive. Rory leaned against a hitching rail in front of the Phoenix Variety Theatre and watched the water wagon roll past and sprinkle down the dusty street. In a little while the town band and various conveyances would line up for the weekly parade of soiled doves new to Durango.

Woody Barrows nudged Rory with an elbow and nodded toward the open door of the combination dance hall and saloon. "Looks like there's some time left before the puddles dry up and the parade starts. I'm goin' in to have a beer with Hench. Want one?"

Rory shook his head and pushed away from the rail. "No thanks. I think I'll wander down the street."

"See ya later then," Woody called out over his shoulder before he disappeared behind the saloon doors.

Rory hoped a walk might help him sort out his feelings. A slow-simmering anger coupled with confusion had been brewing inside him ever since he took payment and they left the cattle at the stockyard. Miss Jessica Stanbridge with her sun-freckled nose, her prim, high-buttoned collar, her bedraggled beige linen suit, and her tempting lips had plagued his thoughts the better part of the drive.

Not only had he contended with Gathers and Tinsley continually sparring over the right to the *orejana* bull, but his mind kept conjuring up unwanted visions of Jess as he'd seen her last. The memory of their kiss had kept him awake long hours into the night. He'd volunteered to take the night watch more often and far longer than any of the others. It beat lying awake on his bedroll staring up at the night sky and thinking of the way her soft lips had parted so willingly at his tongue's insistence and how she had grabbed hold of his shirt as if it were the only thing keeping her upright. It kept him from fighting off the physical discomfort that accompanied the vivid memories.

Trying to lose himself in the crowd, Rory moved along the boardwalk, dodging Saturday revelers and women shoppers, until he came to a wide storefront window where a flash of soft yellow caught his eye. A quick glance told him the place was a dressmaker's shop, and with another look over his shoulder, he made certain none of his cowhands were around. He stopped for a moment, reached down pretending to fasten the buckle of his spur, and peered at the dress in the window.

On close inspection he could see that the soft material wasn't a bright yellow, but closer to ivory, the color of creamy butter. A wide, shiny ribbon adorned the narrow waist; its tails hung almost to the hem. More ribbons, each tied with a saucy bow at the elbows, decorated the sleeves. He was studying it carefully, trying to imagine Jessica in such a frivolous dress, when a small boy in a white shirt and suspendered knickers ran right into him and knocked him on his rear into the flow of foot traffic.

"Sorry, mister," the boy called out, immediately lost to sight as he zigzagged through the crowd.

"Shit!" Rory cursed aloud. He heard a startled gasp and looked up past two well-dressed matrons' skirts to find them staring down their noses at him with contempt. Three shades of red beneath his hat, he mumbled an apology, then stood and dusted himself off. The ladies moved on without looking back.

Before he could change his mind, he opened the door to the dressmaker's shop. A tiny bell chimed as he entered. The store was small, quiet, and empty, he noted thankfully as he closed the door behind him. A short, thin woman with snapping brown eyes and curly, faded brown hair stepped out from behind a counter that stood in front of what looked like a wall of shelves filled with bolts of material.

"May I help you, sir?"

He cleared his throat, remembered to take off his hat, and then looked over at the front window display. "I want to buy that dress in the window."

She looked him up and down, taking in his dusty, trail-worn appearance. "I'm afraid it's very expensive."

He thought of the bank draft in his pocket. The cattle he'd sold had brought a good price; still, he had no idea what an expensive, ready-made dress might cost—but at that moment it didn't matter. He wanted it because he wanted to see Jess in it. "I'll take it anyway."

For some reason the woman became incredibly stubborn. "Without asking the price?"

Was he losing his mind or had she lost hers? "What kind of a store are you running here? Do you want to sell it or not?"

She crossed her arms. "I cater to the best families of Durango, sir. Now, just how do you know it will fit?"

He sidestepped her, carefully skirted a spindly table covered with lace and baubles, and walked over to the window display. Setting his hat on a bolt of cloth spread out on another table, he reached out and lifted the dress form with the butter-colored dress out of the window and stood it on the floor with a sharp thud.

"Now, see here—"

Ignoring the proprietress, Rory put his hands around the waist of the form, ran them up along the sides of the breasts then down over the hips. He lifted the wire form and turned it around, studied the back of the dress, held it up a bit, and eyed the length before he announced, "It'll fit. Wrap it up."

"I refuse to sell this dress to you if you're going to give it to one of *those* women who'll be parading by in a few minutes. I don't do work for the likes of them directly or indirectly and I—"

He wanted the dress bad enough to give her a partial explanation. "I'm taking it home with me."

She seemed to soften immediately. "For your wife, then?"

He retrieved his hat. "Do you want to sell me this dress or not?"

Rory could see the woman wanted to ask more as she slipped the dress off the form and carefully folded it while she walked toward the high oak counter. "I'll wrap it up good then. Do you have far to go?"

"Outside Cortez." He folded his arms and waited, wondering what the charge would be but too stubborn to ask.

He heard the roll of a snare drum and the clash of cymbals down the street. The dressmaker glanced at the window with a frown as she tied a string around the brown wrapping paper. "That'll be six dollars."

Rory hid his shock and dug the money out of his pocket without a word. An off-key trombone could be heard above the other band instruments.

"I hope your . . . well, I hope the lady enjoys it," the woman said as she handed the package over to him.

"Thanks." He shoved his hat back on and headed for the

door just as the drum major appeared in front of the store. The boardwalk was lined with men, and the good ladies of the town pressed back against the storefronts and tried not to be seen watching the parade of whores. Rory tucked the package under his arm and waited for the commotion to die down.

A band led the parade, the musicians' bright uniforms overshadowing their lack of skill. The drummers walked by last and the deep reverberations of drumbeats were soon replaced by cheers and shouts of the men welcoming the week's colorful crop of fallen angels newly come to town via the Denver and Rio Grande Railroad. A fringe-covered surrey led the cavalcade of buggies from the livery stable, all of them full of whores decked out in feathered boas, shining satin gowns, and twinkling jewels.

Rory couldn't help but wonder what comments Jessica would have on the subject, but he was certain she would have a definite opinion on such an obvious display of bad taste. Three girls rode by mounted sidesaddle and dressed even more flamboyantly than the rest. A dark-eyed brunette in a shocking scarlet gown with a feather boa caught his eye, winked, and threw him a kiss. Rory smiled back, tempted to wave and cause a stir amid the crowd of virtuous ladies standing nearby. Instead he watched the girls until they were down the block, turned his attention to the rest of the parade, and when it was finally over, followed the stream of men moving back toward the railroad tracks, which marked the boundary between the more respected section of town and the bars and bawdy houses.

He found his cowhands gathered around a beer-splashed table near the center of the velvet-draped dance hall inside the Phoenix Variety Theatre. Toothless Barney Tinsley was sprawled in a low-backed chair with a brassy blonde seated across his thighs. She was absentmindedly rubbing the top of Barney's bald head with her fingertips as she stared off across the room. When Rory approached, she swung her gaze his way, smiled provocatively, and then snuggled closer to Barney. It was clear the old wrangler had paid for the privilege of the lady's company all evening.

The man they all knew only as Gathers, tall and lean, his right cheek sporting a crescent-shaped scar, sat apart from the rest. Silent as usual, he watched the proceedings from beneath a lowered hat brim. Gathers, who took a barrelful of teasing about the sixty-foot rope he carried with his rig, had been with the Silver Sage for nearly two years now, and in all that time no one had heard him say more than four words in a string. He was a good man around cattle and horses, and Rory, like his father before him, had no complaints about the man or his work.

Wheelbarrow and Hench, the long and the short of the crew, were both teasing a barmaid as she made the rounds with a tray of beer mugs balanced precariously on her shoulder. Just as Barrows reached out to pinch her shapely bottom, Hench swatted his friend's hand away. It was a routine Rory had seen them perform many times before. The barmaid gave them both a cheeky grin.

Rory drew up an empty chair and set the brown-wrapped package down on the seat. After greeting the others, he turned to look at the small stage at the far end of the room. A piano off to the side was nearly hidden by the lush stage curtains. Someone began a tinny rendition of "There Is a Tavern in the Town," and the men in the front row began clapping and singing along.

"Buy me a drink?"

Rory turned to find the same brown-eyed brunette who'd waved to him earlier standing at his elbow. She was nearly as tall as he, with nice legs that were exposed by the swag cut of her scarlet skirt. He looked her up and down as she linked her arm through his elbow.

"What'll you have?" Figuring he had just spent twice what he paid one of the men for a month's wages on Jessica

Stanbridge, Rory felt the need to prove to himself that Jess didn't have any sort of hold on him at all.

The girl on his arm—he could see she was little more than that—licked her carmine lips and tossed her thick curls, so that they played against the fair, unmarred skin of her exposed shoulder. "A beer would be nice," she purred, leaning against him, making certain he was aware of her breast brushing against his arm.

"Two beers," he called out to the barmaid across the table as he dug deep into his pocket and came up with a dime. The barmaid held up her palm. He tossed the dime and she deftly caught it, then hurried off.

The brunette whispered in his ear, "You in town for long, cowboy?"

A shiver shot down his neck straight to his groin. "Nope."

The girl on Tinsley's lap giggled when the old man planted a sloppy, wet kiss on her shoulder. As he swung his gaze away from the sight, Barrows and Hench caught Rory's eye. They were watching him carefully, poking each other in the ribs and laughing as they nodded in approval of the beauty at his side.

Feeling more like an observer than a willing participant, Rory wondered how many times they had all been in this same room, with the same type of girls, laughing over the same jokes. Before this afternoon it had always seemed like enough. Truth be told, he had always looked forward to trips to Durango, but now it seemed that Miss Jessica Stanbridge had not only ruined his ability to sleep and cost him a hell of a lot of money, but she put a real damper on his fun.

When the beers arrived, he drank them both and ordered two more with a quick apology to the young woman hanging on his arm. When he couldn't help but notice that she was looking at him with calf eyes, he smiled into them and whispered, "Why me, darlin'?"

She pulled him around until they stood toe to toe and nose

to nose. Fred Hench hooted. Rory tried to concentrate, not on her cleavage, but on her words. "Because you're not only good-lookin', cowboy, but you still got all your teeth."

He threw back his head and laughed. Still, he found himself wanting more than a quick tumble.

Later, when six empty beer mugs lined the table and Rory was still standing in the same spot holding on to the brunette, whose name was Dovie, she invited him upstairs.

It was the inevitable ending to a visit to the Phoenix. The steep, outdoor stairway behind the brick building led up to the cribs on the second floor. He'd been in nearly all of the small, unventilated rooms since his first trip into Durango and knew they were virtually the same. Each of the five rooms was equipped with a bed, a chair, a small bureau, and a slop jar, or thunder mug, under the bed.

"You comin' along, honey?" Dovie tugged on his arm.

There was no reason in the world why he shouldn't go upstairs with her—still, he balked. All he could think of was Jessica standing against the purpled sunset sky, looking up at him so trustingly from behind her silly spectacles.

"Go on, Burnett," Barrows called out. "If you don't, I will."

Dovie looked downhearted at the idea. She held on tight to Rory's elbow. "I'll help you up the stairs," she volunteered.

"I'm not drunk," he told her. *Not drunk enough, anyway.* Why not go on up? He challenged himself with the question again. *Why the hell not?* More than likely Miss Jessica Stanbridge would soon find exactly what she wanted, pack up her little picks and hammers, notebooks and teacups, and head back to Boston without so much as a by-your-leave.

That settled it.

"Let's go," he told Dovie before he could change his mind again. He tipped his hat back and deftly turned her around so that she could lead him through the room.

"Hey, Burnett, wait!" Fred Hench was standing with the

brown paper bundle in his hands. "You forgot your package."

Rory sighed and let go of Dovie's elbow long enough to take the package from Fred. Dovie turned around to see what was keeping him. Rory looked down at the package, back up at the tall brunette, and then tucked Jess's new dress under his arm. He tipped his head close to the girl's and whispered, "I've changed my mind, Dovie. I won't be going upstairs with you tonight."

"Well, then hell, cowboy." Dovie glanced down at the package in his hands. "I hope she's worth it, 'cause I'm one of the best."

Rory gave her a wry grin. "I hope she is, too," he said, taking small consolation from the package he carefully cradled in his arms instead of the best-looking girl in the room. He shook his head and whispered to himself, "I hope she is, too."

The full moon was such an intense, bright silver that Jessica could almost read by it. Far off to the west heavy black clouds obscured the stars, but to the east the moon was still riding high. A warm, barely perceptible breeze flew across the high plateau, carrying with it the smell of dust and rain on dry soil.

With an oil lamp to add to the moonlight, she sat at the table beneath the awning penning a letter to the museum, pausing occasionally to watch lightning slash the sky in the distance. The electrical display was so far away that the trailing thunder was only a faint rumble. When Whitey warned her of an approaching storm, Jessica told him to be sure that the tent and awning were secure and that the mules and horses were picketed for the night.

Hearing footsteps behind her, Jessica glanced over her shoulder. Myra, looking disgruntled, hurried across the clearing. "I can't find Methuselah anywhere. He's climbed out of the enclosure again."

Jessica laughed. "That tortoise has a mind of his own. He doesn't seem to like it here as much as he did at Camp Zanzibar." Jess set the lamp atop her letter to keep it from blowing off the table and stood up.

"Ever since we moved to Marrakech he's seemed a bit down in the mouth to me." Myra pushed her rolled sleeves toward her elbows and then planted her hands on her hips. "I don't like it here much either. It seems grittier. Things are always a mess."

"How in the world can you tell when a turtle is down in the mouth, Myra?" Jess said, ignoring the comment about the sandy grit that covered everything here in the dry wash. They'd moved from the original campsite three days ago— every book, every box, every piece of china—so that Jessica and Whitey would not have to distance themselves from Myra and the supplies while working on the excavation.

"He hasn't been eating any of the brush I've collected lately. Maybe he's gone off to get some on his own."

Jessica turned away. "Maybe he's just tired of being penned up and is out for a stroll. Maybe he has a family somewhere."

"Well, I'm going out to look for him."

"Myra, please don't. It's dark out there and Whitey's warned us continually to stay in camp at night. You wouldn't see a snake until you stepped on it, and look at those clouds. There's rain in the air."

"With that moon, it's almost as bright as daylight. I'll just walk around the edges of the camp, and I'll take my umbrella."

Knowing that an argument would get her nowhere, Jessica gave up with a mere warning. "Please, be careful."

"I will, dear. You just go on back to whatever it was you were doing." Head down, already searching for the tortoise, Myra walked past the dining table, the hub of the new campsite she had christened Marrakech.

Jessica sat back down, penned a few more lines of her

letter to museum director Gerald Ramsey, and decided that telling the truth was always best; so far she had found the tracks of what appeared to be a very substantially sized Jurassic-period saurian, and one hundred and thirty-seven bones of all shapes and sizes of various, as-yet-unidentified species. She added that although she had not yet discovered anything that might point to a complete fossil of great proportions, she was confident that given a few more weeks and a trip to the mesas, her intuition and study would lead to a find.

Knowing that museum benefactor Henry Beckworth would be anxious for word of any discoveries she had made, Jessica was determined to get the letter off to Ramsey by week's end. She had held off writing before because she had no news. Now she felt more than justified in choosing southern Colorado as her site and was still confident that she had only scratched the surface.

As soon as Burnett returned, she would insist that he take her into Cortez to replenish much-needed staples and post her letter. In addition, she and Whitey had already carefully packaged a crate of the plaster-wrapped fossils for shipment by rail to the museum and they needed to be put on the stage to be delivered to the railway station at Durango. She wished she could be there to see her coworkers when the box arrived, especially Jerome Stoutenburg. More than once she had blessed the fact that he had come down with influenza and headed back to Cambridge, for she suspected that he had really been sent along to keep the museum informed of her progress.

She stared up at the silver moon and wondered where Rory Burnett was tonight. Was he was sleeping out under the stars? Were he and his men still in Durango, or headed back to the ranch? Perhaps he had already arrived home and was taking his time coming to check on them, afraid she would hold him to his promise to take her up to the mesa. Each time she thought of Rory lately, her pulse had involuntarily accelerated and a feeling of heightened anticipation carried a rush of color to her cheeks.

Had it been easy for him to dismiss their kiss? Was she just one of a string of women he rode around kissing? During the past two weeks she had convinced herself that his expertise, especially compared with Whitey's ineptness, could only mean one thing; Rory Burnett was extremely skilled at kissing and had obviously practiced quite a bit.

The very thought made her see red, and the fact that she was obviously jealous over a man she would never see again once her time here was over made her even angrier with herself.

"Miss Jess?"

She nearly jumped out of her skin when Whitey spoke up so near her elbow. "What is it?" she snapped, more out of embarrassment than anger, although she found she'd been more short-tempered than ever as the week dragged on.

"I think we're in for a dousing. Those clouds are spreadin' back this way and the lightnin's gettin' closer." As if to lend support to his words, lightning crackled in twin shards and a peal of thunder followed close behind it.

"Is everything secured?"

"Yeah, but I been thinkin' on it, and maybe it's not such a good idea to be camped so close to the creek bed."

"Nonsense. After all, we're not smack in the middle of it." She looked around at the rocks and scrub oak. "There hasn't been any water along here for years."

He shoved his hat back and winced when the thunder crashed again. "Just 'cause it's dry don't mean there can't come a flood through here."

"And how likely is that, really?" She looked around, unable to believe the parched earth of the high desert wouldn't immediately soak up any rainwater that fell.

He shrugged. "Flash flood could happen anyplace."

Jess looked down toward the dry creek bed and followed it along until she could see the distant mounds of dirt they'd tediously excavated at the dig site. "Is there anything we might do to divert the water if it comes?"

The air was growing still and close as the clouds moved in. The moon was partially blocked now and its light dimmed. He looked prepared to argue. "If it comes, it won't be a trickle, ma'am. It'll be a gully whomper. I think we ought to get up out of here, find a rise, and wait it out."

She smiled to reassure him, anxious to go into the tent, get out of her sticky clothes, and take a sponge bath. "I'm certain my luck will hold, Whitey. Besides, the tents and horses are out of the center of the stream bed. Everything will be all right."

"I hope so, ma'am. Mr. Burnett will have my hide if you're wrong."

"He isn't around to complain about it, though, is he?"

Scratchy Livermore let the screen door bang and moved out onto the back porch. He reached into the open neck of his red flannel underwear and scratched his shoulder as he called out to Rory Burnett, "Storm comin' in. You sure you don't want to wait till mornin' before you light out for them folks' camp? You're actin' like a fool 'cause you ain't et yet."

Rory fought the reins to keep Domino from rearing after a particularly loud clap of thunder and then called out over the mounting wind, "Fix something for the men and I'll have something at the camp." That said, he turned the big horse and let him run, careful to keep to the well-worn road for as far as they could follow it.

Rory figured Scratchy was probably right—he was a fool to head off into the night with a storm riding just over his shoulder, but he wanted to make sure Jess, Myra, and Whitey had fared well in his absence and he wanted to be there in case they needed help during the downpour that was sure to come. As far as he could recall, their camp was on high enough ground to be safe from a flash flood, but it would ease his mind just to ride out and be certain.

Careful not to push his already worn horse past the limit, Rory eased up. It wouldn't do to run Domino into the ground or chance the big Appaloosa's stepping into a prairie-dog hole. The distance between ranch and the camp ran across uneven high desert land dotted with sage, so the going was smooth enough. When he came to a gully or wash, he looked upstream and listened for any sound that might mean an onslaught of rushing water. From the looks of the heavy clouds thick with lightning over the mesas, rainwater should already be making its way down onto the plateau of the vast high desert.

Head close to Domino's mane, Rory spurred the horse on, taking advantage of a break in the clouds, through which moonlight streamed. Before the sky darkened again, he slowed up, sat up straighter, and strained to get a glimpse of the campground, which he thought was just up ahead.

The landscape was empty.

Rory reined in and stared off in all directions in search of a far-off campfire or a trail of smoke beneath the heavy clouds. Nothing.

He pushed on and soon passed the sandstone, flat-topped boulder with the saurian tracks, knowing for certain the camp couldn't be more than a half mile ahead. Why had they let the fire go out?

The black-and-white horse ate up the distance in no time. Again, Rory stopped and stared in confusion then pushed his hat back and wiped off his sweating brow with the back of his gloved hand. He frowned, mad enough to spit. *Damn, Whitey, if you let her talk you into moving her up to the mesa—*

He swiveled around and stared toward the ponderous outline of the mesa. Lightning flashed almost overhead followed by an earsplitting crash of thunder and he was forced to fight for control of his horse. The frightened animal pranced and shook its head, fighting the bit.

Where are they?

Riding over the deserted campground, he located the fire pit they had used as well as the ring of rocks that had formed the tortoise's pen. The remains only proved he hadn't lost his bearings, but he was sure he'd lost his mind. Why else would he be out in the middle of a lightning storm chasing after a damn fool woman after a full day's ride?

Domino turned in a full circle, still fighting the reins. Rory tried to remember his last conversation with Jessica, the one, he reminded himself with a wry shake of his head, where she promised to stay put. What was it she had told him? *Whitey has led me to an exposed section of petrified bone in a dry creek bed not far from here—*

"Damn it!" he roared, afraid the women and the untried youth had moved the camp closer to their find. He knew of only one dry creek that was not far away—a wide, innocent-looking gash in the land that was bounded by a low rise on either side. When it was dry, the creek bed was yards wide. But during a storm it would be the perfect course for a wall of water rushing down from the mesas.

CHAPTER

9

The hot dry wind whipped her hair into her eyes. Jessica stood on the edge of camp, desperately calling Myra's name. She cried out into the darkness beyond the camp, but the words not lost on the wind were drowned out by thunder.

It was one thing to watch a lightning storm from the safety of a second-story flat in the middle of Boston, but quite another to stand beneath an endless stretch of sky about to tear itself apart. Jessica pushed her hair back out of her eyes and ran through the camp in search of Whitey. She found him loading barrels of staples into the wagon.

"What are you doing?" she called out over the noise of the howling wind, the whipping canvas tent flaps, the batting sides of the awning, and Myra's rippling paisley flag.

He shouted back, "I'm doin' what we should have done hours ago—packin' up as much as I can and movin' it up the side of the creek bed. I can't take any more chances.

We've got to move. If that cloud over our heads bursts wide open, we're goners."

"What about the dig? My things? And the crate of fossils?"

Whitey paused long enough to give her a hard stare. "Go get what you can, but do it quick. We should have been out of here at the first sign of a storm." When he reached down to heft a barrel of apples, she grabbed hold of the rim to help him.

"I can't find Myra," she told him, her voice breaking with concern. "She left thirty minutes ago, looking for that stupid tortoise."

"I'll look for her as soon as I help you load that crate of bones. We worked too hard to lose 'em now." Together they walked to her tent, where the carefully packed and labeled crate stood. Counting "One, two, three . . ." they lifted it gently and carried it back to the wagon. Whitey slid it across the wagon bed while Jessica ran to call Myra again.

Whitey was leading his horse when he caught up to her seconds later and shouted, "Which way did she go?"

Jessica pointed toward the edge of camp where Myra had disappeared and watched him ride out and then veer off to circle the camp. She raced to the table and collected her notebook with her letter to Ramsey tucked inside, her knapsack with the maps and hand-drawn sketches of the area, and what tools she could quickly gather.

Hurrying to the picket line, she tried to calm the frightened animals straining against the rope while she untied one of the mules. Pulling, shouting, and threatening one of the great stubborn things with a fate worse than death, she managed to drag it to the wagon and harness it. After checking the brake and tying the mule to the branch of a scraggly bush, she set out after the other.

Lightning lit up the sky. A mighty clap of thunder nearly drove her to her knees. Then, without warning, the clouds opened and she was instantly pelted with rain. Minutes before, she would have welcomed the cooling relief, but now, as her skirt became sodden and tangled around her and the wet, sandy ground sucked at her boots, the rain became just one more hindrance.

With a scream of fear the mare broke free of the picket line and raced off across the desert. Jessica jumped for the line and was barely able to stop the second mule from escaping. Then screaming like a banshee and tugging on the line, she led it to the wagon and struggled to harness it beside the first.

She paused outside her tent and looked around, hoping to see Whitey ride up with Myra, but all she saw through the pouring rain was the forlornly flapping awning. One of the support poles was broken in two. She ducked inside the tent.

With the wind sneaking beneath the bottom of the tent and her wet, shaking fingers, it took three tries to light the lamp. She hung it on the center pole and stood staring around the interior, uncertain of what to haul back to the wagon. First she grabbed the leather folder containing the government permits to search the reservation lands and the proclamation from the museum that gave her permission to conduct field research on their behalf. She quickly pulled her blouse out of the waistband of her skirt, shoved the folder inside, and covered it with the thin material of her shirtwaist.

Next she pulled her helmet off of the peg on the center pole, slipped the strap under her chin, and looked around again. Myra's books lay scattered over the foot of her bed and the bedside crate. Her clothes were in a careless heap in the center of the cot, her boots and shoes on the ground. She wanted to save Myra's reticule, but didn't see it close by. Deciding there was no time to search for it, Jessica knelt down to pull out a small trunk containing her own money as well as a photograph of her mother and father from beneath her cot. She was struggling with the lock when Whitey burst into the tent.

"We gotta go, Miss Jess. Now."

The chest forgotten, Jessica leaped to her feet. "Did you find her?"

In the flickering lamplight, his hat sodden and dripping, his eyes bleak, he looked like nothing more than a very tall child. "I didn't find her, ma'am. What'll we do now?"

The roof of the tent bulged with water in sagging pockets. A slow, steady drip began to fall between them. Outside, the rain was relentless, the lightning and thunder still as loud. The storm had not moved on.

"We'll take the wagon and mules to higher ground as you suggested earlier. Go get your horse and tie it to the back of the wagon. The mules are so skittish I don't think I can handle them myself."

She grabbed her knapsack. He stood aside to let her pass then followed. Her heart was pounding with fear, her pulse rushing so fast she feared the metallic taste in her mouth might have been blood. She swallowed and fought down fear so fierce it nearly crippled her.

Everything will be all right, she told herself. Everything will be fine. The storm will pass and we'll all be able to get things back in order. Myra's probably sitting out the storm somewhere under a rock.

The rain was coming harder. Jess heard more thunder, but this time it had not been preceded by lightning. And this time it sounded low, as if it were tearing across the land instead of the sky. She was almost to the wagon when she felt the ground beneath her feet begin to quake. She glanced over at the mules, at the wagon filled with the supplies and the crate of fossils, the product of a week and a half of backbreaking toil.

She could reach the wagon in a few seconds if she tried, but the ominous roar from up the creek bed kept her from running in that direction. Instead she hiked up her sodden skirt and ran up the slight tilt of land that had once marked the edges of the bed. Her feet slipped on the muddy ground.

She pulled herself up and ran on, up and away from the camp. All the way Jess screamed Myra and Whitey's names as she tried to outrun the wall of water bearing down on her.

Rory rode through the downpour for more than ten minutes. As soon as he found her camp, he was going to haul Miss Jessica Stanbridge's shapely little butt off his land and onto the first available stage out of Cortez.

But first he was going to send that no-account Higgins kid packing for listening to her instead of following orders. Water ran off the brim of his hat and down his back. He was hot and sticky before the rain had started and now he was downright miserable. Not to mention hungry. And tired.

He heard a roar in the distance about the same time he recognized the bloodcurdling scream of an animal. He pushed on through the rain, swearing when Domino lost his footing and almost sent him flying. The roar grew louder. Without ever having witnessed a flash flood, Rory knew what the sound meant. Dear God in heaven, he prayed, keep them all safe.

It was almost too dark to see through the pouring rain. Afraid he would run straight into the floodwaters, he drew up and listened. The sound was definitely off to the right, somewhere in the direction in which he'd been headed. Another tortured scream rent the air followed by the hysterical braying of a mule. The scream was soon carried away as the roar of water faded into the distance.

He reached the edge of the creek, dismounted quickly, and almost slipped down the slope into the fast-flowing water. He scrambled back and wiped his muddy hands on his pants. As the lightning and thunder moved on, the rain let up. Rory led Domino back a good distance and tried to get his bearings in the darkness.

He moved toward the low bank and tripped over what appeared to be a piece of wood. He stooped to pick it up, saw the twisted remains of an iron spring, and recognized it as the seat from a buckboard wagon. He felt as if he'd been gut-shot.

Cupping his hands around his mouth, he shouted, "Jess! Jessica!"

There was no answer, only the sound of the water as it slowed to a crawl now that the fury of the storm had passed.

He hollered again. "Whitey!"

Still no answer. Rory walked along the bank, alternately shouting and cursing, watching for some sign of life, half hoping he would stumble over one of them in the darkness, terrified they had all been swept downstream and he'd never see any of them again.

A quarter of a mile, then a half went by. He kept walking and shouting. He was growing hoarse. The moon gradually appeared from behind the broken clouds to bathe the land in ghostly light. He could see the muddy water slowly churning its way along the wide creek bed. It couldn't be more than two feet deep now.

Just ahead a mule started to bray, weakly this time, obviously injured. Rory started to run through the soft, rain-soaked soil. He found the creature on its side, its forelegs bent and twisted, still trapped within the harness. Pieces of broken wagon littered the ground beside it, a splintered wagon wheel protruded from the mud. He drew his gun and neatly put a bullet through the mule's head.

The silence that echoed after the hideous scream and sound of the gunshot was deafening.

In the deathly stillness that followed, Rory heard a slight sound to his left. It was little more than a sob, but it was enough to give him hope. He started running. Slowly at first, carefully picking his way across the littered ground.

"Jess?"

He was closer now. The sound was more distinct; someone was sobbing. "Jessica!"

In two more strides he found her, huddled up on the sandy bank the floodwater had carved out of the land. "Jess." He went down on his knees, afraid to touch her, afraid that she might suddenly disappear and he'd find out he'd only been dreaming.

Her face was buried against her knees, her shoulders shuddered with the force of her sobs. Her clothing was a tangled muddy mess. So was her hair. She clutched her knapsack in her hands.

"Jess, it's all right." Still on his knees beside her, he inched forward and then tentatively drew her into his arms. Her sobbing grew more intense. He cupped her cheek with his palm and turned her face until she buried it against his chest. She was mumbling against his shirt, alternately crying, talking, and trying to catch her breath.

"It's all right now, Jess. You're all right."

"They're gone. . . ." she cried into his shirt. "It's . . . all my f-fault. I didn't . . . I didn't think anything . . . w-would happen. He tried to tell me . . . but I . . . ."

Rory rocked her gently as he smoothed her wet hair back off her face. Never having dealt with a woman's grief, he dug deep within himself to find the right words. There was a time when he was seven and had to have a broken leg set. Martha Burnett had held him close. He tried to think of the words she might have used. "Shh. Don't take on so. Things will be all right."

Jessica pushed away from him and cried out, "How? How . . . can it ever be all right? I killed them! They're gone and it's all my fault. I wouldn't listen. He wanted me to, but I wouldn't listen to him—"

The panic in her eyes was visible in the moonlight. He gave her a quick, determined shake. "Stop it. We'll find them. Maybe they're sitting in the mud waiting to be found."

She was adamant. "No, they're gone. Myra was missing before the flood. The last I saw of Whitey he'd gone to get"—her breath caught again—"to get his horse."

"Can you stand up? Are you hurt?"

Still clinging to his shirtfront, she shook her head. "I'm not hurt. I can walk."

He stood up and pulled her up with him and could feel her trembling beneath his hands. Afraid she would sink back to a sitting position, still experiencing overwhelming relief because she was alive, he refused to let her go just yet.

With a shrill whistle he called Domino. Head high, the horse trotted to his side. Rory grabbed the reins and held the big Appaloosa steady while he told Jess, "Mount up. I'll lead him along this side of the creek and we'll walk downstream and look for the others."

Jessica stared into his eyes for a moment before she let go of him and turned to grab hold of the saddle. He helped her reach the stirrup and then boosted her up from behind. He handed her the knapsack.

"You all right?" Without thinking, he put his hand on her thigh, all formality swept away.

"Yes," she whispered. "I'm just fine."

He ignored her sarcasm and started walking, leading the horse along the bank. The water was nearly gone now, the only sign of its passing the debris along the newly carved banks. He stepped over and around tangled sagebrush, rocks, twisted pieces of piñon from higher ground.

They passed a broken bentwood chair, one of the three Jessica used at the table. She buried her face in her hands as Rory picked it up, stared at it a moment, and tossed it away. "We'll go on a bit further, then I want to get you back to the ranch house," he said softly.

Her head snapped up. "Absolutely not. We have to keep looking. If there's a chance they're alive—"

Rory began walking again and let his gaze sweep both sides of the bank. It wasn't long before he thought he saw a horse silhouetted against the sky on the opposite side. "Will you be all right if I leave you for a minute?"

Jessica looked up quickly. "Why? What is it?"

"Over there." He pointed across the creek bed.

She gasped. ''Whitey's horse?''

''I'll go see. Stay put.'' He was sliding down the bank before the last words were out. The creek bottom was sandy and soft; his boots sank with every step. Like walking through Scratchy's damn dumplings. He fought his way over to the other side.

The bay horse was saddled, its reins trailed to the ground. As he drew nearer, Rory could make out a dark, ominous shape lying jammed up against the tangled roots of a scrub oak. His steps faltered. He made himself move until he was close enough to recognize Whitey's lifeless body.

Rory glanced over his shoulder before he knelt beside the boy. Jessica was still mounted, just where he'd left her. He knew she was watching him closely, but as much as he wanted to spare her feelings, he couldn't ignore the body lying at his feet. He hunkered down and slowly reached out to Whitey, who lay facedown in the mud, felt for a pulse in the boy's neck, and then rolled him over onto his back. Lifeless eyes stared at the night sky. Without his hat, his soaked clothes clinging to his wiry frame, Whitey appeared broken, defenseless, and vulnerable.

And I left him in charge.

Rory couldn't help but remember how excited the young cowhand had been about the drive to Durango, how he hid his disappointment when he was told to stay behind with the women. If he had only taken Whitey with him and left a more seasoned hand, none of this would have happened. Jessica Stanbridge had blamed herself for Whitey and Myra's disappearance. Rory blamed himself for Whitey's death. Wilner Burnett's boots just grew a size larger. This would never have happened if his father had been alive. He would have known better than to leave a green, untried youth in charge.

''Rory? What is it?'' She was calling out to him from across the stream.

Rory straightened. He hated to have to tell her, but he

couldn't put it off. He couldn't leave Whitey lying in the mud exposed to the elements and animals all night. "It's Whitey," he called back, fighting to get the words out around the lump in his throat. He didn't offer more, refused to call out that Whitey was dead, couldn't send the words out across the creek bed or drifting into the night.

The boy's body was far from heavy, but it was still one of the greatest burdens Rory ever had to bear. He hoisted the black-haired youth across the saddle and then unknotted the leather thongs that held a spare bedroll tied behind the saddle. There was not enough blanket to cover the tall frame. Whitey's favorite boots hung out from beneath the edge of the red wool. Rory stroked the bay's nose before he led the horse back across the creek.

Ramrod straight, Jess was still in the saddle. She had a death grip on the pommel. Her tears glistened in the moonlight. She cried silently now, unable to look at the bay or the body strapped across it. Without a word Rory walked to Domino and started leading him again. There was nothing he could say, no words he dare utter before he had time to wrestle with the loss in his own mind.

His clothes were still wet, his boots sodden. Although the air was still warm, he could see that Jessica had started shivering. She was soaked through.

"I think we should go back. I'll ride up with you," he told her.

She waited so long to answer that he was certain she had no objections. Then she whispered, "What about Myra?"

"I'll send the men out at first light."

"No. Keep searching. We aren't leaving until we find her. I can't leave her alone in the dark."

Fatigue, nerves, and the guilt of an innocent boy's death rode heavy on his shoulders. He turned to her. "We are turning back *now*. We could walk for hours searching for her in the dark. I'm taking Whitey back and I don't want to hear another word out of you."

"But—"

"But nothing. The truth is, Miss Stanbridge, if I don't get this boy back soon, it'll be almost impossible to get him off this horse. You're good with old bones and things that have been dead for centuries, a hell of a lot better than you are dealing with the living, so I don't think I need to tell you what will happen to Whitey's body in a while. He's been through enough. I said I'd send someone out at sunup and I will. Hell, I'll send 'em all out, but I think you might as well face it. She's probably dead, too."

"How can you be so cruel?" she whispered, her eyes intent on her hands clutching the pommel.

"I'm not being cruel. I'm being honest."

He mounted up behind her, refusing to be swayed by the defeated slump of her shoulders or the tears that continued to stream down her cheeks. How many tears did she have stored up inside? Especially since she had probably kept them locked up like Midas' gold for a lifetime. Even now she wouldn't give in to more than tears. She didn't scream or rend her hair, she merely held herself away from him, sat stiff in the saddle, and stared straight ahead into the darkness. She despised him too much to let herself relax and lean back against him. Even after the sniffling and eye wiping had subsided and he knew she probably wasn't crying anymore.

A coyote howled somewhere in the darkness. She began to shiver more violently and her gaze followed the sound. He tried to keep his own mind blank, tried not to think of the curious old woman with a penchant for exotic places and enough frivolity in her soul to tie a paisley pennant to a tent pole. She was out there somewhere, probably as dead as Whitey, lying exposed to the coyotes and night crawlers.

He knew Jessica was haunted by the same thoughts. Still, he couldn't quite find it in his heart to reach out to her, not when his heart was so full of its own pain.

• • •

The ranch house was long and low, she could see that much in the darkness, but Jessica's thoughts were too well occupied with the disastrous events of the evening to care anything about what the place looked like. Weak lamplight filtered out from behind thin curtains in a rear window. When they rode into the barnyard, Burnett gave an ear-piercing whistle that brought two spotted dogs racing out of the barn doors, barking loud enough to carry to the next county. Within seconds, the door to a smaller wooden structure on the far side of the yard opened and men in every state of dress from BVDs to nightshirts spilled out of the dark interior. Somehow they had all managed to pull on their boots. Three even wore gun belts.

The sleep-drugged voices joined in a mixed chorus.

"What happened?"

"Who is it? What's goin' on?"

"Them's Whitey's boots," someone noticed.

All talking ceased.

She recognized Woody Barrows and Fred Hench, the men who had come to tea. The others she hadn't met. They all stared up at Burnett and then their gazes turned on her. She wanted to hide her face in her hands, but instead she simply stared off into the night. They would all hate her now. And with just cause.

A screen door slammed at the back of the main house. Slow footsteps crossed the porch. Jessica couldn't bear to see who else had come out to witness her shame and despair, nor their reactions to Whitey's body draped across the horse; she didn't bother to look. She felt Burnett tense behind her. Without touching her, he dismounted in a quick, lithe movement for so big a man. It was easier to concentrate on Burnett's gracefulness than it was to face the horrible truth of the moment.

Although they were all older than Rory Burnett, there was no doubt as to who was in command of these men when he started issuing orders. "Barrows, get some sawhorses and planks out of the barn and set them in the parlor. Gathers, you and Tinsley get Whitey down and take him inside. We'll lay him out in the parlor until we can bury him tomorrow. Hench, come morning, you and Wheelbarrow can build the coffin."

She remained in the saddle, soaked through, alone and ignored. He hadn't even offered to help her down. While Barrows hurried off to do his bidding, the tallest—a man with a thin, weathered face that looked unused to smiling—took the reins of Whitey's horse and led it into the barn. The other two walked slowly beside the boy's body, an honor guard in nightclothes and underwear.

Jessica sensed Burnett's gaze upon her. She avoided looking down at him by watching the horse flick its ears. He spoke to the only man left, a grizzled old-timer who openly scratched himself wherever the need arose.

"Scratchy, take Miss Stanbridge in the house and put her up in Ma's room. She'll need a hot bath. Get her anything else she wants." That said, Rory Burnett followed the others into the barn.

The old man reached up to help her down and Jessica called upon all of her own strength, afraid that if her legs gave out, she might topple the spindly man right into the muddy yard. She slipped her knapsack over her shoulder and reached out to him.

"Watch your step there, ma'am, it's a fur piece down. There you go." He waited while she clung to the stirrup. Finally Jessica let go. Wiping her hands on her skirt, she turned around, able to follow him at last.

"It's wet enough for a canoe out here," was all he mumbled before he slogged through the mire to the ranch house.

Head down, carefully picking her way through the slush, Jessica forced herself to move, to forget Burnett's cold dismissal, to block out the thoughts that plagued her. The old man held the door for her and she shuffled inside, unaware of the mud she was tracking across the kitchen floor.

"Stop right there, little lady," Scratchy said. "Let's get them boots off you." He whisked a chair away from a long table and set it behind her. When Jessica failed to respond, Scratchy gave her a shove and she sat. He hunkered down and, in the weak glow of a single oil lamp, unlaced her boots and pulled them off.

"Want to talk about what happened out there tonight?" he offered.

She shook her head no.

"Sometimes it helps to put bad times into words, 'specially when you see a man get his lamp blowed out before his time."

Jess balled her hands together in her lap. "He wasn't a man, just a boy," she whispered, fighting back tears she didn't know she had left.

"These things happen. God's will and all." The words made him seem uncaring, cold.

"It was my fault."

Scratchy straightened, her boots in his hands, and shuffled to the backdoor. His muddy tracks mingled with hers. He stepped out onto the porch, put her boots by the door, used a boot jack shaped like an iron cockroach to slip out of his own, and then came back inside. The door banged again.

He picked the lamp up off the table and waited in the doorway. "You ready to go to your room?"

When Jessica stood, every muscle in her body ached in protest. She followed the old man through the darkened hall. The lamplight threw a creased halo over the walls and ceiling. The house was cool; moonlight streaming through the windows created hulking shadows of the furniture. They passed a large room that appeared to be a parlor, a closed door, and then the hall made a sharp turn. The adobe house had been built in an L shape, the bedroom wing obviously added on a room or two at a time. He stopped beside the first door, a rough, unfinished set of planks, that somehow fit the mood of the house. Scratchy reached around her to open it.

Jessica stepped into a room that smelled musty from neglect. The old man set the lamp on a side table near the door and began opening windows. The night air was still cool, but not cold. Within seconds, the room lost its stuffiness. Shadowed faces of Martha Burnett's relations stared at her from behind oval frames. There was a dust ruffle on the high bed, along with a faded, hand-pieced quilt covered with multicolored stars.

She waited in the middle of the room clutching her knapsack until Scratchy lit the lamp on a bedside table. The light further illuminated the neatly arranged room. A rustic chest of drawers made of pine stood against the wall. A rectangular mirror hung above it. Draped over the corner of the mirror was a string of beads.

"There's some clothes in here, night things, whatever you need." He opened the closet doors. "They'll all be too big. B'fore she died, Miz Burnett carried a bit of pork on her hocks, but they'll cover you till you get somethin' more fittin'. Use anything you like."

A riot of calico, dark wools, white nightgowns, and a midnight-black silk were all crowded into the small closet. "Thank you."

"I'll go back and heat up some water for you. There's a bathin' room at the end of the hall, no fancy plumbin' yet, but there's a tub and fresh towels set out. I'll knock when it's ready an' you can go on in."

After the door closed behind him, Jessica walked over to the window and stared out into the night. The barnyard was deserted. Across the way she could see the small building where the cowhands slept. The door was still open. There was a clatter down the hall, wood bumping against wood. Someone was setting up the planks where Whitey would be laid out.

Jessica sighed and turned away from the window. Outside, hoofbeats mingled with muffled shouts. The sounds faded. A low armless rocker sat on a braided rag rug near the window. It beckoned her. Familiar now with the interior of the room, she turned down the wick on the lamp and walked back to the chair. Jessica sat rocking in the darkness until Scratchy knocked to let her know her bath was ready.

CHAPTER
10

Seated cross-legged on the old rocker in a nightgown four sizes too big, Jessica bunched the long flounce at the bottom of the white cotton gown around her legs and brushed her hair with a brush she found in the washstand. She sat in the dark remembering Whitey, his eagerness to help, his boyish, impulsive kiss, the puppy love in his eyes whenever he looked at her. He had been willing to do anything for her. *I'll protect you with my life,* he had said. In the end, he didn't have to give his life; she had taken it with her ignorance.

Although she could hardly bear to think that Myra was lost, too, Jessica couldn't help but remember how excited her friend had been and her enthusiasm in christening the camps Zanzibar and Marrakech. Now she was gone. Myra's beloved books had been scattered across the high desert floor on the muddy wave of water. The pages would soon be blown by the winds across endless miles of sagebrush and sand.

To think of the fossils she had lost seemed callous and unfeeling. Each time an unbidden reminder surfaced, Jessica tried to shove it away. If it would only bring Myra and Whitey back, she would give up paleontology forever.

As much as she fought it, sleep soon crept up on her. More than once she came awake with a start when her head lolled and her chin dipped to her chest. Finally, admitting exhaustion, Jessica walked over to the bed, lay down in the center, and forgoing covers, wrapped the borrowed gown around her feet. She was sound asleep in moments.

A feather-light touch upon her cheek startled her awake sometime after dawn. She awoke to find Rory Burnett drawing his hand away from her face as if he'd been singed. His dark eyes were ringed, the lower half of his face covered with blue-black stubble. He looked as if he hadn't slept at all, and if he had, it had been in the same clothes he'd worn the night before.

All too conscious that she was only wearing the cotton nightgown, Jessica glanced down and found it still tucked about her feet. "I must have fallen asleep," she said, pulling herself to a sitting position.

"You need it."

"You look like you could use some sleep yourself," she told him, glancing out the window. "What time is it?"

"After nine."

She shoved her hair back off her face and swung her legs over the sides of the bed. Leveling an accusing stare at him, Jess said, "You said you'd send your men out for Myra at dawn. Did you? Did they find her?"

He stared at her a moment too long without answering.

"Well?" She shifted uncomfortably.

"Come with me."

She followed, praying he wasn't taking her to see Myra's lifeless body stretched out beside Whitey's. Somehow, though, she knew instinctively that Rory would never intentionally be that cruel.

They stopped at the room beside hers. "There's somebody in here who wants to see you," he said as he pushed the door open.

"Myra!" Jessica paused on the threshold, too relieved to move, barely able to believe her eyes. Myra Thornton was propped against a bank of pillows in a wide bed, primly outfitted in what appeared to be a man's huge nightshirt, a coverlet pulled up under her arms. Woody Barrows and Fred Hench, who both stood the minute they saw Jessica in the doorway, had been seated on chairs on either side of the bed. With her bandaged foot and ankle sticking out of the covers and resting on a pillow, Myra waved her in.

"Oh, Jessica, dear! I've been so worried about you. Are you all right?"

Unaccustomed to having her hair unbound, Jessica tossed it over her shoulders and hurried into the room.

The two seasoned cowhands ducked their heads and, red-faced with embarrassment, bid her a quick good-bye. It was a moment before she realized her own immodest state had caused their discomfort. Jess rushed to Myra's bedside as the men filed out of the room. She sat on the edge of the bed and threw her arms about her friend, unable to hold back tears of relief and joy.

Myra gave her a bear hug. "Why, Jessica, I've never seen you this way. Surely you didn't think anything had happened to me?"

Jessica sat up and wiped her eyes with the sleeve of the oversized gown. The door closed behind them. "I didn't know any such thing." She looked down as if speaking to the coverlet. "Did they tell you about . . . Whitey?"

Myra's smile faded. "Yes, they did. I'm still trying to wrestle with the reasons why."

"That's no secret." Jessica stood up and noticed for the first time that Rory had left them alone. She paced over to the window. Outside, three of the men were working in the corral. "Whitey's dead because of me—because I was too pigheaded to listen to him when he suggested we move away from the creek bed.''

"Now, Jessica—"

"I wasn't raised like you, Myra. I haven't studied the Transcendentalists or Eastern philosophies like you have. I can't just tell myself that it was Whitey's time to die, that his death was all part of some great cosmic plan. All I can do is blame myself.''

"We all deal with grief in different ways, but taking the blame upon your own shoulders won't change things,'' Myra said softly.

"Rory hates me,'' Jess whispered.

Myra folded her arms across her ample breasts. "Oh, posh.''

"He does. Because it *is* my fault. And then last night, when I insisted we search for you before we brought Whitey back, well, that was the last straw.'' Jessica ran her fingertip around the lip of the washbowl on a marble-topped washstand beside the window. "I know it was unfeeling not to want to get Whitey back as soon as possible, but he was already gone and you . . . I couldn't imagine leaving you out there to face the elements alone all night.''

"I was back long before dawn. I was soaking in a hot bath when the sun came up.''

Jessica whirled around. "How?''

"Rory and his men rode out after me as soon as he left you. I could hear them calling and shouting my name. They found me almost two miles from Marrakech. I had become completely disoriented in the storm.''

"Then that means Rory—''

"Brought the men back to look for me immediately. They had a spare horse with them, but I was afraid to manage on my own, so he was kind enough to let me ride behind him.'' She turned bright red, something Jessica had never witnessed before.

"Myra, are you blushing?''

"I had to hang on to Mr. Burnett all the way back. It was quite a thrilling experience. A real-life adventure, and one I'll never forget, to be sure."

Jessica tried to hide a smile. "Tell me about your leg. And the storm."

Myra wriggled her toes, all that was visible of her foot beneath the bandages. "I tripped, that's all. You know me, my body on earth and my head in the clouds. My shoe hit a rock and I turned my ankle and went down. When I was finally able to try to hobble, the storm hit. It must have put out the fire, because I lost sight of Marrakech entirely."

"But the rain, and the coyotes—"

"What's a little water? I had my umbrella. As for coyotes, I saw nary a one, although I had gathered a few nearby rocks and was determined to drive them off. There is only one thing I regret—"

"You never found Methuselah?"

"Oh, no. I found him."

Jessica was amazed. "You didn't!"

"Of course I did. He's under the bed. Mr. Barrows was kind enough to carry him all the way back for me. No, what I regret was that I wasn't there to help you."

The seconds before the flood flashed through Jessica's mind. Scrambling to load the wagon with Whitey. The roar of the water as it rumbled toward them. The screaming mules. Thunder. The splintering of the wooden wagon as it was ripped apart by the force of the water.

Her own ragged breath in her ears as she fought her way to safety.

"I'm glad you weren't there, Myra." Jess picked up the older woman's freckled hand and squeezed it gently. "I'm so very, very thankful you weren't there."

A quick knock on the door was all the warning they had before Rory came in again. His dark gaze never left Jessica. "Are you hungry?"

Gathering the surplus nightgown material across her

breasts, she hugged it protectively. She knew now why his eyes were shadowed and he looked so exhausted. He and his men had combed the darkness until they found Myra. Jessica knew she owed him an apology, not to mention her friend's life.

Myra lay in silent repose, watching them closely. Finally Jess answered him. "No, I'm not hungry."

"At least have some coffee," he urged.

"I'm getting very tired, Jessica." Myra feigned a yawn. "Perhaps you two should leave me alone for a while." Snuggling down amid the pillows, she pulled the coverlet up to her chin, wriggled her toes, and closed her eyes.

Jess had no alternative but to follow Rory out of the room. The hallway was dim; the night's coolness lingered along the floorboards and in the darkened corners. Jessica chose the coward's way out rather than exchange words with him.

"I would really prefer to go back to my room."

She saw him halt abruptly. He turned around and put a hand out on the wall, a nonthreatening but powerful move meant to keep her from retreating into his mother's room.

"I'd prefer you didn't," he said. "We need to talk."

"It can't wait?"

"I don't think so." His eyes were obsidian shards in the darkness. They dared her to refuse.

"You want me to walk around like this?" She held out the sides of her nightgown as if she were about to curtsy.

Why was it always a contest of wills?

Rory stared down at her in the shadowed hallway. She was right. He couldn't take her into the kitchen in her nightgown. After a moment's thought and a longer stretch of silence, he opened the door to his mother's room, stepped inside, grabbed the quilt off of the bed, and was back in the hall in seconds.

The quilt flared like a matador's cape as he swung it up and over her. It settled across her shoulders. He wadded the excess into his hands and jerked it closed across her breasts.

"There." He waited until she took over the task of holding the thing closed.

She had to gather up the bottom with one hand in order to walk. Afraid if he hesitated she would refuse to follow him, Rory headed down the hall and didn't look back.

When they neared the parlor door, he heard her footsteps falter. Whitey was laid out inside, pale and vulnerable. Thankfully the door was closed and Jessica was spared the sight.

Rory walked through the house toward the kitchen, where Scratchy was scraping the breakfast pans. He stopped when they entered and looked over at Jessica. In one quick gaze he took in the quilt, her tousled hair, her bare feet.

"There's coffee on the stove. I'm goin' out to slop the pigs." He picked up a scrap pail by the door and headed out.

Rory walked over to the table, pulled out a chair for Jessica, and then went to get them some coffee. Sitting there bundled in the pieced quilt his mother called Rolling Star, Jessica reminded him of a lost child. Somehow it was a far different perception of Miss Jessica Stanbridge than he had ever contemplated before. Her blue eyes were haunted, her thoughts far from the sun-streaked, planked floorboards she was concentrating on.

Coffee sloshed out of the mug he set on the table beside her. He didn't offer milk or sugar, but gave it to her the way he took his—hot and black.

After a careful sip he said, "We'll bury Whitey this afternoon, around four. By then most of the work will be done . . . and Fred and Woody will have had time to make him a box."

She kept her eyes lowered and ignored the steaming coffee as he went on. "I know the clothes in Ma's closet are all too big, but there's a sewing box in the bottom drawer, maybe you can fix something up for the burial. There's a black—"

"I won't be there." Her voice was a croak. She looked up at him, her eyes pleading for understanding. "I'm sorry."

He hated the way she was trembling, quaking so hard the chair creaked. Would she accept the sort of comfort he had tried to give her last night?

"It's up to you," he said, unwilling to cause her any more pain. "The men will all be there. Maybe it is best you stay with Myra."

"I'm sure I'm the last person they'd want to see."

Blowing on the hot coffee, he looked at her over the rim of the cup. "Don't be so hard on yourself."

"I've never killed anyone before."

His mug hit the table with a loud thud. "You didn't kill Whitey." Leaning back, he rested a booted foot on his knee and spun the rowel of his spur. "If anyone is responsible, it's me."

"Why do you say that?"

"Because I left a green kid out there to do a man's job. Any of the others would have known better than to set up camp in the creek bed in the first place."

"*I* talked him into moving into the dry creek. I wanted to be close to the excavation. He wanted to move as soon as there was any hint of storm."

"An older man would have stood up to you." Rory stared at the colorful stars draped around her shoulders. "He probably had stars in his eyes."

A crease appeared between her brows. "What makes you say a thing like that?"

He knew he guessed correctly when he saw her blush. "Whether or not you want to admit it, Jess, you're a beautiful woman. You could get a boy like Whitey to do most anything."

Guiltily she thought of the way the young man had followed her about the camp, had answered to her beck and call, worked all those long, hot hours on the dig.

The way he tried to kiss her.

Jessica ducked her head again.

Rory hated the jealousy that snaked through his gut. His opinion of himself lowered when he realized he was jealous of a mere boy, and a dead one at that. So far, Jessica Stanbridge had done nothing but twist him inside out since the day she walked into the general store in Cortez. He didn't know where she planned to go or what she intended to do now that she had lost everything, but one thing was for certain—the thought of never seeing her again did mighty terrible things to his insides.

He looked up and caught her staring at him intently.

"Is that all you wanted?" she asked.

He wished he could see into her mind, wished he could absolve her, but doubted he would have any more luck than he was having with his own guilt. "That's all. Unless you want some breakfast. I can fix you something."

Her response was barely audible. She stood up and hugged the quilt closer. "No. I can't eat just yet." Like a prisoner she said, "I'd like to go back to my room now."

"Fine." He stood up.

Jessica moved as far as the door. The length and thickness of her hair amazed him. He never guessed such luxuriance could be bound and hidden beneath her helmet. She was watching him intently, as if gathering the courage to ask a favor.

"What is it?" he wanted to know.

"Will you walk me to my room?"

He knew then she couldn't bear to pass by the parlor door alone. "Of course."

Rory followed her back through the house.

Jessica found the sewing basket in a low drawer in the armoire. It was full of thread, a tattered piece of calico stabbed with pins and needles, scissors, and scraps of paper patterns. Seated on the floor in front of the drawer, she paused briefly to study the jumbled contents. Had Martha

Burnett known the last time she put the sewing basket away that she would never use it again? Or had Rory's mother, like Whitey, been taken without warning, her possessions left in a suspended state, waiting for someone to bring them to life again? Waking up of a morning didn't necessarily mean a person would live to see another day. The sudden, overwhelming realization weighed heavy on Jessica's heart.

Thrusting aside her dark thoughts, she set out to alter one of the calico dresses from the armoire. She chose one with a predominantly blue background. The print made her imagine the Colorado sky covered with tiny flowers of many shapes. Jess moved to the rocking chair and wadded the voluminous material in her lap as she worked. The sound of men shouting to one another as they worked with horses in the corral mingled with a slow, ominous pounding—hammer against nails—as Woody Barrows and Fred Hench put together Whitey's coffin. The sad symphony went on forever.

When her work was finished, Jessica stood and held the dress against her. Even after tucking in the waist, shortening the sleeves, and turning up the deep ruffled hem, the calico was still far from a good fit. The sounds outside had faded, the men had answered the call of a dinner bell. She ignored it. No one came to get her.

Once she had donned the blue calico, she walked over to the dresser and reached up to slip the beads off the mirror. They felt cold against her hand. Jessica closed her fist around them and recalled Scratchy's invitation: "Use anything you want." She moved the strand through her fingers and pictured Martha Burnett as a strong woman, one definitely brave enough to survive the rigors of the harsh environment and the demands of life as a rancher's wife. Perhaps some of the woman's strength, or at the very least, a reminder of it, would come to her if she wore the beads.

Finally, Jessica unfastened the clasp and lay the strand of beads against the bodice of her gown. She then chose another everyday dress with a yellow background for Myra. She thought her friend would fill it out amply. The only thing the dress needed was a new hem. Cautiously, wishing to avoid contact with Rory or any of the men, Jessica stepped out into the hallway and quickly walked to Myra's door. She found her friend still propped against the pillow with a tray resting across her lap. The plate was empty, a cup of coffee half-full.

"I found something for you to wear. When you think you can stand, I'll measure it and hem it for you," Jess volunteered.

Myra's smile of greeting faded. "I'm afraid that might be in quite a while. My ankle's not only swollen, it's black and blue."

"Can I get you anything else?"

Myra shook her head. "Oh my, no. Mr. Livermore, the one they call Scratchy, has seen to everything. Did you have dinner?"

Jess shook her head. "I told them I couldn't eat yet." She crossed the room and hung the dress on a hat rack.

"The food is barely tolerable, but surely it's been hours since you've had anything. Jessica, you have to eat."

Clutching her skirt, Jessica turned to face her companion again. "Not yet, Myra. Please."

"I wish I could go with you to pay my last respects to that dear boy." Myra crossed her arms and stared at her swollen toes.

Jessica felt a rush of anger. Myra's words only served to increase her guilt. "I've never known you to go to a funeral in your life, Myra Thornton. You've always said you don't believe in them. You said the body is only an empty shell, that the spirit is what lives on, and that funerals are only for the living."

"And I still believe that, but somehow burying the dead seems more natural out here, more in keeping with the comings and goings of life. These men aren't worrying about what they'll wear to the funeral, who they'll see, or more importantly, who'll see them. They haven't altered their routine one whit. This afternoon they'll see a friend through the final stages of his life on earth and then probably go out and rope a few cows or whatever else it is they do. Life goes on, Jessica. I have always believed that, but nowhere has it ever been more apparent to me than here. I wouldn't feel hypocritical seeing Whitey buried, but unfortunately I can't walk.''

Jess rubbed her upper arms. Since last night she had been unable to rid herself of an all-pervasive chill.

"Jessica." Myra watched her intently. Too intently. "I've never been one to meddle, but I think you need to go put Whitey to rest. He, least of all, would want you to carry this burden."

Meeting Myra's intense gaze, Jessica sighed. "I don't think I can do it. It hurts."

"Of course it does, but you're one of the strongest people I know. Look at all you've accomplished. You can get through this."

Jess felt cold, bitter laughter well up inside her. It bubbled close to the surface and threatened to escape. "Everything I ever accomplished was washed away in the flood last night."

"And now you're ready to turn tail and run home."

"I don't know what I'm going to do, Myra." Voicing her doubt out loud helped very little.

"I don't know what to tell you, either, dear. You'll have to search deep inside yourself for the answers."

"I'll try," Jessica promised. "You take care of yourself. If you need help, please call out. I'm just next door." She took the tray off Myra's lap, and still too much of a coward to return it to the kitchen and risk seeing anyone, she set it on the washstand and left just as the older woman was nodding off to sleep again.

Afternoon shadows had lengthened in the yard when she

heard low voices somewhere in the house. Soon the talk died away and she heard footsteps on the low, wide porch that circled the house. Standing beside her window, she could observe without being seen. Rory, tall and commanding in a clean white shirt, leather vest, and striped wool trousers, crossed the porch. His dark hair looked damp and neatly coaxed into place. Scratchy followed close on his heels. Behind them came the other four, two on each side of a plain pine coffin.

Jessica leaned back against the wall and pressed her palms against the cold adobe surface. She stared up at the ceiling until the footsteps faded. Her vision blurred, her heart raced, her mouth was dry. "I'm sorry, Whitey," she whispered into the emptiness.

At first she thought she imagined the sudden calm that came over her, but when her pulse slowed and she gradually regained control of her senses, Jessica realized she was experiencing a state of overwhelming peace. She knew what she had to do. Without hesitation she walked to the armoire and slipped the one black gown off the hook. It was well made, of black bombazine, with simple lines. She removed the bead necklace, quickly unbuttoned the calico, tossed it on the bed, and pulled the black gown over her head. Thankfully it buttoned easily.

The gown was inches too wide around the waist, so Jessica dug in the bottom drawer until she found a length of burgundy fabric she had seen earlier. She cut it in half and then banded it about her waist, pulling up the excess material. The drawer provided a pair of black stockings, but they were hopelessly too large, so she abandoned them. Then, realizing she didn't know what Scratchy had done with her shoes, she tugged more of the skirt out of the waistband to lengthen it and hide her feet.

There were no pins to be found, so she was forced to wear her hair down. Sometime during the panic last night she had lost her glasses. She picked up the necklace and put it on again. There was nothing left to prevent her from leaving. She was ready.

Her bare feet made no sound as she darted down the hall and out the door. She paused on the edge of the porch, shading her eyes, and found the men easily. All six were silhouetted against the sun on a low rise not far away. Lifting her skirt, Jessica ran across earth that had been churned soft by horses' hooves. When she reached the edge of the barnyard where the ground was hard and peppered with stones and twigs, her tender soles made the going slower.

By the time she reached the top of the knoll, she realized Rory Burnett had chosen to bury Whitey in his own family graveyard. As she drew closer she could hear Rory's words riding on the breeze. "The earth is the Lord's and the fullness thereof; the world, and they that dwell therein . . ."

The area surrounded by a crooked wrought-iron fence contained four headstones, all with the name Burnett engraved upon them. Not far away an open hole gaped in the earth, mounded dirt beside it, an abandoned shovel planted in the center of the pile.

She drew near, ignoring the rough stones against her feet. Rory's voice was loud and strong as he read from the open Bible in his hands. "Who shall ascend into the hill of the Lord? or who shall stand in his holy place?"

Although no one looked at her, she knew they were all aware of her arrival. As she silently stood behind Woody Barrows the ring of men parted to admit her. Stepping forward, Jessica kept her eyes on the pine coffin deep inside the grave and clenched her hands at her waist.

She concentrated on the words Rory read and the confident, soothing sound of his voice. "He that hath clean hands, and a pure heart; who hath not lifted up his soul unto vanity, nor sworn deceitfully. He shall receive the blessing from the Lord and righteousness from the God of his salvation.''

Jessica looked across the open grave at Rory when he paused. She watched him close the Bible. Although he didn't acknowledge her with more than a brief glance, she was relieved that his gaze held no condemnation.

Rory looked around the small knot of mourners about the grave, the men Whitey considered family. ''Whitey's hands might not have been clean, literally, but he had a pure heart. He wasn't vain or deceitful.'' He paused again, stared down at the Bible, then went on. ''Whitey wanted nothing more than to be accepted as one of us. I think we did that. I sent him to do a man's job, as much as I regret it now. Today I've done a lot of thinking about my decision and the choices Whitey made out there in the desert. I did what I thought right. He did what he thought best. That's all any of us need worry about.''

Jessica shot him a worried glance and found him watching her intently. The words might have been issued over Whitey's grave, but she knew Rory Burnett was speaking to her heart.

''No one knows what God's will is. My ma used to say that the Lord always has good reasons for what He does. We can't pretend to know what those reasons are. I think that's more than true in this case.''

Fred Hench nodded in agreement. Tinsley murmured, ''Amen.''

Rory lifted a handful of red earth. ''As far as any of us knows, Whitey didn't have any family to speak of, so his trail's ending here with my own kinfolk. *Vaya con Dios.* God go with you, Whitey.'' He tossed the soil onto the coffin.

The wiry man with the deeply grooved face put his hat on and took up the shovel. The others bent down to scoop up a handful each and tossed it into the grave. Almost in unison they put on their hats. A pair of boots lay on the ground beside Scratchy. Jess hadn't noticed them before, but she recognized the tooled leather and curled toes. Whitey's boots. She blinked back tears.

She wiped her eyes with the back of her hand and watched while the grave was slowly filled with earth. No one moved to leave. No one spoke. The hollow sound of dirt hitting the wooden coffin echoed as loud as last night's thunder in her ears. She studiously avoided eye contact with Rory Burnett; still, she could tell he was watching her.

Scratchy looked her way and smiled. She nodded to him and then watched Barrows collect a simple cross made of two pieces of wood. He held it steady at the head of the grave as the gaunt man pounded it into the loose soil with the shovel. As Scratchy set the boots in the center of the fresh mound as a last farewell, the men turned away, one by one, and walked back down the knoll toward the ranch house.

They were all alone now, just she and Rory, beside Whitey's grave. Rory stood at ease, the Bible still in one hand. The book looked old and worn. She let her gaze drift away from the Bible to his eyes.

He was watching her, waiting until she was ready to go. She stepped back and let him come round the grave to join her on the journey back down the hill. When she moved, his gaze lowered to the hem of her skirt.

"You're barefoot."

She pulled back the wide ruffle of the skirt until her pale feet showed. "Scratchy has my shoes."

When she looked up again, he was standing in front of her, close enough to touch her, far enough away to be polite. Instead of feeling overwhelmed by his nearness, she felt comforted. He was holding out the Bible.

She took it. He knelt down before her. "Lift your foot."

She lifted her right foot. He cupped it gently in his hands and brushed the dirt off her sole then inspected it carefully. "Now the other," he said.

Jess did as he asked.

When he was through, he said, "It doesn't look like you cut them up. Feel any stickers?"

She shook her head. "No. I'm fine, really."

He stood up, but didn't offer to take the Bible from her. She held it close and stared at the buttoned front of his white shirt. Finally she looked up again.

"Are you sure you're all right?" His eyes were dark, searching.

She knew he wasn't asking about her feet. "I think so."

"Come with me," he said. As if it were the most natural thing in the world, he held out his hand.

Jessica hesitated only a second before she took it.

CHAPTER

11

He led her to a gathering of boulders on the far side of the knoll. From there, a panoramic vista of open plain, mesas, and the dark shadow of Sleeping Ute Mountain stretched out to the horizon line. Rory sat on the top of a low slab of rock while Jessica leaned back against it. Together they watched a covey of quail scurry down through dry brush. He glanced over, found her watching the quail intently, and couldn't take his eyes off her. He had never seen anyone looking as forlorn or as beautiful. The oversized, somber black dress, so pitifully gathered and tied around her waist, made her seem even more vulnerable. He recognized his mother's beads around her neck.

"What are you thinking?" he asked.

She started visibly. "I was just wondering how those quail could disappear so completely and quickly."

He followed her gaze toward the scrub brush scattered over the hillside below. There was no trace of quail.

"If I only had the power, I'd do the same thing," she added.

When she blinked back tears, he found himself wanting to take her into his arms and rid her of her pain. He would make it his own if need be—but he didn't even try, knowing she would be furious at him for calling attention to her weakness.

Instead he said, "I didn't take you for a quitter."

She turned to him. He could see the shadows in the near-translucent skin beneath her red-rimmed eyes. Although she hadn't shed a tear since they left the grave site, her eyes glistened. "I have nothing left. Everything is gone."

"You have proof that saurians existed in this area. Your boss doesn't know you've lost everything yet—"

"No, but before I can go back in the field, I'll have to write and ask them to send the funds to replace everything. But some things are irreplaceable. My notes, the crate of fossils that Whitey and I . . ." At the mention of the boy's name, her voice faded away. She stared out at the plateau again.

"Surely when you let them know you had already found plenty of fossils, they'll replace everything you lost."

Jessica rubbed her forehead with her fingertips and then spoke slowly and carefully. "When I tell them about the tracks and then about the few mismatched and muddled fossils in the riverbed, and when I go on to explain that I have managed, through my own stupidity and stubbornness, to lose not only the supplies but all of the equipment, not to mention a man's life . . . well, I have no doubt but that they'll insist I return immediately. Gerald Ramsey will have no choice but to do what he wanted in the first place; he'll send a man to do the job."

She worked a small pebble near her big toe out of the dirt. In a sarcastic tone she added, "He'll probably send my former assistant, Jerome Stoutenburg, if no one else is available.'' With a lithe movement, she hefted herself onto the rock and sat beside Rory. Her bare toes, dusted with the red earth, peeked out from beneath the ruffled hem of the black dress. ''At this point I wouldn't doubt that he could do a better job of it.''

Her spirits were lower than he thought. Not only did she still feel responsible for Whitey, but she considered herself a failure as well. He knew Jessica Stanbridge tried so hard not to give in to emotion that offering her sympathy and condolence would not work, but goading her might.

''That's about the sorriest speech I've ever heard,'' he said with a snort.

She started to jump off the boulder.

He stopped her with a touch. ''Don't fly off your high horse, Jess. Just listen to yourself.''

''I don't have to listen.''

''Oh yes, you do. I figure you have three choices. You can give up and run back to Boston, or you can tough it out, get back out there, and get to work.'' With a broad wave he took in the high desert around them. ''Write your boss and let him know what you've found so far.''

''But—''

''But nothing. That's all he needs to know right now. For the time being, you can use the ranch as a base and explore the area. I'll ride with you or send one of the men along when I can't. If you find anything new or decide you want to go back and work the floor of the dry creek again, I can loan you what you need to set up camp. It won't be as grand, but at least you'll be able to carry on. Once you've made a find, you can let them know what happened and maybe they'll be willing to credit me for replacing what you lost.''

He could tell she was thinking over his proposal. Then she shook her head. ''I don't know, I don't want to be indebted to you.'' She looked up quickly. ''I don't want to be indebted to anyone.''

''You have to let people in, Jess. Let them help you. You're part of the human race.''

''I've had to fight so hard for what I want,'' she said softly.

''That doesn't mean you have to fight alone. We could draw the deal up fair and square, if that's what bothers you. We'll keep track of every penny I loan you.'' He shoved his black hat off his forehead and squinted toward the setting sun.

Jessica smoothed the material of the black skirt across her knees. ''What's the third option?''

Rory knew then he was three kinds of a fool for even thinking what he was about to suggest. Tipping his face up to the sky, he took a deep breath and then met her intent gaze again. ''You could give it all up, stay here, and marry me.''

''*What?*''

He shrugged, suddenly very interested in the bib front of his shirt. He rubbed a hand across his jaw. In a voice that was barely audible he explained, ''We could get married.''

Jessica was so shocked she couldn't even respond. Instead she placed her palms on the rock beneath her, fulfilling a sudden need to ground herself to the earth. Had he lost his mind?

''Why would you *ever* suggest such a thing?'' Her face was flaming so much that she had to look away to gain a semblance of control. Had she shown such abandon when he kissed her that he felt the need to propose? Or was he merely feeling sorry for her? Certain the latter had to be the case, she said, ''I don't think a marriage based on pity would last very long.''

''I don't pity you.''

''No? Then why a proposal?''

''This isn't Boston, Jess. Out here people can't take time bothering with long courtships. The way I see it, marriage is just one more step in a man's life, like births and deaths and burials. People adapt. They learn early to do what's practical, what suits. In some ways, we're a lot alike.''

More than doubtful, she turned to stare at him as if he'd lost his mind. He wondered if he had.

"How are we alike?"

He cleared his throat. "Well, you're more or less doing what your father raised you to do, and so am I. From the time I was old enough to walk, I've been working the ranch. All any rancher has to put his stock in are his children. In my pa's case, he only had me to pass the land along to. Your father was a paleontologist—"

"A famous paleontologist."

"And he taught you everything he knew."

"He tried," she admitted.

"So that you could take over for him in the same way I've accepted responsibility for the Silver Sage. In that respect, we are a lot alike. We've both been raised to fulfill our fathers' dreams."

She sighed. "We hardly know each other."

"Some folks never even meet before they agree to marry."

"Like a mail-order bride?"

He nodded. "Like a mail-order bride."

"But we have met"—she frowned at him—"and as I recall, that in itself didn't go very smoothly. Most of the time I don't think you even like me very well."

Rory thought of his sleepless nights on the trail, of how he'd volunteered for more night shifts than the rest of the men because she was on his mind so much he couldn't close his eyes without seeing her. "I wouldn't say that."

"Oh no?"

He shook his head. "No."

She still looked skeptical. "And most of the time I don't think I like you much, either."

"You can say what you like, but the way you kissed me tells me something in you takes a fancy to me."

"Please don't bring that up."

"Why not? That's about all I've been thinking about for two weeks now."

Jessica jumped down off the rock. Her feet hit the soft dirt and left shallow impressions when she walked away. Careful to avoid rocks and twigs, she made her way to the edge of the rise. So, he had been as affected as she by their kiss. Before the disaster she had been aroused by the memory of it—more times than she liked to admit. Still, she never expected the brief exchange to lead to a proposal.

The rock shadows were lengthening. The few billowy clouds that sailed against the sky were tinted blush pink. A chunky rain crow scolded a wren. The day was coming to a close. Birdsong would soon cease and the coyotes, owls, and other night creatures would take over the land. The softening of the light, the paintbrush colors that streaked the sky helped to ease her soul. Behind her, Rory Burnett sat patiently awaiting an answer.

The fact that she had always fought so hard to steel her emotions and hide her feelings from the outside world made it easier for Jessica to appreciate the courage it had taken for him to show his. She envied him that. Therefore she refused to do Rory Burnett a disservice by taking his proposal lightly.

The wide-bottomed skirt flared around her, sending up minute tornadoes of dust as she turned around. "I'd never been kissed before. My reaction was purely one of astonishment mingled with curiosity."

"There must be a lot more you're still curious about." He tried to hide a smile and failed completely.

"I have no doubt that you are an expert in such matters," she told him smugly.

"Not hardly," he said.

His response was so immediate she knew that he believed it to be true even though she didn't. Jessica gave him a sidelong look. "Still, you are far more experienced than I."

"Would you be happier if neither of us knew what to do when the time comes?"

"The time is *not* coming. Therefore I don't know why you would propose to me, Mr. Burnett, on the basis of one kiss—unless, of course, you see me as less than virtuous. Or as a mercy case."

"You're about the most virtuous woman I've ever laid eyes on, *Miss Stanbridge*. And if I didn't think you were, then I certainly wouldn't have asked you to marry me."

"Then you pity me."

At that he stood up and closed the distance between them in two strides. He took her by the arms, his gaze so intent that it captured and held hers. "The truth is, for some inexplicable reason, I want you, Jess. I've thought about nothing but the way it could be between us ever since I was crazy enough to kiss you. I want you more than I've ever wanted any other woman, but more than that, I want you to want me."

Shaken by his blunt admission, Jessica was consumed by the images his words conjured. She could only guess at what an intimate, man–woman exchange between them would be like, but it was enough to make her palms sweat.

He had spoken of wanting, of a physical need. She was too clinical a scientist and far from foolish enough to deny that his touch, indeed, his very nearness, aroused certain biological responses in her. Even now she could feel the heat of his hands through the black bombazine. She was close enough to smell the heady scent of his soap, could see the way his gaze dropped to her lips and lingered, much as they would during a kiss. There was no denying her attraction to him, the pulsing need he easily stoked without really trying. She knew for certain that the longer she stayed near him, the closer she came to walking a fine line between giving in to her physical need and holding on to her virtue. Still, shouldn't there be more than physical need and attraction between a man and woman for a lasting relationship?

"What about love?" she surprised herself by asking. "Do you love me?"

"I don't know much about love, but I figure wanting something real bad isn't a bad place to start."

She raised her chin. "I always thought the opposite was true, that loving someone would lead to . . . well, more."

He couldn't help but smile again. "I haven't had much experience with this sort of thing—loving someone, that is."

"All the more reason I must decline your proposal."

His hands dropped to his sides, but he didn't step away. "So you're planning to turn tail and run home?"

She sighed, her senses calming somewhat now that he had let go of her, but still unable to think things through. "I don't know what I'm going to do. I'm sorry that Myra and I have become so dependent upon you. I insist on paying for our food and lodging."

"Forget it, it's my pleasure."

"Thank you, but I will repay you." She thought for a moment longer before she decided, "For now, I think I'll take your suggestion and let Ramsey know what I had discovered before the flood without mentioning last night's disaster. I have a letter all written that I managed to save, along with the official documents from the museum. They aren't much, but they're a start, and a reason for hanging on a bit longer. Besides, Myra needs to rest until her ankle heals."

Pleased that she had agreed to as much, Rory added, "Maybe tomorrow we should ride back out to the dry creek and see if there's anything you can salvage."

"Do you really think we can carry on in a businesslike manner after what you've told me today?"

He folded his arms as he stared down at her. "Miss Stanbridge, I'm sure you'll be able to put my need out of your mind and carry on with your usual fortitude."

"But surely you don't have time, anyway."

Lifting his hat, he pulled the brim low on his forehead. "You're still the boss, remember? As I recall, I haven't been much of a guide for nigh onto two weeks now."

Jessica couldn't help but smile in return. The reaction felt foreign to her after so many hours of sorrow and confusion. "You may be right. There might be something of value left. I'm also interested in what the creek bed looks like. We had quite a perimeter dug around the exposed fossils; I can't imagine what the force of the water might have done."

Behind her, the sun was nearer the horizon, but there would still be an hour before it set. The dinner bell clanged in the distance. Rory turned toward the grave site again, ready to head back downhill. He picked up his Bible.

"Who knows," he said as they walked along together, turning in unison toward the iron fence that rimmed the family plots, too aware of the fresh mound of earth they were leaving behind, "maybe the flood did your job for you. There might be a great big pile of leftover saurian lying right there waiting for you to crate it up and haul it back to Boston."

"There might," she said, more than doubtful, "but I'm beginning to think that nothing comes that easily."

His thoughts turned to the high mesa and what he knew was just waiting to be discovered near a cave in the bluff. The one thing in the world Jessica Stanbridge wanted most was not a day's ride away, but because of past promises, it was not in his power to give it to her. What would she do if she ever found out that he'd known about a complete skeleton all along but kept the information from her?

When she stepped on a sharp stone and let out a yelp, his attention shifted back to her immediately. "Are you all right?"

"Fine. Really I am," she said when he looked displeased.

"I'm glad that wasn't a scorpion."

"So am I." Teetering on one foot, Jess rubbed the sole of the other with her thumb. As he stood contemplating her

Rory realized all too clearly that the one thing he wanted most in all the world was standing there beside him.

With that thought in mind, he slipped an arm beneath her knees, the other around her back, and scooped her up against his chest.

"What are you doing? Put me down," she protested.

"Hold still or I'm liable to drop you on your behind. You're not all that light, you know."

She crossed her arms defiantly, unwilling to hold on and help him in any way.

"I think you should know," he told her, his lips far too close to her ear, "that I don't intend to give up until I get what I want."

"You sound like a spoiled child, Mr. Burnett."

"Maybe so, but I think you should be warned."

She told him as coolly as she could, considering the fact that his lips were now inches from her own, "I was sent here to do a job and I'm going to do my best to succeed."

"That doesn't mean I have to stop trying," he warned.

"That doesn't mean you're going to succeed, either."

Knowing he wanted her in a carnal way didn't help Jessica get to sleep that night. And as for his surprising proposal of marriage—she tried to tuck the knowledge away like a keepsake that she could take out when her days in the high desert were far behind, but Rory's bold proclamation dogged her until dawn.

Giving up on sleep, she rose at first light, dressed in the made-over calico, still tired. But even with the lack of sleep, she was feeling more herself. Scratchy had returned her freshly laundered clothes and someone had even polished her shoes. With a silent blessing for the feel of fresh underclothing next to her skin, Jessica took a look in the mirror over the washstand and proclaimed herself fit enough.

Sunlight streamed through the eastern windows, dust

motes dancing along the sunbeams that fanned out and slanted across the wide plank floors. She hurried out of her door to Myra's room, knocked twice, and entered. Myra was pulling herself to a sitting position, still disoriented and sleepy-eyed. There were three books on the nightstand that had been borrowed from the Burnett library. Jess smiled when she saw the one-stemmed spectacles lying atop them.

"Did you sleep in?" Jessica bustled over to Myra's bedside, helped her to a sitting position, and fluffed the pillows.

"My, you're certainly energetic this morning," Myra grumbled with a jaundiced eye.

Jessica pulled up a chair and sat down, disregarding her friend's expression. "I've come to some decisions and I want to discuss them with you."

Myra perked up considerably. "By all means, go ahead, but first of all, how was the burial? How did you manage it?"

Jessica began slowly. "It was just as you said. I needed to see Whitey through the final step, just as the others did. It was far from pleasant"—she thought back to the solitude of the windswept hillside, of the loneliness of the four graves and the newest one outlined against the crooked fence—"but I'm glad I went."

"Now, what of these monumental decisions? Not giving up, I hope?"

"Not yet. Just before the flash flood I was writing a letter to Director Ramsey outlining my progress. I saved the letter along with my documents."

"How?" Myra wanted to know.

Jessica looked disgruntled by the interruption. "I tucked the leather pouch inside my waistband. Anyway, Rory suggested I go right ahead and post it as if nothing were amiss." She frowned thoughtfully for a moment. "Of course, I'll have to recopy the original letter, as it's a little water-stained. That will give me time to go back out to the dry creek and see if the flood exposed any more of the fossils. I could also scour the area for further discoveries. Rory has even gone as far as to suggest I borrow whatever supplies and equipment I need to complete—''

Myra looked thoughtful. ''I have a little money set aside. I could wire my attorney and—''

Jess held up a hand. ''Absolutely not. You've already spent too much of your savings on this trip.'' She stood and began to pace the room. ''Burnett has agreed to keep an accounting so that any monies or goods he lends me can be replaced by the museum.''

''Once you eventually let them know what's happened, you mean?''

''Myra, do you think I'm being dishonest by withholding the information for a while?''

Myra contemplated the idea for a moment. Her eyelids slowly lowered. Finally they closed all the way.

''Well, what do you think?''

Myra sputtered awake. ''Sounds like a fine idea to me. Let's say you had already mailed the letter off, they'd be learning the facts in the same sequence. Why not go ahead and establish a working site again before you contact them? I'm more than willing to stay on. In fact, I'm quite anxious to start all my sketches over. Besides, I'm not up to going anywhere very soon.'' She yawned again. ''Do you think I could have some coffee? I know that man in the kitchen has probably been up for hours concocting new ways to ruin steak and eggs.''

Jessica knew more than to press Myra further once she had become preoccupied, especially with food. ''I'll see about some coffee.'' She crossed the room and pulled open the door.

''By the way,'' Myra began after stifling another yawn. She was watching Jessica closely, her tone far from matter-of-fact. ''I happened to see Rory Burnett carrying you across the yard into the house yesterday. I have a clear view of the porch from here.''

Jessica closed the door and stalked over to the foot of the bed. After taking a deep breath, she shrugged as nonchalantly as possible, but kept her voice lowered. ''I was without shoes and had stepped on a stone. He insisted he carry me back from the graveyard. That's all.''

''Not exactly the actions of a man who supposedly hates you.''

''Don't look so smug, Myra. And for heaven's sake don't start thinking there is anything between us, because I can assure you that I don't—''

''My, my, my. How did Shakespeare put it? 'Methinks the lady doth protest too much'?''

Jess felt herself blush. Myra's knowing smile set her teeth on edge. ''I'll go get that coffee now.'' She hurried out the door before Myra could mention Rory Burnett's name again.

> Distant thunder in the night,
> Lightning flashes, what a sight,
> Slashes past the eastern hills.
> Four-legged critters hide until
> The quiet rain comes falling down
> Seeping into brittle ground.

With his left leg casually hooked across the pommel of his saddle, Rory contented himself with memorizing his latest poem while he waited for Jessica to cross the creek bed and rejoin him. They had been scouring the area for remains of her former camp and had actually found quite a few.

Sweat trickled between his shoulder blades. He tried to ignore the heat of the July sun as he studied his companion. She sat up unnaturally straight, somehow managing to look like a schoolmarm even in the saddle. He was amazed at how quickly the flesh-and-blood woman he had glimpsed beneath the surface of his proud little paleontologist had disappeared. Gone was the sky-blue calico dress, too large in all the wrong places, but it had set the blue in her eyes dancing. Gone was the streaming fall of golden, unbound hair. In no less than three days she'd turned back into the very businesslike Miss Stanbridge with her high-necked blouse, sturdy shoes, and plain beige skirt. She had lost her confounded spectacles and her silly helmet, which she had temporarily replaced with an old poke bonnet of his mother's. He noticed she was still wearing his mother's beads.

During the three days it had taken Jess to revert to her former self, Rory had a chance to watch her, to memorize every line and curve of her. He loved the way she moved, prim and proper it was true, but ever graceful, sometimes even innocently sensual when she let down her guard or forgot she was not alone. Her fingers were usually stained with ink these days, for she spent long hours rewriting her notes and drawing new maps of the areas she had already surveyed.

At mealtime, while he contented himself with watching the lace of her shirtwaist collar tickle the underside of her jaw, Jess listened attentively to his conversations with the men. Often she asked polite questions about their work, and he suspected her queries were to bring the others out of their shyness and put them at ease. The first morning she joined them for breakfast, his usually boisterous crew was more than tongue-tied with a female suddenly in their midst.

After two days the cowhands were more relaxed in her presence, and he knew that to a man they respected her because she was always gracious, reserved, proper.

The men also saw her as the guardian of Myra Thornton's person. It was no secret among them that Woody Barrows was smitten with Jessica's companion, and although he turned five shades of red, he asked the younger woman's permission to visit Myra—only if chaperoned by three of the others, of course. All the men were trying hard to please their guests. Even Scratchy was scraping together some new culinary surprises. What those surprises consisted of no one could guess, but Rory suspected the changes had something to do with Myra Thornton's very vocal interest in his recipes.

At breakfast earlier that morning, Fred Hench had bemoaned the fact that the book they had so enjoyed one afternoon at Zanzibar had been washed away in the flood. Rory hid a smile when Jess quickly glanced his way. Was she thinking about the haunting love poem she had read aloud or the kiss they had exchanged shortly afterward? He didn't know for certain, but something had set her cheeks afire.

Never one to run for cover, she had looked directly at Rory when she said, "Yes, Mr. Hench, I'm afraid Mrs. Corelli was carried away with the rest of our things, but I'm sure if you'd enjoy another reading session, Mr. Burnett could find something suitable in the library."

Rory promised her he would look.

He repeated the first stanza of his poem again. As usual, he didn't know which direction the work would take, but he thought he might dedicate it to Whitey's memory. As at-home in the saddle as he was the big, overstuffed chair in the parlor, he shifted and looked over his shoulder to be certain Jess was all right. She was off her horse, bent to retrieve something off the ground. She'd been collecting items left by the floodwater, stuffing them into a flour sack tied to her saddle. They clinked and clanked as she rode, the bulges against the muslin giving no clue as to their identities.

That morning, before they headed out, he had called Jess into his office to tell her he had sent Gathers with the list of supplies she wanted to the general store in Cortez. What he didn't tell her was that he didn't have much cash to spare.

He was hoping Willie Henson would extend him credit. Jess had stormed into his office, irritated as hell and trying hard not to show it because two days had passed since Whitey's burial and he hadn't had time to take her back to the campsite. And even though he was now making good on his promise, she still hadn't thawed much, even under the hot sun.

His stomach rumbled like a bobcat's growl. He stuck his fingers between his teeth and whistled. Jess looked up and waved.

"I'm hungry," he shouted across at her. "Let's eat."

Like a homesteader with her face hidden beneath the deep brim of the poke bonnet, Jess cupped her gloved hands about her mouth and shouted back, "Let's just go a bit farther. We've almost reached the site of the old dig." Without waiting for his agreement, she saddled up, led her horse into the dry creek bed, and cantered off.

"Damn," he whispered beneath his breath. "Do I really want to be saddled with a woman like that?"

Since he couldn't think of anything else he'd rather be, he kicked his horse and rode after her.

"I think this is all that's left of our site," Jessica said, dismounting again. She went down on one knee beside a dark smear of rock exposed in the silt.

Knowing they wouldn't be having their meal until she was good and ready, he swung off of Domino and looked down at the faded sunbonnet. "Bad news?"

She stood up and brushed at her skirt. All trace of the digging they had done was gone. "I'm afraid so. It looks as if the fragments were dislodged and washed away. By now they are spread all over the creek bed from here to Mexico."

"Anything deeper?"

She shrugged. "I don't know, but I think if there was anything significant, it would have been exposed by the tremendous force of the water."

"Disappointed?"

He saw her breasts lift and fall as she gave a silent sigh. "Not really. It would be terribly hard to work here again after what happened to Whitey, but I will if this is the only promise of any sort of find. I'll map out the area and come back if need be, but I won't regret a chance to start over somewhere else." She challenged him with a look. "The mesa, for instance."

"Let's eat." Reins in hand, he walked over to two flat stones that stood opposite each other. Jess came up behind him as he began to lay out the food Scratchy had packed that morning.

"Nothing fancy here." He rummaged in the bag and pulled out some sandwiches, apples, and two hunks of corn bread.

"Anything will taste good at this point." She untied the bow at her throat and pulled the hat off. Her sweat-soaked hair stuck to her forehead.

"Don't count on it. Some of the boys have bet that even a starving man would find fault with Scratchy's cooking."

She laughed. "I have to admit it is less than palatable."

"You're being kind." About to hand her a sandwich, he paused. "That's better."

"What?"

"That smile."

She looked away. "I guess I haven't had much to smile about lately."

"As I recall you didn't let yourself laugh much even before the flood." When she refused to pick up his verbal gauntlet, he changed the subject. "July Fourth is in two days. I've talked it over with the men and we've agreed that our annual Independence Day celebration should go on."

"Celebration?"

He took a bite of his own sandwich, chewed, and then explained. "Every year Pa always held a cookout and rodeo followed by a barn dance for any of the neighboring ranchers and Utes that wanted to attend. We've had over seventy-five people come to the Silver Sage for the day. The ladies bring covered dishes, we roast a side of beef, and the men compete in calf roping, bronc busting, and other events. Then we have the dance—of course it's nothing fancy, just a few fiddlers and guitars in the barn—'' He stopped when he saw her frown at the napkin spread over her lap. ''If you're thinking we shouldn't celebrate this year because of Whitey, well, we all knew how much he was looking forward to it and how disappointed he'd be if we canceled it on account of him, so we decided to hold it in his honor.''

''I wasn't thinking that at all.'' Her blue eyes finally met his as she admitted quietly, ''I was just thinking that I've never been to a dance.''

''Never?'' Dancing was a part of every celebration, be it a barn raising or a baptism, but when he thought about it, her admission didn't surprise him any. ''No, I guess you wouldn't do much dancing in a museum basement.'' Somehow he couldn't quite imagine any of the colleagues she so wanted to impress engaging in anything that resembled fun.

''But, of course, I won't be there.''

He had intended to surprise her with the dress from Durango for the occasion. ''If that's because you don't have anything to wear—''

''That's not it at all. I just don't have time for such frivolity.''

''You don't mean to tell me you intend to work that day?''

''I do indeed.''

''There's not a man within miles who'll miss the rodeo to bring you out here on the Fourth.''

''Then I'll work in my room. I have plenty to do.''

He drew his leg up, planted his boot on the rock, and rested an arm across his knee. ''Well, Miss Stanbridge, it's nice to see you're back to normal.''

CHAPTER

12

"What do you mean by 'back to normal'?" Jessica picked up her napkin, shook the crumbs out, and began folding it, carefully avoiding eye contact.

"You've put on those stiff, businesslike airs you wear like a suit of armor."

She used the neatly folded gingham square to dab at the perspiration across her brow. "All I'm trying to do is concentrate on what I was sent out here to accomplish."

When he didn't say anything to that, she finally glanced up and caught him at his irritating habit of trying to hide a smile.

"Is that all?"

Jessica stood up. "That's entirely all, Mr. Burnett."

"So it's as bad as all that, is it?"

"What?" She turned in time to see him stand and move up behind her. Jessica brushed her skirt.

"It's bad enough you hardly ever say my name, now we're back to 'Mr. Burnett' again?"

She swallowed hard. "Since you can't avoid personal discussion, I'm afraid the time for informality is over."

"I don't think that's what you're afraid of, Jess."

Still standing with her back to him, she crossed her arms protectively over her breasts. She felt him move closer. Unwilling to appear the coward she knew she was, Jessica stood her ground. She felt him behind her, sensed the heat he radiated.

When he spoke, his voice was all too near the nape of her neck. She could feel his warm breath across her sweat-dampened skin. "I think you're afraid of yourself," he said just loud enough for her to hear.

An odd warmth crept down her shoulders and somehow wound itself all the way to her breasts. Her nipples hardened into tight, aching buds. A trickle of sweat ran down her temple. She batted it away when it reached the corner of her eye.

Gathering courage, Jessica knew she had to confront him or he would know he had hit upon the truth. She turned around and looked up into his dark, intense eyes. "I was sent out here to do a job and nothing more. I have no other reason to be here."

He took a step toward her.

She held her ground.

"I can give you another reason, Jess."

"Please . . . don't."

"Don't what? Don't make you feel anything? Don't make you admit to yourself that there's a real woman underneath all that starched linen and scientific book learning?"

"Stop it," she whispered.

"You're a flesh-and-blood woman with a need running so deep that you're not going to be able to deny it much longer." He reached out for her, and before she could move away, he had his hands on her shoulders. "You've been trying to prove yourself in a world of men for so long that you've forgotten you're a woman.''

She braced herself, put her palms against his chest, and knew instantly it had been a mistake to touch him. She could feel his heart beating through the heel of her hand. Her voice was shaking. ''That's one thing I'll never be able to forget, because no one will let me, not my esteemed colleagues or you.''

He was watching her closely, staring, she noticed, at her lips.

She started trembling, whether in fear or anticipation she didn't know. She didn't know if she could bear it if he kissed her again—but could she stand it if he didn't?

''If you're set on making life difficult for me, I'll find somewhere else to stay and someone else to help me out.''

''All I'm asking is that you let yourself feel something, Jess, something besides this all-consuming need to succeed.''

''But—'' She could sense her resolve melting away as sure as a candle would melt in the high desert heat. Her elbows unlocked.

''Aren't you even curious about what might happen if I kiss you again?'' Rory moved closer.

She licked her dry lips and lied. ''No.''

''You're fibbing.''

She shook her head. ''No, I'm not.''

He pulled her close, so close that there was no room for even a breath of breeze to pass between them. ''I'll prove it,'' he whispered just before he lowered his lips to hers.

She lost her grip on the bonnet strings. The faded, gathered material dropped toward the ground until the dry wind lifted it and sent it tumbling slowly toward a clump of sage a few feet away.

When Jess didn't resist, Rory pulled her into his arms. He covered her lips with his own and again met no resistance. The way she fit in his arms made him wild for her. Tired of holding back, Rory cursed himself for being as much of a gentleman as he was; still, somewhere deep inside, he knew that he would stop long before he wanted to, knew that he would let her go the minute she insisted—but while Jess remained pliant in his arms he couldn't help but try to convince her with his hands and his lips that they belonged together.

The heat and wind picked up as if fueled by their passion. All around them the air sang with the hum of insects. Birds darted through the low brush as here and there a lizard paused to pant and then slip away across the hot ground. Rory's kiss was fierce, delving, and her lips opened easily beneath his. This time it was as if she knew she couldn't fight the magic between them any longer.

Jess slipped her arms around him and held tight. She could feel the strength that emanated from him, enjoyed feeling the whipcord muscles beneath his shirt as he pulled her closer. He was all hard angles where she was soft curves. For that moment in time there was nothing else but the two of them beneath the wide blue sky and the shimmering waves of heat that rose off the desert floor.

She clung to him as he bent over her and memorized her with his touch. When his fingertips brushed the underside of her breast, she whimpered against his lips. Wanting more, he cupped her buttocks with his hands and pulled her up against him and felt her accommodate him by rising up on tiptoe.

Driven to touch her hot, sweat-sheened flesh, Rory tugged her blouse out of the skirt waistband and slipped his hand beneath it. He felt a thin piece of woman's frippery beneath it and quickly pulled it out of the way. Finally his fingers came in contact with skin, smooth as satin, damp with sweat, as hot as his own.

She felt his hand, hard, callused, seeking, against her flesh. Even as she lost herself to his caress her analytical mind cried out for her to stop, but her body was out of control. That fact terrified the rational part of her more than anything else. Still, she was powerless to protest as he touched her breast, cupped it, let it mold itself to his palm.

Rory sighed against her lips. "Oh, God. Oh, Jess."

He rubbed his thumb across her nipple and teased it until a sweet, all-consuming ache made her knees weak. She felt her insides melt as a rush of moisture between her thighs shook her so badly that she became frantic.

When her control was nearly gone, she heard her father's voice haunting her. *Think, Jessica. Think of all you will be throwing away. Think of your good name, of your reputation, the Stanbridge reputation.*

With an agonized groan she managed to pull away and found herself staring into Rory's smoldering gaze. His hand lingered at her breast. When she fully realized what he was doing, her eyes widened and her lips formed an astonished *O*.

His hand slowly slipped away from her breast. His fingertips savored the touch of satin skin along her ribs and then at her waist. Regretfully he drew his hand away. The hem of her blouse hung out of her waistband and fluttered in the breeze.

He could see the shock and confusion in her blue eyes. "Jess, listen—"

Terrified by her loss of control, she whirled away from him and started running toward her horse.

"Jess!" He took a step and then stopped, afraid of terrifying her any more than he had already. There was no doubt in his mind that the emotion he'd seen in her eyes had been fear.

Jessica ran headlong toward the piebald mare he had loaned her. She tore the reins off of a piñon branch. Her skirt twisted around her ankles before she jerked it up, put her foot into the stirrup, and then hefted herself into the saddle. She kicked the horse into a gallop and didn't look back.

• • •

"Jess!" she heard Rory call out, but ignored his plea. In her haste, she had forgotten her gloves and bonnet, and now the hot, dry wind beat her face unmercifully. The muslin sack tied to her pommel slapped rhythmically against her horse's side. The animal's eyes were wide with terror.

Afraid the mare would run headlong into a rabbit hole, Jess pulled back on the reins and forced the horse to slow down to a stop. While the animal pranced beneath her, sides heaving, Jessica chanced a glance back over her shoulder.

Rory Burnett was nothing more than a silhouette that shimmered in the heat waves in the distance. He wasn't following her. Thanking God for small favors, she tried to control her riotous emotions and wished it was as simple as reining in her mare. Forcing herself to take three deep, even breaths, she tried to shove her shirttail and camisole back into her waistband. It was easier than shoving aside the memory of Rory's hand on her flesh, simpler than trying to ignore the throbbing ache of raw need that only intensified when she kicked her horse into a trot and rode on.

Rory stepped inside the kitchen and let the screen door slam behind him. His mother's poke bonnet dangled from the ties he clenched tight in his gloved hand. Myra and Scratchy looked up from where they sat at the kitchen table. Rory recognized her calico dress as one of his mother's; her injured foot was propped up on a chair. Scratchy sat back, his arms folded across his chest, a deep scowl on his bewhiskered face.

"I was just giving Mr. Livermore here some helpful hints at gravy making," Myra volunteered as she slipped her lopsided spectacles off her nose and set them on the table beside a stack of notes.

Scratchy shook his head. "I don't see nothin' wrong with a lump here or there."

Myra took up the cause immediately. "I don't mean to

offend, Mr. Livermore, but your lumpy gravy is the consistency of glue gone bad,'' she argued.

In no mood to referee, Rory asked, ''Where's Jessica?'' He knew she'd arrived back safely, for he'd seen her horse in the corral. It was still wet and winded and he guessed Jess was off sulking somewhere.

There was no mistaking Myra's look of suspicious curiosity, but she admitted nothing more than, ''In her room. She said something about being overheated.'' She studied Rory a moment too long. Scratchy looked down at the tabletop.

Unwilling to explain, Rory knew Miss Jessica Stanbridge was more than overheated. He tossed the bonnet on the table, drew Jessica's gloves out of his back pocket, and threw them down beside it. That done, he walked out the backdoor.

She didn't appear for dinner. The next morning when Jessica's place was noticeably empty at breakfast, it was quite obvious that she was not coming out of her room as long as he was around. As the last of the men shuffled out the backdoor to get back to the chores they had started before sunup, Myra suggested to Scratchy, ''Perhaps you should fix a plate for Jessica and I'll try to coax her into eating.''

Rory's coffee mug slammed against the tabletop. He'd been in a surly mood since yesterday afternoon and he wasn't about to let Jessica hide in her room until she'd made up her mind to move out. ''If she's too sick to come out, she's too sick to eat.''

Woody Barrows had just come in the backdoor to ask a question. He paused on the threshold, Rory's sharp tone arresting him where he stood. He glanced over Scratchy's head at Myra, who shrugged, then all of them looked at Rory as if he had suddenly sprouted horns.

Leaving the steaming cup of coffee behind, Rory stood up

and left the table, well aware that they were all staring at him and no doubt whispering about his black mood as he stalked down the hall toward Jessica's door.

He paused outside, listened intently, and raised his hand to knock. With a swift change of mind, he shoved his hands in his back pockets and stalked back down the hall and out the front door.

To hell with the ranch, he thought. He pulled a chair away from the wall and out into the center of the porch. Once seated, he propped his feet up on the railing and crossed his legs at the ankles. With his hands behind his head, he stared out over the gentle slope of the valley, at the cattle grazing in the distance and off toward Sleeping Ute Mountain. He sat there thinking of nothing and everything for a long while until finally he heard a soft shuffling sound. When Myra slowly came out the door, leaning on the crutch Wheelbarrow had made her, Rory dropped his feet to the floor and started to stand.

"Stay right there, please. No need to play the gentleman with me. I can manage." True to her word, Myra limped over to a chair beside Rory's and sat down heavily. After she caught her breath, she rested the crutch against her thigh and said, "I love mornings out here. It seems the earth is renewed each and every day."

"I never thought of it like that," he said, "but I think you might be right." *Too bad certain people can't be renewed each day.*

"How many cattle do you have out there?" she asked, staring out across the landscape.

"It varies from year to year. Whatever the land will allow, then there are strays that wander in, range cattle that don't belong to anybody, spring calves. There's a cow camp not far from here. Some of the best stock is up in the hills around there." He could sense her reserve, knew they were talking around the real issue at hand.

Finally Myra said, "Jessica arrived here quite disheveled

yesterday—her hair mussed, cheeks aflame, missing her hat and gloves.'' She watched him carefully. ''That's not like her. I've known her since she was a child and she's never been so at odds. In fact, she's unusually composed at all times.''

For someone so unusually composed, she had certainly come apart in his arms yesterday. ''She's the damnedest, most stubborn, pigheaded—''

''Jessica has a mind of her own.''

''Stuffed full of nonsense,'' he tossed back.

''She's highly educated,'' she countered.

''Doesn't have the sense God gave a goat.''

''Let's stop talking around the problem, Rory.''

He leaned forward, his arms on his knees, and stared down at the floorboards between his boots. ''I asked her to marry me the day of Whitey's funeral,'' he admitted softly.

Her shock was so immediate that Myra dropped her crutch. ''Oh, my! And what did she say to that?''

''She said no, of course.''

''Of course? If you knew that would be the answer, why did you propose?''

There was no way in hell he was going to tell Myra Thornton that he wanted Jessica in his bed, that he wanted to lay claim to her as sure as he did the Silver Sage because he couldn't stand the thought of anyone else touching her.

But for now someone else did have her, or some*thing*— she was devoted to fulfilling her dream of becoming a world-renowned paleontologist.

In answer to her question, he merely said, ''I don't know why I asked.''

Myra shifted in her chair, looked him in the eye, and asked, ''Do you love her?''

He felt his face grow hot and looked out over the open range. ''There's something between us, something I'm not stupid enough to deny, even if Jess is.''

Moving to the edge of the chair, Myra agreed. ''I saw it, too, the very moment we met and I saw the two of you together. I told Jessica back then that there were strong currents between you that couldn't be denied.''

''Well, she's bent on denying them.''

''You have to realize, Rory, that Jessica has been groomed for her work since the time she was old enough to read. It was her father's obsession that she learn all he knew and carry on after he was gone.''

Shoving aside his guilt, he put his foot back up on the rails, certain he wasn't going to get any work done before noon. ''My father left me this ranch when he died, but I haven't let it obsess me.''

''Ah, yes, but from what I have seen, you most likely led a normal life with a mother and father who had many other interests.''

''The ranch was their life, their livelihood, but they had friends, and they had each other.''

''Jessica's mother died when she was eight. She took care of the house and did her father's research work for him when he became the museum director. When she was old enough, she was employed in the museum basement cataloging specimens. Her life revolved between their small flat crowded with books and papers and the museum filled with bits and pieces of the past. She's had no other life.

''She became determined to prove she was just as qualified, just as knowledgeable as any male paleontologist. When her father died, she applied for the job of museum director, but the board of trustees thought it out of the question to even interview a woman. So when she was given this chance to prove herself, she became all the more determined to succeed.''

Rory dropped his feet to the ground again and stood up. ''I'm not asking her to choose me over her work. All I'm asking is that she admit she has feelings for me and to open herself up to—''

Myra stopped him. ''I don't think you need to enlighten me on that point. But if Jessica were to agree to marry you, how could she continue to work for the museum?''

He paced over to the porch rail and rested one hip against it. "I haven't thought that out yet. She could go on with this one project, though, and see it through to the end." He felt a swift flood of guilt. But his promise to uphold the agreement between his father and the Utes tied his hands. Nor did he need a sideshow in his own backyard.

"Do you love her enough to give up the ranch?" Myra asked.

"And do what? Does she love me enough to give up the museum?" he countered.

"Can you please help with my crutch?"

Rory hurried to pick it up for her and then helped her to her feet. Myra shifted her weight off her injured ankle and slipped the crutch beneath her arm.

Myra looked sad. "I'm afraid you've both come to quite an impasse."

"I guess so. But right now I'm going to make sure she comes out of that room."

She watched him walk toward the front door. "Good luck, Rory. Whatever happens, I wish you the best."

Her words made him color with embarrassment. "I'll take the luck," he told her.

Jessica paced her room. As much as she longed to see Rory again, so, too, did she want to avoid him. He was a threat to her future and to the promise she had made her father and the museum. The only thing she could do, she decided, was to leave the ranch and travel into Durango, wire the museum for more funds, and if Beckworth was willing to oblige, start over. If he wasn't willing, then she would have to admit defeat and go home.

Outside in the hallway, Rory stared again at the door that separated them and steeled himself to knock, knowing that if given a choice, she would deny him access. His knock was swift and determined.

Her answer came just as quickly. "Go away," she said through the door.

He turned the knob. None of the rooms in the house had locks. No one had ever wanted to lock themselves away before. She was standing rigid in the center of the room, every hair tucked neatly in place, her blouse protecting her throat, her skirt lying smoothly over her trim hips, flared just enough to hide her shoes. Her eyes snapped blue fire when he took another step into the room.

"What are you doing here?"

"This is my house, remember?" Not exactly the opening he had hoped for.

"Then I'll get out."

His fingers itched to touch her, to rip the pins from her hair and free her from herself. More than ever, he longed to bury himself in her and rid himself of the pain of wanting her. "You can run as far and as fast as you like, but we belong together, Jess. What happened out in the desert yesterday proved that."

"What happened yesterday only proves that I can't trust you."

"Look, I'm sick and tired of arguing with you. I've decided to go into Cortez and see if your supplies are in, then I'm heading over to the cow camp on the far side of the range. You won't have to hide in here any longer."

Swift relief followed by a disappointment she couldn't have predicted assailed her. "And when you get back?"

He held up his hands. "I give up. I won't touch you again. If you're so all-fired determined to turn your back on any chance we have together, then so be it. I'm tired of making a fool of myself." He turned around to leave, then paused with one hand on the knob. "I hope you'll be happy with your books and your boxes of bones, Jess. Just remember, they won't keep you warm at night."

The door slammed so hard behind him that it echoed in her ears, but it couldn't drown out the sound of his footsteps as they faded down the hall.

CHAPTER

13

The morning of the Fourth of July dawned as bright and hot as the last few days had been. True to his promise, Rory Burnett hadn't shown his face at the ranch house for the past two days, and although Jessica didn't like to admit it, she found herself listening for his voice and went to the window each time she heard a horse gallop into the yard.

As long as Rory was gone, she felt comfortable enough to leave her room, visit with Myra, and take her meals with the others. That morning at breakfast, Fred Hench had asked if she could take over feeding a motherless calf from a bottle while he set up the trestle tables that would be used for the covered-dish dinner. Jessica found herself laughing with the first real abandon she'd known in days when the greedy creature nearly pulled the bottle out of her hands as it nursed. It gave her an odd sense of longing to witness something so small and helpless and dependent. When the calf followed her around the barnyard on its knobby legs, she let it trail her to the house so that Myra could watch. Myra was convinced that Methuselah was a far better pet.

Midmorning the wagons began to arrive. Jessica stood in the shade of the wide overhang and watched as the women, most dressed in simple though colorful gowns, climbed down off of buckboards and offered their covered dishes to Scratchy. Myra, standing beside Jessica, mumbled, "No wonder they didn't call this off. It will be the first good meal we've all had in days."

Indian men arrived on horseback. Ute women and children crowded into wagons driven by the older boys. Their clothing was much as Jess remembered from her brief time on the reservation, a jumble of styles. She openly admired the silver work and turquoise jewelry some of them wore. As local farmers and ranchers mingled with the Utes, Myra left the porch to join them.

"Come, Jessica. Let's see what it is those men gathered around that wagon bed are all bartering for, shall we?" She used the crutch to balance herself as she carefully stepped off the wooden porch.

Afraid she would run into Rory, Jess denied herself the experience. She'd heard Barney Tinsley call out to someone that Burnett was back and had cut a particularly ornery bull named Arthur out of the herd. She'd listened in on their talk of the upcoming rodeo enough to know the rudiments of what was about to take place that afternoon. The men had bragged about Rory when he wasn't there to stop them and said he was an accomplished bull rider, but that last year he'd been thrown, knocked out, and remained unconscious for three days. Wheelbarrow announced with a belly laugh that Rory had finally come around, "fit as a fiddle," and that he intended to teach that danged bull a lesson this year.

Beside bull riding there was calf roping, something called bronc busting, a cutting horse contest—during which cowhands and their favorite horses would show how quickly they could cut a calf from the herd—and finally, team roping. All of it sounded dirty and dangerous to Jessica. When the lanky, ever-silent cowboy known only as Gathers was asked to show her his hand and tell how he lost his missing finger "dallying" or fast-tying a rope around his saddle horn during a calf-throwing contest, she decided she was glad she wasn't going to attend any of the events.

"Are you certain you won't come out at all?" Myra asked around noon when the rodeo was about to begin. "They have a few benches set up for the ladies around the corral. You're spry enough to climb the rails and watch if you choose. I can't wait to do a few sketches."

Jessica had made a rash promise to herself to avoid Rory Burnett at all costs because she didn't know if she could trust him to keep his word to leave her alone any more than she could trust herself. She kept to her room, trying not to let the noisy crowd sway her from her decision. Just as she was pulling the heavy serape drape over her open window to block out the view, if not the noise, a swift, impatient knock sounded on the door. She knew it was Rory even before she opened it.

He stood in the hallway, a parcel and what appeared to be a letter in his hand. In a plaid flannel shirt and denim trousers he hadn't dressed any differently for the celebration than on any other day. His dark eyes were expressionless. "This is for you."

Jess stepped back and allowed him to enter. "Thank you." She reached for the letter, glanced at the handwriting, and recognized it as museum director Gerald Ramsey's.

"That was delivered to the Ute reservation. Agent Carmichael had it sent to Cortez. I picked it up when I went in yesterday."

Again she said, "Thank you," and hoped he couldn't detect the way her hands shook. She dropped her arms to her sides.

"Your supplies are in. If you want, you can set up another field camp tomorrow."

He was so curt, so businesslike that it seemed he intended to keep his word. She drew herself up, willing to remain as distant. "I'll have to set Myra to the task of choosing a new name for our next camp."

Just then Barney Tinsley appeared in the hall. He shifted nervously from foot to foot, his hands riding the thick belt at his even thicker waist. His vest revealed a shirtfront that strained at the buttons around his belly.

"What is it?" Rory said, his tone holding a trace of annoyance at the interruption.

"Everybody's waitin' for you to come say a few words before we get started."

"I'll be right there." Rory explained, "My father always started out the rodeo with a prayer."

"Ah." She wished he would go.

He didn't. Instead he seemed to be memorizing every nuance of her appearance. His eyes swept over her, assessing, watching. She wished she had changed, that she wasn't wearing his mother's old blue calico dress. Somehow, wearing the soft, faded fabric made her feel more vulnerable than her own clothing. He held out the bundle wrapped in brown paper tied with twine.

"This is for you, too. I bought it when I was in Durango. I know you better than to think you'd change your mind about coming out today, but"—he reached around her to toss the bundle over to the bed—"I have nothing else to do with it."

Without another word, he turned around and left her staring into the empty hallway. The letter was heavy in her hand. She closed the door and then, alone in her self-imposed exile, Jessica stared at the bundle on the bed. It claimed her attention and her curiosity while the letter only gave her a sense of dread. She carried the letter over to the bed and set it down, deciding it could wait. When she lifted the package, she held it against her for a moment, wishing she could turn back time so that she and Rory would be as they were before his trip to Durango. Things had been much simpler then. Whitey was still alive and she was still innocent of what Rory's touch, his kiss, his very nearness could do to her.

Shouts of children playing near the open window filtered in with the sounds of revelry at the corral. Curiosity compelled her to open the package and see what Rory had purchased for her. She carefully removed the string and then unwrapped the paper. A glimpse of creamy yellow silk caught her eye, but before she unfolded the fabric, she let her fingers feel the delicious texture of it. A heavy lump was beginning to swell in her throat. She lifted the fabric and shook it out to its full length to reveal the most beautiful, most feminine gown she'd ever owned. She held it up in front of her and walked to the mirror over the washstand. The gown looked to be a perfect fit. How had he managed?

Jess tried to imagine Rory in Durango, a dusty, suntanned cowboy who had taken the time to stop and purchase the gown for her. Had he been as embarrassed as she surely would have been buying such a personal gift for him?

When she realized she was tenderly cradling the gown against her breast, Jess immediately held it away. The India silk whispered as she shook it out and spread it across the star quilt on the bed.

Trying to ignore a swell of cheers and laughter outside, Jess picked up the letter and walked over to the small secretary desk in the corner. The letter from Ramsey was dated June 20 and read:

> *Dear Miss Stanbridge,*
>   *Since no communication from you has yet arrived, I am writing to convey my sincere hope that you and Mr. Stoutenburg are meeting with some success in Colorado. It would behoove you to write as soon as possible as our esteemed benefactor, Mr. Beckworth, has been*

in contact with me as frequently as twice a week to inquire as to your progress.

As you know, time is of the utmost importance, as further funding will not be made available unless you are fortunate enough to discover a find of considerable size and scope before winter sets in and conditions become all but impossible for further search.

May I once again emphasize the need for frequent communication? I realize you are far afield, but I am afraid that given the situation, Beckworth is determined to be kept notified of your progress, if any.

Awaiting further word from you, I remain,
Gerald Ramsey, Director,
Harvard Museum of Natural History.

"Your progress, if any—"

Angered by the terse wording and the unwritten hint—"given the situation"—meaning that since she was a woman, Beckworth wanted to be informed of her every move, Jess crumpled the letter into a wad and threw it against the open secretary.

Damn him. She chewed on her thumbnail and stared at the desktop. What had Ramsey meant when he said he hoped that she and Stoutenburg were making good progress? She frowned and then retrieved the balled-up page. After carefully smoothing open the page, she examined the words again. Stoutenburg should have been back in Boston by the time the letter was penned—unless he had been far more ill than she and Myra ever suspected—

Loud whistles and cheers erupted outside. The image of Rory Burnett flying through the air and landing beneath the sharp, pounding hooves of any number of four-legged creatures chilled her to the bone.

She stared down at the letter again, knowing full well the one she just sent after the flood could not have reached Boston yet. Finding it impossible to concentrate with the riotous goings-on outside, Jessica gave up working on her maps and notes. Impatient with herself and her situation, she wished Rory had had the time to take her to the mesa before the conflict arose between them.

She glanced around the empty room. Since everyone was so preoccupied with the events of the day, they would not miss her. Why not ride up to the mesa and have a look around? She would have the early afternoon and evening to explore and be back before dark.

Her mind made up, Jessica hastily changed into her shirtwaist and skirt, then pulled her knapsack off the back of the chair and slipped the strap over her shoulder. Myra had brought her the gloves and the sun bonnet Rory had returned, so she put them in the knapsack with her notebook and pens.

The house was deserted as she slipped out the backdoor. Keeping to the back of the crowd, she skirted the corral and casually nodded to two women standing near the trestle tables by the big barn. One woman's words caught her attention. "There goes Rory Burnett getting up on that same critter that nearly killed him last year."

Her companion sighed and glanced back over her shoulder. "You'd think he'd learn, but he's no different than my Pete. When a man's crazy enough to be set on bull ridin', there ain't nothing a woman can do."

Jess halted abruptly and looked around. The barn appeared deserted for the moment, the door wide open. Men and women had climbed on the corral rails to watch, while some of the older folks sat on low benches set up near the rails. She saw the flash of a red plaid shirt high atop the far rail and couldn't keep from turning in the direction of the corral. Jess sidled up to the back of the crowd, looking for an opening—praying that there would not be one—and then a cheer went up. There was a shifting surge and her opportunity came. She quickly slipped in beside two broad-shouldered farmers in overalls and stood on tiptoe.

One of the men glanced down when he noticed her wedged between him and his companion. He shifted until Jess stood in front of him. Protected by the man's wide girth, she was just in time to see a gate on the far side of the corral open and Rory come flying out of a narrow chute clinging to the back of the biggest live slab of beef she'd ever seen.

Certain the great horned beast must weigh as much as a freight car, Jess covered her mouth with both hands to keep from crying out. Not that Rory would have heard her—the crowd was hooting and clapping, some were even whistling at a deafening pitch. The bull heaved and twisted, bucked and sometimes jumped with all four feet off the ground as it tried to rid itself of Rory in a far more agile way than she would ever have thought possible. Rory flailed around atop the furious animal like a rag doll. The only thing that kept him seated was a thick rope around the bull's middle, beneath which he had slipped one hand.

All too aware that the human spine contained twenty-five vertebrae, Jess wondered how many of Rory's would sustain permanent damage from the brutal pounding.

At one point the angry bull came kicking and bucking near the rail where Jessica stood. She could see the whites of the animal's eyes as the huge, sweating beast lunged and went charging past. Rory's hat flew off. It was quickly trampled, ground into the dirt beneath the bull's hooves.

Nauseated, she wanted to look away but couldn't. Seconds passed like hours. Finally Wheelbarrow began to beat two pans together and the crowd roared. Rory let go and flew off, hit the ground, and rolled away from the deadly hooves.

"He beat the time!" the man beside her shouted as he pounded the other farmer beside him on the back. "Beat the longest ride ever."

"Thought that damn Arthur was gonna kill 'im," the second man said.

While they shouted back and forth over her head, Jess watched as two men rushed out and supported Rory while a man waving a red rag darted across the corral and captured the animal's attention until the others could lead him safely away. Not until Rory slipped between the rails did Jessica take a deep breath and let the tension ease out of her shoulders.

Her legs shook as she pushed away from the rail and said, "Excuse me," to the men who had let her through. They moved aside and she escaped to the shade of the barn, where she leaned against the door frame and tried to collect herself.

Somehow, knowing Rory was safe made leaving that much easier. At least she wouldn't be imagining the worst all afternoon when she needed her wits about her. Just as she was about to step into the shadowed interior of the barn, she recognized the Ute named Piah. He came walking toward her. She looked around, wondering where he had come from. He seemed to have materialized out of thin air.

There was a cold, hard look in his eye, much like the one she had seen the day he visited the dig at the dry creek. He watched her for a moment without saying a word, glanced into the open barn, then back at her. Did he know what she had planned? Could he read her mind?

The man didn't nod or acknowledge her with anything more than a penetrating stare before he moved on. When she was certain he was no longer watching, she looked up toward the mesa. Thunderheads were gathering over the red-stained bluffs. If Piah's glance had not been warning enough, the clouds dampened her enthusiasm to steal away to the mesa. If she had learned nothing else, she knew what deadly power the storm clouds held.

Shifting the strap on her shoulder, she headed across the yard toward the house, careful to avoid Rory Burnett.

Rory dusted himself off, hooked his hand around the back of

his neck, and began to roll his head from side to side. Nothing hurt as bad as he thought it would after the backbreaking ride on Arthur—which was something he had sworn to make himself face after last year's near-tragic accident. His penchant for bull riding was something he never quite understood, especially when most of the men who rode bulls were the wild sort who also liked to shoot up the town on Saturday nights.

But now he'd looked his fear in the face and had held on long enough to break the last time set at the Silver Sage. Part of him wished Jess had been there to witness his triumph, but no matter how hard he tried, he couldn't quite imagine her enjoying a rodeo, which made him wonder once more why he ever proposed to her in the first place.

Punching the dents out of his muddied black hat, he thought about the question Myra had asked him two days ago. Did he love Jessica enough to give up the ranch? Then again, what did it matter how he felt? The way Jessica was acting toward him, he reckoned he'd never be forced to choose.

Rory slipped his battered hat on his head and was just dipping himself a drink of water out of a barrel at the corner of the barn when Piah stepped out of the shadows and headed toward him. He hadn't really expected the man to show up at the festivities. Nor did he look forward to conversing with the sullen Ute again, but there seemed no easy way out of a conversation.

"Piah." Rory nodded a greeting.

"I told you to keep the bone hunters away from the mesa."

Rory frowned. "I have kept them here on the ranch. The women haven't been to the mesa to look for bones at all."

"The spirits are still disturbed."

"What are you talking about?" Slipping a bandanna out of his back pocket, Rory dipped it into the water barrel, wrung it out, and then wiped the back of his neck with it. He glanced around to see if anyone was near enough to overhear. "Let's face it. You're the one who's still disturbed. Why?"

The silver conchos on Piah's hatband reflected the sunlight. His eyes were shaded by the wide hat brim; still, Rory could see the hate reflected there. "I told you to keep them away, but it is of no matter now, for the end is almost here."

He'd heard about religious fanatics who led their people to do whatever they commanded in the name of God. Was Piah about to lead a revolt, or was all this just superstitious talk meant to keep the cave from discovery and desecration like the Mesa Verde dwellings?

"I have done as you asked. I have kept the women away, but I'll tell you right now that one of them wants to go up there and I intend to take her to have a look around. That way I can make sure she won't find the cave."

Rory had the feeling that Piah almost smiled. Almost.

"When?"

"Soon," Rory replied. "I'm not sure."

"It is your decision," Piah said carefully.

"You're right, it is." Rory shifted his stance and glanced over to the corral where two men were team-roping a calf.

Piah walked away without another warning, unable to blend into the crowd because of his height and the tall black hat he wore.

Rory tied the damp bandanna around his neck and looked toward the house. At least Piah wouldn't be held responsible for ruining his day—Jessica had already managed to do just that. He hoped she was good and lonesome sitting inside all by herself.

As he rounded the corner of the barn, intending to watch the rest of the rodeo competition, he spied a khaki umbrella above the crowd. In a few more steps he found Jess wasn't beneath it, but Myra, and none other than Scratchy Livermore was holding the umbrella over her head. Beside him,

Woody Barrows stood twitching his mustache and looking disgusted with the whole situation.

Rory shook his head. Nothing like a couple of skirts around to make us all go plumb loco, he thought.

With her work at a standstill for the time being, Jessica decided to find something to read that might take her mind off of Rory Burnett, Piah's threatening presence, and Gerald Ramsey's letter. She wandered through the house, looked over a dusty row of books on a small bookshelf beside the parlor fireplace, and then wandered down the hall. Rory had offered Myra use of any of his books one evening and told her there were a few newer editions in his small office.

As she entered the compact space at the end of the hall, she felt as if she were trespassing in Rory's private sanctuary. A huge, hand-painted map was tacked to the wall above a rough-hewn desk that took up one side of the room. She leaned over the desk to study the map and recognized Cortez, the Sleeping Ute Mountain, and the Silver Sage borders.

Ledgers were stacked up to one side of the desk; silver-tipped pens, ink bottles, and a blotter had been shoved to the other side. In the center of the desk lay a composition book that appeared to be well traveled. The corners were bent and beginning to fray. There was nothing written on the front to indicate what had been recorded inside, but something about the well-worn condition of the book led her to believe it was much cherished.

She couldn't imagine Rory Burnett keeping a diary or journal. Perhaps the notebook only contained notes and observations having to do with running a big ranch. Her fingers itched to touch it. Jessica glanced over her shoulder. The door to the hallway was open, she could hear anyone who might approach. How could one little peek hurt? Besides, she reasoned, if Rory Burnett ever wanted to look through her notebooks, he was more than welcome to do so.

Her conscience eased somewhat, she reached out as if touching a hot rock and flipped open the cover of the composition book.

The first page was blank. It rustled as she turned it over and stared down at a page of poetry written in a clear, bold hand. There is nothing more personal than staring down at someone's handwriting. It seemed as though Rory were right there in the room.

She sat down on the swivel chair by the desk and was soon lost in Rory's poems. Most of his work concerned life on the ranch, the land, rusty pistols, wranglers, horses, and cow punching. The poems were eloquent in their simplicity. He wrote of blankets of wildflowers, winter's cold embrace, spring's soft rain. She could feel the bitter cold he experienced as he searched for cattle marooned in deep snow. The work spoke of life and death and seasons. The lines were clear and the images strong.

Not until she reached the last few entries did she notice a change in style, as if Rory had reached into his very soul for the words he'd penned. One particular title, "Blue Eyes," caught her attention.

Blue eyes under blue skies,
Though your lips won't call my name,
When you leave you'll take my heart
And things will never be the same.

Blue eyes under blue skies,
Hair golden in the sunset.
I've only kissed you once and yet
I never will forget.

Blue eyes under blue skies,
As I ride beneath the sun,
I tell myself, "Forget her,"

But my heart says, "She's the one."

Blue eyes under blue skies,
There's no place I'd rather be
Than there when the wind slips the pins from your hair
The way I wish you'd let me.

Blue eyes under blue skies
If I could only hold your heart
So close you'd never want to leave,
So close we'd never part.

Blue eyes under blue skies,
How can you walk away?
Knowing I'm nothing without you,
Knowing I want you to stay.

Blue eyes under blue skies
Even though I love you so,
Past promises will make me stay,
Past promises will make you go.

When she read the final line of the last stanza, there was
no doubt in her mind; he was writing about her, about his
feelings for her—expressing them so sincerely that her heart
ached. Never in her life had she dreamed she might be
regarded so tenderly by anyone—but the words on the page
were proof enough that this man had carved a place in his
heart for her, even though she had brought him nothing but
problems.

His marriage proposal had held no such words of love,
but here, hidden between the covers of a very ordinary
composition book, were all the love words a woman would
ever long to hear. Words that moved her beyond belief.

Jess sat for a time, staring down at the last entry, and then
slowly closed the notebook.

Just before dusk, Myra limped in without her crutches,

holding a plate of cold food, a knife, fork, and napkin, and found Jessica sitting in the parlor, an open book in her hands.

"What are you reading?" Myra asked. She set the food and utensils down on a round table beside Jessica's chair.

The supper smelled delicious. "*King Solomon's Mines*." Jess handed the book to Myra as she picked up the plate and proceeded to eat. "It's quite an adventure," Jessica told her between bites. The story was intriguing, but she couldn't keep her mind off of the haunting love poem Rory had written.

"So I've heard. May I read it after you?"

"Of course." Jessica picked up a piece of corn bread so rich it crumbled almost instantly. "Thanks for bringing me some food."

Myra sat down on a wide ottoman near Jessica's chair. "I won't beg you to join us outside, Jessica, but I think you should know that you are the one missing out."

Jessica set her fork down, her appetite suddenly gone. "I have reason enough for avoiding Rory without you badgering me."

Myra looked crushed. "I'm sorry, Jessica, I just hate to see you so miserable. More than that, I hate to see you go through life without really living it."

Jessica set the plate on the table beside her. Lamplight illuminated the tabletop and the arm of the chair. She leaned away from the halo of light, then fingered the beaded necklace as she glanced toward the open door and lowered her voice. "Remember when you said Rory Burnett and I were destined to be together?"

"Yes, why?"

"What if all that is true—"

"I truly believe such things are possible," Myra assured her.

"I'm not convinced, but if it's so, then I suppose it

wouldn't do any good for me to fight any feelings I might have toward him, would it?''

Confident in her answer, Myra smiled. "Of course not. But what is it you want, Jessica?''

"I always thought I knew exactly what I wanted, but right now I'm so confused.''

Myra rose carefully to her feet and tested her weight on her bad ankle. "I think my mental healing is working. You know, Emerson claims that a failure to give the mind control over the body promotes sickness." She pressed down hard once, then once more, but opted to stand on her good leg.

"Myra, what do you think I should do?''

"You'll never figure anything out hiding here in the shadows. I'm going back outside. The barn dance will begin in a few minutes and I think you should be there, that's what I think you should do.''

Jess rested her chin in her hand. "I'll think about it.''

"Well, think fast, because if you don't, you'll miss all the fun.''

Jessica was still alone when the music drifted in on the cool night air. Strains of fiddles and a guitar produced music so merry that it was hard to resist tapping her toes. She wondered if turning Rory down would send him into another woman's arms. She tried to put aside the vision of him dancing with someone else, laughing into someone else's eyes, whispering in another woman's ear. The very notion had her on her feet in an instant.

She'd heard him come in earlier, recognized his footsteps. She had blown out the lamp, listened half in fear that he'd find her in the dark parlor, waited to move until she heard him go back outside again. He hadn't called her name or looked for her. Now, as she entered her own room and lit the lamp, the first thing she saw was the yellow dress still spread across the bed as if he'd left her a silent invitation to join him.

Jessica walked to the side of the bed, reached down and touched the rich India silk, admired its buttery color, and imagined what the fabric would feel like when she slipped it on.

Rory's words echoed in her mind.

I give up. I won't touch you again. If you're so all-fired determined to turn your back on any chance we have together, then so be it. I'm tired of making a fool of myself.

The strains of a waltz surrounded her, tempted her, brought back rich memories of the feel of Rory's strong embrace. What would it be like to dance with him? Could he teach her the steps?

I give up.

What was it he'd said about books and boxes of bones not keeping her warm at night?

I won't touch you again.

What else could he teach her about a man and a woman? With all her education and knowledge she was ignorant of so much. There were still so many things she wanted to know, things she didn't want to live a lifetime without experiencing. *Live life,* Myra had said. She thought of Whitey, of how his young life was snuffed out. Couldn't she give Rory a chance, give herself a chance at love without giving up her dream? Shouldn't she at least try?

Jessica reached up and began to pull the pins out of her hair.

Rory leaned back against the wall and watched the dancers whirl by. Tad Pickering, a farmer near his own age, waltzed his wife past. They only had eyes for each other. Across the room he caught a glimpse of Fred Hench. All decked out in his fanciest boots, tooled-leather cuffs, and a silver bolo tie, the cowboy was fast-talking a farmer's daughter into stepping outside with him. Rory could tell by the couple's worried glance around the room before they slipped away that both of them were afraid of the girl's daddy. The man was known to have a terrible temper.

Woody Barrows sat as close to Myra Thornton as possible on a low bench near the refreshment table. Scratchy was nowhere to be seen. Wheelbarrow may have lost the battle of the umbrella, but he obviously hadn't given up the war.

It seemed like everyone had paired up with someone else. Common sense told him that wasn't true, but it sure seemed that way as he stood alone and watched the others. Some of the wallflowers standing along the back wall had given him the eye. Any other time he would have felt it his duty as host to give them all a turn on the dance floor. But this year his heart simply wasn't in it.

The Utes, who never stayed for the dance, had departed when supper ended. He felt relieved not to have seen Piah face-to-face again that afternoon, but he had caught the man watching him closely and wondered why. He had kept his word and protected the secret of the cave, not only for the Utes but for his own selfish reasons. There was no way he wanted the disturbance that such a discovery would cause, not on his land, anyway. Not if he could help it. But his conscience still bothered him. What about Jess?

Still leaning against the wall, he shifted his weight, crossed his arms over his chest, then crossed his ankles, hoping a lazy attitude would put off anyone who wanted to plague him with idle chitchat. He just wasn't in the mood.

The musicians—two fiddlers, a guitar-playing cowhand, a squeezebox player, and a man with a mouth organ—struck up a lively rendition of "Turkey in the Straw" and a cheer went up from the crowd. Couples who hadn't been dancing took to the floor and the foot stomping commenced again. Dust rose from the straw-littered ground. If anyone noticed the pungent smell of animal dung that lingered on the air, they didn't let it hamper their fun.

It wasn't until the third verse that Rory glanced toward

the open doorway, curious to see if Fred Hench and the farmer's daughter had reappeared. His heart stopped when he caught a glimpse of Jess framed in the doorway, wearing the fancy gown he'd given her.

He pushed away from the wall. The revelers went right on stomping and shouting as if the world hadn't just righted itself. When the dancers blocked his view of the door, he nearly panicked, afraid that when they parted again, Jess would have disappeared. He started shoving his way through the crowd.

"Hey, watch it!" someone shouted.

"Want to dance?" One of the wallflowers had decided to go it alone.

He nearly tripped over a child playing hide-and-seek between the dancers—and then he had Jess in sight again.

She hadn't moved, in fact, she looked bewildered by the chaotic scene before her and obviously hadn't seen him yet. He forced himself to slow down as he stood on the edge of the crowd and simply stared at her.

The music ended and the dancers began to break up and move back to the edges of the floor. One of the fiddlers called out that he had to have a drink or he'd die of thirst. Everyone laughed.

Everyone but Rory. He was too intent on reaching Jess before anyone else saw her. She was a vision, a perfect vision with her sun-kissed blond hair twisted atop her head in a loose bun, pert satin bows at her elbows, the wide sash teasing her waist. More beautiful than any other woman in the room, she stood on the threshold, hesitation in her eyes as she searched the crowd.

He stepped forward.

She saw him at last, but didn't smile.

He closed the distance between them.

Jess straightened her shoulders and primly folded her hands at her waist.

He wanted to laugh, he wanted to shout hallelujah to the

rafters, grab her up in his arms, and twirl her around the room. Instead he merely stepped up to her and spoke just loud enough to be heard over the crowd.

"I didn't think you were coming."

CHAPTER

14

•

She was moved by the relief in his eyes. "I didn't think I would either," she said.

"What changed your mind?"

How could she tell him that she had decided life was too brief to waste sitting alone in the dark? How could she confess that his poetry had given her a glimpse into his heart? That it had melted hers?

"I wanted to let you know that I'm sorry for the way I acted after—well, after the other day. I realize I'm just as much to blame as you are."

He shook his head. "Blame? Why should anyone be blamed for something that was bound to happen?"

"Was it?"

"I'm sure it was."

"I wish I could be as sure."

He took her hand in his "May I?"

Her silence was her only consent. She looked down at her fingers enfolded in his.

He bent down and whispered, "You look beautiful."

Embarrassed, she looked away. No one had ever told her she was beautiful. She'd spent far too many years trying to prove otherwise.

The music began again, and as if fate stepped in, the selection was a waltz. "May I have this dance?" he asked.

Jessica felt a slight sense of panic. "I don't know how," she reminded him.

"I can teach you in a minute." His fingers pressed hers warmly, encouraging her to say yes.

"I'm afraid I'd be too embarrassed." She looked down and noticed he was wearing new boots. They were so shiny that the leather still shone through the dust from the dirt floor and the straw scattered over it. When she looked up at him again, she realized he was wearing a black, bib-front shirt with two rows of pearl buttons she had never seen before.

"Then let's step outside and practice until we have it right." When she balked, he added, "That's all we'll do. Dance."

Jessica let her lead him out into the sultry night. There were other couples in the darkness, some walking together hand in hand, others whispering softly. She felt brazen, excited and scared all at once. When they were out of the shaft of light that poured through the open barn door, Rory slipped one arm around her waist and held her hand with the other.

"Don't look down," he instructed, "just listen to the music and glide with me. One." He stepped forward, but she didn't budge. "You have to move if you intend to dance."

Jessica licked her lips. "I'll try," she promised.

"Again. One." This time when he stepped out, she followed. "Two." They moved forward again, Rory confident, Jessica awkward as a newborn colt. "Now a step back," he said. "Three."

It was slow going at first. Jessica moved without listening to the music, but to the instructions he whispered softly in her ear. "One, two, three. One, two, three." They struggled through the motions until Rory stopped and sighed. "Don't concentrate so hard, Jess. Just let yourself go and listen to the music. I'll do the counting in my head."

"Let myself go?"

"I know that's not something you're in the habit of practicing but trust me. I know what I'm doing."

"I'm sure you do," she assured him.

He chuckled, a low, rumbling sound deep in his throat. "Let's try again."

They did, and this time instead of aiming for perfection, Jessica let herself rely on Rory's skill and gave in to the pulse of the music. After a few missed steps she began to float with him until she was suddenly moving as free and unfettered as a baby bird taking wing for the first time. They danced in the darkness, enfolded by the fertile barnyard scents and clear night air. Countless stars smiled down upon them. When the music ended, neither of them moved to let go of the other, but instead they waited, breathless, until another waltz began. This time Rory moved with her, danced her out of the darkness into the well-lit barn, where they joined the others who were gliding and dipping to the beat of the waltz.

She thought it was wicked for him to hold her so close in front of so many people, but a quick look around told her no one was paying them any mind. Her hand rested lightly on his shoulder. She savored the feel of his shirt and the warmth beneath it by moving her fingertips ever so slightly across it. He noticed immediately, for he tightened his grip on her waist, and when she looked up, Jessica found him staring down into her eyes. She faltered and trod on his toes.

"I'm sorry," she whispered, but he quickly recovered the steps and they moved on.

"You're bound to make a few mistakes in the beginning.'' His slight smile told her he didn't care if she did. ''Myra's had quite a day,'' he added.

Jess looked over her shoulder in the direction he indicated and saw her friend sitting beside Woody Barrows. Although she never took her eyes off the dancers, Myra smiled and nodded as Woody spoke into her ear. When she spied Jessica, her face lit up immediately and she waved. Jess wriggled the fingertips of the hand Rory held in his before they moved on.

When the dance ended, one of the fiddlers called out, ''We're gonna wet our whistles, folks. I suggest y'all do the same.''

Jessica tried to hide her disappointment when Rory let her go. She looked around at the boisterous crowd. It seemed everyone knew each other. ''Do you know all of these people?'' she wanted to know.

''Most of them. Not many people move in or out of the valley. Most of the people my age were born here.''

She realized she knew none of her neighbors back home. Except for Myra, there hadn't been time to make friends outside of the museum. ''You're quite lucky, you know.'' She met his curious look. ''You have so many friends.''

Rory looked around the crowded barn. ''I never really thought about it before. My ma and pa were good at making and keeping friends.'' He rested his hand at the small of her back again. When she didn't protest, he added, ''I'd like for us to at least be friends, Jess, if I can't have more.''

Knowing how much more he really wanted, she said, ''This is hard for me, Rory.''

''Why?''

''Because I've never let myself get close to anyone, except my father, and Myra, of course.''

''Don't you think it's about time you did?''

She glanced around to be certain no one was listening before admitting quietly, ''I wanted to wear this dress for you, and dance my first dance with you.''

"And now that you have?"

"I'm glad I did."

He was watching her talk, concentrating on her lips. Slowly, almost imperceptibly, he lowered his head, but as his lips drew near hers he suddenly stopped, remembering where they were. "I'd like to show you something," he whispered.

She nodded and let him lead her out of the barn. For the second time that night they drifted out into the darkness. The sound of talk and laughter filled the air. Others followed them out. Rory led her to the corral. He leaned back against the fence and was quiet for so long that she began to grow uncomfortable. "What was it you wanted to show me?"

"Look up, Jess."

She did as he asked and saw the intense blanket of stars in the heavens above them. There were so many that it was hard to see a patch of sky. The constellations stood out among the unnamed, uncharted billions.

Jessica told him softly, "I used to stare up at them when we were camping. I even tried to count them one night, but they shimmer, so that it's as if they won't stand still and allow it."

Rory hooked his arms over the rail and leaned his head back. "I love to look up at them, especially when I have problems. It reminds me of how very insignificant my troubles are. When I see all those stars, I tell myself how lucky I am just to be alive and able to see them every night."

She stepped up on the bottom rail and hung on to the top. "Maybe you should write a poem about them."

"Maybe I will," Rory said. He was staring at her again, she could tell, so she tried hard to concentrate on the sky until he said, "Out of all those billions of stars, just like out of all the people on earth, we've found each other, Jess."

Jessica pushed off the fence rail and stepped down.

"Are you willing to ignore that?" he asked.

The music started up again and the other dancers hurried back into the barn. He stepped away from the fence. Assuming she wanted to avoid answering, he said, "Let's get back."

Jessica moved to his side and walked back toward the crowded barn, wishing he would take her hand, afraid to reach out for his and start something she knew she would never be able to stop.

Alone once more, Jessica changed clothes without lighting the lamp. She moved around the darkened interior of her room like a sleepwalker in a dream, still wrapped in the cocoon of pleasurable memories of dancing in Rory's arms. As she pulled the huge nightgown over her head and then let down her hair, she wondered how she would ever get to sleep tonight.

Myra had stopped moving around in the room next door long ago. Jessica smiled when she thought of her outspoken friend and the cowboys who vied for her hand. Myra had made quite a show of her determination to treat both Scratchy Livermore and Woody Barrows, or Wheelbarrow, fairly—but Jessica suspected that Myra would eventually choose her books and her home in Boston over either of them.

But what of herself? What should she do now that she knew the depth of Rory Burnett's feelings for her? He had not proposed merely out of pity—that was all too clear now—but out of love for her. Jess wandered over to the bed and picked up her new gown, shook it out, and tucked it carefully into the armoire. Then she moved to the wash basin, poured a little water from a tall pitcher, and splashed some over her face.

While patting her cheeks and neck dry, she wished it was as easy for her to know exactly how she felt about Rory Burnett. Did she love him? Quite possibly, but there was no scientific formula to help her be sure. If she were to deduce the truth the way she might approach the dating of a saurian, she would simply compare her feelings for Rory Burnett with previous circumstances of a similar nature; but in this case there were no similar circumstances for comparison. She had never been attracted to any man before, nor had anyone every made such serious advances.

She sat down in the armless rocker and set it in motion. The slow movement of the chair lulled her some, but not into restfulness. She crossed her arms and thought some more. How could she carry on with her work with such a dilemma dogging her every step of the way? What if this was her only chance at love?

Mulling over the possibilities of ever falling in love with any of the men she had known, scientists all—well, the thought didn't even bear thinking of. They were her peers, they were knowledgeable—some were even what a woman would call handsome in a refined sort of way—but now that she had met Rory Burnett, Jessica knew she would compare every other man to him.

So then, what is my recourse? she wondered. How could she get past the self-imposed barrier she'd set up around her heart? And once the barrier was behind her, how might she pursue both her work and a life with Rory Burnett?

Enough of this. She stood up, her bare feet soundless on the wide plank flooring. Some warm milk, or at the very least water, would help her sleep. She tiptoed to the door, intent on raiding the crockery jar of milk that she knew Scratchy kept in the little adobe room beneath the water tower outside the kitchen.

Once she reached the hallway, she noticed that the door to Rory's room was open. Seeing by the moonlight filtering through the window that he was still out, she trod carefully. When she reached the kitchen, she carefully opened the backdoor and then the screen door, making certain it did not squeak. She lifted the hem of the long nightgown above the red clay earth as she hurried to the springhouse where the fruits, vegetables, and other perishables were stored.

The heavy door swung inward and Jess followed it, careful not to stub her toe on the threshold. Only weak light from a sliver of moon illuminated the interior of the room. The dirt floor was damp and cool, quite a change from the dry ground outside. The room was scented with an odd heady combination of citrus and mildew. She put her hands out in front of her to feel her way toward the broad shelf where Scratchy kept the milk.

"Who's in there?" A man's deep voice echoed off the walls.

Jess screamed and jumped, dropped the hem of the gown, and then promptly tripped on it. As she went sprawling to the soft, earthen floor, she let out an "Oomph!" as the wind went out of her.

"Jess?" Rory moved toward the white shadow writhing on the floor. "Jess? Are you all right?" He knelt over her and pulled her to a sitting position.

Gasping for air, she grumbled, "Do I sound all right?"

He pulled her to her feet and tried to dust her off, but when his hand came in contact with a pliant breast beneath the thin cotton, she batted it away.

"Please," she said quickly, "I'm fine. Just let go of me."

His hands lingered a moment too long. Jessica lifted her skirt again and turned to head out of the room.

Rory felt her retreat and reached out. His hand connected with the crook of her elbow and he held her fast. "Slow down a minute." He could see her profile in the weak light as she stared toward the open doorway. "Please, Jess. Don't go yet."

She stopped struggling, but wouldn't look back at him. "I wanted some milk. I'm sorry. I have to go back."

"Why? Are you still afraid to be alone with me?"

"We shouldn't—"

"We're not doing anything."

"No, but—"

"Unless you're thinking impure thoughts." He felt her stiffen and her hair swirled around her shoulders and hips as she swung around to argue.

"I'm thinking no such thing."

"Then what's the rush? Let me find that milk for you." He let her go.

Jessica tried not to breathe a too-audible sigh of relief. Squinting in the darkness, she could see enough to know that he hadn't moved. "Well, are you getting the milk or not?"

"How about an orange? We got a whole crate of them at the store."

She wanted to tell him no, to rush back to the safety of her room, but felt her mouth water as she imagined a cool, fresh orange. Jess sighed again. "All right."

He rustled around in the darkness for a moment, then came back to her side. "Got 'em."

"And the milk?"

"I take it you couldn't sleep."

"That's right."

"I found something to cure what ails you."

Handing her two oranges, Rory took her by the elbow again and led her to the open doorway. They stepped outside and paused just beyond the doorway. She could see him clearly now, his new boots and shirt, his hat. He towered over her as he stood there holding a long, slender bottle in one hand. "Midnight snack," he whispered, raising what was obviously a wine bottle.

"What were you doing out here?" she whispered back suspiciously.

"I was making certain everything was cleaned up and all the lanterns were safely out in the barn. I was just about to turn in when I heard someone in the springhouse. By the way, don't ever think about becoming a thief. You're awful noisy."

"As if I would."

"Come on." He tugged on her arm again and reluctantly she followed him across the barnyard.

"Where are we going?"

"Not far. I left the barn open."

She took him at his word and kept walking. He couldn't believe his stubborn Miss Stanbridge was complying with his wishes. Rory slowed down as they passed the bunkhouse, and Jess thought she heard snoring as they snuck past a one-room version of the wood-and-adobe ranch house.

When they reached the barn, he went in first. Against the far wall, a lantern burned low over a long workbench.

"You can come on in," he told her.

She tried to see past the shadows and shook her head. "Oh, no. I don't think so."

"Are you afraid of the dark?"

"It's not the dark I'm afraid of."

He whispered, "I didn't think so, but after the respectable way I behaved myself at the dance tonight, I think you could trust me."

"Somehow I feel like Little Red Riding Hood facing the wolf."

"Come on in before someone hears us and comes snooping around."

"Maybe I want to be rescued," she said, glancing at the bunkhouse.

"Then why are you still whispering?"

"Why don't we go sit on the veranda—"

"Don't go fancying things up. It's a porch."

"The porch, then."

"This is where I come when I want to think. Always has been."

"That must account for your lack of thought lately."

"I have to turn down the light," he told her. As he walked into the barn she followed close behind, careful to keep the long nightgown from tripping her. Rory moved to the back wall and reached for the lantern. Just as he started to turn it down he glanced back and was surprised to find her next to him.

Rory smiled down at her. "Why don't we have our snack right here?"

She swallowed. "Here?"

"Why not?"

She shrugged. "Why not." Her heart was beating triple time as she followed him to an empty stall that was piled high with fresh alfalfa.

"It's not fancy," he said softly.

"We won't be here that long," she said, wondering why she had agreed to stay at all. *You're in dangerous waters, Jessica Stanbridge, and you know it.*

Ignoring her nagging conscience, Jessica smoothed the skirt of the nightgown and sat down in the pungent hay.

"Is this supposed to be comfortable?"

"You'll get used to it. Settle back and relax." Rory turned the lamp down to a soft glow. He sat it on the ground, well away from the hay.

She stayed right where she was, trying to sit up in the soft mound of hay, keeping her eyes on the door, wondering how quickly she could get out if her bravado faltered.

Rory tossed her two oranges. "Start peeling." Then he slipped a pocketknife from his back pocket and began to work on the wine cork.

"And the peels?"

"Toss them on the floor."

"Toss them on the floor," she repeated, as if trying to absorb the meaning behind the words. Realizing there was no alternative, and with a newfound sense of freedom, she did just that and the heady scent of citrus colored the air.

He grumbled all the while he was digging out the cork. Jess held the two peeled oranges in her hands, trying to keep them out of the hay. The juice dripped between her fingers onto her gown.

"Are you about done? I'm a mess."

He glanced over at her. Jess was barely visible in the semidarkness. Rory leaned toward her as if to assess the truth of her statement. "You certainly are, Miss Stanbridge."

"Could you hurry, please. I'd like to get back to bed."

And I'd love to go with you. Rory held his tongue, not wanting to scare her back into the house now that they had come so far.

"All done." He held out the bottle. "No silver cups, no glasses, but would you care for a swig? Oh, and don't mind any bits of cork you might run across."

"I don't believe I'll have any, thank you. Besides, my hands are full." She offered him an orange.

He set the bottle down, took the orange, and then took hold of her wrist. He pulled her empty hand to his lips and began to lick the orange juice from her palm.

At the touch of his tongue a shiver raced down her spine to her thighs. She tried to recover her hand, but he held it fast.

She whispered, "I knew I shouldn't have come."

"And yet you did. Why, Jess?" He let go of her, and although he was waiting for an answer, he pretended to concentrate on separating the segments of his orange.

She wiped her palm on the gown, hoping to still the tingling sensations. "I'm conducting an experiment."

"Then I can assume I've at least achieved the status of one of your ancient relics."

She already knew what he was capable of. It was her own emotions she needed to define. "Not exactly."

"Can I be of any help?"

"I'm afraid there won't be any experiment without your cooperation," she told him honestly as she bit into a luscious section of orange.

Rory finished his and leaned back into the hay. He hadn't even had a swallow of wine and yet he felt incredibly warm inside. It didn't matter what happened, or didn't happen, now. It was enough that she was here, that Jessica Stanbridge had let down her hair, enough to join him in some banter and a quiet interlude. It was enough that she trusted herself and him enough to be alone together in the dark.

He heard her smack her lips as she licked the juice from her own fingers this time. He ignored the aching need that made itself known the moment he found her alone in the springhouse and concentrated on putting her at ease. "About this experiment," he said, truly curious, "when does it start? Or has it?" He reached out for the wine and leaned back again, tipping the bottle up for a drink.

"It began when I agreed to leave the springhouse with you."

When he passed her the bottle, she took a long drink. "My whole life," she began, staring into the darkness that separated them, "I've been taught to ask questions, to be certain everything is carefully labeled and classified. Life is divided into very distinct categories. Sometimes I feel like the part of me that's a scientist is always watching and analyzing my emotional life as it unfolds. I think that's why I find it so hard to 'let go,' as you say."

"So what is it you're curious about?" He felt triumphant knowing what it cost her to open up to him.

She was glad his expression was almost hidden by the shadows. "Today I was in your office looking for something to read."

He went still, half suspecting what she was about to tell him.

"I read your poems."

Rory took another long swallow of wine and passed the bottle back. "So?"

Jessica held the wine on her lap. He was waiting for her to say something. She took a deep breath. "They were very moving, very clear and direct. You wrote love words about me."

"I love you."

He made it all sound so very simple. After a sip of wine she asked, "How do you know?"

"Is this the scientist asking?"

"No, the woman."

"I think I probably loved you the minute I laid eyes on you."

"Then this is purely physical?" Disappointment crept into her tone.

"How about if you let me finish, Jess?" He sighed. "Of course, I didn't know I loved you then. In fact, I thought you were one of the most exasperating women I'd ever met, but I guess that's part of what attracted me to you. You're determined, headstrong. You'll never let anyone push you around or do anything you don't want to do. You know what you want and you're not about to let anything get in your way."

"And you consider those endearing qualities?"

"Well, remember, you're talking to a man who likes to ride bulls, too." He laughed at his own wit, then added, "I wouldn't have thought that's what I'd look for in a woman before I met you, but you worked your way into my mind, Jess, just the way you've slipped into my heart and my life. I can't help it if I like having you here."

Lifting the bottle to her lips, she took another sip and then passed it back to him. Their hands brushed in passing. "I saw you ride Arthur in the rodeo today. It scared me to death. I realized then that my feelings for you ran far deeper than I suspected. Then later, when I found the poems, I wasn't sure about anything anymore."

Rory shook his head, pleased to learn she had been there to watch him succeed where he had once failed. "You were quite a busy gal today, weren't you?"

"Are you mad?"

"Not a bit." He set the bottle aside and leaned toward her. "I'm glad we're getting all this out in the open."

Jessica watched his shadow loom nearer. She waited, breathless, for him to draw near enough to touch.

"May I kiss you, Jess?"

She tipped her face up to his. "Yes," she whispered. "Yes. I'd like that."

Before he did, he reached over and turned out the light, then caught her face between his hands. Her lips were tangy and scented with orange. His lips tempted, tasted, and then delved, yet he purposely held himself back, so hungry for her that he was afraid he might devour her.

Jess moaned and reached out to steady herself. She grabbed his sleeves and held on tight as he deepened the kiss and pressed her back into the prickly hay, but all discomfort was forgotten as she lost herself in the heady sensations his kiss evoked.

When the kiss ended, he gathered up handfuls of her unbound hair, buried his face in it, and then whispered in her ear, "I've wanted to do this for so long. Your hair reminds me of sunbeams. You should never pin it up the way you do. It should be free." Rory ran his fingers through the silken mass again and again until he was hungry for the taste of her lips once more.

Jessica tried to grow accustomed to having him stretched out so casually across her. She had always thought it would be most uncomfortable to have a man's heavy weight pressing down upon her, but now discovered that Rory had a way of leaning on his elbows to keep from crushing her. She let him finger-comb her hair and then kiss her again. In the darkness there was no need to let shyness close her eyes. She kept them open, thankful for the night shadows surrounding them.

His insistent onslaught sent such shock waves through her that she could no longer resist running her hands over his shoulders, down his arms, across his back. He pressed her down into the hay and she clung to him, relishing the feel of his back muscles moving beneath the soft cambric shirt. She felt herself growing hot and knew it was not because of the warm July night. Deep inside she was experiencing a mounting need, one that was growing more powerful with every passing second, one that could no longer be denied.

"I want to touch you, Jess."

Her racing heartbeat intensified. She was not afraid of this man, for she knew now that he loved her, but she was afraid of herself, knowing full well that her control was hanging by a slender thread. He nipped gently at her neck, then her shoulder. His fingers worked at the buttons of the voluminous nightgown.

She let him slip the buttons open one by one and then slide the gown off one shoulder and down past her breast. Jessica hid her face against his collarbone. The night air was alive with the sound of their combined breath, his murmuring against her flesh as he kissed his way from her earlobe down her shoulder to her breast.

When his teeth gently toyed with her hardened, sensitive nipple, when his tongue teased and tempted it until she was writhing beneath him, she ceased to think, to analyze, to fight fate any longer.

He took his mouth from her breast, briefly kissed her lips, and whispered over them, "How's the experiment going, Professor?"

Languidly she trailed her fingertips over his shoulders. "I won't have any results until it's complete."

Rory went very still. He was hard and ready, eager to have her, but that in itself was nothing new. Her acquiescence was. "Are you sure?"

"I'm not afraid."

Certain he had heard her wrong or that he had mistaken her meaning, he asked, "Do you know what you're saying, Jess?"

"I haven't had enough wine to fuddle my mind, if that's what you mean. I wouldn't have stayed if I was scared of what's about to happen. I'm here because I want to know what happens at a time like this. I *have* to know. I may never have another chance."

He was puzzled. Very slowly he drew away from her and sat up. "Then you haven't changed your mind about our getting married?"

She shook her head sadly. "No. I can't even think about that until my work for the museum is over."

"And when will that be?"

"I don't know."

He could see her silhouetted against the hay, could barely make out the ivory skin of her shoulders and breasts. She was willing to give her body to him, but not her heart. He wanted more. He wanted it all. He wanted her with him forever.

"Rory?" She reached out to him again, the warm, liquid ache in her too strong to deny. "Please say something."

"I want you, Jess. But—"

She pulled him down until he was atop her again. "And I want you. I want you to be the one to teach me what love and loving is all about. Before you left for Cortez, you said you wanted me to want you. I do want you. But please, don't make me beg." She reached up and ran her fingers through his thick hair. It was midnight black in the darkness. The tautness slowly left his shoulders and she felt him relax against her again.

"And afterward?"

She refused to tell him anything but the truth. "I can't make any promises."

"If that's the way you want it." He sat up again.

She thought he was going to leave her then and there until she heard the rustle of fabric and realized he was pulling his shirt over his head. Uncertain about how to proceed, she lay still, barely daring to breathe until he had shucked off his boots and pants.

"I wish it was light. I wish I could see all of you," he

whispered as he lay down beside her, his head propped on his elbow.

Sure she would die of embarrassment doing what she was about to do in broad daylight, Jessica blessed the darkness. Without another word, he reached out and trailed his fingers over her breasts again. "I'm going to take off your gown."

Afraid she would lose her nerve, she implored, "Please kiss me again."

He did. And when he had done so thoroughly, Rory slipped his hands beneath the hem of her gown. He ran his palms up her legs, over her thighs and hips, and then encircled her waist. Her gown slowly rose, exposing her to the night air as he explored her body. It amazed her that his touch could be so gentle—so feather light. As her anticipation heightened, fear of the unknown fled.

She sat up as he slipped the gown over her head and then spread the cotton lawn beneath her. When he leaned over her again, she could feel his manhood, hard and erect, pressing against her thigh. Jessica closed her eyes. She arched against him when he dipped his head to her breasts, caressed them with his hands and lips, then began to slide his tongue down the hollow between them. He laid his cheek against her abdomen and hugged her close, then kissed her softly. She buried her fingers in his hair and tugged gently until he slid over her again, covering her with his heat and weight.

When he slipped a finger up inside her without warning, she gasped, then began to moan and thrash as he stroked and petted her until she thought she couldn't stand it any longer. Surely there could be no greater ecstasy than this. Pressing herself up against his hand, she begged for more.

"Shh. Slow down, Jess. We're just getting started."

"Please," she begged. "Please, Rory."

"Please what?" He kissed her again, but his hand didn't stop its maddening movement. "Please stop?"

"No," she gasped. "Don't stop." Her shyness fell away

and she reached out to him, let her hands explore him, clenched him to her, and rubbed her breasts against the crisp mat of hair that covered his broad chest.

Rory shuddered. She was ready for him now, more than ready—she was hot and willing. He had wanted her an hour ago. Now he was ready to explode. Unwilling to wait any longer, he raised himself over her and spread her legs with his knee. She cried out when his hand left her, clasped him to her as a sob tore from her throat.

"All right, Jess. All right." He kissed her temple, her lashes, her lips, and then slipped his hands beneath her hips to tilt her up to receive him.

"It will hurt at first," he whispered in her ear.

She heard him talking but was too lost in sensation to comprehend. All Miss Jessica Stanbridge, paleontologist for the Harvard Museum of Natural History, was conscious of at that moment was the man hovering over her, ready to plunge his hardened shaft into her more-than-willing body. She complied by lifting her hips against him and moaned with delight when she felt the silken tip of his shaft tease the moist opening between her thighs.

Rory nearly lost his composure and then his seed when she bucked against him and teased him with her heated flesh. He dipped into her, prodded her womanhood, tested, tempted, probed further with each stroke until he was slick with her essence. She moaned, thrashed, grasped his buttocks, and raked him lightly with her fingernails.

With each guiding thrust he opened her until he knew it was a matter of tearing her maidenhood before he could bury himself deep inside her.

Jessica was wild with need. Imploring him with her soft cries did not help—he seemed intent on torturing her forever—sliding in and out, in and out until she wanted to scream. There had to be more. This could not be all there was to the art of lovemaking. If there was no surcease, no way to ease the fury of the fire he'd stoked inside her, she would certainly go mad. When he rocked back again, Jessica wrapped her legs around his waist and clung to him, desperate not to let him escape this time.

As he pulled back for the final thrust that would carry him home, he felt her long, graceful legs wrap about his waist and hold him tight. He plunged to the hilt inside her, heard her gasp and then whimper. For a moment he went still, afraid he'd hurt her, until she began to undulate her hips. "Hold on, Jess," he whispered. "Hold on."

He wanted to prolong her pleasure, wanted to bring her to the brink and beyond again and again, but she was beyond thought, beyond reason—and she was carrying him along with her as her movements became more frantic. Panting, crying out, she communicated her need with lips and hands until he felt her arch beneath him and clasp him tight between her thighs.

She screamed when her release came. The sound matched the wild contractions that echoed inside her and brought him to his own fulfillment. Rory couldn't hold back his own cry as he spewed forth his seed with a force and fury that overwhelmed him.

Shaken by what had just passed between them, they were content to lie quiet in each other's arms. Rory gathered Jessica into his arms and held her close, measured the slowing of her heartbeat with his hand, and buried his face in her hair.

She didn't move, didn't speak for so long that he thought at first she had fallen asleep. He closed his eyes against the darkness.

Far from sleepy, Jessica felt him relax, listened to his breathing as it became slow and regular. The clinical description of intercourse her father had given her when she had started her menses was worlds away from the feast of senses she and Rory had just shared. It was a wondrous miracle. A celebration of life that made her feel whole. For the first time in her life she was thankful to be a woman.

"Rory?" When he didn't respond, she nudged him. "Rory, wake up."

He didn't move. "Hmm."

"Is it always like that?"

"No." The word was no more than a mumbled grunt against her shoulder.

Jessica frowned at the pitched ceiling. Had she done something wrong? Could it have been better? "I guess it must not be as pleasurable doing this with someone who's inexperienced."

He raised himself to an elbow and leaned down over her. "*What* are you talking about?"

"I didn't really know what to expect, you know, or what to do. I'm sure it must be so much more enjoyable for you when—"

He put his finger over her lips. "Jess, I'm almost afraid to find out what making love to you will be like now that you do know what to do."

"You don't have to lie."

Rory chuckled, and although he couldn't see it clearly as he'd like, he began spreading her hair out around her like a tremendous halo. "Until tonight I never knew it could be like this. You're a natural, Jess, so don't give it another thought." He ran his hand over her hip and then rested his palm possessively on her thigh. "There is one thing, though."

"Oh? And what's that?" In a daring mood, she linked her arm about his neck and pulled him close.

"I would have lost money if anyone ever bet me you'd be a screamer."

CHAPTER

15

An hour later they snuck back into the house, careful not to let the screen door bang. Rory knew where every squeaking floorboard lay and carefully directed Jessica around them. When she turned to slip inside her room, he grabbed hold of her elbow and spun her back into his arms. She stood on tiptoe and pressed against him to bid him farewell with a luxuriously long, heated kiss.

When it ended, Rory put his lips directly over her ear and whispered, "I love you, Jess. I love you enough to abide by any decision you make, but I want you to know I'm still going to try my damnedest to get you to marry me. Especially now." Then he let her go and turned away.

Still warm and glowing inside, Jessica closed the door, sponged herself off, and crawled into bed.

Far too close to dawn, Jessica was awakened by a light, incessant tapping on her door. She struggled into a sitting position, shoved her hair out of her eyes, and grumbled, "Come in." She could hear men shouting back and forth in the corral and a hammer clanging against an anvil. She was surprised the racket hadn't already awakened her.

The door opened and Myra, dressed in her familiar khaki walking skirt and tailored jacket, barged in. She glanced back over her shoulder in a most secretive way before she closed the door and hurried as fast as her limp would allow to Jessica's bedside.

"Are you all right?" Myra looked her over with a concerned frown on her face.

"Of course I'm all right." Jessica pulled herself up straighter and jerked her nightgown closed. It seemed she'd missed a few buttons in her haste to dress in the barn. "Why shouldn't I be?"

Myra's obvious struggle to give her an answer was almost comical. She folded her arms, unfolded them, arched a brow, and then put her hands on her hips. "Because I couldn't sleep in the middle of the night and thought I had heard you pacing around in here earlier, so I came in to see if you'd like something from the kitchen." She tapped her foot against the floorboards. "I found the room empty."

Jessica felt her color rise and concentrated on the quilt pattern. "I couldn't sleep, so I went out to sit on the veranda. I mean the porch."

Myra limped over to the rocker and slowly lowered herself into it. "That's very interesting, because I went out to the porch to look for you. Perhaps I simply overlooked you in the dark, dear." Her skeptical expression did not match her light tone.

"Well, I did stroll around a bit while I was out. It was such a warm night." She traced the star pattern with her fingertip.

"Rory's door was wide open." Myra laid out the facts like a Pinkerton detective. "I noticed that when I went down the hall. He wasn't on the porch either."

Her unspoken accusation pushed Jessica to respond. "Listen here, Myra. You are the one who has been hoping

Rory Burnett and I would get together since the day we met. Are you now accusing me of having some kind of a midnight tryst with him?''

''Didn't you?''

''It's no business of yours whether I did or not.''

''As your mother's dear friend, as your companion and friend as well, I do think it is my business to step in when I feel the need arises.''

Jessica threw back the covers and stood up. ''And what about your belief in the grand scheme of life, in destiny, in fate bringing Rory and me together?''

''I'm surprised at both you and Rory. I thought him a far more responsible man. Falling in love and getting *married* is one thing, my dear. Becoming a soiled dove in some haystack, as romantic as that may seem, is quite another. And don't try to deny it. You have hay stuck in your hair.''

Jessica's hand flew to her hair, where, sure enough, she found bits of hay. She lowered her voice, unwilling to have their discussion overheard. ''What I did, Myra, was simply take some of your own advice—I just took it a little farther than either of us anticipated. I've decided to live life, to savor it, to wallow in it before it's too late. So don't fault Rory. Ever. He wants to marry me, Myra, in the worst way, but I'm the one that won't agree to that until I know what my future is with the museum.''

''But—has something happened I don't know about?''

Jessica walked over to the secretary to retrieve the letter from Gerald Ramsey. ''Rory brought this from Cortez yesterday. Beckworth is pressuring Ramsey about my progress. If they become too disgruntled, I may have no future at all with the Harvard Museum.''

Myra handed the letter back without reading it and shrugged. ''Well, at least then you could marry Rory.''

Jessica walked over to the window, drew aside the colorful rug, and looked out into the barnyard, hoping for a glimpse of him. She saw Woody Barrows shoeing a big bay horse. "By default? I don't want it to be that way, Myra. I plan to succeed on this dig, and then, after I've returned to Harvard with the find, I'll make a decision."

"And you're sure Rory Burnett will understand?"

"I hope so."

I truly hope so.

Jessica turned back to Myra. "Now that the Fourth of July celebration is over, I can get back out into the field. Rory promised to take me up to the mesa and today I plan to hold him to his word. So if you will excuse me, I'll get dressed. If you see him anywhere, please tell him I would like to leave as soon as possible."

"Before you leave this room, I suggest you brush all the hay out of your hair."

"I expected more understanding from you."

"I'm sorry if I seem to be stepping in where my opinion isn't wanted, and I don't suppose you'll give me your word that you won't carry on again the way you did last night—"

Knowing Myra only had her best interests in mind, Jessica was unable to stay angry. "I can't make any promises. That's what I told Rory last night and he was able to accept it."

"I hope you're doing the right thing," Myra said as she headed for the door.

"I do, too," Jess whispered to herself. As she watched Myra leave the room she repeated, "I do, too."

"Rory?"

At a workbench along the far wall of the big barn, Rory pushed his hat back and looked over his shoulder at Fred Hench. "What?"

"Gathers was tryin' to round up that copper stallion you wanted brought in an' the danged thing jumped the danged fence and took off like a bat outa hell."

As far as Rory was concerned, no one could do any wrong that morning, not after the time he'd spent with Jess last night. He put down the split-ear headstall he'd been attaching to a bit and looked toward the open doorway. All morning he'd hung around the barn half hoping she would wander in looking for him.

"Well?" Hench asked.

He turned his attention back to Hench and noticed the man's curious stare. He usually issued an order instantly, especially when a man stood waiting for one. "Tell him to put that little mare the copper stallion was so attracted to out in the far range and wait for another chance to rope him. That horse has the stamina I want under me for the next drive."

"Right away." Hench started to leave, then added, "Almost forgot to tell you. Last night, somewheres near the middle of the night far as I can recall, I heard somethin' I thought mighta been a bobcat caterwaulin'. Almost got up for a look-see, but I only heard it once then it quieted down right away, so I fell back asleep. Think we oughta put somebody on it tonight? I wouldn't mind baggin' me a bobcat."

Rory quickly returned his attention to the leather headstall and punched in another notch with the hole punch. "I didn't hear Scratchy complain about any chickens missing from the henhouse, so maybe we better wait and see if you hear anything again tonight."

"Right. I'll go tell Gathers about that copper horse."

"Right." Unwilling to have Hench notice the smile on his face, Rory didn't look up again until the man left the barn. "Bobcat." He chuckled aloud and shook his head, wondering if anyone would even believe the howl of the bobcat had really been the satisfied cry of Miss Jessica Stanbridge. He could hardly believe it himself.

His task completed, Rory hung the bridle on a hook above the workbench and headed outside. He'd thought of nothing but Jess all morning, of the way she had surrendered to him last night and the incredible joy he'd experienced in her arms. He remembered the way she looked standing in the doorway watching the dancers as she sought him out. If he could keep that glow in her eyes forever, he just might be tempted to give up everything he owned.

As he walked toward the house in the sunlight, he shoved his hat brim down, hoping to catch her having a late breakfast, to see her again in the light of day. A niggling doubt dogged him all morning; what if she hadn't slept late at all but was back to avoiding him again? What if she couldn't face him after last night because she regretted the whole escapade?

He was almost to the porch when he saw two men ride up at a fast clip. Sheriff John Williams reined in and Rory walked over to greet him as he dismounted. The man was huge, but he carried his weight well. A five-pointed star was pinned to the front of a brown leather vest that was the only item of clothing from his hat to his boots that the sheriff wore that wasn't tan. He sauntered over to Rory and touched the brim of his hat in greeting.

"I didn't think I'd see you so soon after the dance, Sheriff." Rory extended his hand and Williams shook it. The man behind the sheriff wore the badge of a deputy. He was reed slender, with carrot-colored muttonchops that extended to his jawline, a low plainsman's hat.

"We're here on official business," the skinny man told him.

Beside Williams's height and girth, his deputy looked no more than a boy and the two pearl-handled pistols at his waist looked heavy enough to slide down his skeletal body, taking his pants right along with them.

Sheriff Williams introduced the man as Deputy Dexter Hudson, his brother-in-law.

"Why don't we go in and have something to drink?" Rory suggested. It was obvious that Williams, who was usually jovial, was not at the Silver Sage for a mere visit.

Rory led the way into the kitchen. With one foot inside the door he paused, realizing something was not quite right.

Scratchy was standing over the deep soup kettle he usually kept bubbling with some concoction.

The sheriff and his deputy, oblivious to the change, whatever it was, followed Rory in and sat down at the table while he took some mugs out of a tall pine cupboard. When he walked over to the stove and lifted the coffeepot, he realized what was wrong.

"It smells *good* in here," Rory announced to no one in particular.

At that moment Myra walked through the door and smiled. Then she walked over to Scratchy Livermore, elbowed him in the ribs, and crowed, "Didn't I tell you?"

Scratchy, wearing striped wool pants that sagged at his hips and a wrinkled once-white shirt, shot her a bleary-eyed glance and kept on stirring as if four people hadn't just invaded his domain.

Rory offered to pour Myra a cup, but she declined. Then, much to the surprise of the two guests, who'd jumped to their feet at her appearance, she introduced herself to them without waiting for Rory to do so.

"I believe I met you at the dance last evening, did I not, Sheriff Williams?" she asked, staring at him over the top of her glasses.

"We did indeed meet, Miss Thornton," Williams replied, "but I'm afraid Wheelbarrow had you all to himself."

Scratchy made a great show of coughing and sputtering.

"*Not* over the chicken and dumplings, if you please," Myra scolded. She turned to Rory. "I've shown him how to make chicken and dumplings. Of course, it meant he had to turn loose one of those scraggly fowl he calls chickens, but I'm certain it will be better than shoe-leather beef for a change."

Turning a jaundiced eye toward her, Scratchy countered, "Tomorrow we're havin' turtle soup."

"Which reminds me," Myra said, "it's time I go out and

feed Methuselah. He comes running when I call him now—well, not running, precisely.''

Rory laughed as Myra ignored Scratchy, bid the other men good-bye, and left the room. He pulled out a chair for himself and sat down at the table with the others. ''What's up, Sheriff? I take it this isn't a social call.''

Williams put down his coffee and leaned back in his chair. ''I'm afraid not. In fact, I came out to talk to—Miss Stanbridge, is it? She's the one on your arm last night at the dance? The pretty lady that's lookin' for the giant lizard bones?''

Immediately wary, Rory set down his own mug. ''That's right. What's this all about?''

Deputy Hudson shot a glance at Scratchy, then leaned forward and said, ''It's about murder, that's what it's about, Mr. Burnett.''

''I'm tellin' this, Dexter,'' Williams warned.

''Right, Sheriff.'' Hudson contented himself with polishing his star with his shirt sleeve.

''Agent Carmichael up at the Ute reservation sent a man in this morning. Seems he wants Miss Stanbridge to identify a body they found wedged between some rocks in the gorge at the foot of the mesa.''

A cold foreboding lassoed itself around Rory's gut. ''Did they find him on my land?''

Sheriff Williams shook his head. ''Nope. Just off it, though, but still reservation.''

''Why does Carmichael need to involve Miss Stanbridge?''

''From what I understand, the man had some official papers on him, the same kind of papers she showed the agent when she asked permission to search for old bones on the reservation. The thing is, this dead man they found never checked in with the agent. Nobody knew he was up there—leastwise, no officials. They're hopin' she can identify the body.''

Jess had been so upset by Whitey's death that Rory wished he could spare her any more pain. But who was the dead man on the reservation? What connection did he have with Jess?

Williams was still waiting for him to get Jess.

"I hate to do this to her," Rory admitted aloud.

Hudson piped up again. "We got a dead white man lyin' up there in Ute territory who needs to be identified, mister."

"Shut up, Dexter." Williams gave Rory an apologetic look and then finished off his coffee. "I don't relish the thought either, but they claim to need her help. Nothin' I can do but come out here and ask her to go with me."

"Is the body all the way back at the agency in Ignatio? It'll take a good two days to get there."

Williams shook his head. "Naw. Left it right in the canyon below the bluff where they found it. Agent rode out when they came to get him. It won't take that long to ride up there and back. If we get going, you'll be back before nightfall."

"I'll go see if she's willing," Rory said, promising nothing. If Jessica didn't want to undertake such a grisly task, he wasn't about to force her.

"I'll explain it all to her on the way, but tell her not to hurry. The man ain't gettin' any deader."

"Not by a long shot," Dexter Hudson added.

Jessica was on her way out of her room when Rory entered the hall and drew up short at the sight of her. Her hand went to her throat. For an instant she toyed with the pearl button on her high-necked collar, then she dropped her arm to her side. She was not ashamed of what she'd done last night. If anything, she was grateful to Rory for initiating her so thoroughly in the art of lovemaking.

She met his gaze without a blush, although she felt on the verge of one the longer he stood there caressing her with his dark eyes. Would the sight of him thrill her from now on?

Would she feel giddy and tingle from head to toe each time he was in the same room with her, or would the euphoria that came after lovemaking diminish over time?

He watched her stare at him and wondered what thoughts were playing themselves out behind her bright blue eyes. Somehow, even dressed as she was in what he liked to think of as her scientist's garb, there was a new softness to her that she had not previously possessed. And this morning she seemed secure, rather than uncertain, in his presence. If there was any anxiety or regret over what they had done last night, it didn't show in her face or in her eyes. In fact, unless he was a complete fool, he thought that he just might see a glimpse of love shining in her eyes as she looked at him.

"No regrets?" He stepped up to her and took her in his arms, relieved when she didn't stiffen or try to fend him off.

"None whatsoever," she said, looking up into his eyes.

"Good." He dipped his head for a kiss and found himself smiling when it ended. The smile soon faded when he remembered why he'd come looking for her. "The sheriff has come out to see you, Jess. There's been a white man found dead on the Ute reservation."

Whitey's death was still too fresh. She shuddered in his arms and pulled back to look up at him. "What has that to do with me?"

"It seems he was carrying the same sort of official documents that you are."

She stepped away, confused, and threaded her fingers together. "A paleontologist?"

He shrugged. "I guess so. They didn't say for sure, but the Indian agent up there wants you to identify the body."

Her hands covered her lips. She shook her head, then said, "If they found his documents, why do they need me?"

"They want someone to verify it. The papers might be stolen." He waited a moment, then said, "I'll go tell him you refuse, but I'm not sure they'll take no for an answer."

"But—how can this be anyone I know? I'm the only one

from the Harvard Museum who's been sent to Colorado. Surely the man is from some other museum. There may be a remote possibility that I recognize him, but . . ." Had someone already heard of her own work and come to steal whatever find she could lay claim to? The longer she thought about it, the more certain she became that she had no recourse but to find out who else had been working the area.

"I'll go," she said suddenly. "I'll just get the bonnet you loaned me."

"Please"—Rory held up a hand to stop her—"not the poke bonnet. I'll get you a real hat with a brim."

She paused long enough to smile at him. "Don't I have the sodbuster spirit?"

"Let's just say you remind me too much of my mother in that thing." He pulled her close again to nuzzle her ear. "And after last night, there is absolutely no similarity at all."

Jessica shoved him away. "This is no time for such dillydallying. Where's the sheriff?"

"In the kitchen. Wait for me there. I'm going to the reservation with you."

She stopped again, and this time managed to stay out of his arms. "That's not necessary. You have more than enough to do here."

"Listen, Jess, this isn't going to be easy. I don't intend to let you go through it without me."

Five riders moved through the narrow canyon, the sound of hooves striking rock echoing around them. The towering sandstone walls along the canyon were striated with bands of color, evidence of what had begun as ocean, metamorphosed into desert sand dunes, then solidified over aeons only to be drowned again by inland seas. Sediment from swamps and deltas, volcanic activity, and erosion created levels of colorful rock pressed together like pages of a history book that Jessica longed to stop and read.

A Ute scout led them along the creek that wound through the canyon, Sheriff Williams and his deputy behind him. Rory and Jess hung back so that she could pause to observe the rock formations. He stopped to watch and admire her.

Now, as they rode side by side, Jessica put her hand to the wide-brimmed, felt hat Rory had loaned her and looked at the butte above them.

"See anything interesting?" he asked, intrigued by the sight of the white ruffled petticoat hem that peeked out from beneath her skirt.

"Everything." She turned to face him again and smiled. "I wish we weren't on such a dark errand. I would love to explore the canyon wall. I see fragments of dark rock that may be bone, but petrified bone and rock resemble each other so closely that I'd have to examine them to be certain."

They were nowhere near the sacred cave, so Rory felt safe in saying, "We could make the return journey without the others, take our time getting back, and you could explore to your heart's content."

Her joy was immediate. "Really? Oh, Rory, but can you spare the time?"

Seeing the glow on her cheeks and the sparkle of excitement in her eyes, he couldn't bear to tell her no. "I'm still your guide, Miss Stanbridge. We can take all the time you'd like. I can spare a couple of days."

She looked down, watching the trail carefully while her mare trotted over a fallen log. When she looked up at Rory again, her smile had dimmed. When she was certain the others were too far ahead to overhear, she said, "What will they think?"

"Who? The sheriff and his deputy? We'll part company when they head back to Cortez. They'll think we're hurrying back home."

"What about everyone at the ranch? Won't they be worried?"

"Not if we're only gone an extra day. I told Scratchy it would probably be that long before we got back."

She eyed him suspiciously from under the hat brim. "You wouldn't have anything but exploring in mind, would you?"

He bit his cheek and shrugged. "Maybe another experiment or two." Then he leaned closer and teased, "I love it when you blush, Jess."

She completely ignored his observation. "I found out something very distressing this morning."

"Something besides a dead paleontologist?"

"Myra knows."

He frowned. "Knows who the dead man is?"

She sighed in exasperation. "No. She knows about us, about last night."

"How?"

Jessica refused to look at him. Instead she concentrated on the trail, certain this was one of the most awkward moments of her life. "She got up to look for me in the middle of the night and found my bed empty. Your door was open; she knows you were out, too."

"So that proves nothing. Don't worry about it."

"There was more."

"Oh, hell. She didn't wander into the barn, did she?" Their relationship was tenuous enough without having Myra upset at Jess.

Jessica shook her head. "She didn't have to. There was hay in my hair."

Rory longed to reach out to her, to take her hand and tell her it didn't matter, but he knew it did. He had agreed to abide by her decision not to marry him yet, but still, he didn't want her reputation to suffer because their relationship had gone beyond society's established limits.

"Maybe we should go straight back when this is over."

As much as he wanted to spend a night with her beneath the stars, he knew he'd do everything in his power to avoid having her suffer any further embarrassment.

Jessica nodded in agreement, although she had begun to look forward to such a daring idea.

The group up ahead had stopped to water their horses. Rory and Jessica reined in beside them. Sheriff Williams took off his hat and wiped his brow with his sleeve. His hat had matted down his sweat-soaked hair. "The scout says the camp is just around the next bend." He looked over his shoulder at Jessica. "You ready, ma'am?"

Jessica felt her stomach plummet to her toes.

"She's ready," Rory said. "Let's just get this over with."

CHAPTER
16

The deep canyon narrowed until the red rock walls closed in on either side of the stream bed. The only sounds in the hot midafternoon air were the scolding of the jays and the echo of the horses' hooves as they struck against stones.

As Jess followed the others into the temporary camp in the shade of the towering walls, she immediately recognized Webster Carmichael, the agent from Ignatio. He paced impatiently beside the shallow stream. As they approached she easily dismissed the sight of Carmichael, for he had been less than cordial a month ago—but it was impossible for her to ignore what could only be a man's body draped by a dirty canvas tarp a few feet behind the agent.

Rory held her mare while she dismounted. Jessica straightened her skirt so that it primly covered her ankle-high shoe tops. When he smiled encouragement, she became even more determined to get through the next few moments without embarrassing herself.

Webster Carmichael stepped forward to shake hands with the sheriff and his deputy. Without either man saying a word, she sensed the tension between the Indian agent and Rory Burnett. Rory merely nodded in the man's direction and then turned his attention to her.

If Webster Carmichael was sorry for his lack of hospitality when she had first arrived in Colorado, he didn't try to make up for it by thanking her for riding out to help identify the body at his feet. He acknowledged her with a curt, "Miss Stanbridge."

She could almost pity the man. Almost. He appeared too old for the responsibility heaped on his stooped shoulders. Stick thin, a harried expression on his face, Carmichael impressed her as a man who would be more at ease in a schoolhouse than in an Indian outpost. His sparse gray hair and shabby wool coat with too-short sleeves that exposed his thin, blue-veined wrists only made him appear that much more vulnerable. He was out of place in a land where only the strongest of any species flourished.

Jessica moved in closer and was thankful for the solid warmth of Rory's hand at her waist as she approached the tarp and the fetid odor of death and decay hit her. She forced herself to concentrate on what Carmichael was saying and to ignore the pounding in her ears.

"A hunting party found the body wedged between those two rocks." The agent pointed toward a group of boulders that stood against one another like fat, round biscuits in a pan. "From the looks of him, he fell from the top of the mesa."

They all looked up to the flat-topped butte jutting out above them. Silently Jess measured the distance. Then, without warning, Carmichael bent down, grabbed the corner of the tarp, and whipped it back to expose the body.

At first, Jessica was too shocked to move. Filing past a dead man in a coffin was one thing. Staring down at a bloated, battered, decomposed body was another. Blindly she reached out for Rory and he took her hand. She clenched his fingers and forced back the bile that rose in her throat.

The man's limbs were twisted at odd angles. His eyes were staring open and sightless from his grayish-white, battered face. Even though the body was in such a distressful condition, there was no denying his identity. Lying there before her, his hair matted with congealed blood, his skull split open by the impact of the fall, was Jerome Stoutenburg, her former student assistant.

"Stoutenburg." Her lips moved, but no sound issued from them.

"You'll have to speak up," Carmichael insisted. "You know him or not?"

Jessica closed her eyes and licked her dry lips. "Jerome . . . Stoutenburg." The words came out as a croaking whisper. She turned to Rory, wanting to hide her face against his shoulder and tap into the warm solidity of his strength.

Before she could say another word, the pounding in her ears increased to a roar. When she pulled back to ask him for help, his image faded and the world went black.

"Jess?"

His voice came from very far away. She shook her head, unwilling to return to consciousness, some inner defense guarding her from the grisly truth.

"Jess, it's all right. You're all right."

She felt something cool and soothing on her brow. Forcing her eyes open, Jessica stared up into Rory's black gaze. He smiled and pressed his wet bandanna against her cheek. "All right? Can you sit up?"

When she realized they were beside the stream and he was cradling her in his lap, she tried to sit up. More embarrassed than she had ever been, she looked up at the circle of curious faces surrounding them.

"Don't blame you a bit, ma'am," Sheriff Williams said

as he hunkered down to her eye level and pushed his hat back off his forehead. The heat on the canyon floor caused his upper lip to bead with sweat. "Not a very pretty sight."

"Nope," Dexter Hudson put in. "Dead bodies never are. Why, remember that one time down around Shiprock when the wolves got to—"

"That's enough, Dexter," Williams admonished with a wave of his hand as he stood up again.

Even the Ute scout had joined the others, but he silently turned away when she looked at him. Carmichael fidgeted impatiently from foot to foot. "Can you tell me who that man is and what he was doing here?"

Rory shot him a cold glance and said sharply, "Damn it. Give her some time, Carmichael."

Jess laid her hand on his sleeve and said softly, "I'm all right now. Would you please help me up?"

Rory did as she asked, unwilling to let go of her completely in case she blacked out again. Jess carefully avoided looking toward the corpse, which was still uncovered, forgotten in the confusion of the moment.

"It's Jerome Stoutenburg. He was a student assistant at the Harvard Natural History Museum, the same museum I work for as a staff paleontologist. He was assigned to be my assistant and started the journey out here with me and my companion, but he became so ill on the train that I insisted he return to Harvard. Obviously he changed his mind."

Carmichael frowned. "So you think he was looking for you?"

"He must have been."

The agent addressed her again. "Then why didn't he come in to agency headquarters like you did?"

"How would I know?"

"You said he had papers on him," Rory reminded Sheriff Williams.

Williams turned to Carmichael. "That's right. Where are they?"

Carmichael reached into his coat pocket and took out a folded sheaf of papers that was spattered with dried blood. He handed them to Rory, who offered them to Jessica. She shook her head and let him hold the wrinkled sheets as she read them, her hands still shaking far too hard for her to hold the pages still.

The credentials were identical to her own. Issued in his name, they gave Stoutenburg full rights and permission to search the area, including the Bureau of Indian Affairs reservation lands. The documents had been issued by Harvard Museum and signed by Gerald Ramsey, museum director.

It was a double blow to realize that not only was Stoutenburg dead, but that Ramsey had sent her assistant into the field with the same authority she held. Originally only she, as head of the expedition, carried such official documents.

A growing anger and suspicion banished some of her former fear. "I resent the fact that you made me identify Stoutenburg when you already had his papers," Jessica said as Rory handed the pages back.

"The papers could have been stolen," Dexter answered smugly before anyone else could speak.

"That's right," Williams said as he shot a glare at his busybody deputy.

Carmichael defended himself. "I wanted to be sure. Things can get tricky all around when a white man's found dead on the reservation."

Rory pinned the agent with a cold, hard stare. "Now that you're sure who he is, we're leaving. Come on, Jess." He gently turned her away and headed for the horses.

The agent called out, "Just a minute, Burnett. Miss Stanbridge, do you intend to notify the museum, or should I? A telegram should go out immediately."

Rory turned on the man, his eyes flashing with intense dislike. "Listen, Carmichael, she's been through enough—"

Jess whirled around and pinned the agent with a cold stare of her own. "Why can't the sheriff notify the museum? I'm afraid I wouldn't handle the situation very tactfully, seeing as how my director obviously went behind my back to send another representative without telling me."

"I thought he was your assistant?" Williams rubbed his jaw.

"He was until he got off the train—ostensibly to go back to Harvard. Now he shows up with the same authority I have and obviously didn't try to find me before he began searching on his own. He might have asked after me in Cortez, but did he, Sheriff?"

"No, ma'am. He didn't."

"Just as I thought. Nor did he stop in at Ignatio at the agency, which leads me to believe the museum director sent him out here because they no longer had confidence in me."

Rory crossed his arms and stared up at the overhang jutting above them. Just yesterday Piah had told him the spirits were displeased. At the time he thought the man was just bluffing. Now more than ever he knew Jessica needed his protection. Stoutenburg's death might have been accidental and Piah may have stumbled across the body on his way to the ranch, but if Piah was behind it, he had gone far beyond mere protection of the sacred cave. He had murdered an innocent man.

Before he said anything to Sheriff Williams to incriminate Piah, Rory was determined to do a little investigating of his own.

"Let's get going," he said to Jessica, anxious to get her away from the still-uncovered corpse.

She started to walk away and then turned back to the agent. "May I see those papers again?"

Carmichael complied. This time Jess held them without shaking, calmly inspecting every line. Everything seemed to be in order. Everything pointed to the fact that the museum director had granted Stoutenburg the same power he had given her. She was about to refold the pages when her gaze fell to the lower right-hand corner.

Jess held the page between her thumb and forefinger and felt the paper.

"What are you looking for?" Rory was at her side again, watching carefully.

"The seal. There's no seal, no imprint of the museum stamp that makes these documents official."

"Meaning?"

She looked up at him as relief washed over her. "Meaning Stoutenburg must have copied my documents, forged the signatures, and then, after feigning influenza, followed me out here."

"Why?"

Disappointed at his lack of understanding, she slowly explained. "Because he wanted to make a find before I did and steal the credit that would earn him the instant acclaim and respect of his colleagues. Do you see what this means?"

Totally confused, Rory shook his head. "No."

She sighed. "It means Ramsey *didn't* send someone else out to do my job because he lacked faith in me. It means Stoutenburg acted on his own." She suddenly recalled, "Why, he even carried my papers for me once in a while and had ample time to counterfeit his own set!"

"So?"

Exasperated, she sighed dramatically. "Good heavens, you're dense!"

"Why, thank you," Rory said with a wry half smile.

Williams coughed back a laugh and shifted his weight. Dexter and Carmichael continued to listen to their exchange.

"Stoutenburg must have believed I was on the right track, so much so that he was willing to risk his career by forging these documents. Once the find was made, his illicit measures would no doubt have been overlooked because Ramsey and Beckworth would have been overjoyed."

When she realized the rest of the men were still hanging intently on her every word, Jessica handed the forged documents back to Carmichael.

Intending to walk away, she stopped short when Carmichael said, "Just how far were you willing to go to keep this man from making any discoveries before you did?"

Rory took a step in the agent's direction. "What are you trying to say, Carmichael?"

"Rory, please." Jess laid a hand on his arm. The look in his eye was full of fury. Then she turned on the agent herself. "Mr. Carmichael, are you accusing me of cold-blooded murder?"

"I'm just saying you seem more upset that he was out here trying to jump your claim than you are to see him dead."

Jessica had to step in front of Rory to keep him from going for the man's throat. "If you want to question me, Sheriff, you know where I'm staying." With that, she turned on her heel and walked back to her mare. Rory grudgingly followed, but not before he threw a threatening scowl at Carmichael.

When they were alone and ready to mount up, Rory said, "I'm sorry you had to go through that. I'd like to wring the man's neck."

"Don't be sorry. If anything, I'm more determined than ever to succeed."

Rory gave her a boost into the saddle then walked over to Domino. The idea of her newfound determination plagued him every step of the way.

"We're not going to have a choice," he told Jess as he drew up and turned around in the saddle to look back at her.

"What?"

She had been lost in thought; he could see it by the far-off look in her eye and the way she was studying each and every section of the rock canyon wall they rode past.

"We're going to have to camp out here for the night. The sun will be behind the ridge soon. I don't intend to have you on that mare stumbling around in the dark. We'll camp at that sandbank up ahead and there'll be enough sunlight left for me to snare a rabbit for dinner."

"But—what about everyone at the ranch?"

"Can we help it if we can't get back tonight?" He could see her measuring the truth of what he had said. "Really. We'll never make it back before dark."

"You don't have to defend yourself—unless you are trying to trick me into spending the night with you."

"When I see the suspicion in those blue eyes of yours, I can't help but jump to my own defense."

She blushed, her cheeks flaming crimson even beneath the shade of the wide hat brim. After she rode past, Rory followed her to the sandbank he'd pointed out. The soft, coarse sand was high and dry—a perfect place to camp for the night in the narrow canyon. He caught up to her as she pushed her hat back and let it dangle from its rawhide tie against her back and sat astride her mare to survey the area.

She looked back up the stream. "Will the others be coming along soon?"

"Williams and the deputy?" He shook his head. "They'll take the river fork and go back to Cortez that way. It's shorter since they don't have to go past the ranch again."

She had asked an unspoken question and he had answered. There would be no interruption. When night fell, they would be alone beneath the stars. Rory watched her as she digested the information, half expecting her to protest, knowing he'd go along with her wishes and take her back to the ranch if she did.

He swung down out of the saddle and was beside her mare to reach up for her before she moved. She looked down at his outstretched arms and then met his eyes. He shrugged, again asking a silent question. Jessica nodded almost imperceptibly and let him lift her down.

He savored the way she felt beneath his hands. Instead of turning her loose, Rory pulled her closer and wrapped his arms around her. For a moment they stood silent, locked in a warm embrace, neither willing to move or speak and break the spell. The sound of the creek bubbling over the rocks as it meandered through the canyon was soothing in its consistency. He began to sway slightly, rocking her from side to side and felt her nestle her cheek lovingly against his chest.

Rory ran his hand over the back of her head and then began to take the pins out of her hair.

"Don't drop them," she murmured against the front of his shirt.

He carefully complied, saving each precious hairpin as he drew them one by one from her hair. Unwilling to release her, he held her captive with one arm as he shoved the pins down into his pocket. When her hair hung loose and free, he finger-combed it until it spread out about her shoulders and fell with the ripples of moving water down her back and past her hips.

"I should be out hunting up something for our dinner," he said softly, stroking her hair over and over as she stood silent in his arms.

Her words were a whisper barely heard above the sound of the water. "I'm not hungry."

"Not now you aren't, but I'll bet you will be before long."

She shifted, nestled closer, and sighed.

Rory let her take her strength from him.

"Seeing Jerome like that today was horrible, wasn't it?" she said softly.

"Yep. I hated like hell that you had to go through that."

"And I thank you for that. I was afraid there for a moment that you and Carmichael would come to blows."

"It's not the first run-in I've had with him," he admitted. "Last spring the beef rations were short and I let the Utes have what they needed. It's something my pa always did, too, but Carmichael didn't think too kindly of it." He felt her squeeze him tighter as she acknowledged his generosity.

She took a deep breath as if gathering her courage to tell him. "When I recognized Jerome, so many thoughts raced through my mind at once. . . ."

"Such as?"

"I had an immediate surge of guilt. I thought of Whitey, I thought perhaps another young man had died because of me, and if I hadn't told Jerome to go back to Harvard, then he wouldn't be out here looking for me, wouldn't have fallen off the cliff. But then, when I saw those papers and realized what he had done—"

"And you're positive they were forged?"

He felt her nod against him.

"Yes. When I looked at them again, when I had gathered some of my wits about me, I could see that Ramsey's signature was a very good copy, but not perfect. I've seen it enough to know."

When she stood silent again, Rory said, "You know, we took a trip back east once when I was a boy. My mother's sister was ailing. Ma took me to a museum, but all I can remember was that it was cool and dark and musty smelling. There was a hush about the place, too. I always thought anybody who worked in a place like that would be as honest as a looking glass, but what you've told me reminds me more of a nest of rattlers."

She pulled back and smiled up into his eyes. "You have the most unique way of putting things, Mr. Burnett."

He kissed the tip of her nose. "Why, thank you kindly, ma'am. I guess that makes up for my being so dense."

Jessica was suddenly very interested in his top button. "I'm sorry I said that, especially in front of those men."

He chuckled and kissed her again. "What do I care what

they think? I do care about eating tonight, though, so as much as I'd like to stay here and hold you, I think I'd better rustle up some grub.''

''Grub is insect larva. Not a very appetizing expression.''

''That depends on who's cooking.'' He gave her a final hug and tried to ignore the trusting blue eyes fastened on his lips. ''When Scratchy's at the stove, the word 'grub' says it all.''

Rory picketed the horses that had been lazing beside the stream and took off the saddles and bedrolls. ''You want to set up camp while I look for something bigger than a chipmunk?''

''I will. Then I think I'll wander along the stream.''

He sobered quickly, concern for her safety never far from his mind. He looked up- and downstream. The sandbank was located between two bends in the creek, which gave the section of the canyon a secluded feeling, but that was no reason to let down his guard. ''Stay close by. Do you have that gun of yours in your knapsack?''

She nodded.

''Then keep it handy.''

''What are you worried about?''

She was too wise to fool, so he told her the truth. ''I don't want anything to happen to you, that's all.''

''And what makes you think I can't take care—''

He stopped her midsentence. ''Whoa. I didn't say you couldn't take care of yourself.'' He put his hands on his hips, shifted his weight to one foot, and took a deep breath before he admitted, ''I'm not convinced your assistant's death was an accident.''

''Why not?''

''Something Piah said yesterday keeps coming back to me. He acted as if you had been to the mesa. Said he had warned me to keep the bone hunters away. He said the spirits were mad.''

''You mean you *knew* there was a paleontologist out

there somewhere and you didn't *tell* me?'' She looked mad enough to spit.

He took a step backward. ''Now hold on. If you'll remember, up until just now we've had a few other things on our minds.''

''*Would* you have told me?''

''Of course.''

''When?''

''As soon as I remembered.''

''And the sight of Jerome Stoutenburg didn't *remind* you?''

''Don't push me, Jess,'' he warned. ''That wasn't the time to bring it up and you know it.''

''Why?''

''Because I heard it from Piah, that's why, and any mention of his name would have sent those men off on a witch-hunt the likes of which you could never imagine. I'm going to do a little snooping around on my own before I come to any decisions about Piah's guilt or innocence.''

She shivered even though the afternoon was still hot and dry. ''There's something about that man I don't like.''

''Piah? I'll admit he's a strange one. He's caught up in something right now, but unless he turns fanatical, I have a feeling this'll all blow over like a puff of smoke in a tornado.''

''Unless he did kill Jerome.''

He pulled the brim of his hat low. ''Until we know for certain, I want you to be on guard.'' His fingers swept over his own turquoise-handled gun on his hip. If he was going to hunt down something for dinner, he had to get started.

''Rory, wait!'' she called out to him when he was no more than six feet away.

He stopped and admired the way she looked standing there against the red rock wall of the canyon. ''What?''

''A few days before the flood, Piah warned me away from the mesa. He was adamant about the bones of his ancestors not being disturbed. If Jerome had stumbled upon something, some find that might not have been saurian at all, but an Indian burial ground—"

Rory shrugged. "That's what I suspect, but like I said, I'm not going to Williams or Carmichael until I have proof. I've lived too close to the Utes and gotten along just fine for too long. I don't want a band of vigilantes seeing red and yelling for blood."

"I agree."

"You don't sound too sure."

With a far-off look in her eye she admitted, "I'm just tired." Then she smiled as if to reassure him. "I'll be just fine right here while you go hunt down that dinner you keep talking about."

CHAPTER

17

Because his warning and her own suspicions weighed heavily on her mind, Jessica curtailed her urge to wander along the stream. Instead she opened the bedrolls and made a ring of stones for the fire. Then she gathered dry brittle branches of piñon and sage and stacked them before she settled down beside the spring and unlaced her shoes. Once her feet were bare, she hiked up her skirt and waded into the shallow stream. The water barely lapped about her calves, but it offered cool relief from the heat trapped in the gorge.

She looked around at the breathtaking surroundings and was reminded that each time she forgot where she was, reality came sharply into focus to remind her. Southwest Colorado was still a wild, untamed land, a place where life could be snuffed out in an instant by forces of nature—or by the hands of another.

Carefully stepping over the smooth, slick stones in the creek bed, she worked her way back to the sandbank and then sat down, unwilling to leave the water's edge. The water sang a merry tune as she watched the sun sink behind the western wall of the canyon. For a moment she concentrated in disbelief on the blue-green flash that lit up the canyon rim where it met the sky.

With the absence of direct sunlight, the colors along the canyon floor began to fade to varying shades of gray. With the afternoon shadows came a sense of timelessness. She could almost imagine huge reptilian beasts pausing beside the stream, their ponderous bodies leaving deep footprints in the mud.

Had Jerome Stoutenburg found evidence of such creatures before he died? Or had he stumbled upon a primitive grave site? Had the discovery cost him his life?

She heard a footfall echo down the canyon and looked up. Rory waved and began to walk back toward the sandbank. Something dangled limply from his hand. Dinner, she supposed. Jess stood up and brushed the sand off of her skirt and decided to leave her shoes and stockings off. She thought about sleeping beneath the stars with Rory, of how she had blatantly chosen to sleep with him, and prayed she would not suffer for her impulsiveness. But after last night there was no turning back.

She wanted him. She'd be a fool to admit any less. *I want you to want me, Jess,* he'd told her once. Little did she know then how much she would come to want him, how much she would think of him, wait to hear his voice, his footsteps. To depend upon his strength. She watched him stride up the canyon, sure of himself and his surroundings. Each moment she spent with him made it that much more difficult to imagine ever leaving him to return to Boston. He was not only physically powerful, but able to move her through word and deed. Through his poetry, she'd come to know how sure he was of his love for her, but how long would he wait for her to decide to commit her love and life to him?

Until now, her work had been her life. How could she simply turn her back on paleontology?

Dinner consisted of black-tailed jackrabbit roasted over an open fire and beans cooked in the can that Rory had in his saddlebags. Her appetite had not returned. If anything, nervous anticipation kept her from enjoying the little she did eat.

Fully aware that she was suffering a case of nerves, Rory was careful not to push her, even though dragging out the process of cleaning up the supper remains and washing his face and hands in the creek was torture of another kind for him. Finally he settled down beside the fire and waited to see what she would do next.

It wasn't long before she excused herself, pleading the need to answer nature's call and adding a promise not to wander far away. He stared into the fire he'd lit to keep coyotes and other night prowlers at bay. He rubbed his hands on his thighs and noticed the denim of his work pants was nearly worn through.

Her bare feet made a hushed sound as she walked through the sand. Jess returned quickly and waited in silence, standing so close to him that her skirt gently brushed his shoulder. He reached out and slipped his hand around her ankle, ran it up her smooth, well-turned calf, felt the dimples behind her knee.

She reached down and slipped her fingers into his hair and rubbed his head. The shy tenderness of her simple act sent a shaft of heat slicing through him. Rory slid his hand higher and caressed her thigh beneath her skirt. He felt her tremble, but she didn't ask him to stop. He stroked her gently, working his hand higher until he came in contact with her filmy cotton drawers.

Her fingernails raked his scalp, massaging, stimulating, caressing. She worked her fingertips into his ear and traced its shape.

He slipped his fingers up inside the open leg of her drawers and gently explored the silken nest hidden there.

She gasped. Her knees buckled and she sank down beside him, legs spread wide as she welcomed his touch. Rory turned and rose until they knelt face-to-face in the coarse sand. His hand was hidden beneath her skirt, but he could see by the look of heated wonder on her face that his exploration was welcome. He stroked her with a slow even pace until she was panting. Jessica leaned into him, grasped him by the shoulders, and let him take her over the edge. She cried out when her release came and wrapped her arms about his neck. Her warm lips pressed against his neck. She tasted his skin with her tongue.

When the waves of passion subsided, Jessica raised her head and stared into his eyes. Firelight flashed in the ebony depths. "Will you write a poem about this someday?"

"You are a living, breathing love poem I could never put down on paper, Jess."

His words moved her to act. She pressed her lips to his and this time taking the lead, slipped her tongue between his teeth and tasted deeply of his kiss. He returned her offering with a passion of his own, stroked her tongue with his as his hand stroked the moist, heated mound between her thighs.

"Try," she whispered against his lips when the kiss ended.

He whispered back, "If I try any harder, I'll explode."

She shook her head, her excitement driving her to impatience. "No. Try a poem."

"Later." He grasped her shoulders and pushed her to the ground.

She tore at his shirt until it came free of his waistband then feverishly worked at the buttons of his pants until she could shove them down past his hips.

While Jess fought to free him of his clothes, Rory was not idle. He unbuttoned her shirtwaist blouse and pushed it back off her shoulders. She clung to him, raised up off the sand far enough for him to pull the blouse off and cast it aside. The sand had cooled with the coming of darkness—it felt rough and dry against her back.

Rory bent over her, pulled the lacy straps of her chemise off her shoulders, and shoved it down, exposing her to his gaze and hungry mouth. In the shimmering firelight her breasts were as round and firm as they had seemed in the total darkness of the hayloft. Her skin was gilded by the firelight that set the fool's gold shimmering in the sand beneath her. The moment was magic, the night as alive as his blood thrumming through his veins.

He kissed her breasts. She arched against him and moaned, writhed, and begged until her whispered pleas for release softly echoed off the canyon walls.

His breath was hot against her skin as he whispered in her ear. "You want me, Jess? You want me now?"

A shiver raced through her. She was hot and cold, ice and fire. Her body was ready to receive him, she wanted to feel him slide into her, hot and hard. At that moment in time Jessica wanted him more than she had ever wanted anything in her life.

"Yes," she hissed, barely able to speak. "Yes, I want you." Afraid she would climax again before he entered her, she cried out, "I want you *right now*."

He wanted to prolong the torture, wanted to thrust into her and spill his seed and brand her his forever. But as much as he wanted to seek his own release, he also wanted to make this moment last forever. Their relationship was too new, and grounded on such a shaky foundation that he was afraid each time he held her it might be the last.

Rory grasped her wrists and pinned her arms to her sides then slid down her body until he rested between her legs. When he nipped at the tender sensitive flesh of her inner thigh, she dug her heels into the sand and lunged upward with a gasp. He trailed his tongue from her inner thigh to her knee and back up, teased the soft curls over the mound between her legs, dipped into and tasted of her honeyed core.

Jessica was sobbing, heaving sobs that matched the intense thrust of her hips as he delved into her most intimate recesses. Lost in the immense pleasure he was offering her, she closed her mind to everything else, to the hot night, to the multitude of stars carpeting the heavens above them, to the lonesome, plaintive cry of a coyote somewhere on the mesa. For that one intense moment in time he was her entire universe. Jessica gave herself over to him until every inch, every fiber of her being was his to use and control.

When her climax came again, she screamed his name and it echoed against the canyon walls.

Seconds later, as she lay drifting in a satiated void, certain she would never be able to move again, afraid she would never rise from this place in the sand because she had become part of the earth beneath her, Rory released her wrists and covered her with his body.

"We're not through yet," he whispered as he kissed her cheek. She felt his rod, hard and throbbing, tease the fluid entrance to her inner depths.

She moaned as her shattered senses began to come to life again. He prodded deeper, teasing her as he slid in and out of her, centimeter by centimeter. He kissed her shoulders, her neck, her lips and eyelids. He forced her to come alive again until finally, when her fingers dug into his hips to urge him on, Rory grasped her thighs and tilted her to receive him full length.

When she began to increase her pace, to provoke him with a swift undulation of her hips, Rory stilled. "Not yet, Jess. Not yet."

Then, in a swift, fluid move that caught her by surprise, he rolled to his back, carrying her with him.

Jessica found herself straddling him, her knees splayed and buried in the sand. Rory grasped her by the shoulders and forced her to sit up until she was riding him. Her golden hair, shining like midnight sunbeams in the firelight, surrounded them like a curtain of rippling satin.

Too lost in the wonder of the moment to be embarrassed by the brazenness of this new position, she met his heated stare. His dark eyes blazed with reflected firelight. He was sheathed to the hilt inside her, filling her with a turgid strength that was foreign and yet as welcome as a homecoming.

"Ride me, Jess," he whispered. "Take what you want."

It was an easy request to fill. She began to move, slowly at first as she savored the new, pleasant excitement that pulsed through her. It took over until she was demanding more and more of him. He grasped her hips and shoved her up and down as her pace increased. Finally, when she thought she would surely die, he clasped her to him and held her there as his hips bucked and he filled her with his seed.

Jessica was lost. With her head thrown back, she stared up into the starry sky and convulsed over and over with shock waves of her own.

When it was over, she collapsed on his chest and he wrapped his arms about her, enveloping her with his warmth. The coyote howled again, but tonight she was protected from the loneliness of the plaintive cry.

Later, after she had splashed through a makeshift bath in the shallow stream and they had both dressed again, Jess leaned against her saddle and nestled beneath Rory's arm. In silent contentment, they both stared into the fire. "You promised me a poem," she said softly.

He kissed her temple. "Ummm. I'm too tired to think."

She nudged him with her elbow. "No excuses."

"Promise you won't laugh."

Jessica reached out and laced her fingers through his. "Never. There's nothing funny about your poetry."

He watched the coals in the fire pop and break apart. Never in his life had he recited one of his poems aloud to anyone. Maybe it would be easier if he didn't look at her. At the moment he thought it would be easier to ride Arthur again than put his feelings into words. The truth was he'd been working on a new poem ever since they had made love in the barn.

A promise is a promise.

It was one of his father's unwritten laws.

He squeezed her hand and started slowly,

> I'll hold you, I'll love you.
> I want you to know,
> I'll hate it, but take it,
> If you ever go.
> I know now that somehow,
> If we ever part, you've given me somethin'
> To ease this old heart.
> You might go, I don't know.
> I do know one thing,
> While you've been beside me
> You've made my heart sing.

She was silent so long he thought she'd fallen asleep in the middle of his recitation. He leaned over to peer into her face. She was staring off into the night, but the firelight revealed the tears shimmering in her eyes.

"Was it that bad?"

She turned to him. "I wish I didn't have to hurt you. I wish I was certain of what I wanted."

He smoothed her hair back off her face then traced her lips with his fingertips. His touch was feather light. She grabbed his hand, kissed the ends of his fingers, and then lowered it to her lap. Rubbing her thumb along the back of his hand, Jess took a deep breath and sighed heavily.

"I don't want you to say anything because you feel sorry for me." His voice held a note of anger. "You told me once not to marry you out of pity. I sure as hell don't want the same thing from you. You have a job to do and I know you, Jess, you'll do it come hell or high water.'' He laughed at the truth of the old saying. ''I'm not going anyplace. This is my land. I'll be here when you decide you've had enough of that life.''

She measured him with a sidelong look. ''Will you, Rory? Will you still be here?''

''You can bet on it.''

Although his words were meant to reassure her, Jessica's heart was heavy. She closed her eyes and listened to the night sounds around them. The creek sounded louder in the dark than it did by day. The sound made her realize the water moved constantly, day and night, year after year as it carved its way through the canyon floor. There was a rhythmic, solid certainty to this place, one she compared to the security Rory offered. She was again reminded of how much he truly was a part of this land.

''I can see why you love this place.''

He reached forward to prod the fire with a stick and then settled back against his saddle again. ''I've traveled a bit, but I haven't seen any other country like it.''

''It's crept into my soul, as Myra would say. The mesas, the rock walls and buttes. The colors are like a living rainbow, one that never fades, just changes every moment of the day.''

''I never thought about it like that,'' he said. The poet in him couldn't help but admire her choice of words. ''I could show you such wondrous things, Jess.'' At the moment he was not even thinking of the sacred cave and the saurian skeleton exposed in the cliffside near it. There was so much of the earth's history in the area that it would take him months, maybe even years to show her all its hidden treasures.

''You have already shown me wondrous things,'' she whispered. ''Things I could never, ever have imagined. I'll never forget this night, Rory. Never as long as I live.''

Words that should have made him happy felt heavy on his heart. Her admission reminded him again just how tenuous their relationship really was. He looked down and found her staring up into his eyes; the shimmering tears had been replaced by the heat of passion once again.

He bent his head to kiss her as he had earlier, found her lips warm, willing, and much too hard to resist.

An hour after sunup the next day they were nearly out of the canyon. Jessica rode along in silence, wishing she could put off ever returning to the ranch and their separate responsibilities, knowing all the time that it was an impossible notion. Stoutenburg's death complicated everything. If he had not died accidentally and if, as Rory suspected, Piah was somehow involved, then she would be foolhardy at the very least to venture up to the mesa on her own. It was a certainty that Rory would be more hesitant than ever to take her there now that he suspected she might be in danger.

But how long could she tarry? How long would Ramsey wait for her to send him news of concrete findings? If Jerome Stoutenburg had followed her own well-laid plans and explored the mesa at length, he might very well have come across a rare find. But where? And more to the point, how long would it take her to come across such evidence?

She was drawn out of her musing when Rory pulled up short and said, "Let's take that side trail through that narrow crevice over there."

She eyed the narrow walls of the offshoot trail. "Why?"

He reined in again and turned in his saddle. He studied her for a second or two before he said, "Do you think you'll ever do what I ask you to without asking why?"

In her most haughty manner she said, "Probably not, Mr. Burnett."

"That's what I figure." He slapped his reins against his knee. "I was going to show you something you might like, but seeing as how you're not sure you want to follow me, well—"

"All right. I'm sorry. I'll follow you anywhere."

"That's better." He turned around to lead the way.

She muttered, "Unless, of course, I don't care to," but trailed after him without further argument.

After a ten-minute ride they had reached the end of the trail. The narrow crevice abruptly ended where the rock walls met. An indentation in the eastern cliff face was head high, half of it closed in by a broken wall of bricks the same color as the sandstone.

Rory dismounted and dropped his reins. Domino shifted impatiently, but stayed put, trained to stand when the reins dropped. In a move that had become a pleasurable habit in the past two days, he reached up and helped Jess dismount. Her hair, in a long thick braid, swung forward as he helped her down.

Her enthusiasm reminded him of a child's. It pleased him to watch her inspect the ruins in the cliff with such interest. He wished he could take her to the sacred cave, but in lieu of that, he had chosen to take a slight detour from the journey back to the ranch house and show her the remains of a small, well-hidden cliff dwelling.

"I know it's not what you're looking for, but I thought you might like to see one of the old dwellings. The Navaho called the people who lived here Anasazi. It means alien ancient ones."

"It's wonderful." She was rushing ahead of him, carefully picking her way up to the cave and clinging to her leather knapsack. With the same enthusiasm with which she had approached the saurian tracks he'd shown her, she said, "I wish Myra were here to sketch this. She would just love it."

Rory climbed behind her, braced and ready to catch her if she lost her footing. They made it to the opening without incident. Jess studied the ancient crumbling bricks and marveled at the expertise that went into their making. A perfectly square window was set into the wall. Jessica walked over to it, stood on tiptoe to peer inside, then walked to the end of the wall and entered the cave.

It was cool and shadowy inside, the cave itself was no larger than the parlor at the Silver Sage ranch house, but there was enough light to see the paintings on the rock wall. It seemed natural to whisper in the presence of the ghosts of a lost civilization.

"Pictographs." Even though she whispered, the word echoed off the walls. She had seen pieces of an ancient Egyptian exhibit and had naturally read of such findings, but this was the first time she had experienced such a delight firsthand. She moved forward to touch the closest and traced it with her fingers.

Figures of animals and caricatures of men painted in rust and white overlapped and blended together on the wall. Farther along the expanse was a series of handprints of all sizes. Jessica compared them with her own until she found one of the exact size and pressed her hand against it. Rory found another that matched his own palm print a few inches away. As they stood with their palms pressed against the ancient prints on the rock wall, they shared a smile.

"Myra would say we may have made these handprints long ago, in another lifetime."

He laughed. "I wonder if you were just as stubborn back then."

Jessica shrugged and dropped her hand. "Probably so, if you were just as infuriating." She smiled. "Does anyone else know about this place?"

"The Utes, probably. But it's on my land, so unless someone has my permission to be here, it's pretty much a secret." He gave her a measured look.

"I certainly don't intend to tell anyone about it."

"Good." He smiled.

They wandered around in the room for a few moments more.

"Do I have time to make some quick sketches of the paintings?"

Rory walked over to her, knowing that the ranch was shorthanded enough without him taking another day off, but when she smiled up at him, willing to stay or go at his choosing, he couldn't help but assent. "We can't stay too long."

"I'll hurry," she promised, already digging into her bag for notebook and pencils.

Rory walked outside to look down and check the horses. As he walked to the edge of the rock, pebbles rained down from above. Little larger than thick grains of sand, the rocks hit his shoulder before he could step back under the sheltering overhang. The rain of pebbles stopped immediately. He brushed off his shoulder and waited, wondering who or what had dislodged the gravel.

A glance over his shoulder assured him Jess was lost in concentration. He slowly pulled his revolver out of his holster and cocked it, then he stepped out of the shelter of the cave and looked up the cliff face. It was impossible to see over the rim above him. He waited, poised and listening for some sign, hoping he wouldn't have to use his gun but knowing he wouldn't hesitate if Jess's safety was in jeopardy.

There was no sound and not the slightest hint of movement. He held his breath and glanced down at the horses, waiting to hear a gunshot ring out in the box canyon, but nothing happened.

"I'm almost finished," Jessica called out.

He slid his gun into the holster and leaned back against the brick wall where he was once more hidden from above. "Take your time," he told her, knowing full well he didn't intend to leave the shadow of the wall until he felt certain they were in no danger.

• • •

"What's wrong?" she asked him later when they were nearly back to the ranch house.

"What do you mean?"

"What I mean is, you've been looking preoccupied since we left the cave and I can't help but notice you've been looking over your shoulder every few yards."

Trust his observant little scientist. "Nothing's wrong."

"You're a terrible liar."

He tried not to frown, but he couldn't look her in the eye. "Nothing's wrong. I guess I'm just thinking about what I need to do when we get back. Besides, I don't much relish thinking about how we're not going to be alone anymore."

"I've been thinking about that, too."

He arched a brow. "And?"

"And what?"

"Something in your tone tells me there's more."

She wished he didn't know her so well. "And I was thinking that we have to stop this . . . this carrying-on. Myra already suspects the worst and I don't want to put her in an awkward position. And what if any of your men found out?"

"They'd never suspect you of such a thing, not unless they saw it with their own eyes."

"Well, the places you've chosen so far are far from private. We could easily have been discovered in the barn."

He laughed. "Does that excite you?"

"Rory!" She couldn't believe he had asked her such a thing. "I'd rather not chance it again."

"Whatever you say."

She suspected he only agreed so readily because he knew for certain that she'd never be able to abide by her own decision.

CHAPTER

18

By the time they arrived at the ranch house, Jessica wished she could forestall a certain confrontation with Myra, who wouldn't let an unchaperoned night with Rory go unquestioned. As they rode up to the corral Gathers was acting wrangler. He opened the gate to let them pass.

Although she wasn't looking forward to facing Myra and the others, Jess was thankful finally to be off horseback. Unused to such long hours in the saddle, she was stiff and sore and looked forward to a long hot soak in the tub.

"Go on in, Jess. I'll be along after I see to the horses," Rory urged.

She asked halfheartedly, "Do you need any help?"

He shook his head. Unwilling to let her go without a private good-bye, he closed the gap between them and put his hand beneath her chin. He tilted her face up so that he could see her beneath the brim of the black hat. As Fred walked the animals toward the barn Rory glanced up once to be sure no one was watching, then kissed her quickly on the lips.

"Get inside. You'll have time for a bath and a short nap before dinner," he told her.

"I doubt Myra will leave me in peace. She'll want to know all about it."

He tried to look aghast. "I sure hope you don't aim to tell her *all* about it."

She smiled. "Perhaps I will."

His own cheerful expression faded. "Get going, Jess," he said gruffly. "When you look at me like that, I'm tempted to take you right here in the dirt."

Afraid he might just do it, she hurried toward the back porch. Outside the door, Jessica heard Scratchy banging pots and pans in the kitchen and walked in to find him half-dressed as usual in an underwear shirt and wool trousers, muttering to himself as he dropped a poorly peeled potato into a pot of water. Carrot and potato peels were scattered on the table beside the stove and on the floor.

He barely glanced in her direction as she came in before he turned back to his potato massacre and began peeling and mumbling again.

"Something the matter, Mr. Livermore?"

"Yer damn right something's the matter. I'm gettin' sick and tired of gettin' bossed about in my own kitchen, is what." In a falsetto that was obviously supposed to be an imitation of Myra he echoed, "It seems to me that as a culinary expert you would have at the very *least* tried to acquire a collection of spices."

Jessica bit her upper lip to keep from laughing. She could see the poor man was quite put out.

He went right on grumbling. "Then there's all this extra company and whoop-de-do and me havin' to put on the dog for some stall-fed tenderfoot that ain't ever been closer to a cow than eatin' a steak. Up till now thunderberries and sourdough been good enough for this bunch."

Unwilling to admit she had only a vague notion of what he was talking about, Jessica decided it was best to leave Rory to handle Scratchy Livermore's sour disposition. Since he was tired of cooking for extra mouths, she didn't want to bother him further by asking for warm water. Jessica headed for her room, where she planned to content herself with a sponge bath and a short nap—if she was lucky enough to avoid Myra for a time.

Unfortunately the first thing she heard as she left the kitchen was Myra talking to someone in the parlor. Jessica wondered who could be with her at this time of day when all the hands were usually occupied. She shifted the broad leather strap of her knapsack as she approached the parlor door.

"As I said," Myra continued, "I'm sure they'll be back any minute. I've discovered that one never knows what will happen from one minute to the next out here in the West."

There was no response from her companion. Jessica noted a strained, nervous quality to Myra's voice, as if the usually unflappable woman had lost her composure. No matter what Myra might think of her at the moment, Jessica refused to leave her friend in a stressful situation without trying to help.

"I don't suppose you've read—" Myra was attempting to change the subject but was caught up short as Jessica walked through the doorway. For an instant Myra's expression darkened and then an overwhelming smile of relief came over her. Jessica noted instantly that Myra had taken great pains with her appearance—her spectacles were unusually straight. She had neatly tucked in her blouse and her hair was brushed back into a tight salt-and-pepper twist.

Myra rushed forward, grasped Jessica's hands, and pulled her into the room. "Oh, my dear," she began, her voice far too animated, "do come in and tell us what *wonderful* things you have discovered today."

Jessica frowned, about to ask Myra what in the world she

was up to when she saw a movement near the center of the room. Expecting to find the smitten Woody Barrows paying court in one of the wide, heavy chairs near the fireplace, Jessica nearly choked when she discovered none other than the millionaire banker and financier Henry Beckworth standing at attention with a scowl on his heavily jowled face.

She slipped the satchel from her shoulder and absently handed it over to Myra as she crossed the room toward the Harvard Museum benefactor. "Mr. Beckworth, what a . . . what a pleasant surprise."

She suspected the taller-than-average gentleman had been quite handsome in his youth, but now, a life of indulgence had added a portly waistline and heaviness to his cheeks. Still, his skin was clear and ruddy, and his steel-gray head of hair could be envied by anyone, man or woman. His black wool suit was cut of a rich fabric. A thick gold watch chain swagged across the front of his vest and a diamond set in gold winked from a ring on his left hand.

"You don't have to act pleased to see me, young woman, for I can assure you I'm far from happy to see you. I'm only here because that nitwit Gerald Ramsey couldn't put me off any longer. When we received no word from you in over a month, I decided it behooved me to come out and discover for myself if you have accomplished anything at all. And I'm glad I did, let me tell you."

Jessica glanced at Myra, who shrugged and sent her a look that said, "I tried." She turned back to Beckworth. "I will be happy to show you all of my notes and tell you exactly what I've discovered in the past few weeks. I'm sure when you are aware of all the circumstances that . . ."

They all turned to the open doorway as Rory walked in, hat in hand, and stopped beside Jessica.

Beckworth ignored him completely. "I believe I'm quite aware of the circumstances, Miss Stanbridge, far more aware than you'd probably like me to be." He shot a dark glance at Rory and then accused Jessica with a cold stare. "I would like an explanation as to why you and your companion are living here when you should have set up a campsite by now. And don't give me any excuses about a flood. Miss Thornton already tried that on me."

"Mr. Beckworth I can expl—"

"There's really no need to explain," he said, running with a full head of steam, "I can see you've been taken in by the lure of the Wild West and this gun-toting cowboy Lothario."

Shocked, Jess could only stammer, "I . . . can assure you, Mr. Beckworth, I—"

Rory stepped beyond Jess until he stood face-to-face with the banker. Beckworth's ruddy complexion deepened. He drew in his belly and puffed out his chest, obviously trying his damnedest to intimidate Rory.

But Burnett, who stood a good two inches taller, was in no mood to back down. "If you've got something to say to me, mister, then say it. Don't talk around me—and don't ever say anything against Jess."

"*Jess?* So, you *are* on familiar terms," Beckworth snapped.

"Familiar enough for me to take offense at any slander you're willing to throw at her."

"The museum had a hard enough time convincing me she could do the job. When I heard the Stanbridge name, I thought I was hiring a professional. She's supposed to be out here working for me, not traipsing around the countryside whoring with the likes of you."

Jessica blanched. Myra gasped.

Rory went for Beckworth's throat.

The older man might have been heavier, but the elements of shock and surprise were on Rory's side. He pulled Beckworth up by the collar until they were nose to nose. His voice was a low growl, barely audible to the women in the room. He shook Beckworth as if the man weighed nothing.

"Nobody calls Jess a whore. *Nobody*. And you *will* apologize to her. Have you got that straight?"

With Rory's hands still clutching the high stiff collar, Beckworth could do little but sputter. His cheeks slowly turned the color of a ripe plum. He barely managed a nod.

"Good." Rory turned him loose with a shove that sent the man rebounding into the chair behind him. As Beckworth choked and gasped and tugged the material away from his neck, Jessica rushed over to Rory and grabbed his arm.

"Oh, my God, Rory, what have you done?" She pushed him aside and knelt before the older man's chair. Jess tried to help the banker unbutton his collar.

"What have *I* done?"

Truly afraid of the mottled color of Beckworth's cheeks, Jessica took his hand and felt his pulse. "Are you all right, Mr. Beckworth? Can you breathe?"

The banker nodded and continued to rub his throat. Myra stood beside his chair offering suggestions. "Take slow, deep breaths, sir. Relax and let the air flow into your lungs. Think of a quiet, relaxing place."

Jessica glanced over her shoulder and saw Rory watching with a disgusted look on his face. "I give up," he muttered, turned on his heel and stalked out the door.

Beckworth shot a worried glance after him. Once he was certain Rory was gone, he tried to speak but only managed to croak.

"Sir, if you'll just let me explain," Jessica said softly, "I'll try to clear this all up."

"Anything." He rubbed his neck. "Just see that you keep that man away from me."

"I'll get you some water," Myra volunteered, and hurriedly limped from the room.

"I know it must look like I haven't accomplished anything, but believe me, I have, Mr. Beckworth." Jessica hurried off to collect her knapsack from the library table.

She pulled out her notebook and opened it to the first Colorado entry.

Hoping to take his mind off of Rory's assault, she said hurriedly, "We set up camp on the mesa, and then, on the advice of Mr. Burnett, who I met when I hired him as a guide, we moved off the mesa to a high plateau here on his ranch, where I measured and charted five large saurian footprints embedded in sandstone."

At the mention of the tracks, Beckworth stopped rubbing his throat and began to pay attention. Jessica went on. "Then we moved camp to a dry creek bed, where after a week of digging I had cataloged over sixty specimens of saurian bones. They were wrapped in plaster casts, tagged, and ready to ship east when we were hit by a flash flood that wiped out the camp, carried off my supplies, and killed the assistant Mr. Burnett sent out to help me."

At that, Beckworth frowned. "What of that young student who accompanied you?"

Jessica sighed. "That will take a while to explain." It seemed more like it would take forever to untangle Jerome's feigned illness, his forgery, and his subsequent death.

Myra bustled in at that moment with a tall pitcher of water and three glasses on a tray. "Time for a little refreshment before we go on. I have urged Mr. Livermore to make some tea." A worried glance told Jessica that motivating Scratchy had taken some urging.

"I've been through Durango, asked after you at the Ignatio agency, was sent on to Cortez, and have been here since yesterday waiting to get to the bottom of this," Beckworth told Jessica with an exasperated sigh. "A while longer won't matter."

Jessica carefully continued to outline the facts as she knew them, right up to her identification of Stoutenburg's body yesterday afternoon. In no mood to coddle the overbearing millionaire, she described the condition of the body in detail.

Myra left the room midway through her account.

"How terrible for you," Beckworth said, genuinely moved for the first time.

"That's exactly what Mr. Burnett thought. We were late getting back because he wanted me to view some native pictographs in a cliff dwelling here on his ranch." She crossed her fingers beneath her skirt and told him, "I have to assure you, if I could have returned any sooner, I would have." It wasn't exactly a lie. "Of course, what you believe is up to you. I have done nothing I feel guilty about."

"Back to those tracks you mentioned earlier. You say they were three feet long?"

"Yes. I took plaster casts of them, but they were lost, too."

"Do you think you can find them again? The originals, I mean? I'd love to see them." Not exactly apologetic, Beckworth was at least curious and somewhat excited about the evidence she had uncovered.

"They're located here on Mr. Burnett's ranch. I'll have to ask his permission. After what's just happened, I'm not sure—"

Beckworth seemed to be weighing her words. He harrumphed and coughed and shifted in his chair and finally said, "I could apologize to the man if necessary."

She met his eyes. "Not unless you mean it."

He smiled. "I think I can safely say I do. And if you'll accept it, I would like to apologize to you, too."

"Then we'll set up an outing for tomorrow. If that will be soon enough? I'm sure once he's calmed down, Mr. Burnett will lend you a horse and send along one of his men to accompany us. He really isn't as impulsive as he seems."

"Obviously he felt he was defending your honor." Then quickly changing the subject, he told her, "I am more than pleased to learn you were right about saurian evidence in the area. If we can just make a find that will put those bone hunters in Wyoming to shame, well, little lady, I'll write your museum a blank check.''

Jessica didn't smile. How could she be happy when she felt he should have had faith in her all along? She wondered how long Beckworth would stay on at the Silver Sage, knowing full well that Rory's hospitality was already as strained as his temper. Now he would have Beckworth to feed and house.

The only advantage to the present situation was that in all the hubbub, there would be no chance to give in to the temptation for any nighttime interludes with Rory.

Beckworth was so enamored of the area and the saurian prints that he stayed on for three more nights. The morning he finally left for Durango and parts east, it was with two huge plaster casts of the footprints and a lighter pocketbook. He had agreed to reimburse Rory for the new supplies Jessica had ordered, as well as to cover the cost of the team of mules, the wagon, and the horse she lost.

The banker's newfound confidence should have inspired her, but instead the scene in the library and the way she had snapped at Rory after he defended her had driven a wedge between them. Whenever they were together at mealtime or when they passed each other in the hallway, he was decidedly cold.

Rory had already left the house the morning Fred Hench volunteered to drive Beckworth and his carefully crated plaster casts into Cortez, where he would catch the stage to Durango. As the wagon disappeared over the knoll Jessica went in search of Rory, hoping to set things straight. Finally, after looking in all the outbuildings, Woody Barrows told her he was out reburying deadmen.

''What?'' She was certain she had heard wrong.

''He's out replanting buried boulders that hold down the guy wires that keep the fence posts taut. Some of 'em were washed out in the storm. You'll find him about three or four miles southeast of here. If you want, I'll saddle up that little piebald mare for you.''

She quickly agreed, thanked him, and easily found Rory right where Wheelbarrow said he would be. There was nothing around except the crooked fence posts that marched along the land for miles.

He threw down his wire cutters and wiped his brow with the back of his sleeve as she rode up. His tan shirt was open down the front, the armpits sweat-soaked. It stuck to him, outlining his shoulders and muscular back. She waited for a moment to see if he would help her dismount, but instead of walking up to her horse, he turned away and took his canteen off his saddle. While he took a long drink Jessica slid down and waited for him to acknowledge her presence.

He turned back to his work without a word, picked up the wire cutters, and trimmed a section of lethal-looking barbed wire off a roll that lay in the dust beside him.

''So you *are* mad,'' she said without preamble.

''What gave you that notion?''

''It's obvious from the way you've been acting since that scene in the library.''

''The scene in the library,'' he said as he wound the end of the wire around the post and then picked up a heavy hammer and crescent-shaped nails, ''was in your defense. But I guess that doesn't matter to you, does it?''

''I'm perfectly capable of defending myself.''

''Oh, yeah. I noticed.''

''You didn't even give me a chance to open my mouth,'' she argued, finding it almost impossible to keep her gaze from straying to his chest.

He clenched the hammer tight in his gloved hand. ''Damn it, he called you a whore, Jess.''

''And you immediately saw red and jumped down his throat. Was your conscience hurting?''

The hammer hit the ground. He was in front of her in two

strides. "I have nothing to feel guilty about. I asked you to marry me, remember?"

"Don't try to put this on me again, Rory. I told you I can't make a decision until I've finished my work here."

"And now, thanks to that man and his money, you're all set to rush off on that wild-goose chase again."

She planted her hands on her hips. "Oh, I see. You're upset because Beckworth refinanced my work. Now you have no hold over me at all, is that it?"

"I am not upset."

"Then why are you yelling?"

The question brought him up short. Rory turned abruptly and walked back to the fence. Jess followed close on his heels. "Well?"

"Well what?"

"Is that what you're upset about? About him giving me the money to proceed with my work?"

"No."

"Then what is it?"

He continued to stand rigid, his back to her, his arms holding tight to the wire fence. "When I stood up for you, you acted as if I was the one who was wrong. Do you know how that made me feel?"

"I'm sorry—"

"I felt like an uncivilized brute. Then I started to wonder, is that how you still see me, Jess? A little rough around the edges? What was it you said the day we met? That I was . . . *colorful*?"

She reached out to touch his shoulder. He shrugged her off. "Of course not. Don't be ridiculous."

He turned on her again. "Now I'm ridiculous. Maybe what Beckworth said was true. Maybe you're just caught up in the lure of the Wild West. Is that what all this is to you, Jess? Are you just having a grand adventure before you pack up your saurian bones and go back home? If you plan to sell your memoirs, just be sure you spell my name right."

Stunned, she could only stare at him. The sun was nearly blinding. She refused to look away. "Is that what you really think?"

"I don't know what to think."

Deeply hurt, unwilling to let him see how much, Jessica looked down at her hands. She smoothed her torn gloves over her hands and worked the chamois into the crevices between her fingers. "Then there's nothing left to say, is there?"

"I guess not," he admitted.

"I suppose I shouldn't waste my breath talking to you any longer." Jessica mounted, half expecting, hoping beyond hope, that he would stop her.

He didn't.

Rory bent over to pick up his hammer and didn't look back.

Jessica rode as fast as she dared. She let the wind dry the tears on her face and ignored the black hat slapping her on the back as it trailed from rawhide thongs about her neck. She rode on and on, at first racing back in the direction of the ranch until she realized when she returned she would have to face Myra alone for the first time since Beckworth departed. At the moment she could imagine nothing worse than confronting her friend with the unspoken question still hanging between them.

She drew in the reins and paused so that her sturdy little mare could cool down. Jessica leaned over to the horse's neck and gave the animal a pat and an encouraging whisper. When she straightened and scanned the horizon, she realized the grand mesa loomed ahead. It looked closer than ever and beckoned to her with an overwhelming silence.

Why not? she wondered. She had her knapsack, she never went out without it for fear there would be something important to record. Resting in the bottom was the heavy gun—for what it was worth. She'd never fired the thing in her life. She also had a canteen full of water. If she set out now, she could be back before supper.

As far as she was concerned, she didn't care if she returned in time to sit down to the table with the rest of them anyway. Myra was upset with her conduct, Rory had convinced himself she was only using him, and Scratchy blamed her for bringing down Myra on his head and into his kitchen. Let them all stare at each other over the table. She could do without their dour expressions.

She reached into the knapsack and found her father's binoculars. Viewing the mesa through them made it seem all the more accessible. She tucked the leather-encased binoculars away.

Her mind made up, Jessica nudged her horse into a canter and headed toward the striated bluff in the distance.

CHAPTER
19

As if someone kept moving the mesa farther away, it took longer for Jessica to reach the base of the bluff than she estimated. All the way she was careful to keep the most prominent landmarks, Shiprock and Sleeping Ute Mountain, in view so she could find her way back to the ranch.

At the base of the mesa, she paused long enough to take a drink, unsure exactly where the ranch ended and the Ute reservation began. There were no fences this far east. She set aside her canteen, shifted her knapsack, and explored the base of the tableland until she found a place that was gently sloped. She followed a narrow deer trail cut into the hillside with switchbacks so sharp they nearly took her breath away. Once atop the mesa, Jessica was able to cross the land easily, stopping here and there to peer over the rims of the many canyons that cut their way through the land.

Low-lying evergreens, junipers, and piñons that had become so familiar grew in abundance atop the mesa and in the canyons as well. She could imagine the ancient people who once lived in the area collecting acorns from the tangled, scrubby gambel oaks.

She ambled along for an hour, dismounting often to take rock samples or make notations. Each time she repacked her notebook and pencils, she couldn't help but notice the gun at the bottom of the bag. Rory's concern that Stoutenburg's death had not been accidental was never far from her mind. Could she use the gun to save herself? She had learned how to load and fire and knew the gun was ready should she need it, but in the wide-open terrain, it was impossible to imagine that she was in any danger at all.

Although she paused often to look about, she never saw another soul, nor did she ever have the feeling she was being watched. As two hours passed into three she became confident that any fear she had harbored had been groundless.

With little time left to do anything but choose a place to explore at length another time, she came to a quick decision—she would tell Rory that she was going to set up a camp atop the mesa whether he agreed or not. It was impossible to cover the distance from the ranch to the mesa and then venture down into the canyons in a day's time.

Without the brooch watch she had lost in the flood, Jessica wasn't sure of the time, but guessed it was nearly four o'clock. Her stomach grumbled, and as she tried to placate it with more water, she wished she knew which of the various species of berries on the low shrubs were edible. Hunger would no doubt add to the desirability of Scratchy's supper when she got back.

Riding along the rim of the canyon on her way back, she stopped to use her binoculars again. She quickly trained them on the canyon wall up ahead. On her side of the deep canyon, nestled halfway down and nearly hidden by the overgrowth, was a dark crevice.

She surveyed the cave from the saddle, curious to see if it housed another dwelling. Focusing on the entrance, she moved the binoculars left, then right. Her breath caught. She lowered the binoculars to stare at the rock wall beside the cave, raised the eyepiece again, and then homed in on the sandstone wall.

Dark bits of rock were embedded in the sandstone and shale. Whether they were fragments of petrified bone or actual rock she couldn't tell from this distance. Jessica pulled out her map and made a quick notation.

She urged the mare forward. It wouldn't hurt to get a closer look before she started back. Her enthusiasm grew when she was close enough to see a clear route down the side of the canyon wall. Unlike so many other cliff faces, nature had carved a series of notches and ledges in this one that made it look easily traversable.

At a spot directly above the cave, she dismounted, looked around, and tied the mare to a juniper branch. As far as she could tell, it wouldn't take more than a quarter of an hour to climb down far enough to chip a rock sample out of the wall.

That's all I'll do, she promised herself, glancing up at the lowering sun. *No need to get carried away.*

She slung the strap of the knapsack over her head to secure it and pulled the chin strap of her borrowed hat tight beneath her chin. With a last tug on her gloves, Jessica started down. A few steps below the canyon rim, she paused long enough to hike up her skirt and gather it into a knot to keep it from tangling around her ankles as she climbed.

In some places the steepness of the rocks scared her, so that she was forced to crawl on her hands and knees rather than risk tripping and plummeting to the canyon floor.

In no time, sweat trickled down her brow. When a spiny swift lizard of sizable proportions skittered across her path, she let out a squeal, then chided herself.

"Do you know if you had some rather huge cousins that lived around here years ago?"

The lizard watched her curiously and blinked once before

it hurried on its way. She made certain the scaled creature was out of sight before she forged ahead.

A few yards more and she had to scoot out to the edge of the ledge on her bottom until she could dangle her legs over the side and reach for the next foothold with her toe. From that point to the place where she could reach the rock samples, she was forced to use the ancient toe and hand holds the early natives used to lower themselves in to the canyon. Luckily, after only a few easy moves down and sideways, she came to another outcrop, climbed down to it, and rested.

By stretching to the right, she could chisel out a sample of the dark rock. She set the heavy knapsack down beside her, found her chisel, and in a few moments had carefully chipped away a sizable piece, which, upon close inspection, did prove to be petrified bone. Without the gum-arabic solution to give it greater strength, there was nothing for her to do but wrap it as carefully as she could in paper she tore from her notebook and gently add it to the items in her bag.

That done, she took a good look at the rest of the bone shards. Here and there she brushed aside the loose clay-and-sand surface to reveal larger pieces and wished she could climb down to see the entire section from the broad ledge that fronted the cavern. Here was something worth investigating. Here was the proof that had made her entire journey worthwhile. If all of her calculations were correct, she was looking at what would prove to be a complete saurian skeleton from the Jurassic period.

Excited beyond telling, Jess started the long climb back up. Just in time, too, she surmised when the sun dipped below the mesa and the shadows on the cliff wall lengthened. Once she reached the top, she pulled herself to a standing position, brushed herself off, and wiped her brow, more than satisfied with the day's work.

Not only had she found something worth further excavation, but she had managed to put her earlier confrontation with Rory out of her mind for most of the afternoon. Afraid to contemplate what he would say and do when she told him where she'd been, what she'd found, and how she planned to return tomorrow with Myra and her camp gear in tow, she shifted her bag and started toward the juniper where she'd left her horse.

Halfway there she stopped.

At least she thought she was headed in the direction of the tree where she had tied her horse. Jessica looked in all directions, gauged the distance to the spot where she had started down the canyon, and then paced back to the canyon rim.

She came to a startling conclusion. It was impossible to hide a horse in such an open area covered with low shrubs.

The mare was missing.

> If you're goin', then go on,
> If you're set on leavin',
> Then be gone,
> 'Cause I got things to do
> That'll keep me from thinking of you.
> If you're sayin' good-bye, then say it
> If you're playin' a game
> Stop playin',
> 'Cause I got things to do,
> That'll keep me from thinkin' of you.

Whistling a slow tune in time to the rhythm of his latest poem, Rory unloaded what little remained of the barbed-wire roll and jumped off the wagon. Carrying it into the barn to stack with other bales, he decided that he might be damned glad when Jessica Stanbridge left. After all, a man shouldn't have to waffle around while a woman made up her mind about him.

Scratchy had rung the dinner bell the minute Rory had rounded the corner in the wagon. He took off his hat and used it to beat the dirt off his pants as he walked up to the back porch where the others had already lined up for supper. One thing was for certain, he wasn't about to apologize to Jess for this afternoon. As far as he was concerned, no matter how he still felt about her, he knew he couldn't take her indecision anymore, didn't have to take it, and would tell her so just as soon as they were alone. Make it easy on the both of us, he thought.

He elbowed his way to the back of the line of men who were waiting to use the pump to wash up. There was always enough soap, but by the end of the line the towel usually wasn't much good for anything. Standing at the end of the line looking forward to a soggy towel didn't do much to help his black mood.

The men shuffled in amid talk of fences, horses, and the lack of water in certain canyons. It was a familiar routine, reminding him of what life had been like before he had met Miss Jessica Stanbridge. He ducked his head over the bucket and splashed water on his face and neck then used the damp towel to sop up some of it. The rest was left to drip into his collar.

He joined the others in the kitchen. Jess's chair was noticeably empty and so was Myra's, but the older woman walked in the door just as Rory entered from the porch. All the hands stood up and shifted uncomfortably or waited in a half squat until she sat down. She set the leatherbound copy of *King Solomon's Mines* on the table beside her plate.

The heat of the cook stove only added to the close hot air in the room. Scratchy was busy over at the stove plopping potato dumplings in mounds onto the plates. Gathers stood at his elbow, ready to pass the plates around.

When no one else seemed willing to start a conversation, Myra asked Rory, "Didn't Jessica's supplies come in before the Fourth of July celebration?"

"They did. Brought them out myself."

''Well, after reading this''—she tapped the novel—''I'm ready to venture back out into the field. Besides, now that Jessica has Beckworth's backing again, I'm sure she'll be as anxious as I to return to camp life.'' Myra inspected him over her spectacles. ''Besides, I fear we'll wear out our welcome.''

Something in her speculative look made him want to squirm on his seat like a schoolboy in short pants. Instead he added, ''Stay as long as you like.''

Over at the stove, Scratchy slammed a lid on a pan. Barney Tinsley put his hand over his toothless mouth to hide a smile.

''I think it is best if we got on with what we set out to do,'' Myra was saying. ''I have many sketches to replace.''

Gathers set the plates down and for a moment they all stared at the food like condemned prisoners facing their last meal. White dumplings swam in congealed gravy on equally white plates.

Myra pushed hers away, and then, as if she had just noticed her friend was missing, asked Rory, ''Where's Jessica?''

''In her room, I guess.''

Myra frowned. ''No, she's not. She hasn't been here all day. I thought she was with you and that she was just slow coming in from the barn.''

Rory swallowed a mouthful of bread-stuffed mashed-potato dumplings and shrugged, trying to convince himself that it wasn't his concern where Jess had gone to smooth her ruffled feathers.

Woody Barrows spoke around a wad of dumpling. ''I haven't seen her since I saddled up the mare for her 'long about noon.''

The dumpling plummeted like a rock to the pit of Rory's stomach. He laid down his fork. He looked at the men seated around the table. ''You see her, Hench? Tinsley?''

In various stages of chewing, they all shook their heads no.

"Me either," Gathers volunteered. It was one of the first times Rory had ever heard the man comment on anything he wasn't asked directly.

"Oh, dear." Myra took off her spectacles, folded the remaining stem, and laid them on top of the book. Rory could see her gathering her thoughts. "I'm sure she's just out collecting specimens. Maybe she's found a new campsite."

The others kept right on shoveling the food down as if afraid to stop or they'd never be able to force themselves to start again.

Rory's appetite was gone.

"I got biscuits," Scratchy growled over by the stove. "They just ain't done yet."

"How nice." Myra's tone would have melted butter. "More starch. Do you realize that the truly healthy diet consists of leafy green vegetables, fruits, nuts, and seeds?"

Rory pushed away from the table and walked over to the back door, thinking of how Jess had looked about to cry this afternoon when she left him.

Like a fool, he'd been too stubborn to call her back.

Had he made her cry? Would Jessica Stanbridge really cry over him? He'd seen her blue eyes fill with tears when they lost Whitey and hated to think that he had made her cry again. He didn't mind laying claim to her anger, but never her tears.

Blue eyes under blue skies.

One by one, the cowhands laid down their forks. "Want me to saddle 'em up, boss?" Woody asked.

"For me and Tinsley. The rest of you can wait to see if I need you later." Rory knew Barney Tinsley was the best tracker of the bunch, but nothing could help once they lost daylight, and there wasn't much of it left.

Myra was beside Rory before he was off the porch. She

reached for his arm. "Do you really feel there's cause for alarm? I have a firm belief in the universe and I—"

Rory wouldn't voice his fears. "You hold tight to that, Myra. I just don't think it'll hurt for me to ride out and meet her on the way in."

"And if you don't find her?"

Rory pictured Jerome Stoutenburg's battered body and left the porch without a reply.

Nerves made it twice as hard to climb down the ledge to the cave again, and this time Jessica intended to go all the way to the bottom. As she worked her way down she told herself the mare had probably just wandered away, that it would head home, and then, no matter how mad he was, Rory and his men would look for her.

There was no need to be upset. None at all.

She was sure the horse had wandered off because she hadn't tied the reins tight enough. Why, she had been so excited about locating the bone fragments that she didn't even remember knotting the reins around the juniper. No one had taken her horse.

There was absolutely no need to worry.

She reached the cave entrance and wished there was more daylight. There were no matches in her knapsack; she knew that because just that morning she had planned to ask Scratchy for some, but had forgotten. Now there was no way to start a fire to keep the coyotes and other nocturnal prowlers at bay. No water because she had left the canteen on the mare. No bedroll to sleep on, either.

Jessica started to worry.

She skirted the wide mouth of the cave and moved to the cliff face. Not once, but twice, she blinked her eyes, unwilling to believe what she saw. From the upper section where she had taken the sample, it had been impossible to see the fossil field in its entirety. Finally she walked forward and touched the surface of what was definitely a massive femur, only part of what appeared to be the complete skeleton of a four-legged saurian that was already partially exposed in relief upon the cliff face.

Worry fled when she realized she was on the verge of the greatest discovery ever. As soon as Rory found her, she could hurry back for her supplies, wire Beckworth from Cortez, and alert the museum to send a team to the site immediately. Finding a way to get the bones up the cliff would be difficult, but not impossible. She began to pace off the width of the ledge in front of the cave, and when she walked to the right, found a path hidden beneath the underbrush. It sloped uphill at a forty-five-degree angle until it reached the canyon rim a few hundred yards beyond the spot where she climbed down.

At least I won't have to go back up the rocks again, she thought with some relief. There was still the dilemma of where to spend the night while she waited for Rory to arrive.

The cave was dank and musty. The fading light outside did little to illuminate the interior. Jessica walked in as far as she dared, and then fearing that some animal was hidden within, she backed out and hid behind a boulder. It would be a fine place to hide, but sleep was out of the question. At dawn, she would go up the path to the top of the mesa and wait for Rory or one of his men to find her.

She climbed up onto the narrow shelf and set her bag beside her. Removing the gun from the knapsack, she checked the chambers, folded her legs, and set the weapon in her lap. Thus prepared, she was ready to face the night.

As the sky beyond the canyon rim faded from red, to pink, to violet, she heard a stirring somewhere deep inside the cave, a hushed whisper that soon grew to a near roar. Terrified, Jessica crouched behind the rock and grasped the gun, even though she was convinced that whatever was making the hideous sounds could not be stopped by a mere bullet.

With a tremendous *whoosh* and violent beating of wings,

a black cloud of bats poured out of the depths of the cave. Jessica ducked as in one great mass, they swooped out of the cave to greet the night.

When they were gone, she tried to still the trembling that shook her from head to toe. Jess drew her legs up, dropped her head to her knees, and prayed dawn would come soon.

The bunkhouse was a world of its own.

The bunks shoved up against the wood-and-mud walls were each cowboy's private domain. Most of their clothes were on the floor. The walls were papered with newspaper, old calendars, and here and there were pictures of women the men had left behind. The coal-oil lamp stained the ceiling with soot and filled the air with its smell as it burned. Beneath the lamp that hung in the center of the room, Barrows, Gathers, and Hench were hunched over a small table. Woody and Fred played rummy while Gathers worked grease into his saddle.

Rory paused in the open doorway wondering if this was the life he would be leading if the Burnetts hadn't adopted him. Barney Tinsley pushed his wide girth past Rory and threw his hat on the bed in obvious frustration.

Gathers looked up but said nothing. He didn't need to. His dark scowl told them everything they wanted to know.

"We'll go out again in the morning. First light." Rory could barely get the words out.

Woody threw his cards on the table. His mouth worked for a minute, but nothing came out. Hench filled in for him. "We'll find her. She's out there someplace. Miss Jess is smart enough to find herself a place to shelter for the night. You found her after the flood, didn't ya? An' Miss Myra, too. Both of 'em got more lives than a cat, I reckon."

Unwilling to go back to the house and face Myra with the bad news, Rory leaned a shoulder into the door frame. "I reckon."

He wanted to yell, to curse, to pound his fist against the

wall, and there probably wasn't a man in the room who didn't know that already. Instead he issued orders. "I'll tell Scratchy to have grub bags ready for all of you. We're not comin' in until we find her, so pack up everything you need to stay on the trail."

"How far could she get in a few hours?" Wheelbarrow asked no one in particular.

Barney Tinsley spoke up when Rory merely shrugged. "We got back to where you was fixin' the bum fence line and picked up the trail just before it got too dark to see. The tracks led off toward the mesa."

Rory fisted his hands and hooked his thumbs into his belt. "I want everyone packin' a pistol."

Gathers actually smiled.

"You expectin' trouble?" Woody asked.

He told them in as few words as he could about the death of Jessica's former assistant. "I'm hoping it's just as you said, Wheelbarrow. Jess has just gotten herself lost and is waiting out the night—but you should be ready for trouble in case."

"Should we send Scratchy for the sheriff?"

"Not yet." Rory pushed off the door frame, took off his hat, ran his hand through his hair, and then centered his hat again. "I want to take care of this myself. Be ready to ride at dawn."

When he stepped out the door, he nearly knocked Myra Thornton over. "Pardon me, ma'am. I didn't see you there."

Myra stepped back and waited for him to move off the bunkhouse stoop.

"I don't think you should go in there," he said, thinking of the pictures of women in various states of undress tacked to the walls and knowing how the cowhands considered the bunkhouse sacred.

"Heavens! I have no intention of going in there," Myra said, trying to peer around him into the smoky interior. "I heard you ride up and came to see if you found Jessica. Obviously you didn't.''

''Nope.''

He started back toward the main house and she fell into step beside him. When he realized she was limping, he slowed his pace.

''I must admit I'm worried now,'' Myra confessed.

He swallowed. Pulling off his gloves, he said, ''Not as much as I am.''

''Then we must turn our worry into action. What can I do to help?''

''Nothing. The men are going to be ready to ride out again in the morning. Scratchy will be putting together some food. Maybe you could help with that.''

She frowned. ''He's declared the kitchen off limits, I'm afraid.''

Rory stopped when he reached the porch and let her step up first. Myra turned to him when she cleared the top step and said, ''You know, I can't help but think that Jessica would have been back by now if she could have been.''

As much as it hurt to admit it, he said, ''I'm afraid it's my fault she took off by herself.''

''With Beckworth here I haven't had time to talk to her privately, nor to you. I feel I owe her an apology for the way I insinuated she might have . . . that you two . . . oh, dear.''

''She told me you guessed we spent the night together after the barn dance.''

''Oh, my. Was she very upset?''

''Just embarrassed. I want you to know I love her, Myra. You asked me once and I didn't know how to answer. She still can't decide whether to marry me or not. All she's worried about now is finding a damned skeleton for Beckworth.''

''The longer I thought about it, the more I realized it was none of my business what happens between you two—as much as I want to see you together, that is. Things work out the way they are intended.'' She looked off toward the barn and corral. "I wish I had told Jessica that before she rode off today.''

"We're going to find her," Rory said, anger rising at her tone of resignation.

"I overheard what you said to your men. Someone killed Jerome Stoutenburg. That's what you think, isn't it?''

"I don't know for certain. He could have fallen.''

"Who would do such a thing?''

"Someone who didn't want Stoutenburg on the mesa.''

"That same someone wouldn't want Jessica there either," she deduced.

"If that same someone touches as much as a hair on her head, I'll kill him.''

"Violence never solves anything," Myra told him.

"No, but it's a hell of a way to let off steam.''

CHAPTER

20

Sleep was impossible.

Jessica spent the early hours of the night thinking about two things: how excited Beckworth would be when she gave him the news of the find and how angry Rory would be when he found her. And find her he would. She had never read one dime novel where the cowboy hero hadn't been able to follow week-old tracks, broken twigs, or listen with his ear to the ground for his quarry.

Of course, she could never admit as much to Rory, especially now that he was already convinced she had only used him to fulfill a fantasy inspired by such reading.

The mouth of the cave was only visible to her when she stretched up to look over her refuge. Wondering if it would hurt to get up and stretch her legs, she decided to stay put when she heard a slow, shuffling sound deep inside the cave.

Jess picked up her gun and curled into a tight ball. She thought her eyes were playing tricks on her when she saw fingers of light licking the walls and ceiling of the cave's interior.

The light snaked closer accompanied by the now recognizable sound of footsteps. For a moment she was tempted to call out, then decided to wait and see just who was coming.

The light moved closer, arching up and across the walls, accompanied by slow, plodding footsteps. As the light swayed it touched upon huge figures painted on the walls; many of them appeared similar to the ones she had seen in the cliff dwelling Rory had shown her. In the smaller cave the figures had been crudely drawn. Here they were near life size and extraordinary in color and detail.

From where she lay hidden, she could look up at the wide ceiling and see the massive figures clearly. Caught up in the sight of the many pictographs, Jess forgot for a moment she was in danger of being discovered until the footsteps halted somewhere near the mouth of the cave. The smell of lamp oil was pungent, instantly recognizable.

"Miss Stanbridge?" The hushed whisper was magnified in the vaulted, cavernous space. "Miss Stanbridge, are you all right?"

Someone had come from the rear of the cave to find her. There must have been an entrance in the back she had not seen.

Jess sat up and pushed her hair out of her eyes. She peered over the boulder and instantly recognized the Bureau of Indian Affairs agent, Webster Carmichael.

Hearing the rustle of her clothing and the scrape of gunmetal across rock, he turned in her direction and set the lantern on the ground. "There you are, Miss Stanbridge! We've been looking for you."

He reached the boulders and stood waiting for her to climb down. "Here, let me take that before you hurt yourself," he said, reaching out to relieve her of the gun.

Legs stiff from her cramped position on the stone shelf,

she climbed down slowly. "You can't believe how glad I am to see you." She brushed off her skirt and then rubbed her dusty palms against it. "Where's Rory? How did you know where to find me?"

"By searching very thoroughly, of course."

Jessica smiled up at Carmichael. He didn't smile back. Nor did he appear any more cordial than he had before.

"I suppose Rory is madder than one of those bulls he likes to ride," she said.

"I don't doubt it."

She waited for him to lead her out into the night. "Well, shall we go?"

At that moment a lean, dark figure silently entered the mouth of the cave. Instantly recognizable in his tall hat with the silver conchos, Piah stood staring down at her with his dark, expressionless eyes. She was startled to see him there, so much so that she failed to hide her reaction. He ignored her and spoke only to Carmichael.

"You found her. Now you will turn over the—"

"Not in front of the woman," Carmichael said. "I've got the shipment in back. We'll talk after you've gotten rid of her."

The woman? Gotten rid of her? Jessica's gaze swung to Carmichael and back to Piah. Something was going on here that was not right. These men were not part of a rescue party sent to find her, that much was obvious, and she had just handed her gun over to Carmichael. *Think, Jessica. Think.*

Tossing her head, she tried to act as if she hadn't witnessed their exchange. "Well, if you gentlemen will excuse me . . ." She started for the entrance. If she could only escape into the darkness, she stood a chance of hiding from them.

Piah moved slightly and blocked her exit. He grabbed her upper arm with a grip of steel. "You go nowhere."

"Get rid of her, I tell you," Carmichael urged. His Adam's apple bobbed up and down in his reed-thin throat.

Jessica spun to face him. "What are you saying? I demand to know what's going on here." Her knees turned to water, but she forced herself to hold on. There had to be a way to escape. If she was alert, if she was ready—

"Too bad your lover won't be here in time to save you, Miss Stanbridge." Carmichael reached out, pulled a strand of her hair over her shoulder, and rubbed it between his fingers.

She tried to slap him with her free hand, but Piah jerked her back. "Keep your hands off of her, agent. She's mine."

Startled by the venom in his tone, she pulled away. Piah tightened his punishing grip on her arm.

"I want her dead," Carmichael argued. "Take care of her the way you did the other one."

Jessica gasped. "*You* had Jerome killed?" She stared at the fragile-looking man in the fluttering lamplight. "You knew all about his death and yet you went through that charade of having me identify him?"

"Very clever, wasn't it? No one will ever suspect me, but when and if they do, I'll be long gone, thanks to my determined friend here." Carmichael picked up the lamp. His features, lit from below, were twisted, horrifying. "You and your thieving assistant nearly ruined our scheme with your snooping, but thankfully it's come off without a hitch."

Realization came swiftly. "You took my horse. You knew exactly where I was, didn't you?"

Carmichael nodded. "How very astute. We saw the horse, saw you climb down the hill. All we had to do was wait until you were scared enough to come out and be . . . rescued."

Jessica was furious at herself for falling into their hands so easily. She glanced toward the entrance to the cave and wondered how she could ever make an escape. Somehow, some way, she had to.

"I have the gold. I want the guns first and then I'll kill the woman."

Carmichael looked as if he was about to protest, then said, "I haven't got all night. Follow me."

"No!" Jessica struggled to break her hold.

Piah dragged her along as he followed Carmichael through the cave. The lamplight bounced against the walls. The painted figures expanded and contracted with every arc of the lantern's beam. The strange paintings grew nearer as the walls of the cave narrowed down to a tight passageway. The air inside was getting cooler as they walked deeper into the interior of the mesa.

Jessica tripped on a stone in the middle of the passageway and went down on one knee. Piah jerked her upright. She cried out at the pain, but he pulled her along, unmindful of her discomfort.

She tried to slow them down by hanging back. Frustrated, Piah halted, drew back his hand, and slapped her across the mouth.

Jessica reeled. For a moment she was afraid she was going to black out, but she forced herself to ignore the pain and stay on her feet. She wiped her lip. Her hand came away bloodied. They rushed on, following Carmichael. Following the light.

She smelled dampness and an intense, sour smell as they reached an open area. The floor was deep with bat guano. Her shoes slipped in the stuff and she nearly lost her footing. She grabbed for Piah's sleeve rather than fall. The thought of hundreds of bats sent a crawling sensation up her spine.

What if the men left her here to die? She knew she would do anything, say anything to escape this hellhole. She stopped struggling and hurried to keep up, all the time careful to avoid sliding on the thick, slippery goo.

The walls narrowed again. The path descended farther into the earth. Stone steps had been carved into the narrowing passage.

She didn't know if she could stand the closeness, didn't know how long she could breathe if the walls closed in any tighter. Only a fragment of Carmichael's light was visible up ahead as he wound his way through the labyrinth. Her breath was coming in rapid gasps. Shielding her face with her hand, Jessica feared that at the next turn she would run smack into the tight rock walls.

Just when she was about to scream, the passageway widened to reveal another room. Carmichael stopped in the center of it and set his lantern on a long, wooden crate. The cave held eight boxes, some coffin-shaped, others square.

Piah pushed her away from him. She fell against a stack of crates. She sat down on the nearest and fought to catch her breath. There were no paintings on the walls, no light anywhere except for the golden glow of the lantern. She let her eyes grow accustomed to the shadowed room.

"I've delivered the guns and thrown in some dynamite for good measure. Now give me the gold," Carmichael told Piah.

Jessica gasped, "Guns?" She looked at crate upon crate of what could be rifles.

"Winchester repeaters." Carmichael nodded in Piah's direction. "My friend here has decided the Ghost Dancers might need the help of real guns to do away with the whites. I have obliged him—for a slight fee."

"But . . . how could you?"

Carmichael took a threatening step toward her. "How could I? Simply because I could care less what becomes of this reservation or of the ranchers around here. I've had to fight both sides all along. And for what? The Utes hate being here—they're constantly arguing among themselves. Piah's a Weminuche Ute. He and his bunch don't want anything to do with the Mouache and Capotes bands. The ranchers only want to divvy up the land for their cattle."

"So you intend to stand by while they all murder each other?"

He shook his head. "No, little lady, I intend to run as far and fast as I can with the gold they're paying me to turn over these rifles." He looked at Piah. "Now how about it? Pay up."

The Ute hesitated, then reached for a pouch tied at his waist. Carmichael smiled.

Piah's hand moved past the pouch and in the blink of an eye he was holding the pistol he carried in his waistband. "Don't worry about the gold, white man. You will not need it in the spirit land."

Carmichael blanched. He tried to go for his own weapon, but Piah was faster. A shot thundered off the cavern walls. Jessica screamed and covered her ears with her hands.

Carmichael pitched forward. Blood pooled beneath him. It soaked into the sand floor of the cave. Jessica jumped to her feet, the sound of the shot still reverberating in her ears. She darted for the passageway. As much as she feared the dark, the close confines of the labyrinth, the hall of bats, she feared Piah even more.

He caught her before she reached the opening. Using all of her pent-up fear and loathing, she didn't stop struggling until he had wrestled her to the floor. She lay beneath him, panting. He lay still, barely having exerted himself, still calm in the face of the cold-blooded murder he'd just committed.

"You like this," he said as he pressed her against the floor.

She tried to bite the hand that held her wrist. "Let go of me! Let me up."

He lowered his face until it was inches from hers. She could feel his breath, hot, threatening, against her cheek. The floor of the cave was cold, hard, and unyielding. A sharp stone pressed into her shoulder.

"I saw you with Burnett in the canyon. I watched while you rode him beside the stream."

"Stop it!" She wanted to crawl inside herself and hide. His admission made what she and Rory shared seem like filth.

"I knew then it was only a matter of time before he gave in and brought you to this place—showed you the bones. I knew then I would have to kill him, and that I would have you for my own. I know what you like. I will please you greatly, as you will please me."

Jessica screamed. She fought to claw his face with her nails, but he held her back with little effort.

"Save your strength, save the fight you have within for later. You will need it."

He moved off of her and pulled her to her feet. She fell against his sweat-slick chest and shoved herself away. For some reason he had given her a reprieve. Jessica chose not to question him, but used the time to plan her escape.

He had shoved his gun into his waistband again. She stared at it, coveted it, willed the gun to slip into her hand. She was willing to wait until the time was right. As soon as he let down his guard, she would kill him. If she didn't succeed, she knew she wouldn't hesitate to put a bullet through her own head to keep him from ravishing her.

All the secret whispers from her childhood, all she had overheard when her mother and Myra had spoken of the Meeker incident came rushing back.

Did you hear? Josie Meeker was "outraged" by her captor?

There were crowds waiting at every stop along the way when the women were brought home.

Was her mother Arvilla "outraged," too?

They spent days and nights captive.

Piah tossed his hair over his shoulder. "Move." He shoved her toward the door. "I must get my men to bury him and take the guns out of the cave before it becomes light.''

''Rory will be looking for me. If you let me go—''

''He won't ever find you. I will never let you go. You are mine now.''

Refusing to budge, she waited for him to pick up the lantern. ''I can't see where I'm going.''

Lantern in one hand, Jessica's wrist in the other, Piah started out of the room and back through the winding passages. This time they had to climb up and the going was slower. In the bat room he went more slowly than before and let her pick her way through the slippery guano. The smell forced her to choke down a gag.

Once, she stopped to catch her breath. He yanked on her arm. ''Keep moving,'' Piah commanded.

Jessica forced her legs to move. Don't think about the dead man in the cave below us, she warned herself. Don't think about what this one intends to do. Just keep going. *Think about the gun. Get the gun away from him.*

The plan fired her into action. She struggled to keep up with him, to obey, to lure him into a false confidence. Anything, she thought. Anything to escape.

Sleep was impossible.

Rory paced the porch, head down, hands behind him. Every few moments he would look toward the mesa. Although he couldn't see it in the darkness, he knew Jess was out there somewhere, dead or alive, and knew he had to find her.

He had weighed all the options in the last three hours and decided not to wait any longer. Stepping inside the backdoor, he took his hat off a hat rack and shoved it on, then walked to the door of the small room beside the kitchen where Scratchy slept. He could hear the old man snoring inside.

He pushed the door open and walked to the bunk, reached

out, and shook Scratchy by the shoulder. The cook sputtered awake and batted at Rory's hand.

"Whosit? Wha—"

"I'm going out alone. Tell the others to meet me on the mesa. Tell them I'll leave a sign that a blind man could follow."

He left before Scratchy could utter a word, ran into the table in the dark, and slammed his way out of the kitchen. It was a relief to be moving, to take action. In the corral he cornered Pancho, his night horse, the most surefooted after dark. The horse was the pick of the remuda, one he saved for riding herd at night on the trail. In no time he was ready, his saddle equipped with bedroll, double canteens, jerky, and some of the biscuits from dinner.

Dressed in black for concealment, he spurred his horse into a gallop and trusted it to cover ground in the dark without stumbling.

As he rode through the night his thoughts echoed in time to the rhythm of the horse's hoofbeats. *Hold on, Jess. Hold on.*

Bound and gagged since they left the cave, Jessica found herself atop the mesa once more. It was little relief to be outside once again. Piah pushed her toward the waiting horses and heaved her up into the saddle. He tied her bound wrists to the pommel and then leaped on his own saddleless mount, all the time holding on to the reins of her horse.

The ride was excruciating as she bounced in the saddle, unable to balance herself with her hands tied. They crossed the tabletop land and raced down a shallow gully then up the other side until they came upon three men huddled around a low-burning fire behind a rock outcropping.

Piah slid off his horse and left her waiting, still tied to the mare. Wide-eyed above the gag, Jessica watched as he spoke and gestured to the others. Two of them stood, stared at her suspiciously, then mounted up and rode back toward the cave. The third remained by the fire. She recognized him as Piah's nephew. He was watching her closely, speculatively.

Had he, too, watched while she and Rory made love?

Jessica stared at the ground while Piah spoke to the youth in a commanding tone. The boy argued, but eventually left the fire to wander off into the darkness.

Piah came to her then, and pulled her down into his arms. He stood her on the ground. They were alone.

The fire was low, much like the one Rory had burned the night they slept in the canyon. The night they made love beneath the stars—beneath the watchful eyes of Piah and how many others?

She felt as if she had already been violated by this man who had taken her captive, but she refused to let him know it. She stood stubbornly silent beside him, waiting for his next move, watching the firelight play across his sharp features.

"We will eat. And wait. Burnett will come and then I will kill him."

Hours ago she had prayed that Rory would find her. Now she prayed that he would lose the trail, that she could find a way to free herself and warn him before it was too late. If she died, there would be no one to alert the ranchers around Cortez that a faction of the Utes were armed and ready to revolt.

Refusing to give in to her fear, she followed him to the fire. He pushed her close to the fire and commanded her to sit. With her hands tied in front of her it was difficult, but not impossible, to lower herself to the ground.

Piah took out his gun and held it to her temple. She heard the hammer click. "I am going to uncover your mouth. You will not cry out, or I will kill you."

She nodded.

He took off the gag. "Now we will eat."

"I'm not hungry." Contrary to her words, her stomach rumbled. She hadn't eaten since breakfast.

"Starve yourself then." He tore the leg off a small animal carcass that the others had roasted on a spit. As he concentrated on the meal Jessica noted that he had set the gun on the ground beside him. She would have to lunge over him to get it.

A time will come. Wait and see.

She pretended not to care, but she couldn't help but watch each time he bit into the succulent meat. Jessica wet her lips and looked away. Beyond the ring of the firelight the land was black. She could see the outline of low-growing trees on the mesa, but little else. It was impossible to tell where the land ended at the canyon rim. One false move and she would fall into an unseen abyss.

He watched her the whole time he ate, black eyes boring into her, stripping her of her dignity, her nerve. Cross-legged, the man was at ease and confident. Somewhere nearby the youth remained on guard. She guessed the other two men had gone back to watch the entrance to the cave where the guns and dynamite were still hidden.

Carmichael's body was still there, lying in the blood-soaked sand. She closed her eyes.

When he touched her, she jerked awake. Slowly, as he unbound her hands, she looked back at the gun a few feet away.

Determined to keep him talking, to lull him into trusting her, she said, "What are you doing?"

"I cannot undress you if your hands are bound."

Her heart was in her throat. She looked over her shoulder. "What about the boy?"

"He is watching for your lover. Your old lover." He laughed.

"And the others?"

"You talk too much."

Rory would agree, she decided. Still, she pressed him.

"What makes you think you'll get away with this? Rory already suspects you of killing the other paleontologist, the bone hunter."

"I knew he would. It was only a matter of time until our paths crossed."

"He'll kill you for this, you know. He loves me."

Piah laughed again. "He will not get the chance." Her hands were untied. He stared off into the darkness, watching for something, waiting. Stalling for time.

It struck her instantly.

Rory. He wanted Rory to find them, wanted him to witness her ultimate degradation.

Jessica took a deep breath and lunged for the gun.

Before he looked anywhere else, Rory decided to search the sacred cave. It would be just like Jessica to have stumbled across it, for up to now her instincts and knowledge of possible locations of fossils had proven correct.

He hoped Piah had not been there with a welcoming party.

A good hundred yards from the path that led down to the cave, he dismounted. It was slow going on foot as he worked his way down in the darkness and tried not to scatter rocks or gravel that would give his presence away.

As he neared the entrance he crouched to catch his breath and stare into the dark opening. If Jess was inside, she could be well hidden or asleep. If anyone else was there, they would be on guard.

Nothing moved inside the cave. He picked up a small rock and tossed it past the opening. It struck a boulder with a sharp *ping*.

He was rewarded with the sound of a rifle being cocked and readied. A flash of steel along a rifle barrel caught his eye. Someone was indeed guarding the entrance to the cave, and it wasn't Jess.

Footsteps alerted him. A man paced the entrance, watching for movement in the bushes below. Rory threw another rock; this one hit the wall that had the saurian skeleton embedded in it.

The guard stepped out into the opening, an Indian whose bare chest showed beneath an open suit coat. White feathers woven into his braids caught in the low moonlight. Rory took aim between the feathers, then wondered how many more Utes were hidden in the cave. Would the sound of a shot alert them and endanger Jessica if she was captive inside?

He scuffed his boot against the ground and his spur jingled. The slight sound drew the man's attention. The Ute bent low and crept through the overgrowth hiding the path, careful to stay in the entrance of the cave, where it was dark.

Rory held his breath until he could hear the other man breathing. He raised his own rifle by the barrel and swung it like a club. The stock hit the Ute in the head and sent him plummeting over the ledge in front of the cave.

The body hit the ground many feet below, but Rory waited, crouched and ready for another guard to rush from the cave.

Nothing stirred inside. Cautiously he crept forward, moved inside the opening, and waited. He didn't hear a sound. He pulled a match out of his back pocket and struck it on the wall. Holding it aloft, he tried to see how far back the cave projected and noticed that it narrowed down in back and opened into a single passageway.

"Damn it!"

The match singed his fingertips and died.

Was Jess hidden somewhere beyond the passageway? Had she stumbled across this place at all? Had someone taken her down the narrow corridor to the interior of the cave?

Damn it, Jess. Where are you?

Intuition told him she wasn't inside. If Piah had killed

Stoutenburg, as he suspected, the man wouldn't be stupid enough to box himself into the cave. Rory reckoned Piah was smarter than that. Hoping his intuition was right, he ducked beneath the low entrance and left the cave behind.

CHAPTER

21

Lunging past Piah, Jessica reached for the gun. He shoved her and sent her careening toward the fire. Reaching out to brace herself, Jessica's palm hit one of the searing rocks in the fire ring. She screamed and cradled her hand. Piah took advantage of her distress, grabbed her, and threw her down.

His nephew, Chako, came running.

"Help me!" Jessica screamed, imploring the youth.

Piah thrust his hand into her long hair and gave it a hard yank. "Silence!" Then he began berating the boy in their own language.

The pain in her hand was fierce. She cradled her burned palm against her breast and gave in to tears.

Piah's nephew looked confused. Finally, after Piah harshly issued what sounded like an order, the boy left them alone again. Piah turned to Jessica and reached for the front of her blouse.

• • •

Rory had searched nearly the entire mesa top when he finally rode down a shallow gully. His horse tripped and he instinctively braced himself, ready to vault from the animal's back. Pancho recovered his footing, and when Rory reined in, he thought he saw a flicker of light through the trees up ahead.

Dismounting, Rory was careful not to make a sound. He tied the horse to a nearby shrub and unsheathed his rifle. Slowly, soundlessly, he crept between the scattered pine and oak until he was certain he saw the light of a campfire glowing orange in the distance.

He paused, held his breath, and listened for the sound of a guard in the vicinity. Perhaps, he thought with renewed hope, Jessica had found a clearing, made a fire, and was waiting out the night in relative safety.

A twig snapped to his left.

Rory crouched low, taking cover behind the tangled underbrush. He eased his rifle to his shoulder and waited. Someone was definitely moving in on him. He moved left, slowly, cautiously, a few inches at a time.

From his new position, he could see the fire clearly. He almost bolted into the open when he recognized Jessica's long golden hair shimmering in the fire's glow. That was before he realized her blouse was open and that she was not alone—Piah leaned out of the shadows and reached for her. The outline of her breasts was high and proud above her camisole in the shimmering light.

Rory watched as Piah traced his hand along her breasts, saw Jessica stifle a cry. The firelight caught the tracks of her tears.

Hold on, Jess. Hold on a few minutes more.

Instead of moving, he waited for the man trailing him. Come on, Rory silently urged. Come get this over with. He had to get to Jess, had to let her know that she would soon be safe.

The short, smooth needles of the piñon pine fluttered, but there was no breeze. Rory forced himself to be patient when his mind screamed at him to move, to run to Jess, to save her.

Pine needles, crushed beneath his boots, scented the air. He waited, unmoving. Another twig snapped. He felt a slight *whoosh* of air and then saw someone hurtling at him through the darkness. Again he used the gun like a club, unwilling to alert Piah and place Jess in even greater danger. But this time when he swung, he only hit his assailant on the shoulder. The man grunted and then let out a yell.

Rory leaped for the man's throat and drove them both to the ground. One hard right to the smaller man's jaw and he lay still. Rory pulled the attacker up to a sitting position and instantly recognized Chako, Piah's nephew. He let go and the boy crumpled to the ground.

Still in a crouch, Rory spun in the direction of the fire.

When Piah heard his nephew's cry, he pushed Jessica aside, grabbed his gun, and leaped to his feet. She was up in an instant, staring over the fire, her injured hand pressed against her skirt while she struggled to hold her blouse closed with the other. She started backing away from Piah.

In seconds, Rory burst through the trees. Jessica recognized him instantly and screamed, "Look out! He has a gun."

Piah fired a round at Rory, who was running toward them, rifle ready.

"Get down, Jess!" Rory advanced on them.

Jessica took two steps back. Rory fired, but Piah had already hit the ground. The Ute rolled to avoid the bullets and came to his feet not far from Jessica. He reached out to grab her.

"Run, Jess!" Rory bellowed.

Barely escaping Piah's hand, she turned and ran.

When Rory realized where she was headed, he screamed again. "Jess! Stop!"

Jessica ran into the darkness, ran from the terror of her captor, from the gunshots that echoed around her. She ran heedless of the terrain, sought refuge beyond the firelight.

Without warning the ground beneath her disappeared. As she fell through space she screamed and screamed again. Then the earth rushed up to meet her.

Piah was hit. Rory saw the man grab his side and run into the trees. Rory picked up the Ute's gun near the fire, where it landed after he shot it from Piah's hand. He hurled it over the abyss and then, running to the edge of the bluff, tried to see down into the dark canyon below.

"Jessica!"

His cry echoed off the canyon walls and faded away. He called out again. A cry of agony. A plea. "Jessica, answer me!"

Nothing. No sound, no cry. Not a whimper.

It was as if the night had swallowed her without a trace. On hands and knees, ignoring the rocks, forgetting there were any number of poisonous creatures that could bite him in an instant, he felt around for a way to climb down the cliff face, but found nothing. It was a sheer rock wall. He ran back to the fire. A thick branch had not yet burned on one end. He picked up the flaming branch and carried it over to the rim of the canyon and hurled it. With a shower of sparks it flew like a shooting star, then fell, and fell, and fell. By the time it hit bottom, the fire had been extinguished.

There was no way down, at least none that he could see in the darkness.

She was gone and he hadn't told her he still loved her.

She was gone and he couldn't get to her until dawn.

He stood at the edge of the mesa, his hands slack and useless at his sides. When his right brushed the hard, turquoise-inlaid handle of his gun, he knew that there was one thing he could do before he found Jess.

One last thing he had to do.

• • •

There was only one place Piah would go to hide.

First Rory looked for Chako, but there was no sign of the boy. He found his horse and immediately headed back to the cave. Dawn was still a few hours away; he had time before his men found him, time to track down Jessica's killer and avenge her death. In his mind, Piah was just as guilty of killing her as if he'd put a bullet through her head.

There was no one guarding the path to the cave. Rory covered the same ground he had earlier, this time without making any effort to be quiet. He wanted Piah and whoever he had with him to know that he was stalking them. He had no fear of death. Right now he knew he would welcome it.

The entrance to the cave was unguarded. Rory found a dry branch on the ground the length of a man's arm. He took his bandanna out of his back pocket and twisted it around the stick, lit it with a match, and waited until the wood caught fire. Torch in hand, he entered the cave.

Just inside the entrance, half-hidden by a boulder, was Jessica's knapsack. She had found the cave. He picked it up and slipped the strap over his head. The bag had been important to her, part of her. He would keep it. He moved on.

The pictographs danced in the torchlight. They seemed alive, pointing the way. Farther and farther into the deep recesses of the cave he ran until he became aware of two things: the distinct smell of bats and the distant sound of a shout somewhere in the cavern below. Someone was moving along the passage carrying something that made a loud wooden sound as it hit the walls.

He backed out of the passageway. Let them come to me, he decided. *Come on. Come on and taste a little lead.* When he saw torchlight bobbing and weaving from the other direction, he extinguished his own light and tossed it away. Backing out, all the time keeping the others' light in view, he was nearly back in the great entrance room when he stopped and slipped into a wide crevice in the wall.

Two Utes in calico shirts and wool pants appeared in the passageway. They were struggling with a long crate with two smaller ones tied atop it. Piah lagged behind, fighting to hold a torch aloft as he favored his right side. Blood oozed between his fingers and stained his shirt.

Rory stepped out from his hiding place. The two men in the lead were brought up short.

"Drop it and put your hands up," he demanded.

The man in front dropped his end of the crate and translated for the one behind. They raised their hands, nervously shifting their gaze from side to side, waiting for Piah to realize the danger they were in.

Piah called out a curt command to the men but halted when he saw Rory standing near the cave's entrance.

Rory cocked his rifle and shouldered it. "Move away from your men or I'll kill them, too," he warned.

Piah's eyes were shadowed by the brim of his hat, but his sinister smile showed beneath it. "You wish to die like your woman, Burnett?"

"I'm the one holding the gun," Rory reminded him.

"Those crates are filled with dynamite. I am holding the torch."

"You're not that stupid," Rory said.

"No, but I am willing to take you with me when I die."

Without taking his eyes off Piah, he said to the other men, "Throw down your guns and get out now, if you want to live."

Piah lowered the torch to waist height. It burned just above the crates. One of the men tried to charge Rory.

The rifle went off. Piah's cohort was thrown back against the wall with the force of the blast.

The second man watched helplessly, his hands in the air, as his companion slid down the wall into a lifeless heap. A crimson stain blossomed on the dead man's shirtfront.

Rory watched Piah judge the distance between the crate in front of him and the entrance.

"You'll never make it, Piah. That dynamite will go off before you're halfway to the door."

"At least I will have a chance. What about you? Are you ready to die, Burnett?"

Rory didn't feel safe, even in the mouth of the cave. If the crates were full of dynamite as Piah claimed, if they should explode, he risked being thrown over the edge of the cliff behind him.

"I don't care one way or the other," he said honestly.

Piah smiled again. "I had your woman, Burnett. I had her before she died." He lowered the torch still further.

The other Ute yelled something at Piah and ran toward Rory, willing to risk a bullet rather than be blown to pieces. Rory fired.

The man reeled back and fell over the crates.

Piah made his move and tried to leap over the body.

Rory raised the rifle and fired again. He hit Piah between the eyes.

The torch fell from the Ute's hands. Rory realized immediately that it was going to hit one of the crates. He dove for the entrance, hit the ground, gathered himself into a crouch, and ran up the path. Halfway to the top an explosion rocked the mesa followed by a second tremendous blast. Rock and sandstone burst out of the mouth of the cave, shot out into the canyon below, and scattered down the bluff. The cliff face gave way and slid downward. Rory clung to a piñon branch protruding over the pathway as the ground beneath him trembled and threatened to give way. He started to slide down the path as the earth continued to rumble.

Deep within the mesa, in the very bowels of the cave, the reverberations continued as the interior was sealed for all time. When the rumbling finally subsided, when the dust settled and began to clear, Rory raised his head. His rifle was gone, he'd thrown it aside as he jumped away from the blast. He felt for his gun and found it in his holster. He still had his hat and he didn't seem to be bleeding anywhere.

His ears were ringing so badly that he shook his head and tried to clear them. The roar in his head went on, but he managed to struggle to the top of the mesa once again. His horse was gone, frightened away by the explosions. He looked at the sky, guessed there were at least two hours before dawn. He started walking back across the mesa to the place where Jessica had fallen over the cliff.

Come dawn, his men would be riding the mesa looking for him. They could help lower him to the canyon floor, to Jess.

Everything hurt.

Jessica tried to sit up, but couldn't move her arm and shoulder pinned beneath her. She lay still for a time, ignoring the pebbles and rocks that pressed into her side. She wondered exactly where she was and how she got there as the cool night breeze drifted across her face. She closed her eyes.

As the memory of her escape from Piah and her plunge over the cliff slowly came back to her, she wished she had dreamed the entire episode. What of Rory? Where was he? Was he alive or dead? All she remembered was the sight of him as he burst into Piah's camp, the gunfire, his commanding her to run.

She shuddered, afraid of the dark, afraid Rory might be dead somewhere on the mesa. Terrified, she prayed that Piah was not on his way to take her captive again.

Forcing herself to move, she started slowly, one limb at a time. She wriggled her ankles, her legs, and found, incredibly, that nothing hurt. The shoulder she had landed on was numb with pain. Her right arm was twisted beneath her. She rolled over to her left side and pushed herself to a sitting position.

She could hear water somewhere below her. The stars canopied the sky above, but the display offered little comfort tonight. Examining herself by touch, she felt along her collarbone and determined it was broken. Her shoulder had separated above it. Her arm was numb. She cradled it against her, trying to hold it rigid to prevent further injury.

Forcing herself up to her knees, she tried to stand, but dizziness swept over her and she slowly lowered herself to the ground. Glancing over her shoulder, she realized she was inches from the face of the cliff.

She scooted back carefully until she could lean against the rock wall. It was hard, but offered some comfort, and no one could slip up on her from behind.

For a few moments she might have dozed, she couldn't be sure, but she jerked awake with a start when she thought she felt sand sifting down on her from somewhere overhead.

Jessica pressed up against the wall, determined to stay hidden and escape capture. She nearly cried out when she bumped her shoulder against the wall behind her.

A hoot owl called out of the dark. Jessica shivered and pulled the edges of her torn bodice together over her breasts. She reached for the now familiar necklace of beads and found them missing. Her heart sank. She had lost Martha Burnett's necklace in her struggle with Piah. Her mind was wild with images of what had happened to her in the last few hours. Worse yet were the nightmares of what the morning might hold in store.

When she weighed her options, they were few. She was hurt, lost somewhere in a canyon deep in the middle of the mesa. Rory might be dead or dying somewhere above her. She had no food or water, no way to get out of the canyon except on foot. She might wander for miles without seeing another living soul.

Stop it.

Think of something else.

She began to recite the bone structure of diplodocus, one

of the most massive sauropods ever discovered. "Vegetarian's skull, thin pencillike teeth at the front of the mouth. Weak lower jaw. Neck bones jointed and hollow. Spines along neck for muscle attachment . . ." Something small rustled in the dust beside her. She tried to move away and realized with shock that she was on a ledge, and one that was not very wide at that.

Jess snuggled up to the rock wall again and recited faster. "Scapula, humerus, ulna, radius, wrist, hand, ribs, hip socket, ischium, pubis, femur, tibia, fibula, feet."

Oh, God, Rory. Please don't be dead.

"Tail vertebra with elongated chevron, flatter toward midtail. Joints between tailbones; as they narrow, the joints disappear. Narrow cylindrical bones at the very end."

Somewhere very close by, a coyote barked. She whispered, "Diplodocus's tail could be used as a whip."

Her shoulder was throbbing. She licked her lips, discovered the side of her mouth was tender where Piah had hit her.

A drink of water might be nice. Yes, a drink of water would be wonderful.

She forced herself to think, to structure her thoughts so that she might hold on to her sanity. Jessica whispered softly to the night, "Geological ages. Quaternary, Tertiary, Cretaceous, Jurassic, Triassic."

Before tonight she had begun to feel so akin to this land. Now everything held a threat.

She tried to conjure up a picture of the rainbow-hued canyons, the mesa, the high desert plateau. Rory, Myra, the cowhands, and even Scratchy. Methuselah as he tried to burrow into corners of the ranch house.

Jessica fought against sleep, but eventually her eyelids grew heavy and finally closed, effectively blocking out the night sky and the emptiness of the darkened landscape.

Rory sat staring at the ashes of the burned-out fire, watching them break apart as he poked them with a twig. Colorful beads were scattered on the ground near the fire ring. Reflecting the light, they cruelly teased him into recalling the way Jessica was never without his mother's necklace.

He thought back to the day he told her to keep it. The piece had been a rare gift from his father to his mother many years ago and the fact that Jessica found the colorful strand attractive warmed his heart.

"The beads are so beautiful. I couldn't take them," she had protested, although she ran the string of beads reverently through her fingertips even as she refused.

"They're yours," he remembered telling her without a hint of sentiment. "They just hang around gathering dust anyway." He wished now that he had made more ceremony of giving her the beads, wished he had presented them with a kiss and words of love that would tell her how much she meant to him. Now the strand was broken and the beads lay scattered in the dust like the empty hours of a future without her.

The sleeve of his black shirt was ripped at the shoulder, he noticed. His ears had stopped ringing some time ago, but it didn't matter.

Nothing mattered.

Words didn't come to him. The poetry had left his soul.

The sky took on a ghostly gray tint that soon came to life in a deep rose and then pink as the sun started to rise.

He forced himself to stand, worked the usual stiffness from his joints, and walked to the edge of the mesa again. The canyon was still lost in shadows and mist that hugged the floor along the creek bed. The oak and willow growing along the canyon floor were stained dark green in the weak morning light.

He couldn't see Jess on the bottom, but saw enough to know that no one could have survived the fall. Rory balled his fists at his side and threw his head back, unwilling to fight back tears any longer.

"Jessica!" he bellowed. "Jes . . . i . . . ca!"

The canyon taunted him. It threw the word back again and again until he covered his ears, unwilling to hear the sound be swallowed by the land the way his Jess had been.

He wiped his eyes, cursing his tears, his weakness, and walked back to the fire ring. He watched the sky deepen to pale blue.

He heard the hoofbeats first, then shouts and whistles as his cowhands rode into the clearing on the edge of the mesa. They were trailing his horse, Pancho, along with them, as well as Jessica's mare.

Barney Tinsley was the first to reach him. "You find Miss Jess, boss?" He looked around hopefully. The others gathered near.

Barney had called him boss. It was the first time any of the men had done so and Rory wished he hadn't. Not now. Not when he had lost everything.

He looked around at the expectant faces of the men. No single moment in his life had ever been as difficult. "Yes." He nodded and felt his Adam's apple work as he swallowed the emotion that threatened to choke him. "Piah had her. But there was a fight and she . . . she fell."

"Is she all right?" Woody Barrows pressed in closer, pulling up his pants. He looked confused, unwilling to believe the worst.

The men shifted uncomfortably. Gathers spat out a word none of them would ever even whisper in a lady's presence.

Rory looked them each in the eye as he said, "She went over the rim of the canyon." There, he thought. I've said it. It's true.

"You seen her? You been down there?" Woody was so close he was nearly standing on Rory's boots.

Rory shook his head.

Woody, a foot shorter, stood looking up at Rory with a bewildered expression. "Then how do you know she's not alive?"

Fred Hench shoved his friend on the shoulder. "Hell,

Wheelbarrow, she went over the cliff. No man could survive a fall like that. What makes you think Miss Jess could?''

Woody shoved past them all and with his distinctive, squat-legged walk, marched to the edge of the mesa. He tried to see down into the canyon, but could only lean over so far without the risk of going over the edge himself. He knelt down, then lay flat on his stomach with a grunt.

Gathers walked over behind him. "See anything?"

Rory watched them, afraid to hope. They hadn't heard her screams and the deafening silence afterward. He would hear them forever in his mind.

Hench and Tinsley left him and went to join the others. Curious, unable to do more yet unwilling to admit the loss, Gathers, Tinsley, and Hench lay down beside Barrows and peered over the edge of the mesa.

If he hadn't felt so utterly lost, Rory would have laughed at the sight of his weathered cowhands lined up on their bellies staring down into the canyon.

"What's that?" Hench pointed downward.

"Hell if I know, I can't see farther than I can spit," Woody complained.

Tinsley hit him on the shoulder. "Then what the hell are you lookin' for?"

Woody ignored him and bellowed, "Miss Jess!"

Only his echo answered him.

Rory massaged his temples. They were going to drive him insane.

Someone was calling her name over and over again.

Miss Jess! Miss Jess! Miss Jess!

Jessica moaned as she came awake. Groaned when she moved and pain shot through her arm and shoulder. Whimpered when she opened her eyes against the morning light and fully realized her predicament.

She was seated in an indentation in the cliff, a ledge not four feet wide. The gnarled roots of an oak that had tenaciously clung to life in the sandstone wall hung eight feet over her head. Jess looked up and realized the tree roots must have broken her fall.

Oak leaves and pebbles covered the ledge. She shifted, trying to ease the aches and pains that racked every inch of her body. A sound caught her attention. She sat perfectly still, listening.

Voices, indistinguishable words, were coming from somewhere above her.

Piah.

Her fear was so great she couldn't believe the whispers belonged to anyone but him and his men. She couldn't risk calling out, couldn't risk capture, even if it meant she would eventually starve to death here on the ledge.

"Miss Jess!"

Miss Jess. Miss Jess. Miss Jess.

Jubilation swept through her when she recognized Woody Barrows's voice. Before the echo died, she took a deep breath and yelled back. "Here! I'm here!" The words rebounded off the canyon walls.

A cheer went up from the men.

Rory's knees almost went out from under him when he heard her cry. He hurried over to the canyon rim, nearly trampled all of them as he got down on his knees and shouted, "Jess? Are you all right?"

Her heart nearly burst when she heard him call out to her. She waited for the echoes to die and shouted back, "My shoulder is hurt, but otherwise I'm fine."

"Where are you?" he wanted to know. None of them could see her at all.

She frowned, wishing she could be exact. "On a ledge. I think it must be about thirty feet below you."

"I'm coming down to get you," Rory shouted.

"No," she yelled back. "Just pull me up somehow."

Rory turned to Gathers. "Let's put that long rope of yours to good use."

Gathers got to his feet and hurried over to his horse. He was back in seconds, a coiled, braided rope in his hand. He handed it to Rory.

"Will it hold me?"

"It will," the lean, scar-faced man assured him.

Rory looped the rope about his waist and knotted it carefully.

Fred Hench stood up and joined them while Tinsley and Barrows continued to call assurances down to Jessica. "You sure you want to do this, boss?" Hench asked. "I'll go if you want. I'm lighter 'n you."

"Try and stop me." Rory shook his head with a smile. "I'll be fine." He looked to Gathers. "Let's do it."

They walked back to the rim of the canyon and Rory looked over. He took a deep breath and then called out, "I'm comin' down, Jess. We think we're right above you, so when you see me give a holler."

"That is totally unnecessary! Don't you dare come down here, Rory Burnett!" she shouted back. The echo drove the order back to him again and again.

Rory shook his head. "Damn, but I never thought I'd be so glad to hear that woman boss me around again." He got down on his hands and knees and then shimmied up to the edge until he was able to lower his legs over the side. His heart was beating triple time. If Gathers's rope didn't hold, if the knot slipped, he might not be as lucky as Jessica had been. He refused to look down, because whenever he did, he felt his stomach rise up to his throat. Instead he looked at the cliff face in front of him.

"Ready?" Gathers asked.

"Shoot." Rory felt them lower him down the rock wall and braced himself away from it with his boots.

One foot. Three. Six. Ten. They lowered him down.

"I see you!" Jessica called out. "I see you through the tree roots! Go back!"

"I'm not going back."

"Then move to your right."

Rory tried to work his way along the wall. He glanced down once, saw the oak growing out of the side of the cliff, and then made the mistake of looking all the way to the canyon floor. He closed his eyes and swallowed as he tightened his grip on the rope.

"More rope!" he yelled up to the others.

They let him down again, four, five, ten more feet. He could hear Jessica below him. She was calling out encouragement, warning him to be careful, telling him to go back. He ignored her and tried to concentrate on every move.

Finally, after he was low enough to reach out for the tree roots, he pulled himself closer to the ledge, told the men to give him eight more feet, and then finally stood on solid ground beside her. As Jessica struggled to her knees, her face awash with tears, he pulled her into his arms.

"Aw, Jess. Please don't cry."

She ignored him and sobbed against his neck while he cradled her, careful not to hurt her injured arm and shoulder.

It was enough for him to hold her, to feel her warm and alive in his arms. He finger-combed her hair and pulled pieces of twigs and leaves out of it, kissed her ear, rocked her gently. Finally, when her tears subsided and his men were insisting he call out to them, Rory pulled out of her arms and smiled down into her eyes.

His smile faded when he saw the bruise across her cheek and her split lip. Her blouse was rent down the front, her eyes shadowed. Piah's words rushed back at him.

I had your woman, Burnett.

Rory gently fingered the bruise as Jessica pulled the front of her blouse closed.

"Did he hurt you?"

She shook her head. "It was nothing. I'm all right now."

"Did he—"

The word went unspoken. She knew what he was asking.

"No. He didn't rape me."

He pulled her back into his arms. She winced at the force of his hug, but didn't complain.

"Jess, it wouldn't matter. Nothing matters as long as you're alive."

She thought of how close she had come to suffering the fate of the Meeker women, of being "outraged" by her captor, and knew that it would not have mattered to Rory. Still, she offered up a silent prayer of thanks.

"Piah's dead." He never took his eyes off her as he gave her the news.

Jessica closed her eyes. "Did you kill him?"

He reached for her shoulders, remembered her injury, and took her hands in his instead. "Yes. I thought he had killed you. Let's see about your shoulder," he said, carefully lowering her to a sitting position.

"I'm sure I broke my collarbone. I don't know about my arm." She studied him closely as he gently examined her. He had left his hat up on top of the mesa, so she was able to take in the sight of his dark, shining eyes without the overshadowing hat brim. She reached up to smooth back the shock of dark hair that hung over his forehead.

He started to unbutton his shirt. "Glad to see me?"

She let her fingers trail down the side of his cheek before she dropped her hand in her lap. When she realized he was about to take off his shirt, she was shocked. "Of course, I'm glad to see you, but if you think we're going to—"

"Hold on, Jess." He laughed aloud. "I'm going to let you wear my shirt so that you don't have to go around half-naked."

Feeling more than sheepish, she whispered, "Oh."

Slipping out of his shirt, he then helped her slide one arm and then another into the sleeves and buttoned it back up again. "Can I have your petticoat? I'll tear it up to bind your shoulder before I tie the rope around you."

"Are they going to haul me up?" Jess peered skyward.

"Yep. But you're a lot lighter than I am. You'll be back up in no time."

She grabbed his hand as he started to raise her skirt. "I don't think I can do it."

"After what you've been through? This is nothing." He rocked back on his heels. "Now give me your petticoat."

Jessica sighed. "No matter what I do, it seems you're always trying to get my clothes off."

He gave her a quick kiss. "We can talk about that later, when we're home."

Home. He said the word so easily, included her so matter-of-factly. It made her feel warm and wanted and part of his world.

Then she remembered the saurian skeleton she'd seen beside the cave, her promise to the museum, and Carmichael's death.

"Piah killed Carmichael."

"When?"

"Last night. They were working together—"

"What?"

She nodded. "It's true. Carmichael sold Piah guns, lots of rifles, I think. From the looks of the boxes there were enough for an army. Dynamite, too. They were hiding them in a cave, I don't know how far from here."

"I know the place. It's where I found Piah and two of his men. They had a crate of guns and dynamite."

"There were lots more crates and Carmichael's body is inside, too. In one of the underground rooms." She remembered the bats and shivered. "They took me down there. Carmichael wanted Piah to kill me, but Piah refused. He said—" Grim reality came rushing back to her and she covered her cheeks with her hands. "Piah said that he had watched us the night we made love in the canyon . . ." Her voice drifted away to nothing.

He squeezed her hands. "He's dead now, Jess. He can't hurt us."

"Piah wanted me for himself. He promised Carmichael gold for the guns, but he killed him instead. There was something else, too. Something about a spirit dance. They planned to kill everyone in the area, all the ranchers, farmers. Carmichael didn't care. All he wanted was enough money so that he could disappear and never come back."

"The Ghost Dance. Piah tried to spread it through these parts. He learned about it from the Paiutes. He told me there would be an uprising. I guess he thought his ghosts needed a little armament." Rory watched Jessica shrug off her petticoat. When she handed it to him, he began to rip it into wide strips. "I'll have to notify the sheriff."

"They killed Jerome Stoutenburg." Jess squeezed her eyes shut as he slipped a bandage behind her and bound her arm to her side so that it couldn't move.

"I was afraid of that. Carmichael will have to stay buried because there's nothing left of the cave."

Her eyes flew open and she grabbed his wrist. *"What?"*

He knew then that she had seen the saurian skeleton embedded in the cliff beside the entrance to the cave. "There was a little matter of a torch and some dynamite getting together when I shot Piah."

"Oh, my God."

"Right. I was almost blown to smithereens." He knew she was no longer paying any attention when she didn't even react to his last statement. He could see her obvious disappointment.

"The cave is *gone*?"

"Sealed up tight."

"And the cliff? Oh, Rory. You can't imagine what I saw on the side of the cliff. It was remarkable, unbelievable, it was—"

"The largest, most complete saurian skeleton ever discovered."

She looked aghast. "You saw it, too? You recognized it in the dark?"

He tied the last knot in her sling and then untied the rope around his waist. He was afraid of what the truth was going to cost him; still, he voiced it all the same.

"I knew it was there all along."

CHAPTER

22

"You *knew* the skeleton was there?" If he had tossed her over the ledge, she couldn't have been any more surprised. Shock and hurt followed close on the heels of realization. Afraid she already knew the answer, she asked, "When were you planning to tell me?"

"I wasn't." He tested the knot in the riata around her waist and tied another.

"Never?"

Rory looked her square in the eye. "Not if I could help it."

She stiffened, looked down at the front of the shirt he'd loaned her, and straightened the collar. "I see. May I ask why?"

"Because of a promise I made my father. When he settled the land beside the reservation, land that cut through the mesa and the cave, he made a promise to the Utes to protect it because it was sacred land. My father stood by that promise and so did I."

The explanation didn't lessen the hurt. "You didn't trust me enough to tell me about it? At the very least it would have helped me prove my theory was correct, that a find in the area was not impossible." Her shoulders slumped. She stared at the ground.

Rory reached out and cupped her face in his hands, forcing her to look at him. "You had the tracks and the bones you found in the dry wash."

"But—"

"Jess, I just couldn't do it." When she didn't respond, he added, "I didn't want you to have to make a choice."

"Piah warned you away from the mesa because of the guns, not only because of the sacredness of the cave."

"That's true, but I didn't know that then. I was protecting what I thought was a sacred site."

The pain in her shoulder was intense. She was hungry, tired, and on the verge of tears. "I'm feeling ill. Could you have them pull me up now?"

"Jess—"

"Please."

Rory helped her to her feet. When she swayed into him, he wrapped an arm about her. Drawn to the familiar warmth of his bare skin, Jessica instantly straightened and stepped away. She took a deep breath and looked up the rope. It ran up the cliff face and disappeared over the rim. "What should I do?"

"Hold on tight with your good arm. Use your feet to keep yourself away from the rock." He looked up and hollered to the men above them. "She's ready."

The response was a confusion of sound.

Rory could tell Jess was not only hurt, but madder than a rained-on rooster. He pulled her close and kissed her anyway. When he released her, she didn't say a word.

"You ready?" he finally asked.

"Yes." She took another deep breath.

He cupped his hands around his mouth and yelled, "Haul away, boys."

The rope snapped taut and creaked as the cowhands began to pull her slowly upward. Rory's hands left her waist when she was too high for him to hold on to any longer. "Use your feet. Don't look down." He called encouragement up to her while the men above yelled down. Jess held her breath until she began to feel light-headed, then forced herself to breathe. She tried to ignore the sharp ache of the rope around her waist as it cut into her and kept a tight grip on it with her left hand.

Inch by inch she moved up the cliff. She used her feet to push herself away from the wall, but at times the sandstone was a mere handsbreadth away from her face—shards of rock, bits of shell. Clay. She moved upward, watching the veins of color pass, layers of time pressed one upon the other. The cowhands argued among themselves as they worried over her safety. Finally, when they could reach out to her, they pulled her up and over the rim.

She couldn't help but blink back tears when she saw the eager, familiar faces glowing in welcome.

"Are you all right, Miss Jess?"

"Miss Jess, how'd you get yourself into this pickle?"

"Miss Myra's sore worried about you, ma'am."

They all spoke except Gathers, who was intent on unknotting his rope so they could use it to pull Rory up. She touched him lightly on the sleeve. "Thank you, Mr. Gathers," she said, amazed when his hard gray eyes softened. She looked around the circle of faces. "Thank you all."

Woody Barrows cleared his throat and nudged Gathers with his fist. "We're just lucky we got this long-roper here ridin' on our side."

One by one they returned to the edge of the mesa to retrieve their boss. In a quarter of an hour, he was standing beside Jessica again, leading her over to the horses tied to the branches of the low pines.

"You found the mare," she said quietly as she stroked her mount's nose.

He hated the way she avoided meeting his eyes. Any fool could see that she was hurting and it nagged him to know that his deception was behind it. She was angry, too, and typical of her, fighting not to show it. There was no way he could change what he had done, nor would he have done anything differently. He was frightened to think that she might never understand how he could keep the secret of the saurian skeleton at the cave and still profess to love her. But if there was one thing he knew she did understand, it was commitment. She was as committed to the work that was her inheritance as he was to his. When they were alone, when she was rested, he would try to talk to her again, to convince her that he was only doing what he had to do. For now, all he wanted was to hold her and ease her pain.

"The boys found the mare wandering on the mesa. They found Pancho, too. But you're riding with me." He made certain there would be no argument. "I don't want you alone on a horse with that bum shoulder."

Jessica watched him as he walked bare-chested over to his horse. With his back to her, he loosened the leather ties on the back of his saddle and shook out a lightweight wool jacket. She felt a surge of relief when he slipped into it to cover his upper body. Jessica pushed her hair back off her face and tried to look away. It was one thing to know what lay beneath a man's clothes, to feel his smooth flesh in the dark. It was quite another to face taut muscles and bronzed skin in the light of day.

Rory looked over his shoulder and caught her eye. She blushed, infuriated to think that even as upset with him as she was, she could still be moved by the sight of him.

Rory walked over to the campfire and picked up her knapsack. He dusted it off and carried it back to where she stood staring off into the canyon. He tapped her on the shoulder.

"Here." He offered the knapsack to her.

When she reached out to take it, tears filled her eyes. "You found it."

He helped her slip it over her good shoulder. "In the cave."

She hugged it close. The contents of the smooth, worn leather bag—her father's binoculars, her notebook, compass, measuring tape, maps, chisel, brushes, pencils, and pens—felt lumpy, but oh so dear. Here were things she could trust, things she knew and could hold on to. "Thank you." She paused briefly as she continued to hold the knapsack close. "I lost your mother's beads," she confessed. "They must have been broken when Piah—" She glanced down at the borrowed shirt she wore.

Rory wanted to do more, but he contented himself with reaching out to brush aside a stray lock of her hair. "Forget about the beads. You can't imagine how I felt last night when that knapsack was all I thought I had left of you."

Reading the sincerity in his eyes, she remembered what it had been like to sit on the ledge in the darkness and wonder if he was dead or alive. "I think I do."

"Ready, boss?" Fred Hench was the last of the men to mount up. They sat their horses, waiting for Jessica and Rory, looking everywhere but at the couple standing in the midst of them.

Rory wanted to tell them all to head back to the ranch so that he would have Jess all to himself, but one look at her face told him the effort would be useless. Not only was she exhausted, but obviously in no mood to talk about what had happened.

"All set," he told his men, then he remembered the boy, Chako, who had escaped into the night. "Tinsley, you and Gathers look for Piah's nephew. I doubt he'll give us any more trouble, but see if you come across him hiding anyplace up here. If he was in the cave, I didn't see him."

As the two men rode off Rory helped Jess mount Pancho and then swung up behind her. When he put an arm about her waist, she settled back against him, but didn't say a word all the way back to the ranch house.

Three days later, after moving cattle to a spring-fed canyon, Rory rode up to the ranch house and noticed Myra seated on the front porch with an open book in her lap. When she waved in greeting, he waved back and then reined in before the porch and dismounted.

Looping the reins over a hitching rail that fronted the house, he then used the cast-iron boot scraper on the bottom step to wipe the cow patties off the bottom of his boots before he walked across the porch. Myra slipped her glasses off her nose and laid them on the book.

Rory pulled up a ragged cane-bottom chair and settled down before he said a word. He put his boot heels on the porch rail, crossed his legs at the ankles, and rested his head on the back of the chair. He pushed back his hat and then smiled over at Myra who had watched him patiently.

"You'd make some cowboy a good wife, Myra."

Her eyes widened and she laughed boisterously. "What makes you say that, Mr. Burnett?"

"You know when to talk and when not to."

She picked up her spectacles and fiddled with the single stem. "I sensed you have something on your mind. I believe a person needs quiet contemplation to straighten out his thoughts."

"Is that what Jess has been doing? Straightening out her thoughts."

"I'm certain it is."

Neither of them had to remind the other that it had been three days since Rory brought Jess down from the mesa. At first, pain had been her excuse to stay locked away from the rest of them—and indeed, when the doctor finally arrived, he found that both her collarbone and one wrist were broken. But it had been three days now and she still refused to see him.

Myra hesitated before she asked, "What really happened on the mesa, Rory?"

He swung his gaze over to her. "What do you mean?"

"I know that agent conspired to sell guns to the Utes and that the man called Piah was behind it. I know he took Jessica, that she fell, that you and your men rescued her. I know everything except why she won't talk to you."

"She hasn't told you?"

"No. She hasn't."

Rory was in no mood to explain. Instead he told her, "I need your help, Myra."

Armed with new purpose, Myra drew herself up and assured him, "You have it, young man, if your request is within reason."

"I need to know all you know about Jessica's work, how she searches for those damn fossil bones, and the kinds of places she might look for them."

Suddenly a willing conspirator, Myra scooted up to the edge of her chair, glanced over her shoulder, and whispered, "Where would you like to begin?"

The outcrop on the graveyard knoll was bathed in early-morning light. Jessica sat alone and watched the sky come to life. The high plateau was patterned with color, not unlike the carefully pieced quilt that covered her bed. The morning sun highlighted the wildflowers and set afire yellow blazing stars on their slender stems and snakeweed topped with golden blooms. On the hillside at her feet, the pink and scarlet penstemon that thrived among the rocks danced in the morning breeze.

The air was fresh and dry; the sunlight warmly kissed her cheeks. She looked down and watched as the deep ruffle of the long black dress Rory's mother once wore brushed the dust when a gentle draft pressed it back against the toes of her brown shoes. Absently she reached up, found the knot in her arm sling, and eased it away from her neck. With her sling and bandages, it was far simpler to get in and out of Martha Burnett's dress than her own tailored clothes.

As she stared out at the high plateau she couldn't help but let her gaze slide over the mesa. It was hard not to recall all that had happened there. It had been days now since she'd left the house, nearly a week, and in all that time she had not seen Rory. Last night Myra had tried to convince her that she couldn't hide forever, that she had to face him and talk over whatever had caused the breach between them, but Jessica refused to discuss it with her friend.

But last night Myra wouldn't give up. She had cornered Jessica in her room and argued, "I don't know, nor do I want to know, what happened between you two, but I do know Rory has been equally hurt, Jessica. He loves you and you've shut him out entirely."

Jessica remembered picking up her hairbrush and brushing her hair while Myra paced the room. "All right. If you must know, I'm upset because he knew exactly where a huge saurian skeleton was located and didn't trust me enough to tell me. And you say he's hurt?" She laid down the brush and faced her friend squarely. "That is nothing compared to what I'm feeling right now."

"And what is that?"

"Betrayed."

"He must have had good reason for keeping it from you. Up until now he's seemed more than willing to help. What about the tracks he led you to?"

"An offering to keep me occupied."

"Surely—"

"I just can't discuss this, Myra. Please."

"I suppose you have a right to decide how you want to deal with this. Exactly where do we go from here?"

Jessica knew Myra had every right to ask. Days were

slipping by rapidly while she took the coward's way out. She tried to tell herself it was because she needed time to recover from the shocking events she had witnessed. The real truth was not as easy to face; she had made love with Rory Burnett, not once, but twice, because she thought he loved her. He still professed to love her.

And yet he'd kept from her the very thing she needed most.

This morning, before she walked to the top of the knoll, she had told Myra, ''I've come to the conclusion that there is nothing left to do but go back. I can't work with my injuries, and when Ramsey and Beckworth learn about this latest fiasco, they're certain to withdraw their support and appoint someone who can stay out of trouble.''

Someone who won't be taken in and fall in love with the first person they meet.

''They'll send a man to do the job.''

Myra crossed the room and sat on the bed. ''You can tell me anything you please, but I know you still love Rory—''

''Things have happened that I can't put aside, Myra.''

The older woman stood up and sighed. ''I'm trying to remember that the universe is in command of this situation, not me.'' She took Jessica's hands in her own. ''Let me know if you change your mind. You know I'll abide by your decision.''

A thought had struck Jessica just then, one that she never thought to ask her friend before. ''Is there any reason you don't want to leave here, Myra? Have you . . . are you . . . I know Woody Barrows has been courting you—''

''Oh, good heavens!'' Myra colored deeply and shook her head. ''I'm no more smitten with Mr. Barrows than I am with that Livermore creature in red underwear masquerading as a cook. Oh, my goodness, no. There's nothing holding me here. When you say the word, I'll be ready to leave.''

Now, as Jessica watched the sky deepen to a dark blue, she wondered if she could actually leave without seeing Rory at all. Even now, after he had betrayed her by not showing her the skeleton and giving her the chance to decide what to do about it, she didn't know if she could bear to face him and tell him good-bye.

What her mind wanted and what her heart felt were two distinctly different matters.

He had stopped trying to see her days ago. Since then, she never caught as much as a glimpse of him through the window, nor had she heard his voice in the hallway or parlor. Rory Burnett was avoiding her completely, just the way he had before the Fourth of July celebration.

With a last look across the plateau, she stepped away from the boulder and began to cross the knoll. When she reached the crooked fence around the graves, she leaned out to grasp the rusted iron and stared down at the freshest mound of earth that marked Whitey's grave.

"Good-bye, Whitey," she whispered, and then, lifting the fabric of the bulky gown, she started back down the hill.

Jubilant for the first time in days, Rory slammed the screen door and stepped into Scratchy's kitchen. The house reeked of boiled cabbage. Crossing to the stove, he lifted the lid of a deep pot, and sure enough, bubbling away was one of the old man's favorite concoctions—red cabbage and boiled beef. "Smells ripe, Scratchy," he said with a smile.

Rubbing his patchy beard with four fingers, Scratchy asked, "What's lit your lamp? You were lower than a diamondback 'fore you left."

"Life's good, Scratchy. That's all. Life's real good." He tore a hunk of bread off of a loaf cooling on the tabletop. Rory left the room, walked through the hallway, and stopped outside Jessica's door. He didn't knock, not when he knew damn well she'd deny him access. Instead he opened the door, found her standing beside the bed in the long black gown she'd worn to Whitey's funeral, and was two steps inside before he realized what she was doing.

"You're packing?"

Jessica painstakingly finished folding the yellow dress he'd given her and placed it in the open valise on the bed. Although she hadn't yet looked in his direction, she could sense his slowly mounting anger. Finally she turned to him, but didn't dare move closer. "I'll ship your valise back when I get home."

"You might as well unpack, because you're not going anywhere," he said, taken by the contrast of her light hair and eyes and the heavy blackness of the gown.

His dark eyes bored into hers as if he dared her to try to get by him. She shifted, reached out, and took hold of the oak bedpost. "You can't force me to stay."

He crossed the room until he was standing just inches away. Reaching up, he took off his hat and tossed it on the bed. He wiped his forehead with his red plaid sleeve and shoved his fingers through his sweat-dampened hair. "Do you love me?"

"Rory, please, I—"

He smelled of the fine layer of dust on his clothes, of horses, of the outdoors. He loomed over her, pinned her with his eyes. One of his hands gripped the bedpost just above her own, but he didn't touch her.

"Do you, Jess?"

"I can't . . ."

"Can't say it? Or can't love me? Are you saying you'll never forgive me for holding to a promise I made years ago? Are you saying that it's all right for you to stand by your word, but it's not all right for me to do the same? Is that what you're saying, Jess?"

All the hurt and anger she thought she'd locked deep inside suddenly erupted. Her fingertips pressed against the bedpost until her knuckles went as white as her face. "You lied to me," she cried, unable to hold back any longer, furious at him for unleashing her emotion.

He kept his voice low, calm. Thankful to have finally penetrated her shell, he said, "I never lied, Jess. I just didn't tell you something I was bound not to tell you."

She pushed off the post and stepped back. "You said you loved me and I believed you. What am I supposed to think now? That you loved me just a little? That you loved me enough to *use* me but not to trust me with your secret?"

He went after her, grabbed her good arm, and held on tight to keep her from moving farther away. "I used *you*? I seem to recall you being quite willing to use *me* just to satisfy your own curiosity."

She flinched. "How can you say that?"

"It's true."

"It is *not* true." She jerked her wrist out of his hold, turned, and paced to the window.

He followed close on her heels, started to reach out to her, and dropped his hand. He wasn't going to give up until she admitted what he knew to be true. He lowered his voice again and said, "Then tell me you love me."

She dropped her head and covered her eyes with her hand. "Stop badgering me!"

"I just want the truth, Jess."

She whirled around. "You know I love you. And because I let myself love you, you've taken everything—my work, my trust, my heart." Broken, she stared up at him through tears, daring him to deny it. "What am I supposed to do now?"

"I didn't take any more than you were willing to give, and no more than I wanted to give you in return." Unable to let her stand away from him, he reached out and tried to pull her into his arms.

She fought him as hard as she could while protecting her injured shoulder. All the while, he continued to hold her—held her without hurting her, held her to keep her from retreating into herself and shutting him out forever. When she realized her efforts were fruitless, she quieted. He stroked her back, soothed and calmed her, measured the beat of her racing heart as it pressed against his own.

"Say it again," he whispered against her hair.

Defeated, unable to stand against his tender onslaught, she looked up at him through tears and whispered back, "I love you."

His relief was so great that he sighed and pulled her closer. With his cheek against the top of her head, he smiled. He felt her hand brush against his back and settle on his waist. The movement was grudgingly given, he could tell, but given just the same.

"What now, Jess?" he asked her. "Where do we go from here?"

He barely heard her whisper, "I don't know."

Rory took her hand and pulled her over to the bed. The mattress sagged when he sat on the edge and drew her down beside him. He threw an arm over her shoulder and held her against his side hip to hip, thigh to thigh. They sat staring at the window across the room, aware and at the same time not aware of the men and horses, the dust and dry wind moving beyond the rippled glass.

Finally he said, "I can't let you go, Jess. I can't make it without you, you know that."

"And if I stay?"

"We'll be married."

She sighed.

He tightened his hold on her shoulder. "I'll work like the devil to make you happy."

"What about my own work? What will become of me without it? Even though I love you, I still can't imagine myself as a rancher's wife."

He held her close with one arm and laid his hand on her thigh. "You won't be just any rancher's wife, you'll be mine. I think we can find enough to keep you busy."

She threw him a doubtful look. "We can't do *that* every minute," she mumbled.

With a laugh he responded, "Why couldn't you continue to work from here?"

"What do you mean?"

"What's to stop you from searching for saurian fossils, prehistoric leftovers? You'll always be a paleontologist, your knowledge is one thing no one can take away from you. What does it matter where you live?"

"I couldn't work for the museum—"

He could tell by her tone that she was mulling over his idea. "There are plenty of men like Beckworth out there, rich men willing to fund you even if you worked independent of the museum. Do you think a man like that really cares where a paleontologist hails from as long as she's successful?"

"I guess not, but—"

He pressed the point. "I met the man, remember? He didn't strike me as loyal, just eager to get his hands on what he wanted. After all, he was ready to fire you when it seemed you were on the wrong track."

"I suppose I could still obtain the necessary permits to search government land once I've exhausted the search here on the ranch. And your neighbors might not object to me going over their land, either." She looked at him for the first time. "But how would you feel about me digging up the place? You told me once that you didn't want a circus here, that you were afraid the Silver Sage would be overrun with scientists and curiosity seekers like the cliff dwellings. If I found another skeleton, I'd have to call in a team—it could take weeks of excavation. The news would leak out."

"If you're willing to marry me, I'm willing to put up with a few more bone hunters around here. Besides"—he leaned down, unable to ignore her pouting lips any longer—"if you'll marry me, I'll buy you a whole damn circus tent and charge admission if you want it."

"Really?" She couldn't take her eyes off his mouth as he bent closer.

"Really." Unable to resist any longer, he pressed his lips to hers and found them warm and willing. Enfolding her in his embrace, Rory pressed her back against the pillow and headboard, relief and thanksgiving in his kiss. Tenderly he held her and traced her lips with his tongue until she opened to him. When the kiss ended, she sighed softly, then kissed him again.

The sound of a soft footstep in the hallway drew them back to reality. Rory sat up and looked around in time to see Myra standing on the threshold, a stern expression on her face. "Sometimes," she said, drawing herself up as far as her short stature would allow and thrusting out her substantial bosom, "the universe needs a champion! I have let things run their own course for far too long." She stepped into the room, advancing on the two of them with a suspicious frown on her face. "Exactly what is going on here? Maybe the two of you have taken leave of your senses, but I have not. It is broad daylight and you have not even deigned to close the door. Jessica Stanbridge, I am nearly at the end of my tether with you. One moment you profess to love Rory, the next you feel betrayed.

"And you"—she rounded on Rory, who was helping Jessica to an upright position—"I have listened to your excuses once too often. Young man, are you trying to compromise her beyond all reason?" By the time she finished her tirade, Myra was trembling in her high-button shoes.

Rory started to defend himself when a slow, curious thumping began in the hallway. The three occupants of the room watched as Methuselah slowly but surely worked his way into the bedroom, bumping against the door as he turned the corner. Rory bit back a smile. He glanced at Jess and found her trying to gain some composure. Her lips looked too well kissed to deny what Myra had seen anyway.

"I plan on compromising her for the rest of her life, Myra." Rory took Jessica's hand. "She's finally agreed to marry me."

Myra looked from one to the other, smoothed her skirt, tidied her hair, and then cleared her throat as Methuselah ever so slowly disappeared beneath the bed. Undaunted by the sudden news, Myra raised her forefinger and pronounced, "Once again the universe has successfully accomplished its plan unaided. I should have had more faith."

With that, she turned to leave, but not before pausing in the doorway. "I will inquire as to the details of how this outstanding decision was made and exactly when you will carry this plan to its conclusion, but for now I intend to wait until you have extricated yourselves from this most disturbing tableau." Head high, she left them to ponder her words.

"What did she just say?" Rory asked.

"She said you need to get off me."

He frowned. "You have no excuses left, Jess. Have you changed your mind?"

Jessica shook her head. "I am not a fickle female, Mr. Burnett. Surely you know that by now?"

"I didn't think so." He stood and pulled her up after him. "Now, before Myra comes storming back in here, let's 'extricate ourselves from this disturbing tableau.'" With her hand in his, he headed for the door.

CHAPTER

23

Miles from nowhere, Jessica Stanbridge Burnett sat atop the high-sprung seat of a buckboard and held tight while the wagon creaked its way across a sage-and-rock-strewn plateau. Time and again she glanced over at her husband and grew more frustrated with every passing second.

A wreath of rosebuds and wildflowers rode askew atop her head. Her hair, neatly twisted into a thick topknot a few hours ago, had begun to unravel. Her long stray locks were lifted by a breeze so hot it felt like an oven.

She could feel a drop of sweat slide between her breasts, but the high starched collar of the exquisite lace gown she wore prevented her from reaching down to wipe it away. Instead she pressed the neckline of the gown against her skin and let the sweat soak into the white lace. Her fingertips swept across the newly strung necklace Rory had presented to her before the ceremony. She was touched to think he had known how much they meant to her, known her so well that he had sent one of the men back to the camp-

356

site on the mesa to gather up as many beads as he could find.

She watched Rory expertly guide the team of draft horses. What was he up to?

"Where *are* we going?" Although she had already asked at least ten times, Jessica remained ever hopeful that he would finally let her in on his secret.

"You'll see." He nodded at the road ahead.

Jessica sighed. She stared at the broad rumps of the huge horses carrying them to some mysterious destination.

"You might have at least given me time to change," she said.

He shot her a dark glance, his ebony eyes reflecting the black hat he'd pulled low on his forehead. "I plan on being the one to take your wedding gown off you on our wedding night, Mrs. Burnett."

Jessica folded her arms in defiance. The wagon jolted and she was forced to grab the seat again. "By the time we get wherever it is we're going, I'll be covered with dust."

"It won't matter." He smiled. "Clean or dirty, you're beautiful."

She blushed furiously and smacked him on the shoulder. "We left everyone standing there in the parlor waiting to celebrate."

"We'll have our own celebration."

"But—" She would never forget the looks on Myra and the cowhands' faces when the brief ceremony performed by a traveling minister ended and Rory took her by the arm and led her away.

"Besides, they have all that cake and chicken to put away. I left a bottle of whiskey, too, so don't worry your pretty head. They won't suffer without us."

"I should have stayed to see Myra off," she said.

"The preacher said he'd get her to Cortez and from there she can take the stage to Durango. You're not worried about her being alone with the preacher, are you?"

"Not as worried as I am about the preacher being alone

with Myra. I'm sure by the time they reach Cortez he'll be well versed in Emerson and New Thought.''

"Is she taking that turtle?"

Jessica smiled. "I'm afraid so.'' Three or four bumps later she added, "I'll miss her.''

Rory snapped the reins and laughed. "Not for long. She said she'll be back for Christmas.''

"You don't mind, do you?'' She watched him carefully, hoping to gauge the truth of his answer.

He turned to smile into her eyes. "I want whatever makes you happy, Jess.''

"I love you.'' She reached up to touch his cheek and almost fell off the high seat.

Rory laughed, winked, and said, "Hold on, Jess. You've already got a bum shoulder. I don't want to lose my wife before the honeymoon.''

Jessica blushed again and let a few silent moments pass while they bounced along. They seemed to be heading for a high-walled canyon. Behind them, the contents of the wagon shifted and rattled beneath a tarp. She had no idea what he'd brought along—that, too, was a secret.

Two hours later, just when she was thinking, 'some honeymoon,' they entered the high walls of a river canyon that she recognized as the same one they had traveled through on the way to identify Jerome Stoutenburg's body, the canyon where they had spent the night beneath the stars. She looked to the rim far above them and thought of Piah, of the night he had watched them make love, and she shivered.

Rory was watching her. He reached out and took her hand, covered it with his own, and squeezed her fingers gently. "Don't worry. No one can hurt us now.''

Having given up on asking him about their destination, she simply inquired, "Are we almost there?''

"Just about.''

Jess studied the canyon. The river was still shallow, but

the water rushed clear and steady over the rocky bed. Willow and cottonwood grew along the canyon floor. One wall was shaded, the other still ablaze with late-afternoon light.

"What are you thinking?"

"I was thinking about the canyon walls. The formations are subdivided into a lower marine series and an upper or freshwater series of strata. The upper are the Jura; thus the term 'Jurassic' is given to the period in which it was formed." When she realized she had slipped into a professorial tone, she turned to him. "What were you thinking?"

"I was wondering just how long it would take to get you out of all that lace. How am I supposed to get all those little tiny buttons open?"

"If you'd let me pack, I would have included a button hook," she told him primly.

He merely smiled.

Rory pulled up on the reins, let the wagon slow to a stop behind the horses, and then set the brake. "We're here," he announced.

Jessica let go of the wagon seat and stared around the canyon. They were two miles south of the place they had once spent the night on the sandbank, alone with the song of the river and the sky clear and blue above them.

He jumped down, walked around the wagon, and helped her down. "Watch your dress," he warned, grabbing the hem as it nearly caught on the high, spoked wagon wheel. When he had her safely on the ground, he kissed her, bent her over his arm in a romantic embrace worthy of the cover of a dime novel.

Breathless when he released her, Jessica smiled up at him. "I must look a sight," she said, trying to straighten the crown of flowers that rode atop her hopelessly ruined hairstyle. He reached out, removed the pins one by one, handed them to her, and then gently untangled the wreath of flowers from her hair. She shook her long hair free until it hung down her back.

"There," he said, carefully setting the flower wreath on the wagon seat, "now you look perfect."

"Perfect? I'm dusty, disheveled, sweaty, and starving."

"The first three sound delicious. I can take care of the starving." He walked to the back of the wagon and began to untie the tarp. Throwing the ropes aside, he felt Jessica walk up behind him.

"What is all that?"

"A picnic basket, well stocked. Your valise—kindly packed by Myra—bedrolls, pillows, a tent in case it rains, a fry pan, a few bottles of wine, various and sundry other surprises." More than pleased with himself, he tucked his thumbs in his pockets and rolled back on his heels.

Jessica entwined her fingers and shrugged. "Where do we begin? I've never been on a honeymoon, you know."

"Well, seeing as how the dress has, I was thinking it might just fall off of its own accord."

She shook her head. "I don't think so." She looked down and smoothed the intricate lace. "Do you think your mother would mind my altering it?"

He closed the distance between them and took her hand. Bringing it to his lips, he kissed her palm, her wrist, and then the bend of her elbow. "I don't think she could be anything but pleased with the woman inside it."

"Really?"

"Yep."

"Rory?"

"What?"

She looked up at him from beneath lowered lashes. "Maybe it's time we got down to the honeymoon part."

"No doubt about it."

The long row of nineteen covered buttons didn't pose a bit of a problem, nor did the removal of Jessica's high-button shoes. Rory smiled triumphantly as he slipped the long, silver buttonhook back into her valise and turned around to help his bride slide the heavy lace off.

"You're beautiful, you know," he told her as he kissed her shoulder and then carefully pushed her dress down to her waist. Her breasts rode high and firm against the frilly trim of her chemise.

"I love you," she said in response.

He held her hand while she stepped out of the dress, then he picked it up off the ground and laid it across the wagon seat. Jess wrapped her arms around his neck and boldly pressed against him. He dipped his head to kiss her, explored the inside of her mouth with his tongue, and didn't stop until they were both eager for much more.

Rory bent down and slipped his arm beneath her knees. She hooked hers about his neck and let him carry her to the back of the wagon. He set her on the wagon bed and she frowned, disappointed when he didn't jump up beside her.

"Where are you going?" she said, pouting. "Do you just plan to leave me sitting here in my skivvies?"

"Not for long. Pretty soon you'll be sitting there in nothing."

She planted her hands on her hips. "What are you doing?"

"Looking for a good place to set up camp."

"Do you have to do that right now?"

He stopped and turned around. Mimicking her, he put his hands on his hips and gave her a knowing half smile. "Do you plan to boss me around for the rest of our natural lives?"

Jessica folded her arms beneath her breasts and didn't say another word until he turned away and then she mumbled, "Only when you need it."

A few minutes later he had spread out the bedrolls near a fallen log, set up a fire ring, and filled a bucket with water. "Can I get down yet?"

"I'll lift you down," he said, making good on his word.

He led her to the pallets, held her hand while she sat down, then sat down beside her. He handed her a clean towel that was folded at the end of his bedroll. "I thought you might feel better if you washed off some of the dust."

"Is it that bad?"

"Here." He took the cloth from her. "Let me." Dipping the towel in the bucket, he wrung it out and then slowly, carefully, moved the soothing, tepid dampness over her cheeks and nose. Jessica closed her eyes and he pressed the cloth gently against one then the other. She tilted back her head and he swabbed her neck, her shoulders, the crevice between her breasts.

Jessica licked her lips and opened her eyes. Immobile, he was staring down into them.

"Let me," she said, wresting the cloth from his hand. As he unbuttoned his white pleated shirt and pulled it out of his waistband, she dipped the cloth back into the bucket and then squeezed the water out of it. He was bare to the waist, his biceps knotting as he unbuttoned the front of his trousers and slid them down.

"Damn it," he grunted.

"What?"

"Boots. I forgot to take off my boots."

Jessica giggled and pressed the wet cloth against her forehead while he struggled to get his boots off, shuck out of his pants, and keep his balance on the bedroll.

"You can look up now."

She did. He was sitting naked as a newborn on the blankets, but there was nothing that resembled a babe about him. Except maybe the glow beneath his tan cheeks.

Jessica got to her knees, pushed him back until he lay across the blanket, and began to stroke his eyes and then his lips with the wet cloth. She brushed it across his shoulders, down his chest, and followed the dark trail of crisp hair that tapered down to the thatch from which his manhood sprung erect and throbbing.

She touched him there, moved the wet cloth over him again and again, slowly at first, then faster—gently at first, then with added pressure. He groaned aloud.

Jessica smiled. "I think I'll take to this marriage business."

He could barely utter the words. "I knew you would if you gave it a chance, Professor." Then he grabbed a handful of her hair and pulled her down beside him before she could torment him any further.

"Wait. Please." She sat back up, hastily took off her underclothes, and then stretched out next to him, lying on her uninjured shoulder.

He stroked her neck, traced her ear, cupped her breast. Jessica slid up against him, felt his skin next to hers. She slipped her fingertips into the swirls of hair matted across his chest. His heart was beating hard against her palm.

"Make love to me, Rory," she whispered. "Don't make me wait."

He gently shifted her until she lay on her back, then rose above her, amazed to find her slick and ready for him already. "Are you bossing me around again, ma'am?"

"I said please, didn't I?"

"No. But it doesn't matter," he said.

Jessica lifted her hips, nudged him, teased him, begged him without words until he slid into her so far that she gasped and then cried out, unable to hold back.

Rory steeled himself while she shuddered around him. When she settled down, when her cries subsided to mere whimpers, he began to move again. Over and over he drove into her, bringing her back to life, rekindling the fire inside her until she was dewed with sweat, clinging to him, riding him high with her legs wrapped about his waist.

He dipped and bucked, felt her rasping breath as it teased his ear, heard her moans turn to mewling cries, and knew he was about to explode. "Hold on, Jess. Hold on to me."

She did. He drove full length inside her and let go his

seed. Their cries of release blended into echoes that rever-
berated off the canyon walls.

He kissed her temple and held her close as she slept in his
arms. The afternoon was almost over, the sun slipping out of
the canyon. Rory knew he had never felt as happy or as
complete, and now that he had Jess, things would only get
better.

He thought about getting away long enough to prepare
dinner and then awaken her with a kiss. She snuggled closer
and he let time pass by without moving. He closed his eyes,
willing to join her in sleep for a few more moments, until a
shot rang out.

He dove over her, covering Jessica with his body. She
woke up screaming.

"What is it? Who's shooting at us?"

He shoved her head down and pinned her there. Where
was his gun? Why in the hell didn't he have it nearby?

Cursing himself for not wanting to wear a gun on his
wedding day, he heard another shot ring out. It splintered a
rock nearby and sent fragments shooting in all directions.
Another bullet followed almost immediately and pinged off
of a boulder not far from the wagon.

He grabbed Jessica's arm and shouted, "Come on!" and
in a crouch, ran with her to the side of the buckboard. They
huddled beside it, Jessica shivering, her arms crossed over
her breasts.

"Who is it?"

"I don't know, but I'm sure as hell gonna find out." He
reached beneath the tarp and pulled out a rifle and his gun
belt. He handed her the revolver.

Another bullet cracked through the canyon, the sound
reverberating off the canyon walls. "Whoever he is, he's up
there." Rory pointed to a spot halfway down the canyon
wall. "You aim that way and fire. Don't use up all the

bullets at once, space them evenly. I'm going to run up to that boulder and try to get closer.''

"Oh, god, Rory. You're naked.''

Another shot hit the dirt close to the wagon wheel.

"Honey, I'd rather be naked than dead. Count to three and start shooting.''

She counted and fired. He ran. Jessica squeezed her eyes shut and pulled the trigger a second time. The hidden gunman shot back. Rory crouched low behind the boulder, waiting for the man to reveal enough of himself to make a target.

Jess fired again.

Rory's head went up over the rock and a bullet ricocheted beside him.

Jess screamed.

"Keep shooting. Don't worry about me,'' he told her.

She fired again. Two bullets were left.

There was movement on the ridge. Rory's rifle barrel flashed and a shot rang out.

With a shout, the man on the ridge stood to his full height. Rory fired again and their assailant pitched headlong into the canyon.

Jess dropped the gun in the dirt and ran to Rory's side. His gaze never left the place where the sniper's body disappeared into the brush. He slipped his arm around Jessica.

"Are you all right?'' he asked her.

"Still shaking. Are you?''

He kissed her temple. "I'm fine. Get dressed. I think that was Chako, Piah's nephew.''

"Do you think he was alone?''

"He was alone or someone would still be shooting at us.''

She dressed and waited with the loaded gun in her hand beside the wagon. Still shivering despite the heat, she didn't move until Rory was back.

"It was Chako."

"The boy?"

"Yep. He's dead."

She set the gun down and stood up. "Do you think any more of them will come?"

He shook his head. "No. From what I heard from the sheriff when he notified the BIA and then went over to the reservation himself after Carmichael's death, Piah and his men were acting alone. The rest of the Utes either had no knowledge of his plan or wanted nothing to do with it."

"But the boy—"

"He was never seen again after the night Piah and the others died. I thought he might have died in the cave or run off, but he must have been hiding out here in the canyon. When he saw us, he probably thought he could avenge Piah's death." He moved away, intent on starting a fire.

Jessica looked off toward the spot where the boy died. "It's all so terrible."

Rory paused with an oak branch in his hand. "It's all over now. I covered him with rocks, the way his people would have." He looked into her eyes, tried to measure the depth of her fear. "If you want, I'll take you home."

She frowned. "What do you want to do?"

"Well, I would like to stay until morning, at least. It'll be easier traveling in daylight. We aren't in any danger, but if you don't want to stay, I'll understand."

Dusk had settled around them. She knew he was right. Still, she wondered if she would be awake all night waiting for someone else to attack them. "How did you feel when you knew you had to get back on Arthur the bull?"

He smiled. "Scared out of my wits."

"But you did it."

"Yep."

"Well"—she sighed and resigned herself to facing her fear—"I guess that's about how I feel right now, but I'll stay."

He dropped the wood into the fire ring and went to her side. "Good. I'll make it worth your while."

Early the next morning, Jessica carefully scrambled over rocks, artfully avoiding branches and gravel as they worked their way up a sloped slide area a few yards downriver from the campsite.

She hollered up to Rory, "Where are we going now?"

"Keep moving." He paused to watch her struggle upward. "Do you need help?"

Quite testy, she snapped back, "Of course not. Let's just get this over with."

"I don't know why you're so out of sorts."

"Me? Me out of sorts?" She huffed and puffed, praying no one rode into the canyon and caught her running around in her underclothes. Jessica told herself not to worry, that it was his land after all, that he had warned his hands away from the canyon for at least four days. "I don't know why you think I'm out of sorts. After all, yesterday was my wedding day. I was up before dawn, married, trundled off in a wagon, dressed and undressed, then shot at. Today you force me to march up the side of a mesa in my chemise and pantalets." She stopped to catch her breath, dared to look downhill, regretted the move, and then yelled up at his back, *"Of course I'm not out of sorts!"*

"You forgot to add the part about lovemaking."

"Where are we *going*?"

"We're almost there."

She trudged on until he stopped, then she stopped, too, gauged the distance between them, decided she could make it, and climbed the remaining few feet. When she reached his side, he waylaid her by draping his arm over her shoulders.

"I love you, Jess."

She was hard pressed to hide her smile, but she feigned a

reasonable frown. "Couldn't you have told me that down there?" She nodded toward the riverbed.

"Nope. I brought you up here to give you your wedding present."

Certain he had lost his mind, she decided to humor him. She waited patiently, given the circumstances, for him to take a present out of his pants pocket. Instead he put his hands over her eyes, led her five steps forward, and then said, "I hope this is something you can use."

For a moment she was dumbfounded as she stared at the cliff face and then the rocky ground on the wide shelf of land. "I don't see—"

And then, unable to utter another word, she moved forward, staring in disbelief at a partially exposed fossilized skeleton of a large-boned, obviously reptilian creature embedded in the shale and sandstone.

A pick, shovel, and broom she had not noticed until she looked over the mound of fossils lay close by. Jessica knelt down and ran her hand over the exposed vertebrae.

"It's not as big as the one at the cave," he said.

She looked up from where she knelt in the dust. "Someone's been working the excavation. How did you find it? Do you think this was Jerome's?"

"Nope."

"How can you be sure? Perhaps—"

He looked down into the canyon. "I found it, Jess. I don't know how I did it, but I did. Myra told me what she knew about where to look—"

"Myra?"

"Yep. Anyway, that's where I've been for two weeks. I started looking back when you wouldn't speak to me after you found out about the cave. Then, once we got everything settled, I went out searching again, and as I said, I don't know how I did it except I ran into a streak of luck when I saw that strip of backbone peeking up out of the ground."

''But you've dug out almost a quarter of it, if I'm judging correctly by the size of the femur.''

''I wanted to uncover as much as I could to surprise you with.''

She looked up and saw him standing there, wearing nothing but pants and boots, genuinely intent on making her happy, and couldn't stop the tears that sprang into her eyes. ''Oh, Rory.''

''Did I break something?''

She got to her feet and went to him. Her arm went about his waist. He held her close. ''No.'' She sniffed back a sob. ''No, it's perfect. Just perfect.''

He kissed her hair.

She wiped the tears from her cheeks and looked up into his eyes. ''Maybe you should give up cattle and poetry and take up paleontology.''

He kissed her lips. ''I'll leave that to you.''

''How about a poem? Do you have a new one for the occasion?''

''The bones aren't enough?''

''I love your poetry as much as I love you.''

''You are my poem, Jess. You're all I need.''